Take the Fourth

Jeffrey Walton

authorHOUSE®

AuthorHouse™
1663 Liberty Drive
Bloomington, IN 47403
www.authorhouse.com
Phone: 1-800-839-8640

First published by AuthorHouse 3/30/2011

ISBN: 978-1-4520-8928-7 (sc)
ISBN: 978-1-4520-8929-4 (dj)
ISBN: 978-1-4520-8930-0 (e)

Library of Congress Control Number: 2011900409

Printed in the United States of America

There would be a few more trees left standing, one less book on the shelf, and a ton of ideas still bouncing around in my head like lotto balls, if it wasn't for the daily doses of support and patience that I received from my loving wife Wendy. Through her encouragements and perseverance I took my first steps of placing keystrokes to liquid crystal displays and developing characters, plots, and subplots and eventually turning them into this novel before you. I thank her for that. I love her for that and for that I dedicate these bounded words to her, my Wendy. These words are as much hers as they are mine.

"The right of the people to be secure in their persons, houses, papers, and effects, against unreasonable searches and seizures, shall not be violated, and no warrants shall issue, but upon probable cause, supported by oath or affirmation, and particularly describing the place to be searched, and the persons or things to be seized."

Preface

An excerpt from a thesis entitled "DATA"

A visionary is one who can foresee the realization of technologies based upon innovations and inventions that do not exist today.

Joseph Woodland was a visionary. In 1949, while relaxing in his beach chair, he invented the barcode by placing Morse code in the sand with his fingers. There were no barcode readers or lasers at this time and computers were in their infancy stage. Over time the new technologies bloomed and the barcode made strides. Lasers became scanners, scanners became fingers, and the barcode became a language, a language spoken throughout the world, by computers throughout the world.

Look around today, barcodes, barcodes, barcodes, on milk, DVD's, FedEx packages, assembly lines, luggage, bottled water, drugs, cars, furniture, greeting cards, t-shirts, passports, lumber, and even people. A series of lines in the sand becomes the universal methodology of tracking—tracking what we buy, where we are going, when we do so, how we do it, and who we are. Each time a barcode is read it becomes raw data—raw data analyzed in the most mundane way, raw data analyzed in the most personal way.

Think about it. At the grocery store, the shopping cart becomes a basket of information. Scan a bag of potato chips and the price automatically appears on the screen with the total. Scan a bag of potato chips and the computer will delete an entry out of its inventory. If the shelf inventory is low a message automatically appears on the LCD window display of the stock boy's PDA. If store inventory falls below a predetermined amount it will automatically file an order for more potato chips with the purveyor. Information provided to the purveyor will be used in ranking the store's profit margin based on its product of potato chips. This in turn will be used to determine delivery priorities. The more the store sells, the faster they receive their product. Scanning saves the store money, less time for error, no need to call in orders, no need to do inventory. Scan the bag of chips and handed with the receipt are coupons for future purchases. These coupons could be for the same product or its competitors, buy Coke and get a Pepsi coupon, buy Lays get a Herr's coupon. Competitors use this information to gain insights to their market campaigns and insights into their rivalries.

Harmless information, 1's and 0's, are just sitting on a database in the middle of Kansas somewhere. Harmless information used by the store to help run its store. At any exact moment in time, inventory can be taken and supply statistical information on product sales and profit margins. Decisions can be made whether to increase shelf space for a particular product or remove a product altogether, find out if the in store bakery is churning out dough or stuck in dough, if fish sales actually increase on Fridays, whether or not to put those 40 cases of almost flat soda on sale based on its limitation of shelf life, or how many dozen eggs were sent back based on expiration date. They can predict the future, project inventory for next week, next month, even next year, all by analyzing their raw data.

Now scan a supersaver card, punch in a phone number, pay by debit/credit card, swipe a finger, have a retinal scan (not rectal mind you, though that would make checkout lines a little more interesting) and this bag of potato chips becomes linked to an individual along with the date and time. Raw data becomes information; information transformed into who bought what, where, and when.

Along with the Herr's bag of potato chips, Marcy Peterson purchases Little Debbie Snack Cakes, 3 Lean Cuisine's frozen dinners (meatloaf, lasagna, smoked turkey), two 2 liter diet Cokes, loaf of Wonder bread, 24oz jar of Skippy peanut butter, Dial soap, Kotex, bottle of Advil, mint flavored Scope, two pints of Ben & Jerry's (Cherry Garcia, Fudge Brownie), 40 watt GE light bulbs 2-pack, string cheese, a Starr magazine, and a pack of Tic-Tacs. Marcy's total $129.86 deducted from her Fidelity checking account on July 18, 2005, at 5:45p.m. in the Winn Dixie, Jacksonville, Florida, store #23345. Marcy uses one $1.00 coupon.

With this data, a store can pinpoint its customers' demographics. What's the gender majority? What's the average age of the customers? What's the average income? Who's the best customer? What's their average spending per visit? How much did they spend last year? Do they use coupons? Food stamps? Are they married? Have children? With this data, they can ask themselves—Should a pharmacy be installed, buy more carts with child seats? Should the fresh vegetables and fruits be upgraded? Sell a cheaper grade of hamburger? Add more family only parking? Charge a fee for bank withdrawals when they use a debit card? Add more types of shampoo? Change their magazine types at the checkout counters? Add a self-checkout?

Now grant access to the database with outside vendors, let them query to their hearts content—for a price of course, and here is where the scary part starts.

This same information, the same 1's and 0's sitting in the middle of Kansas can become personal without knowing it. That same Marcy applies for some health insurance. She calls on the phone and is connected to a salesperson. After taking some general information, the computer whirls, spins, chugs, and spits back a monthly dollar amount all within less than a minute. The processing power behind this monthly dollar amount is staggering. It used to be just a quick look-up in the actuary tables based on age and race, not anymore. It's a very complex process, basically a computer program, broken into many parts. The first part of this massive thinking machine deals with the entered data—name, telephone number, social security number, date of birth. This data is used for search parameters, search parameters for databases; many databases, one of them being the Winn Dixie database in the middle of Kansas somewhere. The information stored there is harmless—who bought what, where, and when, but in this specific case the search parameters are: Marcy and all items bought within the last year. The raw data is returned—it's just mindless information to the naked eye. Most people wouldn't give it a second glance if they saw the information scattered on a piece of paper—just a bunch of numbers and names, no big deal. The second part of this complex process is the data scrubbing; turning this mundane information into something of use. From analyzing the data (another part of this computer program and the most complicated of them all) it can be determined that Marcy Peterson lives alone and buys food for roughly 3 days during each trip to the grocery store. Her average cost per shopping trip: $65.12. She rarely buys fresh fruits, vegetables, and never buys fish. She mainly purchases prepackaged meals and snacks with an average daily consumption of 3589 calories per day. Checking other databases and a search for any type of health club membership turns up empty. Last time she bought a pair of sneaks was 2 ½ years ago. Clearly Marcy is not health conscious and there is an 82.34% chance that she is overweight. Cha-ching—increase base insurance amount by 33%. Combined this information with her yearly driving distance and any traffic violations reported at the local DMV, and it is assumed she is a safe driver—deduct 1.5% off the base amount. Next, incorporate the type of work she does via her social security number, her Friday night bar bills or liquor bills taken from her Master Card, any doctor visits taken from her PPO card, or find out if she's a non-smoker and the base amount fluctuates up and down depending on the outcome of each search.

Raw data can become extremely personal as well. A vendor such as Johnson & Johnson can query a store's database and access one or all customers. They can find the average sales per customer, per age group, per visit, per year, per product, or products. They can determine the results of their most recent ad campaign per anyone of the demographic statistics thus helping them to analyze their marketing scope and in turn formulate new strategies to increase sales. Anyone can see the benefits to this information—these bits of 1's and 0's sitting in the middle of Kansas somewhere. Information is the key to success and marketing gurus will take advantage of this fact. Say J & J might want to convert a user of a competing product to their brand under a new marketing campaign, how about Kotex to their Stayfree.

Querying that same Winn Dixie database we find Marcy Peterson once again. She last bought Kotex on July 18th. She uses the competition but does she always? A simple query would suffice. Turns out, the answer is yes and with the enclosed dollar coupon. In the database is Marcy's demographics file containing address, age, phone number, etc . . . Presto—send a coupon; send all users of Kotex a coupon in the mail, maybe even a free sample. Better yet, a timely coupon so it is fresh in the memory and not lost or thrown away. Querying the database again yields that Marcy Peterson buys Kotex on average once every 4 to 5 weeks and using a simple calculation it can be surmised with a 96% accuracy that her next period will fall somewhere on the week of August 15th, therefore to assure the maximum benefits of a marketing campaign, the coupon should be sent no earlier than a week before her period. She gets her coupon on the 12th and uses it on the 16th, all without ever knowing that the big conglomerates are watching and learning from her every move, they even know when she's menstruating. The timely campaign is a success with a 62.76% switch rate just by sending a coupon. Follow it up with one or two more and hopefully buying Stayfree becomes a habit and gains a customer for life or at least until menopause.

●　●　●

Chapter 1

She heard tires squeal, the roar of the engine, and looked in that direction. A dark car could have been blue or black, hard to tell with the sunlight and shade of the trees during this afternoon. It was one of those old muscle cars, Nova, Camaro, again hard to tell, she wasn't an expert in automobiles; they got her from point A to point B; that was all that mattered, even though she drove the top of the line Mercedes sedan. The car she saw had big fat tires, that she remembers and a vinyl roof—black, nothing else stood out in the mind. She watched it as it sped down the street, five maybe ten seconds it was gone. "Humph," such an asshole she thought, "speeding around a children's playground, should string him up, they should have put in speed bumps". She was pissed.

As the echo of the car wafted in the summer air, her ears and mind came back into focus. She heard children crying, startled by the sounds of the loud asshole no doubt. She turned to her little ones, picked up Samuel who was crying and looked for Ripley who was playing on the gym, fort thingy that was bigger than some people's house—cost more too. She scanned the horizon and Ripley's pink tee shirt was nowhere to be found. She scanned again, looking at the swings, then to the sliding board, still no luck. She moved closer to the fort area hoping to get a glimpse that she was inside.

"That's an unusual name?"

"She was named after Ellen Ripley."

"Who?"

"Well actually after Sigourney Weaver."

"Sorry I still don't follow you."

"Sigourney Weaver's character in Alien; one of my husband's favorite movies, he just loved the name Ripley."

And so the questioning by the detective continued.

●　●　●

Chapter 2

Gunfire. Automatic gunfire. Screams. Blood curdling screams. Shattering glass. More automatic gunfire. Ricochets. More screams. More blood curdling screams. More shattering glass. Even more screams. Sounds of horror. More screams. More gunfire. Panic. Panic. Panic. Utter pandemonium. Running footsteps. Trampling footsteps. The sounds of the terrified. The sounds of war. Crying. Sobbing. The sounds of despair, grasping for air. Crying. Sobbing.

The bullets stopped. The loud and deafening sounds stopped. For a brief second, as the confusion began to set in, almost complete silence fell upon the area, then the wailing and screams of the injured became predominant as they drowned out the song "Winter Wonderland" playing over the mall's speaker system. There were bodies and blood everywhere, in front of the Modell's sporting goods store, in front of Macy's, in front of the shoe store, in front of the jewelry store, in front of the pretzel stand, in front of Starbucks. There were bodies and blood everywhere. There was a mother who was bleeding profusely holding her dead son. An elderly man who was shopping for his grandchildren was clinging to his dead wife. An entire family lay bullet stricken with the mother still clutching their smiling family photo with Santa taken moments ago. There was a set of twins in strollers with no more life to give along with a proud father whose life had also been extinguished while the mother laid unconscious and unaware of the horrors that lie ahead. There were teenagers with iPods who will no longer experience one of life's little pleasures, that of song. There was a twenty-something who hadn't taken her first sip of a mocha double latte. There was an Asian couple who will not see the birth of their first child. There was a young man holding a ring box for a very special Christmas present who will never hear the word "Yes". There were people with presents who will never feel the joy of giving. There were people who will never feel the joy of receiving from a loved one. There were people who were in too much of a rush to say "I love you" before heading to the mall. There were people who were full of life and the Christmas spirit just moments ago. There were bodies and blood everywhere.

There were seventy-eight people in total who will not see the New Year, sixty-two of those people died in a mall outside of Philadelphia just two days before Christmas, the others all died of complications shortly thereafter.

Two of the seventy-eight people who perished in the nonsense were the assailants themselves. There were five in total. These two walked out of the garage holding a plastic clothing bag, the kind one receives during checkout with a new suit or jacket, and then walked calmly up the stairs to the top level of the mall right past California Pizza Kitchen and Bloomingdales. They staked out a claim at the other end of the mall, right in front of Macy's department store. It was a busy intersection of the mall with views of both the upper and lower decks and very close to the parking garages. There were plenty of people here at any given time of day, even more so since it was the season. They checked their watch. Right on time—a few seconds later the mall echoed with gunfire and screams.

Reynolds was in the middle of the mall doing his last minute Christmas shopping. He was at one of the high end jewelry stores picking up some sterling silver Christmas tree ornaments, his annual gift to his wife of twenty-seven years. She had enough ornaments to stuff the gills of an eleven-footer with such decorations, she didn't need any more but it was an annual thing; besides it was a no-brainer of a gift and Reynolds liked those kinds of gifts. He had ten ornaments on the counter of various shapes and sizes, from bells to balls to snowflakes and reindeer and was just about to hand over his black American Express card when he heard the first shots echoing through the mall. Having been in combat, being a marine (for once a marine, always a marine) in certain parts of the world, he knew what automatic gunfire sounded like. Reynolds was quick on his feet for a man of fifty-one and was a rare individual who moved towards the sounds of bullets and screams. Even though he had been out of the marines for a good twenty plus years, the training embedded deep down inside of him came back like riding a bike. He reached for his 9mm that was tucked in the back of his pants just under his coat. He never went in public places without it, for it was moments like these he feared being without one. Within seconds he was within eyesight of two individuals wielding automatic guns and firing at anything that moved. He quickly ducked into the Gap which was a corner store, fully disregarding any injured or dead in his way. He watched them empty a clip and tried to reload, now was his chance. He acted without thinking. Thinking would have caused even more lives. He was about twenty-five feet away when he took his first shot. It missed, as did his second one. He was closing in on the gunmen and was close, so close he heard the locking of a clip into one of the guns. He fired again, this time catching a gunman in the fat part of the thigh just below the buttocks. He screamed in pain. Then Reynolds made a conscious decision and fired a head shot. "Shoot the fuckers dead," he thought, "no pleas of temporary insanity for these assholes." It was a clean shot as was the other one. The two assailants were dead. "Five rounds, three hits, two kills not bad for a fifty-one year old. Game over for these fucking assholes. I win. You lose mother fuckers," he said aloud as he reached for his inside coat pocket for the cell phone, while he tuck the 9mm back into his pants.

On the other end of the mall there were three shoppers, standing right between the three anchor stores of Nordstrom's, JCPenny's and Sears. They were well dressed with Dockers and a festive sweater or buttoned-down Polo with a jacket, each had carried a bag which appeared to contain gifts. The shoppers were all white males, clean shaven, in their late teens to early twenties and any one of them could pass for the traditional so-called Mainliner (Philadelphia's high society, private schooling suburbanite). In an instant, the shoppers transformed into methodical gunmen; dropping their bags and producing automatic weapons of some sort. It took a second or two to notice what they were doing. In that amount of time it was too late for most. The first to go were two rent-a-cops on Segways. They posed as the greatest threat but proved to be inconsequential and fell without even a chirp from their walkie-talkies. Then it was the public's turn. While one gunman concentrated on the lower level, spraying bullets like he was watering plants with a garden hose, the others concentrated on the top floor where there were mass amounts of holiday shoppers. They timed their burst, since a forty round clip only lasts a few seconds, by allowing one to fire while the other waited or loaded a new clip so there seemed to be a constant flow of bullets. They each deposited three clips into the befuddled crowd and when all was said and done, less than a minute had elapsed.

After their clips were emptied they turned around and ran through one of the stores, to the back, out the service entrance, and into the maze of service corridors behind and between each store. They knew their way around. They were outside in less than forty-five seconds and into a parking garage walking calmly to their car. Since the news of the inside eruption hadn't yet made its way to the outside world, no one ever questioned the holiday shoppers, why would they? Before long they had taken a ticket for the PA Turnpike and headed west towards Ohio, stopping at the first service station for a cup of coffee. They waited a total of fifteen minutes got into the car with their java and didn't say a word until they were on the other side of Harrisburg.

"You know," looking at his cup, "the lady who sued Mickey D's over that hot cup of coffee"

"Yeah"

"She probably would have been the first to bitch if the coffee was cold"

"What made you think of that?"

"The words on this coffee cup—Contents may be hot. Well no shit, I just ordered coffee and coffee is served fucking hot. You can't go anywhere or buy anything without some sort of warning. Ever buy an extension cord, damn thing has more warnings then a nuclear power plant. Don't use for tying. This is not a toy. Do not use outside, blah, blah, blah, blah. I mean buy a toaster and there is an illustration with a man on a rubber raft, with the toaster on his lap in the middle of a lake, and it has a big red "X" through the picture. I mean no shit, what do they think, we are morons?"

"They have to do that or they'll get sued, hence the warning on the fucking cup."

"Why, because people are such fucking morons, that's why we need to tell them everything we can and cannot do with a product. What ever happen to plain old common sense? If you are out in the middle of a torrential down pour and decide to make toast and get electrocuted, you have no right to sue because you are fucking stupid, you'd also be dead but that's beside the point. Stupid people should have no rights, even their significant others should have no rights. Natural selection at its finest . . . Darwin would be proud."

"Well, what happens when you use the product the correct way and it kills you?"

"Not the same thing."

"Yes it is, the people who made the product are fucking idiots."

"True, they may have not conducted every test possible, in which case they are responsible but still you shouldn't have to tell me I shouldn't use your product in the rain if it has a plug on it. Ah, that is not always the case either, is it? Take, umm what was it some cold medicine . . . I can't remember it but someone tampered with the bottle put some kind of poison in it and it was out of the hands of the makers and seven people were killed."

"Yeah, it's because of that, I can't open a goddamn Snapple bottle when I'm thirsty or open a little Debbie snack cake when I hungry, all that goddamn shrink-wrap."

"I have a theory."

"On what," half paying attention while tapping on his iPhone?

"Shrink-wrap. The guy who poisoned those six or seven people was indeed the inventor of the shrink-wrap machine. Think about it. Kill seven people and make millions upon millions. That . . ."

"Tylenol."

"What?'

"I looked it up on Wikipedia, the person used cyanide in the Tylenol tablets."

"Okay, pardon the rude interruption, like I was saying that little piece of plastic gives the illusion of protection and people feel so much more secure. He took away their security but then gave them security . . . . a fucking genius I tell ya, a goddamn mother fucking genius. The illusion of security."

"Just liked we talked about."

"Yep exactly like we talked about, give the public the illusion of doing something like preventing them from taking three ounces of liquid per bottle on a plane. Really, what the fuck does that stop. Not a goddamn thing, yet people comply because they think the government knows best. Utter bullshit."

"Hey, back to the aspirin, why is it they have armored guards in the aspirin aisle yet the fruits and vegetables are in the wide open?"

"Shut up, and gimme that phone for a minute," and he proceed to go to Yahoo. "Wouldn't you know it boys we are the number one news story in the world right now, how about them apples."

The driver of the vehicle didn't enter the conversation. He couldn't help but think this was a scene out of Pulp Fiction; they just killed innocent people in a mall and are now talking about coffee and shrink-wrap. Beads of sweat started to form on his forehead as they still headed west.

At the suburban mall things were a tad different. Media trucks now outnumbered the emergency response vehicles. Every network had vans, satellite linkups, and hordes of reporters, cameramen, and equipment. "The Mall Massacre," "Christmas Carnage"—the networks were trying to come up with a catchy tagline for commercial breaks, one network even tried "Season's Senseless Slaughter" but soon opted for the seemingly standard "The Holiday Mall Massacre" as it gave a little more punch to the present giving season. There were the in your face interviews with the confused family members, store employees, holiday shoppers in other malls throughout the country, doctors, trauma units, the police, the so-called psychologists to discuss feelings and other SME's, democrats, republicans, rock stars, movie stars, the governor, the President, and of course security experts given their much needed opinion as how we can stop this from ever happening again. There were pictures and video of bloodshed, body-bags, and diagrams out the ass on every network across the globe. Images that will stay with many throughout their life. All this was just the tip of the iceberg for the things to come in the following days and weeks, well at least until the media can no longer milk the cow called terrorism.

They paid their toll of $13.60 and entered Ohio with making one additional stop for gas. They drove for another hour and back to their home town. The driver dropped off both passengers at separate locations and headed for home himself—still feeling quite queasy. Within three hours, three different doors in three different locations were flanked by some of the finest S.W.A.T. members. They were poised and ready for the final "ok". It was given and just like a scene out of any given action flick, the good guys stormed the buildings and apprehended the suspects. Okay, apprehended was the wrong word.

Behind door number one, a teenage boy who sat behind a computer monitor, fingers a flailing on the game pad, wearing headphones, and playing of all things a first person shooter type of video game—the press would have a field day with this one. He was oblivious to his surroundings until it was too late. The door crashed open and the game pad was mistaken for a gun; the kid laid in a pool of blood from five shots to the chest. Door number two was almost the same story, except he was watching the news. Every station carried his deadly deed and he watched in awe. Again the door crashed opened but this time there was no game pad, there was no gun. He just turned around and glared at his oppressor and smiled. It was this cocky smile that landed him in hell and the shooter a desk job for life; for it was this smile that the S.W.A.T. member saw, he knew right there and then this guy was guilty and was the cold blooded killer who took away Christmas for many, and not just the people who were murdered. This smile made him squeeze the trigger and put a round right between the eyes; well, it was a little off-centered and more so to the groin area (it did the job of removing that fucking smile off his face quite nicely), but the second round, an instant later was the killing shot, right below the left eye socket. Explaining these two shots to the captain took all but one word—guilty mother fucker (one word in his eyes anyway). The third door was crashed in pretty much the same manner. The S.W.A.T. team searched the downstairs with precision that match a fine Swiss watch and found nothing. Two members went on to search the basement while the remaining ventured to the second floor. It was the bathroom where they had found the seemingly lifeless body. The body had a faint cut across the left wrist in what appeared to be a failed attempt at suicide probably because of the pain involved. The pills he took instead did the trick. They thought about calling in an ambulance since there was a slight chance that he could have been coaxed back to life but they waited and opted for the coroner instead.

Evidence was then gathered at each house or apartment and the authorities assumed the operation was a complete success. They found detail plans of the mall, itemized lists that included budgets for things like bullets, food, and hotel but the most interesting piece of the plot was another set of detail plans, not a plan b incase this one failed, but a plan for another full frontal assault on the very same mall, planned for exactly one month later just to prove the point that no one was really safe. The mall would have beefed up its platoon of guards and installed more cameras but besides the fact that they were not going to search everyone entering the mall, the mere façade of security would not have been enough to stop another attack. The fact of the matter was no one is truly safe and the shrinking freedoms proposed by the man in charge, Homeland Security, or the other extensions of government and law enforcements are not going to make one iota of a difference but on this day, the day of the massacre they had to feel justified in their plight. Within nine or ten hours of the Mall Massacre, all five suspects were flushed out and killed, except for Mr. Suicide, and a second attack thwarted.

Security camera tapes at the mall were reviewed by the FBI and the gunmen's facials were caught and enhanced. Matching these pictures up with the security cameras at the turnpike was a cinch, for each toll booth has several built in mini cameras at varying heights and take about 8 shots of each vehicle as they pass through the toll. Using the latest facial recognition software known to man, searching the turnpike's picture database, and narrowing the query via on ramps close to the mall, produced identical matches to the assailants within a 98.97 percent accuracy margin Searching the turnpike's computers again provided a cashless ticket, proving they were still on the main artery of Pennsylvania, heading west. They also predicted their exact location within five miles. Once the gray Chrysler passed the checkpoint camera it was an easy mark to follow. From there members of the FBI and local S.W.A.T. force coordinated their efforts through both ground and air. Simple really—people make mistakes, especially young men, inexperienced men. They made the mistake of not wearing masks, taking a toll road, not looking for cameras, staying on a toll road. They made many mistakes. That is the story the media will tell and they are none the wiser.

"Scott, Reynolds here, listen, something really bad just went down at the mall, it's a cluster fuck, we need to do something and fast."

That one call started a chain of events. Just as the President was about to have a quiet late lunch with his family—a first in almost two weeks, Scott entered the main dining room, just roughly two minutes after his call with Reynolds. He briefed the President on what he knew. In a matter of seconds the President rationalized his nod to Scott. It didn't have anything to do with the campaign or Homeland Security or the Patriot Act; it was the right thing to do, being so close to Christmas and all was just a bonus.

As media reports started to flow over the airwaves, Langley was a buzz. Conference rooms and conference phones were jammed packed with analysts from all corners of the globe. Was it terrorists, demonic adolescents, or Tom Clancy copycats? Hows and whys were being asked and no questions were being answered, just speculations at this point. Computer monitors, televisions screens, pda's, blackberry's, cell phones, and any other form of technology was ablaze with speculation. Nothing was clear this early in the game. In the midst of what may seem to be utter confusion to the outsider, the direct phone of someone deep within the National Intelligence rang—bypassing any secretaries or phone taps. It was Scott Norwood calling.

"Listen, obviously you've heard the news about the mall and that two assailants were taken out, I've just talked with the President, he gave the nod, I need as much information within the hour so it can be fed to the proper channels," a click was the next thing heard and that's how the real story started.

● ● ●

Chapter 3

Today Jorja Carson came in and sat at her desk, not her desk where she spent the better part of her life just a month ago, but at her desk in her new office, her new office with windows, her office with the name on the door and her own personal secretary out front, the office of the Deputy Director of the DS&T or Directorate of Science and Technology. The DS&T as stated on the website is responsible for leveraging technology to assist in critical intelligence problems within the boundaries of the CIA. This was Jorja's job. Being the new deputy director to DS&T, Jorja was connected at the hip to her counterpart, the CIO of the Office of Director of National Intelligence. The DNI was the premier overseer when it came to intelligence as put forth by the Bush Administration in the later part of 2004. After 9-11, Homeland Security was supposed to be the glue, the liaison between the CIA and FBI but a new committee was needed to encompass the entire Intelligence Community. This Intelligence Community consisted of not only the CIA, FBI, and Homeland, but all branches of the military, DEA, NSA, Department of State, and a slew of other government agencies, sixteen in all. They were the change machine that funneled all the information and sorted it to the appropriate wrapper or in this case, an agency, for further analyses. Jorja had to make sure that the information they received from DNI was routed to the correct department within the CIA in a timely manner. Prior to her move she spent many of days and nights floating between Langley and an undisclosed location close to the White House drafting budgets, going over communication protocols, and sorting through piles of documentation in what amounted to be an internship for her new position. As her learning curve seemed to lessen, she grew more comfortable with her title and surroundings with each passing day, though she still wasn't used to having an office of her very own.

Jorja's new office was still sparsely decorated but she made room for her only prized possession—the full one sheet movie poster to "2001: A Space Odyssey," hanging right next to her poster from "Silence of the Lambs". This was no ordinary movie poster, oh no, this was indeed a rare specimen. She first laid eyes on the poster when she was on a field trip to New York City and she visited MoMA at the age of twelve. Right there and then she vowed to herself that one day she would own such a work of art. Two years ago she forked out over thirteen thousand greenbacks for her holy grail at an auction down in Dallas. Yes, thirteen thousand—it is that rare. In the collectors' circle this poster is simply dubbed the "Eye" poster. It consists of a close-up shot of a human eye in orange and blue and the famous Star Child in its pupil, with a tagline that reads "the ultimate trip." The poster was produced to promote the 70mm relaunch in New York and was supposed to appeal to the movie goers who entered the theater half way through the film stoked by the wacky weed and wanting to finish out their trips amidst the stars and music. The fact that this poster was used for wilding, the act of pasting posters at construction sites, on fences and walls throughout the city, very few survived, very few survived in this pristine of a condition. It cost Jorja another thousand to frame it and protect her investment. The day she got promoted she knew this piece would be making the ultimate trip to her new digs so she could enjoy it each and every work day, which amounts to almost seven days a week in this job. Getting this piece from apartment, to car, through the parking garage, through security, in the elevators, to her wall was comical at best but was worth every smile and light profanity under her breath. As she smiled and stared at her eye, she sipped her morning cup of Joe—jet black, none of this half skim milk double foam mocha latte five dollar a cup crap . . . she loved the taste of coffee so why mask it with sugars and cream, besides look at all the money and time she saved by not going to some overrated Seattle coffee joint. Time was money as the old saying goes but so was coffee; at about five bucks a day for some glorified handpicked java beans and hot city non-filtered water, that adds up to a little over eighteen hundred dollars a year (weekends included). Place that in a money market account and over twenty years that's a tidy sum, maybe help finance a boat or vacation home for retirement or even another poster. She sipped her free cup of bitter as she waited for her computer to boot and entered her login, password, and for even more security as opposed by the federal government in regards to biometric scans, she swiped her index finger. Jorja was now plugged into the network, one of the most powerful networks in the world and it was not even seven in the morning.

Before joining the CIA she worked for the Office of Naval Intelligence as a project manager for some sensitive development projects; her uncle, a Senate Armed Service Committee member recommended her for the job. She entered the CIA eight years ago on her own merit but unbeknownst to her, her uncle might have had a little talk with a certain somebody, given a gentle tap on the back, and paid for a round of drinks—favors are the true currencies in this town—she fully earned the position of Deputy Director of DS&T through her hard work, dedication and smarts—in other words no help from her uncle this time around. Jorja was a smart cookie, always had the flair for electronics, be it computers, cell phones, digital camera, and not once did her VCR ever blinked 12:00. She cruised through computer courses at college, got one of her degrees in software engineering, the other in network engineering. She didn't go to an Ivy League school, though she almost could have if money were not so tight. Her father did the odd jobs here and there to get by and raised his daughter the best he could after her mother was killed in a freak boating accident on the Chesapeake Bay. Her mother had masoned a good solid foundation in her life though common courtesy before she passed on from this world. She died just before Jorja entered school, before her first A, before her first school recital, before Jorja's first kiss, before her first boyfriend, before the prom, before graduation, before life began. She accepted her mother's faith early on in life. Her father was not so lucky. He loved both his daughter Jorja and his wife Caroline. Caroline was the love of his life, he truly missed her everyday and everyday he looked at his daughter and every day the similarities reminded him of his loss, the love of his life, his Caroline. There was no doubt that Caroline and Jorja were mother and daughter. Jorja had her mother's green eyes, vibrant green eyes; it was the first thing people noticed when she wasn't wearing her wire frames. She had her mother's cheekbone structure and wavy sandy brown hair which she wished was straight as all women with wavy hair do. At age thirty-eight and standing at five-eight, Jorja was a spitting image of her mother, there was no hiding that fact. What she did hide was her fit figure, hidden behind unrevealing cloths which seemed to be the norm when working for the government. She also hid the fact of her father's health. It wasn't Jorja's fault but her father fell into a state of depression. Every time Jorja was successful in a turning point of life, her father would dwell on the fact that his wife was not here to cherish in these moments. The more successful Jorja became the more depressed her father became and his broken heart just couldn't take it any longer. Her father died late last spring.

She opened her email glanced at the headers and before she got any urges to open them, she accessed the report server and dialed up a report labeled—IP Addresses, She entered today's date, punched enter on her ergonomic keyboard and waited a few seconds but before she could analyze the report her phone rang, then it rang again, and again, her inbox was starting to fill up, and before she could breathe it was way after lunch. Again she noticed the IP report but again she was interrupted, she noticed a buzz in the air, like chaos was about to erupt. Then an emergency alert appeared on her screen which blocked out her entire desktop. A wave of data is about to be upon us, she thought, the chaos she thought. She picked up the phone and at the same time fired off an alert to her staff—meeting in conference room D in fifteen. Then as predicted, the wave hit and all hell broke loose; news about the shootings had hit the airwaves.

She had a few minutes of air while her staff collected any data prior to the meeting; she thought about replacing her cold coffee but instead glanced at the prompts for the IP report that was still open on her desktop. Having been promoted within the past month she has found many new encumbrances, report reading of IP addresses was not one of them; she simply could not let her old responsibilities fade away. This report was latest and greatest list of all the IP addresses (a number similar to a phone number that identifies the device such as a computer or printer, on a network) that were flooding the routers of the CIA on a daily basis. The report was divide into countries in regards to ordering, whether or not the address was incoming or outgoing, and the number of hits each IP address received. Sure hackers could spoof IP address but not necessarily the traces placed on them from the CIA. Very few people had that kind of smarts—there were other reports for those individuals. At the very top of this report was an IP address with no country and a few hits in the outgoing column—meaning the hits to this machine originated from within these walls. Odd she thought, the address looked familiar, like a federal IP number but if it was a federal number it would have been marked under the United States. Her curiosity peaked. She ran the IP address against a few databases, all coming up blank. Her curiosity peaked even more. She quickly checked her past reports, before she was the deputy director—she saved everything; she was a pack rat. No mention of this IP address anywhere, none. Before she could investigate any further Jorja made her way to conference room D. She gathered what little information there was and laid out her plans to her staff and was back at her desk within forty minutes. The IP Address report was still open but that wasn't her priority now. Her curiosity was still peaked and she quickly went to the router's configuration file and blocked access to and from the IP address until she could fully confirm its identity, then she wrote the number down on a sticky and attached it to her monitor. If someone needs it, someone will scream she thought.

●　　●　　●

Chapter 4

It worked like a charm, each and every time, he was four for four. He carried a picture of the cutest little puppy, walked up to his little girl and asked her if she had seen Max. He used the name Max because it was the most common pet name in America—learned that one from a Snapple top he did, number 415 to be exact. The answer to his "Have you seen Max?" was always the same of course, "no," then he would ask her to help find his lost puppy. He carried an empty leash which made it more convincing, not that a five year old would pick up on such a thing but it was just a precaution for any of the adults in the vicinity. He learned this trick from one of the daytime talk shows, probably Oprah, on how to prevent your child from getting kidnapped—daytime television was full of good ideas and the other nice thing was no one could really track what you watched, not like that internet thing—who knew who was watching on that thing or how it could be done. He acted on impulse and did very little planning, it was more of a gut feeling for him. Drive around a little, don't make it too obvious, look for a playground with lots children and very few parents or nannies, of course. He didn't want to stake out or learn the habits of an individual, too much risk involved, someone might catch on, someone might see. He didn't want to be obvious.

His parked the car out of sight because that was the smart thing to do, and headed out of sight around the corner of a building, all while calling out "Here Max, here boy" and of course the little girl was in tow. He checked and double-checked, even triple-checked and made sure no one was watching. He stop by the back of his car, squatted down to look underneath, the little girl followed suit.

"Do you see him?"

"Mmm, no."

He stood up and the little girl followed suit. He then reached into his jacket pocket and fiddled with a zip lock bag, inside the bag was a rag doused with a little bit of homemade chloroform, which he learned was a mixture of bleach and acetone from an old rerun of CSI Miami. In what appeared to be one single motion he lifted the lid to the already unlocked and slightly ajar trunk with his left hand and in his other hand grabbed the rag and from behind his little girl, placed it over both her nose and mouth, all while picking her up and placing her in the trunk. She didn't put up much of a fight, unlike his last one. He noticed this one was still breathing even though she was out cold, also unlike his last one. Things were going his way this time around. He closed the lid to the trunk, checked, double-checked and even triple-checked, no one was watching. He entered his car, took off his bright red baseball hat and with the turn of the key started the engine. The radio was already set to the news station, his air was on the lowest of temperatures, and his gas tank read a little over half full; he was good to go for his seventy-one mile trip back home, just out of reach of the major city's network news. He knew that his local news would carry the missing person report, they did so before, but after a day or two they moved on to more important things like the drought or the price of gas or another shooting in the city, they always did. Before he put the car in drive, he donned his out-of-style Raybands put on his favorite Yankee's cap, checked his mirrors, checked and rechecked and he was good to go. He popped the stick into d and pressed the gas pedal. Shortly thereafter he cursed under his breath calling himself an idiot for he didn't want to draw any attention.

"Camaro, early to mid 70's, dark green or blue, black vinyl top, big wheels. Kidnapping suspect." This went out over all the airways, police band, both am and fm radio, and most important television. This was a Levi's Call, Georgia's own interpretation of the Ambler Alert System put in place by the Georgia Bureau of Investigation (GBI). It was named after eleven year-old Levi Frady who was abducted in October of 1997—his killers were never found. This was the best they could do and the detective in charge reassured and promised this was his best line of action. Both mother and father were unconvinced. Ripley was their daughter, their five year old daughter and she has been missing for over two hours and this seemed like an eternity. They both wanted nothing more than to go running up and down the streets shouting her name to help find their precious daughter but they were made to run the gauntlet of emotions down at police headquarters.

All three family members were stashed in a little brightly lit, tan room with sparse fixings that consisted of a table that has seen better days and a few chairs, the most comfortable being an olive green foam padded chair over metal sitting in the corner and that was occupied by Ripley's brother. He was holding a can of A & W root beer and didn't understand one iota of what was going on; he was very well behaved though. The other metal, non padded chairs were arranged in the typical interrogation fashion, two contained the parents of Ripley on one side, the other side by the detective in charge of their case. A pad of yellow lined paper, a pencil, a black phone, and two glasses of water were the only things on the table. Nothing hung on the wall except, well not actually hung, more like mounted was the typical interrogation one-way mirror, which nobody was behind.

"Why are you both in town today?"

"Two reasons, I had an early morning meeting, then I was going to meet my wife and children for lunch and all of us were going to take Ripley to her appointment?"

"Her appointment?"

"Yes, doctor's appointment just a few shots for her allergies, we never changed her doctor, since we moved, It has been about a year and a half and we wanted to get s little bit further . . . farther from the city life but still have all the comforts of the city, such as quality doctors, shopping, and whatnot. We never really worried about," searching for the right words but chose, ". . . something like this, either when we lived here or our new place."

"What type of allergies?"

Ben knew he was just trying to put them at ease and asking simple questions before he pressed harder, basically trying to trick the emotions so they wouldn't get in the way of the more difficult task that laid ahead. "She has some really bad food allergies, she has to stay away from anything with peanuts, and pollen makes her wheeze, tree pollen is the worst so thank god it's almost summer."

"Seems more and more kids these days have a peanut allergy, back in my day this was unheard of . . . probably something to do with all the steroids and peanut oils they use in processed foods now. What line of work are you in?"

"Tough one really. My full time position is now borough manager of my now home town, but I dabble a little as a business analyst for some pharmaceutical companies, it's not steady work but the pay is rather good."

"And you?," directed towards his wife Lindsay.

"Same line of work, that's how we met, but mostly I've been a mother of two and only work when I want to."

"Okay, can you tell me why you took them to this park?"

"Well, ummm . . . . Ben's meeting was just a short distance away and umm, I, we, used to live right up the street, ummm . . . it was Ripley's favorite park, Samuel was too young to remember, it just seemed like a logical place to spend some time together."

"When was the last time you visited this park?"

"I don't know, I . . . I . . . I just don't remember . . . . ," she was trying not to cry, "Before we moved I think . . . ummm . . . yes, before we moved, probably on a Saturday in late October . . . we moved in November."

"Okay," and the detective took a brief moment, scribbled a few words down on his pad, "Do you have any enemies or people you distrust?" A question from seemingly left field.

"Excuse me?"

"I apologize, I have to ask, you just never know?"

Lindsay was taken back from the question especially the enemies part . . . she hesitated, stared at her husband Ben then glanced at her son, trying to make some sense, trying to find an answer, "we have a lot of friends, we get along with all of our neighbors," the words seemed harder to come by, "Both of my parents are no longer with us, Ben's whole family is . . . ummm . . . I mean I truly love them as my own . . . . I've even stayed on good terms with my ex."

"Ex? When was the last time you saw or talked to him?"

"A few days ago, he called me and ummm . . . told me he was moving to a new townhouse, but . . . . but I'm sure, no I'm positive he wouldn't do this . . ."

"Don't be too quick to judge, more times than not a biological parent is involved."

"He's not her father, Benjamin is, my ex is like an uncle to her . . . . I know what you are thinking, strange that I'm still on good terms, we were just young that's all, we both had wandering eyes and both wander quite a bit when we were in our twenties . . . . but still we have maintained a good friendship, Ben and Terry even go to ball games together."

"Can you call him?"

"Will I call him? Yes, but not now, I just cannnn . . . can't at the moment . . . . I just can't tell him Ripley is . . . ."

"The sooner the better."

"I'll call," and Ben pulled out his cell phone and dialed but the detective nudged him, "Can you use a land line, we want to tap and record this."

Ben felt guilty for Terry was a very good friend to him but he always had this feeling in the back of his mind, you just never know. So he complied with the detective in charge, put his cell away, and dialed a number he knew by heart.

"Terry, it's Ben."

"Hey Ben, what's up? You ready for the game tomorrow night, I've got great seats."

"Terry, bad news, real bad, so listen to me."

"It's not Lindsay?"

"No . . . . Ripley," he took a deep breath," . . . . she's missing".

"Dear god, when, where . . . . what can I do, where are you . . . I'm coming over," the sheer panic set into his voice. With those words "she's missing," still lingering in the air it sucked the wind right out of Lindsay, she broke down and started sobbing. Ben as well, couldn't keep his eyes from wallowing up. Samuel looked up at his mother and father crying and he too started to cry. He didn't realize the situation with his missing sister; he was just upset because both his parents were upset—it was a natural reaction to a child of three. After that call, Ben was as visibly disturbed as his wife, reality was really beginning to set. Before the detective left he had just a few more questions.

"Do you have an answering machine at home?"

"Yes but . . . ."

"Do you have the capability to check your messages when you are away?"

"Yes but . . . ."

"Please, check your messages for me."

With that Ben used the land line once again, entered his four digit pass code and waited.

"You have no new messages."

Ben finally realized what the officer was suggesting . . . as in every missing person case there is a chance it's a kidnapping and the ransom note/call is a possibility.

"Please, there is nothing more you can do here, I have a few more people from the park to interview, you need to go back to your home and wait, I'll send one of my officers with you." And with that the detective parted ways for he knew time was of the essence and he didn't want to spend precious time consoling emotionally distraught parents. It seemed callous but that's what made him good at his job.

Before his other interviews Detective Charles Lynch went to grab a cup of coffee and a smoke but before he could make his way to the break room he was stopped by one of the young rookies.

"Detective Lynch, I was just coming to get you, a Camaro fitting the description was just found just a few miles from the park. A neighbor heard the news and called it in . . . The car is supposed to be in the garage."

"Yeah, but what are the chances this is our car?"

"Well the neighbor who called it in, said he came home around an hour ago"

"Who owns the car?"

"Not sure yet sir."

"You have to know the address and who lives there?"

"Yes, we've checked on that sir but the Camaro is not registered to any of the members of the household.

"Okay, send a crew, now."

In the back of Lynch's mind he knew the odds were against him, but this just might be a lucky break. Sure most cases were solved through hard work and dedication but every so often one just needed a little luck to push it towards closure. This could be just that break. Lynch grabbed his coffee, nixed the idea of having a smoke and went back to interview a few more people from the park and thinking to himself—hopefully, very shortly I'll have another person to interview—strike that, interrogate, he meant to think.

And just like clockwork four squad cars were called into motion, eight officers in all and they surrounded the single family rancher in typical two by two standard cover formation, their guns drawn, with the lead officer and his partner taking the front door.

They rang the bell, heard some rumblings, then "Just a sec., if it's a package just leave it."

They rang again.

"Okay, okay, just a sec," and he opened the door to much his dismay. When there's a kid involved little time is wasted on formalities and pleasantries. He was quickly escorted out the door, handcuffed behind his back, and asked if he owned a Camaro and it wasn't the other way around . . . "Yesssss," saying in a baffled manner.

"Do you mind if we search the house?"

"Huh . . . what . . . . why am I . . ."

"I'll say again do you mind if we search the house?"

His mind raced, the cuffs where tight against his wrist, he wondered if he left anything in plain sight. The officer raised his cuffed hands forcing pain to both his rotator cuffs, much like the pain when being forced to say uncle, only this time it was not meant as a school yard ritual, it was meant to inflict a great deal of deep pain."I'll ask one more time, can we search the house?"

"Yesss," was the painfully response this time.

With that the officer knew he had full rights to search the premises, since the suspect had just forgone his rights granted by the fourth amendment. The four officers who were around back were quickly called to the front and permitted to enter and begin their search. The remaining officers went to the detached garage and indeed there was a dark green 1974 Camaro, black vinyl top, and big ass rear tires. The officers did a quick search of the vehicle, popped the trunk lid, and found nothing—in fact the car was pretty much spotless, like it had just been cleaned. Inside the house the officers started with a quick search, each taking s separate room in the house. They searched closets, under beds, the attic, and the basement, and no little girl was to be found. They then brought in two well trained police dogs to help in the search for Ripley. One dog, the biggest German Shepherd anyone has seen, took off immediately for the basement, down the stairs, and around the corner towards a shelving unit. The dog started barking because that's what he was trained to do when he found what he was looking for . . . so he barked and waited for his master's arrival. When his master arrived he barked and scratched behind the shelving unit. The shelving unit was a massive wooden structure consisting of old paint cans, electrical wire, and other household maintenance items that are rarely used. The officer was joined by his partner and both sets of muscles were needed to move the shelf even a faction of a foot. After a minute or two they were able to step behind the monstrosity and they found what the dog was barking at. A reward was justified. Affixed to the back of the wooden shelf was a bag of pot—a little more than an ounce. Besides this, the house looked in normal working order albeit from the dirty kitchen sink filled to brink with unsoaked dishes from many boiled pasta dinners with canned sauce and those shaky cans of filled preservative parmesan cheese that seemingly never goes bad. And no little girl, no Ripley Newenberg age five was to be found . . . time was of the essence

This time Detective Charles Lynch was mono a mono in the same brightly lit interrogation room and this time there were people behind the mirror. This time was different; this time there was a suspect in the room, a suspected in his early twenties.

"Empty you pockets please and take off that hat." He recorded the contents of his pockets in his yellow pad, "What were you doing at this house?" and so the question and answer session began.

"Why am I here, I . . . . I . . . Don't understand."

"Answer my questions first," in his best intimidating voice.

Silence as the young man contemplated his options, then, "I . . . I'm allowed there . . . it's my step dad's . . . he's away, out of town, comes back next week."

"And your mother?"

"At home . . . can I call her, don't, can't I make a phone call or something?"

"Again I'm asking the questions . . . do you understand? Where is she?"

"At home."

"Home? She wasn't there when we brought you in."

"I said that's my step dad's house, that's not hers."

"Can you explain?"

"Explain what? I don't understand, I'm confused, why am I here?"

"You were staying at your step dad's and not your mothers?"

"My dad, my real dad I have no idea where he is, if he's still alive, my step dad is the only father I really know of, he and my mom divorced a few years ago, we had a fight, my mom and I, I still live there but she hates me coming in late, she hates that I have a life outside of hers, so I moved into my step dad's, for a little while."

"Does he know you are there?"

Silence again filled the air . . . . "Well uhh, no . . . . but but I have a key, he wouldn't mind . . . I've done this before . . . call him, he'll tell ya."

"Where is he?"

"On vacation in . . . . in . . . . fuck I forget."

Unphased by his abrupt use of the f-word, "does he have a cell phone?'

"Nope, ... I . . . think . . . never mind."

"What?"

"No, nothing, ... I was just going to say, he always forgets to pay his phone, sometimes I call and its turned off, he just forgets sometime . . . he has money to pay, he just forgets sometimes, that's all . . . that's why I live with my mom, at least when I go back home if I turn on a light there will be light . . . not that way at my dad's house . . . step dad's"

"What do you do?"

"You mean job? Well, I, I, do things for people."

"Like sell drugs?"

"What, no . . . no . . . no, I'm like a handyman, you know fix a screen door for my neighbor, mow the grass, odd jobs, small jobs, I was pretty good in wood shop in high school and work construction during the summer."

"Why aren't you working now?"

"We are in between jobs, I work tomorrow, I have to be on the job site six sharp."

Satisfied with his answer, "Is that your car in the garage?"

"What, the Camaro?," shaking his head, "no, no way in hell, I couldn't afford the insurance, that's my dad's baby. He's had that car for like forever, as long as I can remember anyways."

"Anyway, no s, it's in your name."

"I know, someday it may be mine, and as far as my mother is concerned, it is mine . . . . he placed the car in my name just before things got ugly with the divorce."

"Do you ever drive it?"

"He'd kill me if I took it out of the garage."

"You didn't answer the question?"

Silence again, then a "no" in an all knowing lie.

"Well, your dad's is on vacation right?"

"Yes," knowing all too well that he knew the truth and he sunk further into the chair.

"The car, that car, your father's Camaro was spotted entering your dad's driveway about two hours ago, if he wasn't home, then who was driving your dad's baby?"

Knowing all too well he was caught, "Me."

"Explain."

"Explain what, yeah I did take his car out, just for a ride, I went to the mall."

"Where else did you go?"

"I just rode around, that's all . . . . did someone report it stolen or something, it's my dad's . . . . step dad's I mean, listen it's in my name right? . . . . yeah this is the first time I took it without permission but . . . . I know, I know, dad doesn't even know I'm here this time, and I took his car, his baby without permission . . . . that's my trouble isn't it?"

He seemed to be grabbing for straws as to his predicament, as to why he was sitting in the room down at the police station. Detective Lynch was starting to question himself as well and stopped with the questions for a few moments while he gathered his thoughts. Charles glanced at his yellow pad of paper and his notes from the previous interviews, he flipped a few pages, flipped again . . . and looked at the table and again at his notes. His notes from the last interview stated a man with a red baseball cap was seen at the playground—on the table in front of the twenty year old, laid a Philadelphia Phillies baseball cap, bright red, with a white "P". He was ready to start questioning again.

"When you rode around, where else did you go?"

"Just to the mall I said, I wanted to get new sneaks, but didn't have enough money, they were like eighty dollars. I even parked the car way out of the way as it wouldn't get scratch or something."

"How much were the sneakers?"

"Eighty dollars."

"Wow, that's a lot for sneakers . . . Did you drive around the vicinity of Ash and Georgia?"

"I don't know where that is . . . I might have . . . I don't know."

"So you just went to the mall and nowhere else, you didn't stop for a hot dog, or watch kids play at the park, or stop and get gas?"

"No, none of that."

"What if I were to tell you, that this car was seen at the playground by Ash and Georgia?"

"I said before, it's possible, I don't know where that is."

"Your car was last seen at Ash and Georgia, a playground is nearby, a young child was taken, kidnapped, a five year old."

He was grabbing for air, he didn't know how to respond. "I . . . I . . ."

"Have you seen her? Did you take her! Where is she? Where, where is she!," as Lynch stood up and was pounding on the table, letting his emotions get the better part of him and he knew he just made a grave mistake in the interview process. He let it slipped that the victim was a girl.

"I . . . I . . . . don't, . . . don't know . . . what you are talking about," as his voice started to grow shaky and scared.

"Damn it you, you better come clean, right now, goddamnit, right now!" in a voice that could be heard down the hall.

"I . . . I . . . I . . . swear to you . . . I swear," with the last part barely audible over breathless sobs.

Detective Lynch watched his reaction and eased back into his chair. He was beginning to think he was on a wild goose chase, his gut told him so, and he always listened to his gut . . . not just because it was the biggest part of him. He glanced over his yellow tablet again and didn't say a word; he was just about to write the time down on his yellow pad indicating the interview was over when he glanced at the contents of the pockets.

"You said you were at the mall."

A very quiet "Yes," was heard.

"You were going to buy sneakers," more of a statement of facts then a question

"Yes," shaking his head at the same time.

"You said, they were eighty dollars and you didn't have enough money."

"Yes," again shaking his head at the same time.

"Curious, why didn't you buy them?"

"I didn't have enough money, I was short a few bucks."

"You bad at math?"

"Huh, . . . bad at math . . . no, no, not that bad, I measure angles, square footage and stuff like that."

"Well, on the table you have eighty-seven dollars and some change . . . that's Cleary enough for your sneaks, expensive as they may be."

"At the time I was going to buy them I didn't have enough money."

"Did you raid your dad's . . . I mean step dad's cookie jar when you got back home?"

"No."

"Visit an atm machine on your way home?"

"No."

"Just curious, then where did you get the extra money?"

"Some guy."

"What do you mean some guy?"

"Some guy came up to me at a stop sign and asked what year my car was, he said seventy-four was the same year as his old one, then he handed me ten bucks and asked if I wouldn't mind waiting there while he went to go get his camera, he said there was another ten in it for me and he would be no more than five minutes. He wanted a picture of the engine, he seemed nice enough but he never returned, I waited like an extra ten minutes."

"And then?"

"Nothing, I got tired of waiting . . . more like pissed, so I punched it a little and squealed my . . . the tires."

"Where was this?"

"I don't know."

"Was there a playground around?"

"I don't re . . . . wait a minute . . . I remember looking in my rearview mirror . . . seeing if this guy was going to return, I remember seeing a big red sliding board. But, but that's all I remember."

Detective Charles Lynch wrote the ending time of his interview down on his yellow pad.

"Officer Roberts here is going to take you down to see one of our sketch artists."

And just like that, the detective was out the door . . . no apologies . . . he didn't have time, time was of the essence. In his mind now this was a bonafide kidnapping case and the Levi's call placed by the GBI was justified.

● ● ●

Chapter 5

"Access Denied" Strange he thought and tried it again—"Access Denied". He tried another search, and the same reply was shown on the screen "Access Denied". He didn't get a "Server Unavailable" or a hundred other messages implying database backups or system maintenance. It was he himself that was being denied access which was strange in and unto itself for there were only three other people who had access to the machine and knew its purpose and two were at the White House and one them had asked for his help in the research. It was only a matter of time until the phone rang. He tried to circumvent his point of entry to no avail. He tried backdoors and other tricks of the trade and each and every time, "Access Denied." Someone shut him out but whom? Why? Just as the phrase "son-of-a-bitch" was echoing through his brain, the inescapable ring of his cell phone sounded. It was indeed Scott.

"How did you do?"

"I was able to pull names, dates, times, and locations and was in the midst of creating a solid timeline of events but . . . ."

"But what?"

"I was locked out!"

"What do you mean locked out?"

"Exactly like I said, I got an access denied message, from what I gather it was placed by someone in house. I've tried other venues but they pretty much have them locked as well."

"Who has access to shut down something like this?"

"I could only speculate that it was from the top in the department either Peter or ummm Mike, and neither of them have a clue and why would they sudden shut us out, it's not like they know about the network?"

"Good question. Send over what you have so far, I'll try to access this as well, if not I'll call Peter. I'll be back in touch shortly. Give me fifteen minutes." Click.

Scott immediately pulled up his virtual private network (VPN) on his laptop, logged in, and scanned his index finger. During the few seconds in which it took to connect, he cursed under his breath. He simply didn't have time to do his own research; he was the point man to the President, he was the man with the answers, he didn't dig for data, he didn't comb through meaningless information, he didn't analyze the mundane, he had an inside man to do just that, one who used to have access.

"Fuck!"

On the screen "Access Denied".

He flipped open his cell, punched in a number on speed dial and within a few seconds the direct line to the director rang.

"Hello Scott, make it fast please I'm in the middle of shit storm as you can imagine"

"I know I'm working on the same from my end, I was trying to piece together a timeline but I was shut out of a system I need for completion. The President wants this information yesterday so helping me restore my connection is imperative. I got an access denied message."

"Understood. You coming in from the vpn?"

"Yes."

"Okay, during a crisis we always block some sites on the outside, it keeps the traffic down. Do you have an IP?"

"Yes, ends in twelve dot one six eight."

"Just a second, I'll put you through to one of my techies . . . . On second thought it'd be faster if I would do it for you, hold on." Peter's fingers raced across the key board as he open the main servicing center command window. Yes, he was the director, the head fromage so to speak but he knew his way around the network, besides it would take even longer to explain things to a peon and he wanted Scott off his back as soon as possible. The last thing he wanted was the President to shuttle even more responsibility to Homeland Security after being deemed uncooperative whenever the "T" word was uttered, ". . . ummm . . . . yes, it looks like it was manually blocked. You should be back in business."

"Thanks Peter."

"You're welcome, if you find out any information, keep me in the loop will ya?"

"Absolutely Peter, thanks again." he was already out of the loop Scott thought.

The call and even more importantly the IP address was a fading memory to Peter on this very hectic day. Not so was the case just a few doors down the hall from the director. The truth to the matter, the IP address was not available to the outside network, it resided somewhere on the network at Langley. It was just made to look like an outside address. The reason it was contained inside was that it needed the protection from the very best firewalls the planet has to offer.

● ● ●

Chapter 6

". . . . but the people at the top are controlling this world.

And to top it off, they get taxed less than you . . . . oh it may seem like a lot, thirty-five percent, but take that from an annual salary of ten million dollars. That's three and a half million dollars. Chump change I'm telling you. Are they telling us they can't live on the six-point-five million dollars per year? Boy I sure hope they can pay their minimum wage housemaids in a timely manner. Now take the average American earning thirty-five thousand dollars a year, take twenty percent of their salary for taxes. That leaves them with twenty-eight thousand—the average American car cost more than that. Twenty-eight thousand dollars, twenty-eight thousand dollars left to feed a family, pay rent and utilities, insurance, healthcare, and any other living expenses. Barely getting by.

Then we have the middle class—a middle class that is declining at an unprecedented rate. We once had the biggest in the world. Not anymore, not today. The middle class is shrinking, and they are not moving up my friends. We are heading for a two class system. Lower and upper. The upper class is controlling this country. They streamline, they merge, and in turn, they cut jobs. Cut jobs of good people, hardworking people. They never reinvest in the people, they never reinvest in the people that made them rich. They just take and take all while distancing themselves from the common folks—see the limos in their driveways, see the gates at the end of their driveways? They see it coming. We are heading for trouble. Don't believe me? Just ask France or the Bolshevik's. You say an uprising, a revolution cannot happen in this day and age . . . think again . . . . who's going to stop it?

Who is going to stop it?

I am . . . .I am . . . . I can help. Help Now! My solution—tax the people who can afford to be taxed not the ones who can't. They don't want to reinvest in the people who made this country great . . . we'll reinvest for you. Reinvest in America, in its people, the American people. Believe me, the money makers of this world can live on what they've got . . . it's the people who don't got, that can't live. I'm telling you now this has got to be done, done now!!! Or we're heading for trouble"

Click.

"Stacy, get Scott in here now!"

Scott Norwood, or as some call him Wide Right after the famed Buffalo Bills' place kicker, forty-six, stands an inch just shy of two yards (six feet for those following at home), pepper gray hair that has been that way for the past six years, Brown Alumni, Georgetown Law—top of his class in both. Arrogantly intelligent, so much so, he always brags about getting eighteen hundred on the SAT's, "I've even did the extra credit on the back," he proclaims. Truth is, he can back up his smarts and is always two to three steps ahead of the competition. He was a member of the Senate Committee on Intelligence for four years and on the Nation Security Council for one, then stepped into the job of deputy director of the CIA, and now, Chief of Staff.

It takes a special person to be his friend. He doesn't have many and those who are, are friends for life. The President is one of those people, a friend, a friend for life. Met in all places, a corner bar on one of those lettered streets in D.C., the kind of bar that has been around since the turn of the last century. Not many people his age walked up to a bar and ordered Lagavulin, in a snifter, one ice cube, especially at eleven in the morning. He wasn't young, in his mid to late twenties, but he wasn't a man, not in this town, not yet and Lagavulin was a man's scotch—like drinking a cigar. It just so happened to be the only scotch Jonathan Whitaker drank as well. In fact, it was his personal bottle behind the bar. Before reaching for the bottle, the bartender glanced at Mr. Whitaker for permission to pour and a nod was given, all without Mr. Norwood knowing.

"Scotch is best sipped at night," Mr. Whitaker jested.

"I wholeheartedly agree, unless it is celebratory in nature," Mr. Norwood replied

"So what are we celebrating this early in the morning Mr.?"

"Mr. Scott Norwood, Scott I prefer. Passing the Washington Bar Exam."

"So you received your letter today. Congratulations are in order."

"No sir, Mr.?"

"No?"

"No, I just finished the last two and a quarter hour session today, hence the celebration."

"But official letters don't go out in the mail for another seventy-one days."

"I don't need a letter, I know I passed. Aced it is more like it."

"So, you are that sure of yourself?"

"Yes, always am."

"Mr. Jonathan Whitaker, Jonathan I prefer."

"Not Jon?"

"No, far too many in this world I'm afraid, I like to stand out and be seen. So, why my scotch?"

"Your scotch? It's like smoke in a bottle. Never much acquired the need for cigarettes but I do get a craving for this gem of a drink from Islay but I save myself for special occasions."

That was a special occasion over twenty years ago and Jonathan Whitaker knew it; unbeknownst to Scott.

● ● ●

Chapter 7

She did as she was told; Stacy summoned Scott Norwood to the President's study just off the Oval Office. Scott's office, though tucked in the corner of the West Wing, was in earshot range of the President if he was truly pissed but in this case he was just annoyed at the donkey named Blair Anderson he saw on TV. Although still a few months away from the primaries, everyone knew Anderson was going to get the democratic nod for the ticket, the democrats knew it as did the republicans, and Jonathan Whitaker knew he wanted him lined up in his sights. In order to put him in focus within the crosshairs, he needed Scott.

"Good you have the game on I see, my Hoyas had control at the half," as Scott walked into the President's study.

"Well now it's a different story, they're down by six with under a minute to go." They watched the last minute of the game which took about ten minutes with commercials and time outs. Georgetown ended up losing by two against Villanova as they never regained the lead. "So did you catch Blair on Primetime?" Jonathan asked.

"All of it, he certainly can talk the talk."

"And that's all he can do and that's all I want him to do, is talk. He's going to give us trouble in a few months."

"Are you saying he's going to be a contender?"

"Scott don't go blowing shit up my ass again, I know you know the facts so what are they?"

"Unless he's doing his intern, strike that, he'd probably be more popular, the only other person the democrats can throw at us is Parker but I bet the only state he would take is Wisconsin, then there are always third parties and not since Perot has there been anybody close. So Blair doesn't have a chance against us, you," knowing of his mistake that it is always about Jonathan.

"I know that and you know that . . . . it's the American people I'm worried about, numbers don't mean a goddamn thing when it comes to November . . . and dammit Scott I want another term, you got that!"

"We all want another term."

"Well I need you to see to that."

"Meaning?"

"Don't give me this meaning shit, you know damn well what I'm talking about, open some doors, rattle some cages, look under the bed if you have to."

"We've been down this road before with Blair."

"Listen you don't have to concentrate on Anderson, look elsewhere, the reason I have you on my team is that you're always one step ahead of the game, so . . ."

"Actually," interrupted Scott, "I've been looking at his potential running mate, Floyd Carson, seems to be of the same caliber as Blair. I know it's way too early to choose his partner for the big dance but all signs point to him, he'd be crazy not to, they are best of friends. The only other contender in my book would be Bowen out of North Carolina but they don't see eye to eye on everything."

"What's your confidence level that it will be Floyd?"

"One hundred percent."

"You cocky son-of-a-bitch, you can never be gray about anything can you?"

"I'm only one hundred percent sure since I saw an email to Carson from Anderson asking him if he would consider the vice presidency Carson never hid the fact that the White House was his primary goal and this would get him one step closer to that door."

"I'm not even going to ask how that email crossed your path."

"And you shouldn't."

"But I want the White House door closed and locked for this duo, you got that?"

"Understood."

"By the way, I think Georgetown will lose their third straight come Saturday against my boys."

"I don't see it, I think Providence will lose by at least five."

"Don't give me that goddamn one hundred percent crap again."

"Then how about odds?"

"Just get the hell out of here and get back to work," Jonathan said with a slight smile.

No skeletons, no snakes, not even a parking ticket, nothing, Floyd Carson was clean, squeaky clean. Floyd took his life seriously, never venturing outside the lines, a straight shooter as they say. His opinions and views are formulated from his facts and thoughts and no one else's. If he felt it, he believed it no matter what other people thought. That's what made him tall, strong, and almost unstoppable. When debating Floyd, if he didn't have all the facts, he never offered a word on the subject at hand, he simply stated "I'll have to get back to you on that when I have more information, I apologize for being unprepared." Few people saw this as being weak, most saw it as having the balls to say "I do not know"—politicians do not need to have all the answers. Floyd Carson fought his whole life against this stereotype and he also fought his whole life to get where he is today but he wanted more and he was going to fight even more. He knew Anderson was going for top dog and he also knew Anderson was going to ask him to be his running mate. It was just the fact that vice president was a vice more than his ultimate goal. Yeah every kid growing up uttered the words "I want to be president," few kids actually knew the true meaning of this statement—Floyd was not one of them. He grew up and saw the power of the presidency, saw a president bring down the wall and really change the world—he wanted to do the same. "Start out small," he thought, "don't bite off more than you can chew." And when he became class president he took those thoughts in stride. Floyd knew all too well the class president was elected on popularity and not leadership, so he became popular, a well liked individual by every clique from the geeks, to the motorheads, the potheads, the cheerleaders, and the football players. Everyone knew Floyd Carson but most important, everyone liked Floyd Carson. He won hands down, wasn't even close, a landslide as they say, no one even knew who ran against him. Once elected, Floyd immediately took into action, stepped up to the plate of leadership and challenged school policy and kept a promise to his fellow students. He had many changes he wanted to make but he remembered "start out small, don't bite off more than you can chew"—he did just that. His first successful challenge was the school's dress code, one line in particular—it simply stated no shorts for boys. Put it this way, when spring was in bloom, so was a new dress code, along with sexy legs everywhere. He was successful in removing a dead-beat teacher and creating more parking spaces for the students and a senior lounge. He didn't win every battle but he learned from his mistakes, and learned well. He moved into college where he honed in on his skills, the college presidency could have been handed to him on a silver platter if he wanted it but elected not to run. He wanted more, to learn more, and not be bogged down with school policy . . . . he had already done that, instead Floyd took to his studies. History, critical thinking, statistics, public speaking, and yes he even took political science and was entrenched in the ROTC program. He graduated with a three point eight. He then went to law school to hone his skills even more, never once did the thought of becoming a lawyer ever cross his mind—just wanted to learn how they think was all. He wanted to know how to lie, manipulate words and statistics in order to combat them we he needed. Two years of his life were spent there, in the bowels of deceit, the pit of hell with the scum of the earth, the future ambulance chasers, future rape and murder defenders, future law makers—worth every penny. Fresh out of law school, he took the bar in his home state of Virginia and passed—would have been a shame to have spent all that money and not prove yourself. From there his stepping stones took him to an internship at his state's congressmen's office where he honed his political skills. The stones grew bigger as he became a congressman, then the senator of Virginia for four consecutive terms. The only thing missing from his repertoire that might hinder his ultimate goal would be a tour of duty in the armed forces; after all, it is hard to be the Commander in Chief without an ounce of actual field experience running through the course of your veins but it has been done before.

At age fifty-five, Floyd Carson has been around the block a few times and knew Washington like the back of his hand. It was a given that when Blair Anderson would ask Floyd Carson to be his running mate the answer would be a resounding "YES". In fact Senator Carson already had his letter of intent drafted and waiting. He and Blair were great friends and most important great allies. It was hard sometimes to tell their views apart—they believed in the greater good and that there was still hope that the trust was not betrayed in the American public. The past few years it was particularly hard for the American public to trust anyone again, from lying under oath about sex and taxes, to too close to call elections where you needed your brother's help to recount votes in his governed state in order to win. Really who knows what terrible secrets are still hidden beneath the stories of 911 or on the oil fields of the Middle East. The trust is almost gone; hence the duo's campaign slogan would simply read "Trust." Just try to unearth any skeletons or snakes, as said before—squeaky clean.

Most of the past year of Floyd's life was spent at twenty-five hundred dollar per plate dinners with Anderson and businessmen wanting to gain an ear of a possible future president. He hated it but was a necessary evil—they needed the campaign funds—millions of them. Because of this, time with his family was nearly nonexistent. Even this past Christmas was cut short and the last time he made love to his wife was almost a year and a half ago. There just weren't enough hours in the day for his family and his political career to coexist. He had to prioritize and it wasn't ever easy. He too missed that special bond with his wife of twenty-seven years—the wife that stood by his side in every decision he has ever made, even guiding him when morality seemed to dissipate in the wind of political lies. It was his wife Grace that he loved dearly and he too could see the tension forming between them. Wining and dining, debates, conference calls with god who knows who, little sleep, meetings and more meetings took their toll on their marriage. There was just no time for even himself yet alone Grace. She stood by her man though, with big smiles through thick and thin. She just might one day be the first lady; little did Floyd realize that was the last thing Grace ever wanted Scott Norwood came to this conclusion as well after he read a personal email from Grace

●　　●　　●

Chapter 8

His remark for calling himself an idiot earlier was the fact he removed his hat and put on another pair of glasses and his lucky baseball cap, to someone watching, in his mind, this was a sure tell sign of someone changing his disguise. "Idiot, it's the little things like that, that will be trouble down the road," he thought to himself. Seventy-one miles later clocking in at just under two hours and fifteen minutes, he was in his driveway. He made just two stops along the way, stop one was to check on his little girl and slip a gag over her mouth, the other was to the laundry mat to pick up his clothes that were placed in the dryer earlier that day. A clever ruse so he thought, for when he pulled into his driveway, he popped open the trunk, grabbed the big canvas laundry bag and the detergent and calmly walked into his house. He wished he would have thought of this earlier it would have saved him from trying to come up with a last minute schema during his third attempt. That time he panicked when he entered his driveway for he simply didn't think it through. He ran into his house and pondered the situation. He pondered his dilemma way too long, for his prized little blonde died from heat exhaustion in the back of his trunk. Not this time, it was pure brilliance so he thought and this time his prized little blonde was safely inside the house. He carried the bag down into the basement, the bag that contained his little girl. She was still out cold. He moved her into a bedroom, a bedroom he finished not long ago, a bedroom for a little girl, his little girl. The room was far from perfect from a builder's perspective and would have never passed inspection. The electrical work was shoddy at best, the drywall buckled near the top, the drywall tape showed through the bright pink paint, and the trim was uneven but the room was perfect for a little girl. There was a bright pink shag carpet on the floor, and the furniture was pine painted in white, trimmed in gold and not new, there were many scuffs marks on the legs from a vacuum cleaner maybe, and a few deep scratches on the bureau. The bureau was filled to the brim with little girls clothes in all types of sizes and the same was true for the nice size closet—nothing seemed to be missing in the wardrobe department for a little girl, from shoes, sneakers, hair barrettes, little undies in every color, to bright t-shirts also in every color, sweaters and jeans, one or two very nice dresses appropriate for church attire and even a cute little jean jacket with rhinestones in the shape of a daisy. There was a nightstand with a white wicker lamp with a white wicker lampshade that provided the only source of light in the room . . . there was no natural light whatsoever. The bed was small but still perfect for a five year old and had a canapé with white ruffles around all the edges. Fresh linens and a big fluffy comforter on the bed disguised the fact that it was used. Pink throw pillows and a stuffed panda bear completed the ensemble. There was a book shelf with many new and used children's book with such classics as Chris Van Alsberg's The Polar Express to the Grim Brothers' Fairy Tales and the complete collection of the Chronicles of Narina. On top of the bookshelf were a record player and some old children's records. There was even a fairly new Barbie's dream house with pool and swimsuit Barbie along with her corvette in the one corner. On the walls were a few nicely framed prints of beach balls and a sandcastle and some seashells, and a full length built-in mirror on the opposite side of the bed. She even had her own bathroom with a toilet, a small tub and sink, a pink toothbrush and a pink plastic rinse cup, along with pink towels and a bathmat that matched. The bathroom was badly tiled all in white ceramic tile and would have made it sterile looking if it wasn't for all the pink accessories. Any five year old girl would have thought this was heaven . . . . if not for the dead bolts on the steel door.

He opened his canvas bag, took out his little girl and placed her gently on the bed . . . . like sleeping beauty. He bent over and kissed her on the forehead, she did not wake—unlike sleeping beauty. He picked up the canvas bag, walked out the door, and clicked all three locks to their locked position. His little girl was safe at last; his little girl was home at last.

•   •   •

Chapter 9

The chaotic day of the Mall Massacre came and went, it was closing in on early February, and it seemed as though the FBI had things under wraps and Jorja was back to the mundane work of poring over budget reports. Working at the DS&T was not a glamorous position by any stretch of the means; one could justifiably be called a nerd. It entails a flare for technology, analytical skills, as well as a vast comprehension for numbers, a lot of numbers and not just the ones and zeros of the digital world. Jorja is good at this part as well, strike that—great; this, more than any other characteristic was what propelled her into this position, the characteristic of her vast comprehension for numbers, numbers of the general ledger kind. She is responsible for budgets that involved payroll, computers, servers, routers, T1 and T3 lines, fiber optic lines, databases, satellite uplinks, software, pagers, cell phones, email, operating systems, and any other form of communication device that links people and people, computers and computers, and people and computers. She is responsible to report these numbers directly to the Deputy Executive Director of the CIA. She is responsible for running a tight ship and running a state-of-the-art ship—a ship that has to stay one step ahead of the competition, the thieves, the terrorists, the hackers, and the governments—both hers and theirs. She is responsible for learning on the fly, learning from the past, and learning from mistakes—both hers and theirs. Green eyed Jorja Carson, age thirty-eight, has many responsibilities as Deputy Director of the DS&T. and her most important responsibility is that of security.

As one can image, security at the Central Intelligence Agency is top priority—"the" top priority. Everything is checked and checked again, then checked again. All software must be review, line by line, by the best in the business. If a company didn't supply the source code (the actual code written in a language understandable by humans) or the CIA would not be allowed to compile the code on their own, the software package was simply not permitted in house, even Microsoft had to go through this rigorous ordeal, no exceptions. The hardware side of things must also be checked and checked and checked again, from disk drives, to computer memory, to the keyboard and the mouse. A few years ago a company who shall remain nameless, supplied the CIA with replacement keyboards. The keyboards failed quite regularly and replacements were always supplied with a speedy smile. They failed due to planned obsolescent, in plain English, the return key was made with shoddy parts—on purpose. The keyboards were also made with a few added perks that went under the radar of the agency for over two years. They were made with a memory chip and a small processor that logged the first one hundred or so keystrokes each and every time the computer was turned on. In other words, the first thing most people do when turning on their computers in the morning . . . . they log on . . . . capturing their usernames and passwords. It wasn't noticed until a devious little CIA techie was performing an April Fool's joke. The joke was to place a music chip, like those contained in a greeting card, and hook it up to the caps lock key. Why the caps key lock? The caps lock key is linked to a small power supply in order to light up the small LED to notify the user that the caps lock is on (located on the top left-hand or right-hand of almost any keyboard). All the joke needed was to solder a few extra wires from this power supply to the music chip, when the caps lock key was pressed it supplied power to the LED and at the same time, the music chip, and music would begin to play. When the joke worked most people assumed the annoying little ditty came from their computers and not underneath their keyboard, driving them and their neighbors a little batty while trying to adjust their volume on their computers. On one particular early morning of April 1st a keyboard was opened and a little secret was revealed. That same caps lock key light was used to supply just enough power for a memory chip to capture the first one hundred or so keystrokes each and every time the computer was turned on. Then when the keyboards failed, the chips were swapped out with each new keyboard the CIA received. Ingenious. Needless to say, the ingenious company has since perished along with many of their employees. The former security officer was in a wee bit of hot water over that one but he managed to survive just long enough to open his golden parachute. The techie who discovered the device was given a small reprimand for his devious stunt but in the long run it was totally worth it; he was given a promotion and is now the security officer reporting directly to Jorja. If Jorja was ever to remain in her position and receive her chute, she would need help from people she trusted and the techie reporting directly to her she trusted with her life. She trusted Greg Manoski.

Greg was plain and simple—a stereotypical nerd, aside from the fact he was trim even though he lives on junk food from the vending machines. He drinks the Dew like it was going out of style, dresses in grays and blacks, not for the slimming effect but because it was easy to look coordinated with minimal effort—learned that one from Albert E, has the driest of humor that even an Englishman would consider wet, occasionally has the same flair for the word fuck as the military, and could spout a quote from the popular Tracy Ullman spin-off quicker than two teenagers getting off in a backseat of dad's car. If he wasn't sleeping, he was in front of his array of computers pounding away to the ends of the internet and running reports out his ass and that's exactly what he was doing on this Sunday,

This Sunday was a slow yellow day. "Elevated" was the term provided by Department of Homeland Security on their five color-coded scale. Funny, no one can ever recall if their scale was ever set to their lowest color green or "Low" . . . don't want the terrorists hitting us with our guards down do we? "Hey Amad, look, it's green on the website—no one's watching, let's go, bring the nuke." Yes it was a slow yellow day with CNN churning out their liberal slander, forest fires in California, and something about the latest femme fatale who drug overdosed right after her concert the night before. Yes, a slow yellow day for Greg as well; sitting in his cubical running daily reports, looking for suspicious activity among library book checkouts (kidding on that part . . . . but possible), and theoretically making the world a better, safer place. He was working on his fourth can of crab juice, aka. Mountain Dew, so aptly named by one of his colleagues while watching a Simpsons' episode involving the World Trade Center and some low-bit toilet humor, when an automatic email appeared on his

Blackberry. It read "Fingerprints". This was a message generated from a program in which he wrote years ago. It was to inform him that a file was on its way. The file contained all fingerprint records to be uploaded to IAFIS (Integrated Automated Fingerprint Identification System owned by the FBI) through various Police departments around the country. The normal channel of delivery for such a file was through the FBI network; after all it was the database owned by the FBI. Being the smart guy Greg was, he intercepted this file prior to arriving on the FBI's network. He had listeners installed to retrieve any packages of information with specific headers verifying it was indeed a Federal Bureau of Investigating IAFIS file and he simply routed this to his/CIA network first. From there he would download the file into the CIA's database and cross-reference this with any known undercover agents, CIA's wanted lists, or VIP's in the system. The program was requested by the former Deputy Director of DS&T after the FBI exposed one of their ops in the field. It was an accident but try explaining that to his widower and only child. Since this program was installed there have been several incidents that have gone under the radar of the feds at the bureau and for good reason. Once the file was scanned it was placed back into the queue for IAFIS, uploaded with a new timestamp and maybe, just maybe a few key pieces of information deleted or changed and everybody was none the wiser. The whole process of cross-referencing was an automatic process but there was a manual process in which Greg alone was responsible—it needed a pair of human eyes and the touch of human logic that a computer could not provide in order to evaluate the hits within the CIA's database. It was rare that a hit occurred but when it did he would have to investigate the matter and sometimes call his supervisor in order to continue. As luck would have it on this slow yellow day one such hit flashed on his screen after he opened his trusty old program.

It was from a police report from Saint Michael's Maryland dated 1978. The IAFIS system came on line in 1999 but since then there has been a tremendous amount of backlog with getting old files uploaded. The typical scenario would be when an officer responsible for caseload had any downtime; they would gather any unsolvable crime or missing person reports and batch them together to be sent to the feds. Some departments worked better than others, some took their time; after all, a thirty-year old unsolved case rarely took precedent over a case that was in the here and now. The scenario in Saint Michael's was they just forgot until some newbie wanting to make a good impression, entered the department. That newbie found a few files in a forgotten box by a forgotten file cabinet in a rarely used room. He noted a few fingerprints and decided on his own to send them to the good folks in Washington. There was not one officer left in the department who worked on any of these cases.

Greg did a double-take when he saw the name, the name belonging to the fingerprints, the name that should not belong on a missing person report, and the name he knew all too well. He had mistakenly put two and two together and came to the wrong conclusion; that conclusion being the owner of the fingerprint was missing. He read the summary and corrected himself. He then went on to read the entire report. He noted the date, the time, and of course the name and location. These fingerprints were lifted at the last known scene of the missing person, they were found on a vessel drifting afloat in the Chesapeake. The report claimed that Ms. Nash was an avid boater, who enjoyed sunset cruises and tossing an occasional trap into the waters for the tasty Maryland Blue Crab. The report claimed Ms. Nash was by herself at the time, confirmed by the neighbor who stayed at home to watch her daughter in return for a few crabs and by another boater who waved to Ms. Nash upon passing her within a mile from her home. Ms. Nash's husband was still at work. The boat was found the next day with a small amount of blood belonging to Ms. Nash and a few dead crabs. One of the crabs in particular contained some of Ms. Nash's blood within its claw. There were no traps on board and a few pieces of chicken used as bait. Also on board were two wine glasses and no wine bottle. The glasses contained one set of prints belonging to Ms. Nash, the other to an unidentified person. No other liftable prints from the unidentified person were found on the vessel. The case remained opened since a body was ever found but the conclusion was that she fell overboard during the retrieval of one of the crab traps. The officer working the case wrote a brief note saying no foul play was involved and deemed it an accident but never officially closed the case due to the missing body. The blood was caused by a poorly placed hand and the claws of a captured crab.

After Greg read the entire report, he reread it again just to be on the safe side. He knew this file could be detrimental to the name belonging to the fingerprints even if it was over twenty years old. He also knew this was a call out of his hands, so he called the Deputy Director of Science and Technology, he called Jorja.

"Yes, Greg"

"I just received a hit off our incoming IAFIS file . . . and"

"And what?"

"You're going to want to see this, and see it now"

"Anybody we know?"

"Yes, everybody is going to know."

"Send it."

"Will do, it's on its way. Just remember I'll need you to embiggen more power to me in order to change the timestamp a sap."

"Embiggen?"

"Yes embiggen, it's a perfectly cromulent word."

"Cromulent? Now you're making things up."

"No, no, no . . . that's in the Webster's Dictionary, look it up."

"Never saw those words on my SAT's."

"That's because they didn't exist until about 1995 or so."

"Oh let me so guess . . . . your favorite yellow family, the Simpsons?"

"You got it, season seven," with that he hung up before she could even ride him about it and sent the file via the normal encryption to Jorja's desktop.

Almost instantaneously it was on her computer monitor. Almost instantaneously she was in shock. Almost instantaneously she knew she had a big decision to make. Greg was more than right; everyone knew the name of this person. It was indeed a VIP and possibly a future VP. It was the name of Senator Anderson's best friend. It was Jorja's uncle. It was Floyd Carson. "But why were they on a missing person's report?" Even before she read the report summary she came to the conclusion to change the file and yes, mainly because it dealt with her uncle. She immediately picked up the phone and dialed Greg's extension. As she waited for the connection, which was almost instantaneously, she glanced at her monitor and glanced at the report.

"Hey Jorja, told you, what do you want me to do?" There was silence. "Jorja?"

On the other end of the phone Jorja was now truly in shock. She was trying to reel her mind around what she just read but couldn't grasp it. It went blank. Then she finally heard Greg on his fourth attempt.

"Jorja, do you want me to flag this?"

"Yes, flag it, flag it now, I'll call you back," and she hung up the phone and started to read the entire report. Her eyes stop at a specific word. She stared at this word and couldn't move past it. It was as if her eyes blurred out all other surrounding words on purpose, as if this word was in 3-D, and burning into her retinas. The word wasn't really a word at all. It was a name—the name of Nash. She hadn't thought of that name in quite some time and now that name opened a floodgate of memories.

Greg got his answer. He removed the report from the file without so much of a reaction. His nimble fingers glided across the keyboard typing various commands and hitting various function keys and before any amount of time had elapsed the file was on its way back to the FBI with a new timestamp—a new timestamp and a missing report that would have seriously caused questions and concerns for a campaign duo that could take on the White House. Greg knew why she had flagged the report, although he thought he knew; given the circumstance he'd have done the same, and almost did but he wanted that decision to be hers. He didn't need his ass on the line and what a thin line it was. Greg returned his eyes to a copy of the report he had just confiscated and reread it yet again. He took note of the facts and wanted to dig a little more, he wanted to find out who was the mystery woman, who was Ms. Nash. Again his fingers flew around the keyboard and not before long he had his answer. His jaw dropped as he read her file. One word stood out from the crowd, yet it wasn't a word at all. It was a name, a name of a daughter, the name of his boss, the Deputy Director of DS&T, the name Jorja Carson. Now he knew the real reason she had him flag the report.

She shook her head, she tried to gather her thoughts, but her mother's name brought back memories of a gentler time, a happier time. Her mind filled with senses of long ago, containing sites of holidays, family, home, and smiles, containing smells and tastes of seafood, especially crab with old bay seasoning, and containing sounds of seagulls, waves, and her mother's soothing voice. Her mind was so filled with joy from the past she didn't notice the tears filling in the corner of her eyes. She remembered walking down to the dock in her backyard, stepping over the few loose boards, and seeing her mother's boat. Carolina's boat was huge . . . okay maybe not huge but to a six year old it was huge. It was her mother's pride. It was aptly named The Carolina Crabber. Her father never ventured on the boat; he didn't very much care for the water; he could never swim, so he was afraid of water but her mother . . . . well her mother should have been born with fins. She loved it. Jorja remembered boarding the boat and her mother immediately making her put on one of those puffy, smelly, bright orange life vests that was two sizes too big for her and very uncomfortable, but "them the rules" her mother would say . . . "them the rules". Caroline was very well educated but always liked that phrase no matter how incorrect it seemed. Jorja remembered turning the key at her mother's command and bringing the engine to life, then the ropes were lifted and the waters of the Chesapeake were theirs. They would ride to a secluded inlet, drop anchor and await the bluish crustaceans. Jorja's favorite method to catch the critters was to tie a chicken leg on a piece of string and lower into the water with a big old lead weight. After fifteen minutes or so, she would slowly, oh so very slowly pull the string into the boat, one finger at a time. It would take almost ten minutes to pull the string to where she could see the chicken leg beneath the surface. More times than not, there would be a crab floating to the surface with the chicken in its claw. With her mother's help, a net would be lowered, the crab snatched, and hauled into the boat, and then the process would start all over again. Her mother had the typical crab traps where each of the four sides of the trap would open when they hit the floor of the bay, when the rope was pulled all sides came up trapping inside any crabs nibbling on the bait. "What fun was that?," Jorja often asked. Thinking back to these times Jorja suddenly couldn't recall the last time she had had crab, two years, maybe five, maybe even ten years ago, maybe even longer. She couldn't comprehend why this was so. She loved crab. She was close to crab. She still lived by the Chesapeake, still lived within the boundaries of crab country, yet for some reason she never craved the delicacy of the bay since her mother's disappearance, that is, not until now. Her trip down memory lane was interrupted by her inbox ding, her eyes focused on her desktop, and she glanced upon the police report again. Her mind shifted back to reality. She reread the summary and now probing thoughts were clanging in her head.

She tried to remember events of that day but they had dissipated over the years, plus she was very young at the time, all that was left were snapshots in her mind. She remembered that her mother didn't wait for her after school. She remembered the neighbor, Mrs. G, was waiting for her with a snack. She remembered how dark it was and staring in the direction of the empty dock. She remembered her father saying everything was going to be ok, and her father crying. She remembered the police coming to the house. She remembered waking up and looking out her bedroom window and still there was no boat, actually she remembered she did this almost every day in hopes that her mother would one day return. She never did. What she didn't remember was any type of funeral or church or cemetery or hearse or tombstone; she tried but she couldn't. She didn't remember ever officially saying goodbye and with this she felt her heart ache, she felt a sudden empty hole that was always there but just ignored until this day, and then she felt angry.

Again she shook her head and tried to gather her thoughts but the barrage of unanswered questions pounding inside her head made it difficult to think straight. New information always brings to light new revelations to a story and now she was forming new questions as what really happened that day. Her memory wasn't cooperating and all she could do was form questions that led to unthinkable notions; this was partially due to her background at the CIA but still, she now had her doubts. "Why were my uncle's fingerprints on the boat, how well did he know my mom, did he have something to do with her disappearance, or worse her death, is that why he took me under his wing, did he feel guilty, could he even be my father?" Jorja had a lot to think about and she did so in the weeks that followed.

● ● ●

Chapter 10

Detective Lynch went back to his office sat at his desk and gave life to his computer monitor. He entered all his notes to the case file which took about seventy minutes or so, after he finished he did a few searches of other files within the police database. Research was the primary key to solving most crimes; it was also the most tedious. His first attempt at finding answers was to find any other missing children within a 25 mile radius of this town within the past year. His search parameters returned 3 hits. One of them being his case the other two marked closed. He read their case files anyhow. He continued his research. He widened the radius to fifty miles and received two more hits. Again both cases were closed . . . one had drowned at a nearby lake, the other was taken by her mother to California. Again he widened the search by another twenty-five miles, three more hits and two more closed cases. The third was marked opened, ongoing investigation. He read the file and found many similarities. The missing person was blonde, a female, under 6 years of age, and vanished from a park near the parents home. He quickly punched the number of the investigating officer into his phone.

"This is officer Orlando Garfield, I am currently out of the office, please leave a message and I'll return your call at my earliest convenience"

"Hello, this is detective Charles Lynch of the Forest Park, police department . . . I have to . . . . goddamnit," and quickly hung up the phone. He didn't have time to play phone tag. He dialed another number.

"Taylor County Sheriff's office, how may I direct your call?"

"Hello, I'm Detective Charles Lynch of the Forest Park police department, I need to speak to Officer Garfield."

"I'm sorry, he's not in today, may I patch you into his voice mail?"

"No, I need to speak with him immediately, can you tell me where he can be reached?"

"I'm sorry detective but today it's his day off."

"How about a home phone?"

"Well . . . I . . . can't . . ."

He cut her off even before she answered, "This is about Tanya Drake and her case, I may have some more information."

Everybody at Taylor County Sheriff's Office knew of the case . . . first missing persons case under the age of 15 ever . . . . it stung a lot of people hard, there were still color photographs all over town and it was almost a year ago,. Not quite a year but close, but no one in this town forgot so soon.

The dispatcher quickly confirmed Lynch's identity then supplied him with Orlando's home phone.

Six rings later, Officer Orlando Garfield was on the phone.

"Hello."

"Officer Garfield?"

"Yes?"

"Detective Charles Lynch sir, I'm sorry to disturb you at home but I'm in the midst of a missing person case and our cases sound very similar but mine is just a few hours old."

"Similar in what manner?"

"Both blonde, under 6, female, within a 75 mile radius of one another and vanished from a playground near the parent's home."

"Excuse me for being blunt but that's it? Doesn't sound like much to go on."

Lynch could tell right away he liked this guy's style. He's to the point just like him. "Quite right, just a hunch is all. I need to follow it up. I always go with my gut feeling. So can we share some information?"

"Sure, whatcha ya got?"

"A pencil sketch of a suspect."

"How soon can we meet?" was the reply from an officer with an almost year old unsolved, still open missing person case.

●　　●　　●

Chapter 11

Easter was early this year and she dreaded the holiday, always did, even as a child, just too religious for her tastes. It never made any sense to her how the non-Christians accepted it with rabbits and eggs and speaking of eggs—hardboiled and dyed were not her cup of tea, neither were the ham and dried paska bread that her Aunt Gracie served on the holiest of Sundays and this coming Sunday would be no different. She knew she couldn't back down from the invitation; she never could, only if there happened to be another holiday massacre, which was very unlikely but unlike past Easter Sundays, she was looking forward to this one. She wanted very much to call her uncle out on the carpet and question his fingerprints straight up but she needed to be tactful, besides she did still love him.

Though Grace and Floyd never had children for reasons unknown to Jorja, aunt Gracie came from a rather large family, so every seat was filled at banquet sized table in the opulent dining room. There was chatter from each section of the table with almost everyone trying to seize some talk time with the man of the hour, the one who just might be vice president some day. Jorja knew this was not the time or place to speak of the past.

Dinner was unmemorable as remembered with dessert becoming the highlight of the feast. Jorja and Gracie, along with Robin, the maid but more like family, gathered a few dishes and wound up in the kitchen. Robin returned to the table to finish the clearing.

"Honey, what's up? You're not yourself," the perceptive aunt questioned.

"You could always read me, couldn't you," a rhetorical statement, "I don't know, it's just lately . . . . well lately . . . ," and Jorja stopped with silence looking for a way to finish.

"Come out with it girl, I didn't know you to beat around the bush."

Jorja seemed to gather her thoughts, "Okay . . . it's just lately I've been thinking . . . . thinking about mom," and she said it as though she was embarrassed to say it in front of her aunt, "It's been thirty-two years and I really never . . . . never questioned anything about her, my memories of her seemed to be fading . . . . I mean you and uncle Floyd have played a huge part in my life . . . . it's just that . . . it's that I feel a little bad for bringing this up now I guess."

"Honey, you never have to feel that way about talking about your mother . . . . It has been a long time, too long and I have to apologize for not mentioning anything sooner myself, I guess I wanted you to bring it up . . . . deep down I knew we'd have this conversation I just thought it would have been earlier in your life . . . truth is I placed it on the backburner because I really didn't know how to approach you . . . then time passed and I guessed I hoped it would simply fade away. May I ask why now?"

"Strange really, the other day I was looking at a menu and realized it had been ages since I had crab, it got me to thinking about crabbing and how mom and I always went out on her boat every Friday after school, then a flood of memories hit me but I know there were more that I can't recall, then questions started to form, questions I could have never asked at that age," as she told her convincing lie.

"Alright, Robin can finish up here, do you want to go to the study, away from the crowd and talk a bit?"

"If you don't mind being away from your quests?"

"Honey, they are family, you are family, I'm here when anyone needs me, how about another cup of coffee first?"

"Yes please," and with that they made their way into the study. It was a manly room, with dark wainscoting, shelves with books and nautical trinkets, and of course Uncle Floyd's bar stocked with nothing but the finest. Aunt Gracie closed the pocket door and they placed themselves into rather large leather parlor chairs in front of the small fireplace, though it was a chilly March evening the fireplace was not glowing with ambers.

Jorja glanced at the original oil above the mantle that pictured a schooner cutting the waters of the Atlantic; it was by some famous artist whose name she did not know, then with a sense of purpose, she asked her first question.

"Where is mom's grave marker?" No beating around the bush this time for Jorja. This caught Aunt Gracie way off guard and was slow to answer before Jorja chimed in again. "See I don't recall a funeral for my mom, I don't remember visiting a grave site and bringing flowers . . . I don't remember saying goodbye."

"None of us really said our goodbyes, it hit your father the hardest, he never got over her death."

"Her body was never found, right?"

"That is true, that's why there was no funeral. Your father refused to give up hope and having a funeral would mean that his hope was lost. Oh, how he loved her so, truly adored your mother, worshiped the ground she walked on . . . even though she was pretty much a free spirit and never had the same admiration for your father."

"So are you saying . . ."

"Wait, no, I'm not saying your mother never loved your father . . . she did indeed love him, she loved him for being the father of her child, she loved him for providing the foundation of the family, she loved him enough to say I do."

"Then . . ."

"What I'm trying to say, is that your mother's true love had already passed, she knew this, so when the opportunity of a serious relationship came around for a second chance, she grabbed it. Your mother took that chance with your father. She wouldn't have married him if not for love, it just wasn't as deep as your father's. This is not a bad thing. It is or was the same with your uncle and I. I fell head over heels with him in college. I would do anything for him but Floyd was a different breed, he had goals in life that seemed more important than family. I married him anyway hoping, as do most us women, that one day he would change. He hasn't yet. Oh I still love him and he still loves me it's just not the deep love that two people share like when you are . . . . when you're soul mates."

"Uncle Floyd must have loved you enough to spend the rest of his life with you if he asked you to marry him."

"Well looking back I was blinded and stupid. I knew he really didn't love me for the same reasons as your mother," saying this as she didn't want to continue with the rest of the conversation

"What, that he too missed his opportunity regarding his soul mate?"

"Sort of but . . . it's . . . a tad more complicated than that . . . . ," as if she were searching for the right words.

"Aunt Gracie? . . . . Aunt Gracie?'

"It was all such a long time ago."

"What?"

"College. That is where your mother's true love was found . . . . I was dating Floyd, sophomore year, and his brother came to visit with his newest girlfriend for homecoming . . . that girlfriend was your mother. Needless to say my sophomore and junior years were pretty rocky for me . . . I almost didn't graduate."

"Why?"

A deep sigh, "The connection between your mother and Floyd was almost instantaneous. We all saw it, yet no one wanted to admit it. Over time it grew harder for me to stand by and watch and eventually we broke up, and I left him . . . only to come back later to pick up the pieces."

'Are you saying . . . that . . . . that . . . my uncle and my mother dated?"

"As I said, it was more than that . . . and it's complicated. See your mother and . . ."

"Wait, wait . . . . my father's brother stole his girlfriend, my future mother, then somehow magically got her back and married her?"

"Well . . . . yes . . . . see your mother and your uncle were romantically involved, they were inseparable in their sophomore year and into the summer. It hurt your father something fierce, that's why there has always been tension between the two of them and to be quite honest I don't blame him one bit. He took that tension to his grave. Your father was never the kind of man to ask for help regarding himself, yet when your mother passed away he had no one left to turn to. He opened the door just enough to let you into our lives but he stood in the doorway, never entering."

"You said they were involved into the summer, but?'

"Yes, but then something happened between your mother and your uncle."

"What was that?"

"I'm not sure . . . he won't talk about it, never has and I think he never will. The two of them started to part ways in the beginning of their junior year. I was still very much in love with your uncle and your father was still very much in love with Carolina, it seems that the heart never fully recovered for each of us. You kind of gloss over things when blinded by love. So . . . so as I was saying, they started to part ways and I think we both just chalked it up to them both being free spirits. If you have two free spirited people each wanting something completely different in life, then no amount of love can be enough to hold them together. Anyway, their junior year was on again off again and Carolina couldn't take it anymore and eventually dropped out of school midway through the second semester and went back home. It was probably a year or so later that she ran into your father. You father picked up exactly where he left off, just like me. It took some time for Carolina to come around, especially since your father was Floyd's brother, but she finally said yes to marriage. She didn't see Floyd until their wedding and it was awkward at best, your father lifted his hard-pressed foot from the floor because he didn't even want to invite his only brother but your mother wanted him there. Floyd and I got married shortly afterwards and looking back on it, I think it was for spite rather than love, besides a political career just looks better with a wife by your side."

"Aunt Gracie, you really can't mean that?"

"Looking back at it after all these years . . . I think I really do . . . but I cannot complain, I've had a good life, I have lots of family, though no children of my own, I always considered you my daughter. I was able to watch you blossom into a great sophisticated woman . . . . your mother would be so proud . . . . I'm so proud of you Jorja," seemingly holding back the tears.

"Aunt Gracie . . . ," Jorja so wanted to ask more question, deeper questions, but she could see her aunt was trying to not cry, so she reached across and grabbed her hand.

"It's alright child . . . like I said I've had a good life . . . . I have loved in this life . . . maybe I feel a tinge of regret because I have not been loved the way I always dreamed of . . . but . . ."

"But Aunt Gracie . . . I do love you."

"Yes I know, I know child, I love you too, so very much . . . it's just that . . . ," and the tears started to roll down her cheeks, as though she just had an epiphany. She stood up to grab a tissue from Floyd's desk and Jorja stood up as well. The hugged each other for awhile and neither said a word until Aunt Gracie caught her composure. "I still have much to tell you about your mother and what a wonderful person she truly was."

"Another day perhaps?"

"Some day real soon, my child."

"Aunt Gracie . . . . thank you . . . . thank you for always being there for me . . . I know I don't say it enough . . . I do love you . . . I love you like a mother."

"Thank you for making me feel so proud, I love you too," and with that they each wiped their eyes and headed back out to the family room where the rest of the family was still hanging on Uncle Floyd's every word.

Now Jorja had a lot on her mind. She had a beyond a reasonable doubt that just maybe, just maybe her uncle was her father, especially learning of their romantic involvement. She could easily see two people being such in love, were always going to be in love with each other, then one day out of the blue they reconnect. She also had in that analytical mind of hers the fingerprints on the boat. Why were my uncle's prints on that boat? Only one person really knew the answer to that and she would eventually have to talk to him.

● ● ●

Chapter 12

She started to stir and he watched through a full length one-way mirror. He was watching ever since he locked the door. His watching room was like a little closet, very dark with the only illuminating light coming from her wicker lamp in the pink room. There was an air vent from her room to his room which permitted audible sounds to enter in both directions. He had a dining room chair with a thin burgundy striped cushion and a box of tissues and some bottled water. There were no other comforts of home in his watching room. From his seated position he could see almost every inch of her room . . . even into the bathroom for there was no door on that room. He watched her closely and again she stirred. Within 15 minutes her eyes were open. She didn't move. He could tell she was confused.

"Mommy," just as faint as could be.

No answer of course. He just sat there watching ever so intently.

"Mommy," just a little louder this time.

Still he did nothing, just watching like a cat watching its prey. She sat up but barely, as she used one arm for support. She wasn't just confused she was nauseous and her forehead was scrunched from her pain. This time the "Mommy" was a bit loud; it startled him. He assessed his wise investment in sound proofing the walls. It wasn't any fancy sound proofing that one would buy at a high-end audio/video store, it was just a bunch of rubber mats and some sliced up used tires wedged in between the studs and ceiling joists. He was satisfied that no sounds could be heard for he did an earlier test with the record player turned onto its maximum setting. It could barely be heard from the bottom of the cellar stairs. Again, "Mommy," even louder than before, so loud it caused her great pain and she began to cry. She made her way off the bed with tears rolling down her cheeks and went to the first door she saw. She opened it. It was the closet. Her confusion deepened. She glanced in all directions and found what she was looking for—another door. She approached the steel door and moved the handle, it didn't budge. "Mommy," again as more and more tears were streaming down her face. She knocked on the door and it echoed a hollow thud. She knocked again to no avail. "Mommy, mommy . . . . mommy," in between sobs and a sniffling nose. He could tell she was in pain and that is was a headache which he assumed was from the chloroform. Her eyes were starting to grow puffy and red as wails of pain and confusion did not dissipate, even for a minute. He wanted to help, he wanted to hold her, tell her everything was going to be all right, he knew he had to wait, he knew he had to wait for love to take its course. Her crying, sobbing, and sniffling went on for another thirty minutes all the while he sat in silence and just watched. Finally she made her way back to the bed and fell asleep from deep exhaustion and pain. He took this opportunity to open the door and place a few items of food on the bureau. He placed an apple, a banana, a box of animal crackers, some peanut butter cookies, bottled fruit juice, and a bag of pretzels, then turned to look at his precious little girl, he briefly thought about another kiss but decided against it—there was plenty of time for that in the future. He walked out the door and clicked all three locks to their locked position. His little girl was safe at last; his little girl was home at last.

He made his way upstairs to tidy up a bit. He fixed himself a nice dinner which consisted of chicken Marsala and asparagus and poured himself a generous glass of cheap chardonnay. For a time in his life he worked in a restaurant. Started out as a dish washer and because he never took a day off and was always on time they moved him to food prep where he never took a day off and was always on time. From there they made him a line cook and there he stayed. He wasn't the best, especially in busy times but he held his own. He was good at pasta, his secret being adding a ton of butter just at the end of a sauce for a creamy rich finish, even though butter was never a key ingredient explained to the customers—they loved every bit of it—no questions asked. He always had to laugh because most customers just assumed pasta was on the healthy side, especially if a bunch of vegetables were thrown into the mix but with about a quarter stick of butter in each dish, this was highly unlikely. After the new owners moved in, they cleaned out the kitchen staff and started from a clean slate, so he was without a job. He tried to find other jobs as a cook but no such luck, so he fell back to construction work in which he learned during the summers while still in high school. He hated it. He hated the outdoors, the hot sun and sweaty days. He didn't last long and he found a job away from the sun and at night . . . he now cleans offices after closing hours.

He clicked on the evening news and as expected one of the top stories was indeed the little girl, Ripley Newenberg age five. He learned her name. He learned her age, then he learned the most shocking news yet . . . as the news reporter stated—"Earlier today Ripley Newenberg, age five was taken from this Forest Park recreational park, just slightly before eleven this afternoon, right before she was to have lunch with both parents. Ripley Newenberg is from Fort Valley and is the child of Benjamin and Lindsay Newenberg. Benjamin is the borough manager. Police are doing everything in their power. If you have any information regarding the missing little girl you are urged to call immediately . . . ." Whatever the reporter said after that fell on deaf ears, for all he could dwell on was the town Ripley was from, Fort Valley, that town was the next town over . . . "son-of-a—bitch" he said aloud, then thought, everything went so well and now this. Then a pictured flashed on the screen, a pencil drawn sketch more like it and he heard the words from the reporter, "walks with a limp". He was shocked . . . . and relieved, the picture looked nothing like him . . . . so he thought.

•   •   •

Chapter 13

With that free cup of Joe in one hand and adjusting her frames with the other, Jorja started to glanced over the daily budget for the 8th of April; there was such a thing as a daily budget, even though it was a Saturday, even though it was her birthday she was in the office, working, not off, not with her family or what was left of her family, not with friends, not opening any presents, not blowing out candles, but working; there was no birthday celebration for Jorja. She had an invite to her uncle's but it just didn't seem right to be there, something in the back of her mind was churning and she knew she would ask the wrong question or questions during dinner so she took the safe bet and opted out with the work excuse. She really wasn't into work and her mind drifted to her mother, her father, her past and all those nagging questions she had yet to ask. She remembered her mother's favorite dress, it was yellow, she was trying to remember the last time she saw her mother in it and before she knew it she was lost in a distant memory. When she refocused her mind she found herself looking at the yellow sticky attached to the corner of her twenty-one inch LCD screen. The yellow sticky had just a series of numbers, ending in twelve dot one six eight. She wrote this number down just before or after the shootings at the mall, she couldn't remember when. She completely forgot about the sticky, it just became part of the monitor, along with other various fruit stickies from apples, bananas, and oranges. They were cheap decorations, a little collection of hers which simply faded into the bezel of her monitor. Then she started to remember why she wrote this IP address down in the first place, and quickly started wondering, wondering where this IP address led. There was some phrase amidst the back of her mind, something about a cat, something about curiosity, as she opened a DOS prompt and tried to communicate with the IP address. A simple command really: ping. Ping and the IP address and hit return. So ping she did and too much surprise she received a reply, very much like dialing a phone number, listening to it ring, and then someone picking up—basically proving that the number was indeed valid. Her answered was returned—three lines on the screen, each with the same exact IP address in return—meaning she was able to reach the computer, the computer that owned that IP address. The IP address ending in twelve dot one six eight. The IP address as of several months ago she herself personally locked down. The IP address that was somehow magically opened without her knowledge. The IP address that she couldn't find the owner. The IP address that shouldn't exist. The IP address ending in twelve dot one six eight.

She dialed up the report server and ran a report. The same report that was once her responsibility; the same report she ran on the day of the massacre, the same report that showed the IP address; she just couldn't leave well enough alone. She ran her report for December 24th and it showed nothing. It didn't show the IP address in any of the back logs since the massacre. No one seemed to have hit the IP address which was a good sign, a good sign until she ran the report for today, for her birthday. Again the report showed not one hit. "How is that possible?," she questioned herself. She had just pinged the IP address and it returned an answer. Unsure of herself she double-checked and pinged again. Same reply, same exact three lines on the screen. She was able to communicate with this computer and the hit should have registered on the daily report. She ran the report again and again and still nothing. Then she ran it for the day of the massacre. "Strange," the IP address didn't show, it seemed to vanish into thin air but she saw it with her own two eyes just a few months before. She blocked it and wrote it down on a yellow sticky which she affixed to her flat screen monitor, yet that IP address didn't exist on the report when she reran it for the day of the massacre, the 23rd. She quickly went back to her saved report from that day. Sure enough, the IP address was correct. The IP existed on this old, saved report yet somehow magically disappears when she reran the report for the 23rd at this present time. She should get the same results. It is like it didn't exist, yet she was able to ping this computer, she was able to see this computer, so it did exist. So instead of dealing with the report server she went directly to the router's interface, the piece of hardware that helps communicate between computer and computer. She redid her steps to block the IP address again, basically denying access again to anyone who would want to communicate with this machine, just like she did on the day of the massacre at the mall. Again she couldn't leave well enough alone. Again she pinged the machine and again it came back with a reply. "Impossible," she thought. "Impossible," she just blocked that IP address at the router level yet she was still able to communicate with the machine. No one should have access, not even herself. "Odd," she thought, "Very odd indeed." Perplexed she just turned around and stared at her orange and blue eye on her wall and was hypothesized for a brief moment. She went to refill her coffee cup and stared some more, thought some more. The coffee got the best of her and she made her way to the lavatory. While rinsing her hands she noticed the fine wood, then she noticed the nice marble floor with inlay, then she noticed the stalls, how each unit was closet like, more private, she noticed the lighting was a bit dimmer, the towels just a little thicker—it was almost as good as home. She felt strange in the sense she was here before yet never noticed, in and out so to speak. Then she realized, "the restrooms on other floors are not like this". They were the usual metal stalls, tile flooring and walls, very bright, and cheap paper. "Ah, the perks of an executive, this is nice." Then it hit her like a piano falling from a five story building. "Access level."

She made her way back to the computer and brought up the security protocols. She brought up her security level and it read level two. She could not change her own even though she was the top guard dog of security. She was at level four before her promotion. This could explain a few things but not all of them. Again she went to the report server this time bringing up a report entitled "Security Clearance for Reports". This one stated all the report names and the security levels of each report. On her IP Address report, FULL ACCESS was granted to only the level one security holders, LIMITED ACCESS was granted to level two and below. "A wall . . . . dammit!" She had the same level access as when she was a peon in a cubical. But just like that old pair of roller skates she refused to throw out from the eighth grade, she dove into her old pile of junk, aka, her hard drive, searching for buried treasure, a clue, an old report. After several minutes of digging, she found the same report entitled "Security Clearance for Reports" from over a year ago. The report of reports showed a level two for FULL ACCESS, and not a level one for the IP Address report. Between this report of old and the report of new the level access was changed by someone, good money on the "when" was placed on within the last several months. Now that would explain a lot but not the "why" or the "who". She reached for the phone and dialed Greg's extension knowing all too well he would answer, even though it was the weekend.

"Happy birthday, Jorja."

"What . . ." and caught her off guard.

"I said happy birthday, your last year in your thirties I do believe."

"Um . . . . thank you but . . ."

"Come on, you really don't need to ask that now do you? I know lots of things."

"Yeah, I know but . . ."

"Listen I could tell you where you ate dinner last night and even make an educated guess as to what you had for dessert, but why did you really call?"

"Reports," finally getting to her but.

"What about them?"

"Who has access to change their access level?"

"Well, you for starters but you know that, well only the ones you have full access to, then there's Mike or Pete, that's probably about it . . . . oh and then there's me of course."

"You?"

"Jorja, you should know by now I can hack my way around even the best laid CIA's securities."

"Which brings me to the point of this call, can you do some snooping?"

"Sure thing, name your poison but I bet it has something to do with report access."

"I need you to find out who and when changed the access level on the IP Address report. I have one from a year ago which states a full access by level two and above, but when I run it for today it shows only level one has full access."

"That's strange to say the least, that report has always been level two, ever since the day I created it."

"Then I'm taking to the expert."

"You sure are, I'm on it, shouldn't take long . . . . and by the way, home and nothing."

"What?"

"Home and nothing, the answers to the questions where did you have dinner and what for dessert."

"You know me so well."

"That's the plan."

"Well then, thanks for my birthday greeting."

"You're welcome, and by the way, I have a present for you . . . . nothing much mind you."

"What?"

"It's just that I will refuse to end this conversation with a Simpson's quote."

"Well thank you, that was a gift from the heart, now remember, I want the answers now or eventually! Facts are meaningless. You could use facts to prove anything that's even remotely true," and she quickly hung up knowing all too well there was a man sitting in front of an array of monitors that was flabbergasted.

"Holy fucking shit," he beamed. She used not one but two Homer Simpson quotes and he wondered just how long she was saving them. He had the biggest of smiles and couldn't help but to giggle a little while he went to work, searching for the answers. He dove right away into the database searching for the journal files which contain information that has changed on the system. He didn't find any changes pertaining to this event. He then pinpointed the main players that could change the report level, Mike, Peter, Jorja, and he omitted himself since he knew damn well he had nothing to do with it. Again he found nothing. He tried a few other back door queries, and again nothing. At the moment he was stumped. He pulled his hands away from the keyboard and closed his eyes and contemplated for a few seconds. His mind then snapped into gear and his fingers flailed while doing the alphabet dance. As quickly as the bulb came on, it went out like one of Edison's first attempts at lighting a horse hair filament. It was another fizzle. He thought some more. If level access was changed then there should be a paper trail or in this case journal files, unless, unless someone erased them as well. If that was the case, then he might have a chance looking at the reciprocating database—a database that was an exact mirror copy only not located in the basements of Langley. In reality the CIA had many mirrors and he was going to check everyone. He did and nothing. He even checked the backups. Nothing. He thought some more. He thought out of the three main players, none of them had the expertise to erase a change such as this. So he decided to play the waiting game. His plan was to hack in and change the IP Address report access level back to two, then place a wee bit of code in order to track the perpetrator the next time he or she changes the access level. He did this with minimal effort. By doing so he would have to call and tell Jorja it might take some time but . . . . but then thought about it, he thought about the "why". Why would anyone want to change the level access of this report? Only one reason came to mind, to mask certain IP addresses.

With his quick hack he ran the IP report with full access set at level two.

Almost immediately he saw the same thing Jorja saw, an IP address at the top of the report ending in twelve dot one six eight; he too did not recognize it. He reset the level access at one and reran the report. He did a difference on the two reports—sure enough the only difference was this IP address was now missing from the report. It had a governmental look and feel to it, the first set of digits in the IP address gave that away but there was something amiss, something not quite right. Before he forgot, he rehacked the IP report and set the access level back to two. He'll play the waiting game as to who changed this but for now he had an even bigger piece of meat on his plate to cut. He ran the IP address through the likes of whois.com and various other domain registrars, and even through the CIA's databases, all of them turned up nothing. Then he did the same thing Jorja had done and pinged the address, sure enough he received a reply.

"That's good," he questioned, "maybe I can find the who by the where."

He adjusted his firewalls and made his computer look like it was outside the CIA network; very few people in the CIA had this type of skill-set. Once outside the network, he could put a trace on his message when he tries to ping the machine again. From this trace he could find the location with ease. It took him close to an hour to apply the right settings for the trace but once all was in place he was shocked with the results.

"This can't be," was his immediate reaction and he rechecked his steps and reran the trace, again taking almost an hour. Same results—nothing. No trace information was available. He tried to ping the machine, again nothing, no response. It's like it vanished into thin air. He thought some more. He thought about rechecking his steps but didn't want to waste the time, he thought some more. He was caught in a flurry of over complicating the matter. His brain was racing, searching for an answer but it wasn't his analytical skills that first found the answer, it was his eyes. He noticed in the bottom right-hand corner of his screen, a little icon was flashing. That icon meant his firewall was off and he was still outside the network. He turned it back on and reran the trace, this time he was shocked even more.

Greg ran an in-house trace and received his information alright. This IP address resided somewhere within the CIA network and that somewhere was in the mountains of Virginia. So now he had the "where," not the who just yet, and certainly not the why. The receiver was in his hands.

"Whatcha got?"

"What I don't got, is an answer or a Simpson's quote."

"You liked them didn't you?"

"Hell, I thought it was my birthday, you're such a clever girl, more on that later. That IP report, I don't know who changed it, they covered their tracks pretty good, they erased the journal files and entries from the backups and mirrors."

"So we are talking who exactly?"

"Your answer is as good as mine but the next time they change the report access level I will have them, I wrote a wee bit of code into the report to trap the user id."

"That could take a while I expect."

"Yeah, maybe, not something you check on a regular basis, we, I mean you, might have to force their hand with something."

"I'll have to think then."

"I'm sure you will being such a clever girl and all, also I reran the IP report with full level access set to two and found something weird."

"What?"

"A strange IP address."

"Let me guess, ending in twelve dot one six eight."

"Damn, you're good, shall I call you Carnac the Magnificent."

"It's like someone changed the access just to hide this one IP address."

"I know, and the strange part is, you'll find this interesting, the strange part is that the server is located within our network."

"Ours? Where?"

"Oh, you know the place, in them hills," with his best southern drawl.

Right away she knew in the Blue Mountains of Virginia, "there must be some highly classified material on that server."

"My thoughts exactly, can you comb through your budget reports to see if this is mentioned anywhere? After all, you are probably paying for it, the DST deputy director should be aware of all its toys."

"I will but that's going to take some time, in the meantime, I want you to find out as much as you can about that machine, someone has taken some pretty good precautions to hide it, hide it from me, but why, who?"

"I will."

"Do you need anything more from me?"

"What? . . . . Uh, no . . . . on my deathbed I will receive total consciousness . . . . so I got that goin' for me."

"Huh?"

"Gunga, gunga-galunga."

"What . . . ," Jorja said quizzically.

"The Dalai Lama, himself. Twelfth son of the Lama. The flowing robes, the grace, bald . . . striking . . . . come on . . . . you're killing me Smalls."

"I thought you said no Simpsons quotes for my birthday."

"It's not . . . it's from Caddyshack?"

"Never saw it . . . . sci-fi is my forte."

"Never saw it? What . . . you've been living on Altair 4 your whole life?"

"Forbidden Planet, 19 . . . . 1956 . . . . see, see I know my stuff in that genre . . . . now tell HAL, Gort, and Robby to play nice and see what you can find me."

"Okay, I'm impressed." The mere fact that she mentioned three of the top computers/robots in cinematic history brought a clever smile to his face but the fact she knew the planet Lesile Neilson visited in the classic tale of the Tempest set in space floored him to no ends.

"Just remember that the facts . . ."

"You used that one last time, give me something new Jorja."

"I was going to say before I was rudely interrupted, the facts can be dangerous, tread lightly my good friend, live long and prosper."

Upon listening to the dial tone, he smiled and reminded himself, that's the reason he loved his boss so much and would do anything for her, she was a nerd just like him, that and she was always quick with a sci-fi quote. He quickly slapped on his headphones and got to work while jamming to Metalica's Sandman—"hush now baby, don't say a word, never mind that voice you heard, it's just the beast under your bed, inside your closet, in your head."

●   ●   ●

Chapter 14

It took Garfield two hours to arrive at Lynch's office; he went to his station first to gather all the evidence. He knew it was a long shot that both cases were connected but something in his gut told him otherwise—something both Orlando and Charles had in common. They met at Lynch's office since this was indeed the hot case and it was best for Detective Lynch to stay close to the phones. Garfield was not what Lynch was expecting. He expected someone much like his build, a bit girthy around the middle. Garfield was just the direct opposite, in other words, nothing in common, and at six-two, black, and built like a stone wall, Charles and Orlando were ebony and ivory to the stereotypical extreme . . . they could never make a cop buddy film that was serious.

"Thanks for coming down on such a short notice, Officer Garfield."

"What do you think the chances are . . ."

"We'll know much more shortly. I was thinking, if the cases are related that the date might be significant."

"My thoughts exactly . . . I pondered that very thought during my ride down here. They are only a week apart but a year apart . . . . I was thinking anniversary or something."

"So was I, so I did a bit of research and expanded my original search parameters to five years to see how many more hits we'd receive."

"And?"

"And I found only one other missing child at or around our time frame . . . that was three years ago and was a four year old boy . . . that case is still unsolved as well."

"So we are thinking the same thing here, no longer just a missing person's report but a kidnapping. This could have been a first attempt, then switched to girls for some psychological reason."

"I always thought it was a kidnapping, I'll keep this bookmarked for the time being . . . so I've read your case file, very similar indeed, do you have all your interview notes with you?"

"Yes, but there was only one other person at the park that day and the only real clue that I received was a man in his late twenties or early thirties was seen looking for a dog."

"Hmmmm, the eye witness report we received stated he was in his early forties, maybe late thirties."

"Yeah, how did you manage to get a sketch of your perpetrator?"

"Well, a kid in his twenties was paid ten bucks so he could have a picture of his car."

"And?"

"And that's it . . . just a coincidence I know . . . but it happened on the same street as the park and within the same timeframe and I thought it was odd . . . how many people walk up to a complete stranger and ask for a picture of his car?"

"Good point, maybe it was some sort of three card monte . . . . you know make them look here, when the ace is over here . . . How long was the kid waiting?"

"In total about twenty minutes, so we are on the same page here, he pays a kid to sit and wait by the park, hoping some onlooker will take notice. The car was a hot rod of sorts so plenty of people could pick it out of a lineup if asked; the bone is thrown over here, while he gets away in a plain Jane over here . . . three card monte as you say." He paused a bit, glancing at Officer Garfield's notes while completely blocking out Garfield's next set of questions to where he only heard gibberish. After several seconds he then came back online with "Goddamn mother fucking bingo!"

"Excuse me?"

"Sorry . . . but these cases are the same sick twisted bastard . . . . I just read your notes from the interviewee . . . walked with a limp."

"That should have been in the file."

"It wasn't."

"Sure it is . . . . oh wait, right here . . . . on the back . . . . we did put out an APB but received no hits."

"This is the same guy. I'm sure . . . and I bet my life on it that these two little girls are not the only ones."

"You know looking at these two pictures side by side, these girls could be cousins or even sisters . . . same height, same build, almost the exact same length of hair . . . just shoulder length."

They compared notes for a good solid hour until the phone rang. It was the Newenbergs. He just didn't have time to comfort them. He basically told them he had a few solid leads and his prayers were with them . . . even though he wasn't a religious man by any stretch of means . . . . far too much evil he saw in this world to be convinced otherwise. After the abrupt phone conversation, Charles pulled out a map of the state hung it up on his cork board and placed a red thumb tack where each little girl vanished, he was old-school. He then used an old fashion compass and drew two circles that signified a seventy-five mile radius from the vanishing points. The two circles overlapped much in the way a Venn diagram does.

Garfield stated, "There is a good chance that the sick twisted bastard lives within these circles somewhere."

That brought the first smile to Lynch's face since he started this case this morning.

"How do you take your coffee?"

"Like me."

"Excuse me?"

"Like me . . . . black."

That brought the second smile and Charles quickly walked to the break room for two cups of straight black coffee and a badly needed cigarette break. Five minutes later he arrived back at his office and Orlando was standing by the corkboard holding the compass. There were now three interlocking circles on the board and the one he drew also contained the two red thumb tacks.

"Here, hot and black"

"Thanks, I hope you don't mind but I took the liberty and drew a third circle, originating from Ripley's hometown. Tanya was taken from her hometown so I just wanted to see if the two overlapped."

"Okay, it looks as though we have a bit more research to do. I only did research from my crime scene outward. I didn't think to look from her hometown outward . . . maybe she was followed, stalked."

With that Lynch brought up the case database on his computer and Orlando moved in just over his shoulder. His new search parameters started at a town right in between Ripley's and Tanya's., a seventy-five mile radius and within the past year. There was one hit, still open . . . so he drilled down to read the case file. Becky Timberstone, age four reported missing on May 4th of this year, disappeared from a playground, and the kicker . . . also blonde. No reported witnesses.

"What's your gut telling you, Garfield?"

"That our anniversary theory is shit."

Their map was beginning to look like a pond after someone threw in a handful of pebbles. They drew seventy-five mile radius circles from Ripley's hometown, Tanya's hometown, Becky's hometown, and they found a few more hits in the database. They divided the case load and Lynch hooked Garfield up with a colleague's computer and password. After an hour or so they each came back with one possible match. Five in total and all within the past year, although one was slightly older at age eight but all other statistics matched . . . female and blonde and still way too young.

For several minutes maybe more like ten or so they focused on the map and its circles, knowing all too well that the sick twisted bastard lived within one of them—not one word between them during this time. Each of them had a mind moving forward, thinking and rethinking.

Garfield broke the silence, "Do we have a picture of Anna, the eight year old?"

"No, it's not in the file."

"Can we get someone on the phone? . . . We need a fax or email."

It was coming in on eleven at night but the Barnsville Police department was more than helpful and at roughly 11:07 they had a picture of Anna. Garfield walked up to the map and removed the Anna thumbtack, then grabbed a yellow highlighter from Lynch's desk and highlighted a circle . . . it contained all four remaining thumbtacks, it contained all four of the missing little girls, it contain Ripley's hometown, and it also contained Ripley's vanishing point. And just like that it was a clue that could break the case wide open or even better, return Ripley home but time was ticking ever so fast. Eight year old Anna had short brown ear length hair. It was a gut feeling both men shared.

● ● ●

Chapter 15

So now Greg had a task at hand. It was a challenging task to say the least but he was about to embark on his favorite journey, one that was even better than Frodo or Bilbo Baggins', a journey where he got to play with his toys and prove just how smart he was to Jojra, to his boss. With that in mind he brought all his monitors to life and cannonballed into the data pool.

His first order of business was to see if he could talk to the machine. He quickly opened a command prompt and tried a few commands. The first was to ping again, and yes he received a reply. The next order of business was to open a line of communication and he tried to telnet into the box. This was a standard communication protocol between computers. He received no response. He tried another protocol called ssh, then ftp, nothing, then he tried another, and another, and yet another, no response each time. Next was plan B. If he couldn't communicate with the box, just who can? He brought up the IP report again and tried to find an average hit ratio, just how often was this box being used. It seemed as though over the past months, the number of hits grew; he pinpointed some of the past months' highs and lows. One particular high hit day was Dec. 23rd of last year, another was for a few weeks ago, right away Greg knew Dec. 23rd would be forever etched in his brain right alongside of nine-eleven. He thought that was a strange coincidence. The other high note, he did a bit of research, turns out that day was a high level alert day at airports across the country. He then rationalized that this might have something to do with the boys of Homeland, "but why was this machine on our network, they have their own network?" He needed to set up a trace so he could see where the hits to this IP address originated. He would need Jorja's help to do this since she had the authority to maintain hardware protocols and this was going to take more than a few lines of coding but before her help, he proceed to plans c and d just in case.

Jorja was back at her desk also doing her part in the investigation. She brought up the inventory report and narrowed in on the stuff over in the hills of Virginia. She could probably tell how many rolls of toilet paper were left in the janitor's closet if she wanted to . . . . this thing had everything on it . . . . well almost everything, she quickly realized the janitor's closet was bigger than she anticipated. She also thought about doing a manual check but she didn't know how to quite pull this one off . . . she had never been to the hills and just couldn't go waltzing in without the proper credentials, besides she would need that from her boss and she didn't want to tell her boss about anything just yet. Everybody had secrets, she knew that much, especially people in the CIA, especially people with higher credentials, yes Jorja needed to soft-toe around the water cooler that's for sure, and she had to watch her back along with Greg's.

She went back to her thoughts, back to her reports. The inventory reports turned up nothing; next she checked the budget reports. She was searching for that proverbial needle in the haystack. The CIA had billions at their disposal and trying to find a legitimate figure within the two hundred dollar toilet seat covers was next to impossible. She wondered just how big this server/machine was, how powerful it was, that could tell quite a bit and give her better odds at finding it. She was hoping it wasn't some cheap server, something just about any fifth grader could build these days. Jorja has built her share of computers and servers were no different. All that was needed was a motherboard, cpu, hard drive, some internal memory, software, and then from there it was pretty much plug and play and all that could be done for under $200. No Jorja was hoping for something much bigger, much more powerful, something from the likes of IBM, SUN, or HP. Her hope waned as she spent the next several days reading page after page of figures in her spare time. She even looked through hardware requests and approvals and found nothing. It was though someone just brought in a computer and plugged it into the network. Something like that just does not happen on the most powerful network in the world. Someone plugs something in, and someone somewhere knows about it and sure as shit someone knows about this little puppy, someone, somewhere.

For Greg, things were no different. It took him a few days to execute plans c and d and just like Jorja, they turned up zilch. He needed to go to plan b. On his way back from the vending machine with a mid-afternoon caffeine pick-me-up in his hand he stopped by Jorja's office.

"Come on in," Jorja said as she was coming back from a meeting, "You find anything?"

"No luck whatsoever, which I have to tell you, is strange for me."

"No luck on this end either, I think I've combed through every report that we have to offer."

"I have a plan b."

"B? You are only on plan b, I'm disappointed."

"No, no, no, I thought of plan b right after plan a, but proceeded to c,d,e,f, geez I forget where I left off maybe w, well anyway, plan b involves hardware installation. We have to swap out the main hub in the server room and it's not like I can go prancing in without proper authority. Those guys in there hate me."

"Hate you, why?"

"Because just about anything they can do, I can sidestep, with the exception of swapping out hardware to bypass hard coded encryption chips within the hubs."

"You have access to the mail room, you can make the switch there, actually go ahead and order what you need, I'll okay the request, then once we have the new and improve hub with the right encryption chip for your needs, I'm sure you can Photoshop a legitimate shipping label, then we'll just ship it to the IT department, and they'll install it for us, just when you do, order the newest hub, make sure it's their latest top of the line model. It's always easier to force a swap when there is an upgrade involved."

"I already have the label printed," he said with a smirk, "and we want the ic5300 with 32 gigabit ports, this baby is going to fly."

Over the next few days Greg and Jorja were on the same page in regarding this IP address. They wanted to know more. It took a few days for the new hub to arrive and it was just a matter of swapping out the encryption chip that Greg had obtained through improper channels. Hardware encryption was one of the hardest to break but if one had the right chip and knew the encryption methods the odds were in their favor. Greg had friends everywhere; that's one of the main reasons he was so valuable, though most of these so-called friends could very well have ended up on the FBI's most wanted list with ease, if it wasn't for Greg's ability to keep them under wraps and under the radar. This chip Greg had obtained came out of Taiwan just days before and shipped to a drop off place, from there it was simply placed in one of those Amazon a to z swish cardboard boxes and shipped right to his cubical. Jorja had the hub sitting in her office and the switch was made there and sent to the mail department. From there it would be installed within a day once the IT department received it along with the hardware request form signed by Jorja.

Two days later they were in business. The new chip within the hub allowed Greg to peek inside the message header of the incoming request to this server. Each time a message is sent from one computer to another this message is wrapped in a package much like the analogy of a letter and envelope. The package contains the original message, along with the address as to where this information is to be sent then wrapped in any encryption protocols that is needed along the way. At any one time if someone or something would receive this package and take a peak, they would only see gibberish unless they had the actual keys to break the encryption. This is where Greg's Taiwanese chip came in handy. He was able to break the encryption because he had the keys to open the lock, although he only had the keys to decrypt the address layer of the message. The rest of the message was still encrypted and even the best of the CIA computers couldn't crack a 128 bit encryption method quite easily, that could take months, years, even decades to do even with the most powerful computers man had to offer. Greg didn't care, he just wanted to see the address layer, where the information was coming from, and after a few moments he had learned all its secrets, and was shocked as hell as he and Jorja saw the address flash on their monitors.

One of the most famous addresses in the entire world flashed on his screen, 1600 Pennsylvanian Avenue, the White House itself. Both Greg and Jorja gasped for air and didn't say a word. It was made clear that the president and his chief of staff Scott Norwood had hit the server the most. What the hell did they just stumble upon? Yeah the president and his chief had access to the CIA's network at a moment's whim, even Homeland Security, and the FBI, but hitting a server well hidden from just about everybody, well then, they wanted to know more. But they also knew they were in dangerous waters, very dangerous waters, shark infested waters, shark infested waters with blood. This added yet another layer of complexity to the situation. If this box was used by the president then why didn't anybody know? The network of friends had to be complex as well. They both thought privately amongst themselves then Jorja broke the silence.

"Greg, what are you thinking?"

"Oh how I wish we didn't know what we know now . . . . knowing what we know now I want to know more."

"Ummmm, yeah . . . my thoughts but not exactly, it's like my Silence of the Lamb poster."

"Why?"

"It's a picture within a picture."

"Excuse me?"

"Take a close look at that poster."

"Yeah?"

"See the moth?"

"I may wear contacts but I'm not blind."

"Ever see within the moth's head," before he could answer, "In the moth's head, there is a picture of a skull, it's plain as day when you first notice it, sort of like the hidden arrow in the Fed Ex logo, once you see it, you always see it."

"So a picture in a picture, like the Droste Effect."

"Not exactly, that's different, that's the same imagine being mirrored over and over. Looking even closer at the skull on the moth, you'll notice something even more; you'll notice the skull is actually a picture of seven naked women from a famous Dali photograph."

"Well I'll be damned."

"Well I have the feeling there is a lot more to this computer then meets the first glance."

"I know, I know."

"There is something very peculiar in this IP address, first it's embedded within our network, next it's hidden in the hills, and now it seems to be only used by the president and his chief of staff."

"Not to mention, I forgot to tell you, that the hits to this server seem to peak during a country crisis."

"What are you talking about?"

"I was able to pull average hits from the IP report and there happened to be a correlation with hits and crisis, take the Mall Massacre, there were over five hundred hits on that day alone, most days it seems to be about ten to twenty, again, remember a few weeks ago, the high level alert at the airports, over three hundred hits."

"The more and more we talk the more and more my curiosity peaks, Greg, I need you to take the next steps, we found the who and the where, now we need to focus on the why, we'll worry about the how later."

"In order to do that I'm going to have . . ."

"Don't say it, I think you know what I'm talking about."

And without saying a word, Greg knew it meant spying on the president, but he too could rationalize it, everyone had to be monitored on the system, be it the president or Jorja, no surfing for porn on the company dime, they save that for the boys over at the FBI, searching for child pornography was their excuse.

Greg was also able to decrypt the communication layer, now he was able to talk to the machine, well sort of, it was asking for a login and password. He went straight for root as the login and root as the password but couldn't be so lucky. He stop there knowing full well if he were to attempt anymore break-ins a flag would be raised and if they, the ones who configured this server knew what they were doing, his first failed attempt should signal the red flag. He was praying they were not bright but then reality had set in realizing who ever set this up in the first place knew pretty damn sure how to hide it, and hide it from pretty much the best in the field, himself included.

● ● ●

Chapter 16

It wasn't hard to hack the president's password, the biometric scan of his finger was not needed for this point of entry, which only got you into the network, he was already hooked into the network but he needed the password for the box itself. People are creatures of habit, that's what made the hacking of his password like child's play. Habit—the habit of using the same old passwords over and over . . . why does one need to remember separate passwords for Amazon, Citbank, E-Trade, your email, your network, your voice mail, your laptop, your life . . . . when one will do . . . the same one over and over. Most people do this, all people do this, that is if they don't write them down somewhere, somewhere close. The human mind has a limited capacity to remember insignificant strings of letters and numbers, so people stick to easy things to remember like names and special dates. The president, like everyone else, was a creature of habit and to expose his habits the first place to look was the In-Q-Tel network. In-Q-Tel is a nonprofit venture capital firm that invests in information technology for the CIA. One of their key goals is to tie company databases together through the wording that was put in place by the Patriot Act. Any company that has an online database could be searched for information in order to protect the American citizen. A series of scans within the In-Q-Tel, lead to several companies that kept passwords stored in the clear, in other words unencrypted, a bad idea and unacceptable in this day and age but it still happens even in this day and age. People are lazy or just don't know any better. Anyone can create a website today and anyone with an idea to sell—be it porn or popcorn, can make money by providing an online point of sale. Give the public a false sense of security by asking them to supply a username and password before they supply their credit card or bank information, after all, who is going to hack into a website's database that sells dog toys or gummy worms—the government that's who. Again people just don't know any better. They store this personal information—user name, password, credit card number, address, and phone number, right into an open source database, thinking their eyes are the only ones looking. It's the ignorance of the public that really makes his job easy. After only a few minutes Greg had several likely candidates for passwords. All of them were created before he became president. One password was from a flower shop for roses which seemed odd since most secretaries were given the job to keep track of birthdays and anniversaries, one came from a rare online book store where he paid fourteen hundred for a first copy of Mary Shelly's Frankenstein, another from a cigar website where he bought a fifteen thousand dollar humidor to be used as a gift since he bought three of them within six months, and there were a few others as well. The passwords were all pretty easy to decode, there was m3llss4 which is number letter substitution for Melissa, which was not his wife and correctly deduced that's who the flowers were for, another was abc123, which is a very common one, then there was sdfghjkl, which at first glance, maybe even second third and fourth looks very random but turns out it's just sequential letters on a keyboard. Then there was 3dogmai, *dogmai, and 1dogmai. It looks as though he found a pattern, more importantly he found the president's pattern, his old standby, his forget-me-not, his password. On top of that he found the president was way overly conceited.

With a few passwords in hand he was about to do the unthinkable but he wasn't about to do it alone. He was going to try to log in as the president of the United States, the repercussions, well, he couldn't even begin to image if he got caught—he dialed Jorja.

"I think I have a way in."
    "Come to my office."

Within minutes Greg was within the walls of Jorja's office after making a brief stop for yet another caffeine buzz. He walked behind her desk, placed his Dew on the desk blotter and pulled up a chair. He felt very comfortable sitting close to Jorja and noticed she changed her perfume.

"A new scent?"

"Pardon?"

"You've changed your perfume."

"Good nose."

"Why thank you, now before we get started I need you to get me the president's login name."

"I should be able to get that," and within minutes she had it

"Here it is, CICJW54."

"So I'm betting he was born in 54."

"Who? The President?"

"Yes."

"How do you . . ."

"Commander in Chief Jonathan Whitaker, 1954," before she could finish her question. "Okay, are you ready?"

"I guess."

"Listen, there are going to be some red flags going up if I hit this server with incorrect passwords, I don't know how much time I have before that happens but once in I should be able to find the files that hold the passwords and statistics and reset them."

"And if you don't?"

"I'd rather not worry about that, beside I'm going to try and mask your IP address and make it look like it's coming from the White House, that will at least buy us something . . . . what though I'm not sure."

With that idea, Greg accessed some of his special software located on his home computer and after about fifteen minutes he was ready for his first attempt.

"Okay my dear, are you feeling lucky, well are ya punk, which one would you like to try first. Here's the list."

"First off the exact quote is . . . . I know what you're thinking. Did he fire six shots or only five? Well, to tell you the truth, in all this excitement I kind of lost track myself. But being as this is a .forty-four Magnum, the most powerful handgun in the world, and would blow your head clean off, you've got to ask yourself a question: Do I feel lucky? Well, do ya, punk?"

"I thought sci-fi was your forte?"

She smiled then Jorja perused this list of six passwords, all of them looked very much the same, with the exception of a number before or after the main body of letters, then asked, "Are you sure about these. They don't . . . hold on dogmai . . . is that Latin?"

"No, but trust me, if you know Jonathan, one of these will work . . . . think, think onomatopoeia."

"Like pow, kaboom, bang . . . I always think batman with those words."

"No sorry I always get them confused . . . . I mean . . . . a . . . palindrome I think . . . . well sort of."

"Like Able was I ere I saw Elba?"

"You're good, very good but I was always keen on rise to vote sir."

She nudged him in the ribs and said, "Ha, I see it now, 1dogmai . . . you're right, then again you're mostly right."

"Mostly?"

Ignoring a replay, "How about we go with 2dogmai?"

"Sure why not, it's your neck in the noose," then he created a connection and the prompt LOGIN: was staring him right in the face. His fingers tensed and his breathing had almost come to a halt, the idea of hacking the president's password was again causing his stomach much upheaval.

He entered CICJW45 and just before he hit return Jorja shouted, "Wait!"

He saw his nervous mistake, damn transposition he surmised, always got him into a heap of trouble. He backed spaced and entered CICJW54. PASSWORD: Now the moment of truth. He entered 2dogmai.

"Invalid Login or Password." replied the IP address ending in 12.168.

"Jorja are you sure about that login id?"

"Pretty sure."

"On a scale of one to ten?"

"Eight . . . maybe seven."

Greg rolled his eyes and thought to himself, "a difference between a B and a C, not up to my standards."

"Do you want to try another one or a variation of this one . . . . . you know like substitute the o for zero or i for one?"

"No I want to try another one."

"Are you sure?"

"Yes, *for I am* positive, make it so," accenting the "for I am" in her best Jean Luc Picard voice.

And without another word Greg entered CICJW54 being mighty aware of his first error, then slowly and methodically, using his old hunt and peck mode, he entered dogmai4 and hit return.

"Invalid Login or Password," replied the IP address ending in 12.168

"Shit," was Greg's answer to the message, "That's not good, we're done for the day."

"Done? Why?"

"I told you about those red flags, we just failed twice, one more failed attempt and I am pretty sure, no . . . . one hundred percent certain, we will lock out the president. Then when he goes to enter this machine and gets a user blocked error all hell will be loose."

"But I know the reason."

"I don't care Jorja, we can wait, we must wait."

But before he could say anything else, Jorja grabbed the keyboard and starting typing. She hit return.

"Invalid Login or Password," was not the reply from the IP address ending in 12.168.

Instead both she and Greg were starring at a dollar sign prompt.

$

"Holy fucking shit Jorja, that took some balls, what did you enter?"

"Come on genius, surely I haven't stumped you," he was, "Now what?"

"We take a look around."

"That's a Unix box."

He entered his first command which did not work, then Greg spotted the caps lock key light was still on. He wasn't stumped anymore just one more reason to love that woman.

Greg entered a few commands and the machine seemed to be at his beckon call. On the monitor now was a list of all the directories on the machine. He printed them off. Then he did the command ps—ef and hit return. A list of all the processes this machine had running was now displayed on the monitor. He printed that as well and at the $ prompt he entered exit and hit return. The screen went blank.

"Why in the hell did you do that?" Without a word Greg went to her printer and gathered the papers, then handed them to her. She looked them over, and then spotted what Greg saw just moments ago. Two of the processor belonged to the president. They being one of them, the other meant the president too was online, dangerous territory they were in, shark infested waters, yes shark infested waters with blood. Hopefully no one noticed.

They were out of the machine but they had plenty to do. They had to analyze the directories and processes if they could. This would be a good spring board as to what this thing was doing on the network. They had "the who," "the where," "the what," now they needed the why . . . the how would come later.

They each had their adrenalin rush for the day and they each needed to calm their nerves. Greg suggested getting Jorja a coffee but she declined and instead joined him in his quest for another can of caffeine. During idle chit chat, Jorja was running things in her head, she knew damn well Greg wouldn't leave well enough alone but she had to convince him to lay low. Meanwhile she wanted to take control, she knew her way around a Unix box and she had one thing Greg did not . . . . she had the presidents daily itinerary, which meant there was a very good chance she knew when the president would most likely not be in the system.

"Greg I don't want you in that system unless I'm there right beside you."
"I understand."
"Greg, I mean it, if you go in and get caught I cannot help you, it's my responsibility, got that?"
"No, no, I understand fully, so when's the next time you want to do this?"
"How about this coming Saturday, the president has his banquet with his dwindling allies in the Middle East."
"Sounds like a plan . . . I'll bring the wine." Deep down Greg was thinking about abandoning her words, deeper still he realized he would do anything for that woman even take the fall for what they just had done

but even deeper the idea of working besides Jorja on a Saturday night, he couldn't plan for a more romantic evening, hacking code with his green eyed boss, yes, yes, yes he will stick to his words. He then slipped a dollar bill into the vending machine, pushed one five seven, watched the item drop, reached in, and handed Jorja her very own Kit Kat Bar.

"You scare me sometimes."

"Everyone knows your mid afternoon snack," Greg then calculated about just how many people that might be and that he knew he was the full majority. He had the facts on green eyed Jorja Carson, most of them anyway.

●　　●　　●

Chapter 17

After diner he finished watching the local news, then the world news, and even watched the first round of Jeopardy, in the first round he rarely got any answers so why watch the Double Jeopardy round, although he was in full glory when he answered a $100 or even $200 dollar question and considered himself a top contender. He shut off the boob tube then finally made his way downstairs to his little dark room. His little girl was again awake but she laid in silence on the bed. No food or drink was touched so he assumed she stayed where she was. He just watched his little girl in silence and deep down he felt a sense of joy he hadn't felt in a long long time, almost a giddiness. She was the one, she was his little girl. After about forty minutes or so, Ripley climbed out of bed and made her way to the bathroom. Ten minutes later she was out. He noticed she was such a good girl she even used soap and rinsed her hands. Her mother taught her well. She then went on an exploration of her room. Ripley first went over to the food. She was starving. She grabbed her favorite right away. She liked them because they were fun to eat. She peeled back the barely ripe banana and broke off a piece of the tip and placed it gently in her mouth . . . almost like she was unsure of how it tasted. It must have tasted like she remembered because she continued breaking off pieces and eating them like there was no tomorrow. She held the empty banana peel and looked for a place to throw it away. There was no waste basket to be found. He cursed himself as he watched, "how could I be so stupid?" She placed the peel back in almost the same place she found it. Next she grabbed the red bottle of juice and took a sip. She made her yucky face, probably because it was very warm. She took another sip and decided against it. She placed the cap back on and placed it in almost the exact place she found it. He made two more mental notes, one that she was pretty tidy and another was he needed to find a way to keep the juice cold—he'll use the ice chest he concluded and smiled yet again at his wisdom. She didn't touch any other food at the moment. She then knelt down besides Barbie's Dream House and glanced in the windows. She didn't touch it. She just looked with that child wonderment. She spent almost an hour on the floor and he was beginning to get antsy and uncomfortable. He stood up to stretch and knocked the box of tissue on the floor. She turned towards the sound, towards the mirror. It wasn't a loud sound, just a small slap of cardboard hitting concrete. She got up and walked right in front of the mirror. On the other side he was motionless. He was in awe. Ripley was more beautiful then he could have ever imagined. That blonde hair and those steel blues eyes . . . everything he remembered. His girl was beautiful. The two stood and stared at each other, only Ripley was staring at herself unknowingly of who or what was on the other side of the glass. To her it was just a mirror; to him it was a window into his soul. Unphased by the previous sound she went towards the closet and opened it up. She glanced through all the clothes like she was looking for something; she then made her way to the bureau and again rifled through all the clothes like she was looking for something. She looked again in both the closet and all the drawers. She was seemingly becoming upset. Earlier that morning she had a fight with her mom because she wanted to wear her favorite lime green shirt with the embroidered rainbow turtles on the front—it was a gift from her granddad when he came back from California. She couldn't find it, she couldn't find it anywhere. She knew none of these were her clothes. She immediately went to the steel door again and tried to open it, again it did not budge. "Mommy," at the top of her lungs, then a change of tune . . . "daddy . . . daddy . . . daddy . . . I want out daddy . . . please daddy . . . please." He so wanted to say something right there and then but he needed more time. The sobbing worsened. It turned into sheer panic and screams . . . "Mommy . . . daddy . . . . mommy . . . daddy . . ." and so it went on for at least an hour. He knew she was going to cry but he expected nothing like this . . . he too was beginning to panic. He couldn't bare it any longer. He exited out of his watching room, went upstairs, peeked at his watch and got ready to go to work

Chapter 18

On the contrary to Greg sticking to his words Jorja was planning a night of her own. She knew how to get into that system on her own and she also knew the password now. She couldn't wait to get off work. Somewhere in the back of her mind that cat was meowing louder and her curiosity was taking control. Just a few more hours, a few more budget reports, a few minutes in the car, actually with traffic more than a few, but she would be at home doing her own bit of investigating.

And just like that her day had ended, traffic was the usual heavy load on the beltway, no accidents or rubbing-necking which was good and pulled in the driveway at almost the usual time when on the rare occasion she didn't stay late. She opened her garage, walked into the mud room and tossed her keys unto the kitchen table on her way to the fridge. She studied her selection but her pickings were slim, today was normally her shopping day but that would have to wait. She grabbed a bottle of vitamin water, strawberry yogurt, and a slice of whole wheat bread which she also kept in the fridge, then made her way to her office. Here was a pretty elaborate setup that was state of the art with the fastest computing power Silicon Valley had to offer. She upgraded her system quite regularly and always had the state of the art, even sometimes before it was available to the general public . . . she had connections as well She booted up her system and while she waited for the log on screen she pulled back the foil of her yogurt and spooned in a mouthful. Her computer was fast but she almost downed the entire thing before the login screen appeared. It was gone before her personal settings appeared on the screen. Jorja then went straight to email, did a quick glance and nothing was crucial, she fired off a quick email to Greg on some other minor project, did another quick glance and clicked on the VPN network that would take her to her final destination of the evening. To her it was almost a vacation destination to an exotic land. She didn't know what quite to expect as the anticipation was killing her. Then she saw the all too familiar login prompt.

Jorja hesitated. Her mind starting playing angel devil but came to the rationalization that she should proceed. After all she was directly and indirectly in charge of security and she didn't know what this machine was doing on her network and she knew someone went to an awful lot of trouble to hide it on the network. When the password prompt flickered on the screen there was no hesitation, no doubt and she was at the all too familiar dollar sign prompt. She did the same commands as Greg did, only in reverse. She went straight to the see the processes running on the system to make sure the president wasn't on the system. He wasn't but Jorja knew exactly where he was; it was an informal dinner at the White House with his congressman friend, the republican senator from his home state of Rhode Island. She noticed there were a few processes taking up a pretty good bandwidth of the processors but in no way was this going to hinder Jorja at all. She printed her own list of directories and pulled all six pages from her colored laser printer. She pulled out a highlighter and went to work on a few suspicious names. There were quite a few. She then went to the home directory and listed the folders. She saw folders for CICJW54 and COSSN17 and correctly assumed the other one belonged to Scott Norwood but didn't know what the 17 stood for, she also saw root, and another home folder, CEOFS01, but couldn't even take a gander for she was not logged in as that individual and knew she'd get a permission error had she made an attempt. She opened up the president's folder and found not much to work with. She perused a few other content folders and directories making notes on her paper where appropriate but she really didn't find much of interest. She was pretty disappointed in the first two or so hours that had gone by, that is until she reran the command to display the processes. She had totally forgotten about the processes that were eating at the cpu's power. She saw the directory they were hitting and made her way there. Here was a world she did not recognize, not one iota. She saw things like menv, mumps, and just the letter o. She went to the o first and did a list of the directory. Hundreds of items scrolled before her. She summarized that these were computer routines of some sort since they all ended in dot o or object routines that really only machines can read. They were of no use to her. She went up a level and tried to open the mumps directory

The screen flashed and she was at a new prompt that just had an M>. "Never seen this one," she thought to herself. She punched in a few Unix commands and each returned the message Invalid Command. She tried help and nothing, stop and nothing, upper and lowercase and nothing, she tried control characters, function keys and nothing, every time Invalid Command. It was like she was stuck in the damn maze of the popular MUD game Zork.

Go West,

You are in the maze.

Go East

You cannot go that way.

Go south

You cannot go that way. Your lantern has gone out.

Go west. You cannot see and have fallen, you have died. You are in an open field west of a big white house with a boarded front door. There is a small mailbox here.

Everything led back to the M prompt no matter what she tried. She started just banging letters on the keyboard in frustration and some combinations of letters, she didn't know which ones, she found herself back at the $ prompt. She looked at the clock in the corner of her screen and cursed under her breath. It was 2:24 and she had a very busy day planned and it was going to start in less than three hours from now. She thought about staying awake but quickly nixed the idea for she was tired now and any bit of sleep would help. She would have to tackle the system another day. She called it a night.

At 5:15 her alarm clock sounded and she was pissed—pissed because she knew no amount of the wonder brew was going to get her through this day. She fought her way from beneath the covers and exposed her naked self to the elements of the house. She walked into the bathroom and started her hot hot shower. It was approaching 6:15 before she took her first sip of coffee and that was from her travel mug as she backed out of her driveway and prepared for the morning commute. In between long lights and the stops during the GW Parkway crawls, she checked her email on her blackberry as did most of D.C. but she was very careful not to type and drive unlike most of D.C. Once she was in the office it was business as usual with meetings out the ass and the feeling at the end of the day nothing was accomplished. On top of this all she was dead tired and unlike Jack Bauer, she needed something to eat and a good night's sleep. She stopped at the store bought a nice piece of halibut, fresh fruits and veggies and made herself a nice healthy meal. It was almost nine o'clock before the system even entered her mind. She approached her computer sat down at the comfy chair and before logging in she felt her body cry for the pillow, this time she listened. She had shed her clothes, climbed under her dark paisley comforter and was out before sheep number seven jumped the fence.

● ● ●

Chapter 19

The next day was pretty much the same as the last with the exception she had recharged her batteries with that good night's sleep. It was Thursday and in the back of her mind, no in the front because that's about all she could think of, was the system and how Saturday was quickly approaching. She wanted to find out more before Greg starting his poking but it didn't look like tonight was going to happen either due to the president's schedule.

Friday night was typically get out of work and get drunk night around the greater D.C area, especially in Georgetown but of course Ms. Carson never participated in such events. Sure she would drink but only to the tune of enjoyment. She was a big Amarone fan, the raisined grape of the Valpolicella. She fell in love with the wine on her first and last trip after high school to Venice. She always dreamed of going probably because she remembers her mother's love for the watery streets and gondolas. Although she could afford to drink it every night she saved it for the weekend and the bottle would last the entire weekend. Upon entering her car after work, she was transported to another world. She turned on the local jazz station and visualized her evening. She was in much anticipation. She would kick off her shoes grab a wine glass, and pour herself a glass from the bottle of Masi that she had already mentally chosen, and of course she knew the president would be busy until the following Monday. She hoped to have plenty of time to explore before Greg was to come over, possibly into the wee hours of the morning and into the afternoon if need be. She had already informed her staff to only call in dire need, if there was some sort of emergency she would be alerted no matter where she was located.

So as planned, Jorja entered the mud room just off the kitchen, threw her keys unto the table, kicked off her shoes, grabbed the osso and popped the cork on her favorite drink from the god Bacchus and poured a full glass of the red velvet liquid. Then she recorked the bottle and made her way into her office. She grabbed the glass by its stem, just like she always did as to not warm the wine from the temperature of the hands—the way she learned from the Italian waiter in the watery city by the Adriatic. She took her first sip as the monitor flickered. She ran the wine across her tongue, swished it between her gums and teeth and tasted the softness of plum on the finish. It will be even better once it breathes, she always says to herself, and it always was. She put the glass of wine down, logged in and tried to remember where she left off to what seemed like ages ago. Then she remembered the M prompt. She needed to do a bit of research but didn't know where to begin, so she went to where just about everybody does their research these days, google.com. At the prompt she almost entered just M, but almost immediately she knew her mistake, then entered "m prompt" in quotes and a whole bunch of nothing appeared on the screen, nothing of any real use as she quickly processed the data. Then she tried M> in quotes and got thousands of hits, all from mathematical equations. She then pulled out her pages from the evening and glanced at the directories. She saw the word mumps and thought that was strange. She thought of the childhood disease and why it might pertain to this computer. Was this some sort of biological server and found herself thinking of pure evil along the lines of the Andromeda Strain. She decided to enter mumps in the Google search. As expected it spitted out sites such as WebMD, Wikipedia, doctors, and symptoms sites. She scrolled through a few pages and nothing. She went back to the first page and clicked on the Wikipedia site. She clicked open the one hundred percent relevant link and she read the information on mumps, a glandular problem yada, yada, yada. She went back and click a ninety-seven percent relevance link, same thing, then she click on the seventy-two percent link and read Massachusetts hospital, she was just about to click back when she read the words programming language. Her interest peaked.

Here MUMPS, the acronym for Massachusetts General Hospital Utility Multi-Programming System or M Technology as it is known today is a database language that was developed in the sixties and is still in wide use today by hospitals, financial institutions, including top tier best in class banks, and the government. Jorja took a moment on that one—the government. Interesting. She has never heard of this language and she was a computer major and on top of that the government used it, her government. She knew Java and HTML and C and C++ and even Pascal. She heard of FORTRAN and COBOL, even Basic and Assembly, although she never studied them but MUMPS, she'd have to do a bit more research. She read the in-depth article on Wikipedia; she clicked on few links that took her to various companies that offered the language in a more robust form. Almost everybody claimed the language as super fast and cheaper to run than its competitors. It sounded too good to be true. She then found a link on SourceForge and downloaded an open source, basically free of charge, version of the language. She also downloaded the documentation including the installation guide. This free version seemed to have all the bells and whistles and later found out that major startup companies opted for this version as opposed to shelling out the big bucks for an Oracle license. In a little over three hours Jorja had a database using M up and running on one of her homemade Unix machines, where the installation guide failed, and they almost always did, she was able to piece together the rest of the information from newsgroups and forums and even entered an online chat room for some tweaking advice. During her install, Jorja knew she was on the right track by comparing her directory structure to that of the machine ending in 12.168, they were pretty similar.

The time was now a little before twelve and Jorja had a new language to learn. As with most computer languages the concepts are basically the same only the syntax is different. From what Jorja had gathered so far, there were not that many commands in MUMPS and it seemed fairly easy and straight forward. She learned that commands can be shortened from the word to just the first letter, a real timesaver but makes for reading the code a tad more cryptic. She also learned that MUMPS is both a compiled language and an interpreted language, meaning programs can be written and saved to run at a later date or at the M prompt one could enter a series of commands and execute them immediately by hitting the return key. She also learned how data was stored in the database. It was a strange concept but she caught on rather quickly with the help of an online chat partner aptly named measles2. He helped by saying that everything is stored in arrays or variables and by putting the little hat or carrot character in front of the array or variable it will be saved to the database and becomes a global variable, meaning everyone can use it. Her very first commands that Jorja wrote were in the form of Hello World. Every programmer knows the Hello World example. It usually is the very first piece of code written when learning a new language. It's usually quite simple and in this case it was no different. Jorja simple wrote

```
M>set ^X="Hello World" write ^X
Hello World
```

She now had a variable called X in the database that was equal to the value of "Hello World" and could retrieve it anytime she wanted to or change it or delete it when she wanted. After a few more hours she was getting quite good at the syntax of the language but what was really difficult to her was seeing the things stored in this database without having to write down the information she created within it. She went back to measles2 and stated her problem. He understood and shipped a small program that would help in her situation. With this program Jorja was able to traverse the database with ease and see what was stored there. There were many nuances to this new language but Jorja had a firm grip on the overall gist of the idea. Over the course of watching the sunlight peak through the shades and feeling her stomach grumble Jorja felt like she was back in school again pulling an all-nighter, only she was deeply engrossed with enjoyment. Once her eyes started to lose focus, Jorja called it quits. She hadn't even entered the president's machine or taken another sip from her wine glass. She left her computer on but locked it out of habit then picked up her leftover Amarone and went into the kitchen. She pulled a used bottle of wine from the cabinet over the stove, removed the corked, grabbed a funnel and poured her remaining wine into the bottle. Any wine left over, which is pretty rare in this household, she saves to use as red wine vinegar. Adding different grapes and vintages makes for a highly complex and tasty vinegar to be used as salad dressings and whatnot. She placed the bottle back in the cabinet, went to the fridge and poured herself a glass of cranberry juice which she used to wash down a piece of multi-grain bread and a hand full of vitamins. From the kitchen it was to the master bedroom where she closed her blinds to remove most of the sunlight for it was closing in on eight a.m. She sought comfort between the sheets long before the notion of brushing her teeth ever entered her mind. She adjusted her alarm clock and tried to remember when Greg was coming over, she didn't quite remember but assumed it was the typical picking up the date time, between seven and eight. She rustled a bit with her pillow, tossed and turned looking for the perfect spot and was soon asleep. She was up just before twelve and felt sort of refreshed after her shower. Then she made her way outdoors to do a few errands before Greg arrived.

● ● ●

Chapter 20

Orlando and Charles worked most of the night solidifying their case. It was more than a hunch, now that all four of these cases were connected and there was indeed a common thread that was woven through each of these missing little girls—the color of that common thread was indeed blonde. The first missing girl was Orlando's case—Tanya Drake, yes the case was still open but no one, not even the parents, expected her to return to a normal life. Every law officer knows the first twenty-four hours are the most critical in any missing person's case and both Orlando and Charles knew they were fast approaching that time constraint with Ripley. It was like waiting for the guards to unlock the cell and bring the prisoner to the gas chamber. Each time the secondhand hit twelve it was one step closer to the inevitable, one step closer to meeting the creator, and one step closer to lights out forever. The clock on Lynch's desk read 4:37, just a mere seven hours until the . . . . until the . . . . neither one of them wanted to think about that . . . . there was still a chance and that's what they were going to hold onto—a chance. They were getting closer, they could feel it. There was still much hope left for Ripley Newenberg. Yes, there was still hope for Tanya Drake but it was a superficial hope, not a hope to finding her alive, just a hope that one day they would find the body, give her a final resting place before god and officially close that chapter of her life.

Tanya was three days away from her sixth birthday on the day she vanished from the park oh so very close to home. She was cute as a button and was the only child to the Drakes. She was their miracle child for they tried every natural method of conception under the sun before they chose one of the many medical treatments. Almost sixty-five thousand dollars and four years later Tanya came into their lives. She was the world to them. Although they could have easily given her the world, the parents were well grounded and did not spoil their daughter. She was well mannered, well behaved, and loved her parents. She always had an ear to ear grin, she was always happy, like she already knew how difficult it was to get here, so she enjoyed it as best she could, always making her parents proud no matter what she did. It was heart wrenching three days after her disappearance when the doorbell rang and Mrs. Drake answered it. There stood before her was Alicia, a classmate of Tanya's, dressed in the most adorable white taffeta dress holding a present for Tanya's birthday. She was on vacation with her parents and did not hear the news. She didn't understand the tearful response she received from Mrs. Drake and she too started to cry. The motherly instinct took over in Mrs. Drake; she opened the door and hugged Alicia like she was her found loving daughter. She wouldn't let go. Alicia's mother had to get out of the car and come to the rescue. She herself didn't understand the situation until Mr. Drake came to the door, took her aside and explained things. Mrs. Drake was never the same after that and still to this day lives on prescription medication.

Colleen Rhinehardt was the second little one missing from a playground also close to her home. She was from a family of five, excluding her natural father. It was Colleen, her mother, her elder brother, and two smaller sisters that made up the household. The mother barely made ends meet but she did manage somehow to put one decent meal on the table each day, be it breakfast, lunch or dinner, though most of the time it was breakfast just because it was the cheapest to make—pancake batter can go a long way. After calling the officer in charge of the case at a little after one in the morning, Garfield and Lynch learned there were no witnesses and he had the sense that the mother had an unnatural feeling of relief—basically saying that was one less mouth to feed. She was at the playground on September 23rd, unsupervised by an adult, her older brother age eight accompanying her to the park but failed to bring her home. It wasn't until the next day the mother called the police about her missing Colleen, age 5. She was almost identical to the other girls, shoulder length blonde

hair, cute as a button as well, and vanished from a playground within the seventy-five mile radius of Ripley's hometown. The case was still marked open but no one wasted much time on this one for all intents and purpose it was a cold case, a closed case, there were just no leads to follow.
.

Becky Timberstone was the youngest of the little girls at age four. Her case was still very hot being only a few months old, though hope of finding her safe return had diminished as well. The officer in charge of this case was away on a much needed vacation. He worked himself to the bone on this one because he played the "what if" game, what if it was his little girl, age five, he could not even imagine. He worked so hard on trying to find Becky that his family life was in jeopardy, he actually was neglecting his fatherly responsibilities, his little girl. His partner finally helped him see the light. His partner Josh Cerrito was due in Lynch's office any minute now. Josh thought about picking up the phone and calling his partner but didn't want to give him any false sense of hope; he'd better go investigate this new lead until proven otherwise. And so as it was, Officer Cerrito hopped in his car and at 6:36 am he pulled into a visitor's space just outside Detective Charles Lynch's building. Lynch was waiting for him outside with a cigarette between his lips.

"Officer Cerrito?"

"Yes, Detective Lynch?"

"Yes, come on up, we're just about to do a press release," with that, Lynch did a deep drag on his last bit of smoke to the point it glowed almost bright red and before exhaling, flipped it onto the ground and squashed it with his black shoe. "Coffee," as trails of smoke followed his question?

"No thanks, don't drink the vile stuff, I had my morning can of Coke to get my caffeine fix."

"Suit yourself," and they made their way to Lynch's office without another word.

Garfield looked as tired as Lynch and did the normal exchange of introductions and pleasantries, funny thing was he had yet to do this with Lynch; from the moment he walked into the door it has been all business.

"Okay now what about this press release?"

"We found four cases, yours included that fit the same exact mold all within a year's time frame. We are coming up of the twenty-four hour marker with the Newenberg case and you know what that means, we now need as much help as possible, so we'll ask the help of the public—the more eyes looking for . . . ."

"The sick twisted bastard," interjected by Orlando

"Perpetrator," Lynch said with a smile, "the better we'll be . . . and now that we have a serial kidnapper on our hands the public will go ape shit and that's just what we need, an angry mob with eyes. By the evening news tonight this will be a national story for sure with all kinds of clips on how to protect your children. What I'm most concerned is for all the households that lie within that highlighted circle there, to keep their eyes open."

"Okay, I'm with you but our descriptions aren't even close. In Becky's case we are searching for a kid in his late teens to early twenties in a red Mustang."

"That was what Orlando here calls the three card monte, same thing happened on our case but it was a 74 Camaro and a twenty-two year kid behind the wheel. There are not that many cars like that so finding the needle in the haystack was a so called piece of cake. Turns out he was paid by our guy to basically sit and wait. I'm sure the same thing happened on your end."

"That's your theory?"

"Sticking to it until we see otherwise."

"Alright I'll roll with it . . . . for now."

The release went out on the AP wire just two minutes prior to seven and it wasn't five minutes later that the phone call came in from one of the major networks . . . just so happens CNN is located a stone's throw away in Atlanta. The first interview was with the local station WXIA, they were the first to cover Ripley's disappearance and never left . . . they knew the first twenty-four hours hadn't elapsed as well. At fifteen past the hour, two out three local news segments within the national daily morning shows covered what they were now calling the serial kidnappings, within a half hour the third and fourth were on board. CNN followed suit but their broadcast was national. People already in their daily commute who were tuned into "all news all the time" heard the description as well. Even people bouncing around the dial or glued to their visionless porn and dirty talk stations heard a glimpse of the serial kidnapper, described as medium build, white male, thirty-five to forty-five and walks with a limp. Ripley's case was no longer just a missing person's report. Ripley's case was no longer just a local story. More importantly Ripley's case was no longer just a local case. The mere mention of kidnapping is enough to wake the dead. Couple this with the word serial and the three letter acronym most commonly seen on cheap t-shirts signifying "female body inspector," the FBI, was already on route from their Atlanta based office.

While the media whipped the case into a frenzy, the Forest Park police, with the help of the GBI, prepared for the arrival of the men in blue. Lynch waited for them outside and just before he lit another non-filtered Pall Mall, two nondescript dark blue sedans with government plates pulled into the station's parking lot. He was expecting each of the g-men to be wearing some sort of dark sunglasses to invoke that mystique he has heard so much about—none of them wore any shades. He let them walk right past him without saying a word. He knew there would be hell to pay but he didn't want to pay it just yet. He also yearned for just going home and trying to get some rest, he wasn't as young as he used to be and this working through the night shift was for the birds—mainly the owls, but he decided to have yet another smoke hoping to get his fourth wind from the nicotine fix, besides, he was a cop at heart and he needed to find this sick twisted bastard and find him fast. With that need in mind, he extinguished his Pall Mall and decided to pay the piper. He expected the non-shade wearing FBI guys to have commandeered his office—that was not the case but no sooner did he sit down in his chair, Orlando summoned him to the conference room on the second floor. He grabbed his lukewarm cup of coffee, his yellow note pad and away he went. Upon entering the conference room he quickly noticed it looked like these guys already made themselves at home. Maps, folders, laptops, various forms, and paper were scattered on the table, everyone had a cup of coffee except Josh who was holding his third can of red and white, there were a few pastries at one end of the table, and two seats that were open for he and Orlando at the other. It seemed Josh brought the feds up to speed and they were already planning their first move; that move being to focus on the man with a limp.

●　　●　　●

Chapter 21

Greg stuck to his word and mostly fantasized about how his evening with Jorja was going to play out. Each one of his dreams ended up in the same shape or form, that being in bed with his green eyed lady and humming to the tune by Sugarloaf. There was one where he brought champagne and strawberries and after their work was done he pictured himself snuggled up on the couch with Jorja watching the Simpsons. There was another one where he opens the fridge grabbed this and that and prepared a five star meal even though he could screw up making cereal. Then there was his favorite where he set up an elaborate ploy with a system on the network and him and Jorja would hack the system together only to stumble upon a secret code that Jorja could break and it would profess his undying love to her.

It was Saturday and Greg was as a giddy as a school girl showing off a new pair of shoes. He was counting down the hours with fevered anticipation but then he remembered he didn't know the time. He did a quick check of his email and it turned up nothing, then he flipped open his cell and was about to call Jorja, then decided he'll play it by ear and say between seven and eight but closer to seven. He assembled his laptop and a few disks they may need, and a nice pen drive with a few coding hacks reserved for backdoor entry into locked documents, spreadsheets, and a password protected operating system or two. One of his so called buddies in the shadows wrote that piece of code, if Microsoft only knew Yes he was ready, and if need be he could tunnel into his machine at work or his machine at home. He was hoping that would not be the case; there were many things on his home machine to keep from prying eyes, many, many things and lesbian videos being the least of his worries.

His car was half way to Jorja's house and his dashboard clock read 7:06. With the hour upon him, Greg was growing rather nervous. Deep down he knew none of his dreams would materialize into reality but he always had hope. Before he knew it, he was in front of his boss' house. Only once before had he been here and that was for a small informal Christmas party when he first entered her department. He really didn't know her then, just idle chit chat but right away he melted every time he looked into those eyes. He parked, exited, and was just about to collect his composer and ring the bell when the door suddenly opened. Jorja heard him coming. She had her hair pulled back in the normal work mode ponytail, she had a pair of nicely fitted jeans which was not work mode at all, and neither was the white t-shirt draped over by an unbuttoned oxford. Greg felt a little overdressed in his spanking new loafers, Dockers, and the rest of his business casual attire. He handed Jorja a bottle of wine which he picked up earlier this morning. She thanked him and looked at the label. Though it was not her favorite Amarone, it was pretty damn close, it was a Valpolicella. Her mind quickly went back to the comment "I know a lot of things" and she had a moment of uneasiness.

"I don't know if it's any good, to be honest it was on sale, I was going to get this Spanish wine, it looked pretty close to your name, something like Rio Ja, but some lady convinced me to get this one at almost the same price," which was a convincing lie.

Jorja, smiled at his mispronunciation of the Spanish staple wine and her uneasiness dissipated. She pulled out a magic marker and simple wrote "Greg" and the date on the label.

"Why did you do that?"

If we don't drink it tonight, I'll place it in my wine rack, and when I do open it I will remember who gave it to me and first toast that person."

Greg was hoping they didn't open it tonight.

"So did you get anywhere," Jorja asked?

"Kept my word I did, looked over the directories I did, noticed a thing or two I did."

"Alright Yoda, shall we get down to business?"

Greg could only think of one thing at that moment and it had nothing to do with work, "sure," and added "I can," finally following her inquiry.

She lead him into her office, Greg had been here before but the office seemed different, it was more cluttered, more like his workspace at home, with routers, modems, and from what he could see three computers, tons of computer parts, books, cables, a few backup powers supplies and enough cords coming out of two surge protectors to warrant a fire marshal investigation.

"Nice layout."

"Coming from you I certainly appreciate it."

"No seriously, I mean it, I feel right at home, almost like being on the star ship Enterprise."

"I think you mean something a bit more like a Ferengi Freighter."

"You know, you and that sci-fi brain of yours . . . okay let's begin," with that Greg pulled out his laptop and hardwired into Jorja's home network which was eventually logged into work. He put his laptop aside and pulled out his list of directories, he too had highlighted a few. Jorja pulled out hers and compared notes.

"Where did you get those Greg asked?"

"Same place you got yours," she replied, "I printed out an extra set in the office."

Greg was sure he remembered and he remembers not printing two but he chalked it up to a being completely lost within her eyes or maybe she did a little investigating on her own, either way he didn't question any further.

They each had highlighted the word mumps. Jorja played dumb.

"Why would mumps be on this thing? I mean what does this machine have to do with diseases?"

Greg had a slight chuckle, "That's not a disease it's a database, that's why I highlighted it, something is stored there and we should be able to find out what."

"A database? Do you know anything about it?"

"Sure do, I have to, a lot of financial data, some huge banks, investment firms, and securities have this type of db, a wealth of information at your fingertips, no pun intended . . . not to mention hospital data since this was written by Neil Pappalardo for Massachusetts General Hospital somewhere around 1967. I would like to poke around this machine a bit more, find the size of the machine, its memory, capacity, etcetera."

"Is there anything more you can tell me about this mumps?"

"Yes, but it's boring, it's just another language to learn, fairly easy, I'll show you once we are in."

Greg was able to get into the database without the little utility Jorja had up her sleeve. He was able to see the table structures of the database but one thing he learned over the years—a mumps database is unlike the database systems of today. Granted, there are engineers who have placed rather complicated data schemes on top of this database making data queries a piece of cake to anyone with a little knowledge but underneath lies total chaos and this is where Greg was looking, all while giving Jorja a play-by-play on the language syntax. Unlocking the secrets without access to the data structure could be next to impossible even for a seasoned veteran familiar with the mumps language. It appeared to Greg that he would have to dig a little harder to uncover the meaning behind the data. He listed out some of the raw data and most of it looked like gibberish, with the exception of some words here and there. Nothing made much sense at first glance, even at a second glance or third. He tried counting records in a few folders/tables but it took too long to come back with an answer so he aborted his previous keystrokes. He then looked at the allocations for data storage and realized this thing was a monstrosity and he checked the current block size of a few tables. He did a double take when he wanted to reconfirm his findings because the numbers he originally obtained were now out of date; they were always out of date. He rechecked again and again the numbers were even higher. They were growing at an unprecedented rate.

"Jorja, this database is being used, look at these numbers, they keep growing."

"From?"

"I have no idea, but see these two files here . . . these two files are growing by leaps and bounds. There is a lot of data being poured or calculated into this machine, a lot of data, every second."

"Can we see the data?"

"Sure," and with that Greg punched in a few commands and the screened filled with numbers, "My god it's full of stars . . . . I mean tons of data."

6075781211, 411945138, -82.6171865, 37.37015718405753
6075781211, 411945146, -93.076171825, 44.902577996288876
6075781211, 411945456, 75.3662109301, 42.779275360241904

6075781211, 411945897, -112.0605468789, 34.23451236236987
6075781212, 411945906, -75.0585937582, 39.90973623453719

And they kept scrolling and scrolling to what appeared to be no end in sight, hundreds, thousands, maybe even millions of entries. They noticed the first set of numbers appeared sequential even though there were many duplicates, the second set of numbers were sort of sequential but with no apparent next number algorithm, well without a paper and pen anyway.

"Greg, what do you make of this?"

"I don't know, it appears to be a pattern and then again, no. Without the data schema we would just be guessing."

"It looks like the first number is always a ten digit number and the second always a nine digit number, the third always a negative."

"See, not always the case, the third number here is positive . . . and . . . and this one here has the last number negative."

"Do a screen print will ya," and with that the toner cartridge became a little lower.

"If we don't know what kind of data this is it might help to find out where this is coming from, there has to be something else in the pipeline supplying this amount of data."

"Divide and conquer then, I'll take the numbers and try to find meaning, in the meantime see if you can pinpoint the data stream." With that they both went their separate ways, although they were still in the same room together.

● ● ●

Chapter 22

Two hours had gone by and Jorja's eyes were numb; she had been staring at the stream of numbers on her printout trying to gather some sort of relationship and nothing came to mind. She had a pencil in hand and scratched together various patterns and algorithms to give the numbers a purpose and nothing came to mind. She subtracted, added, divided, she tried modulo division, she played with prime numbers and Fibonacci sequences, she played with dates and time, and still nothing came to mind. She accomplished nothing, no sense of purpose; in fact she was no further along than she was at the beginning of her quest. Greg was very much in the same boat. He checked processes running on the machine, he checked the open ports of the machine, and couldn't find the entry point of the data stream, leading him to believe the machine itself was generating this data. He was systematically picking off each of the running processes on the machine but still had a ways to go, a long way. It was closing in on eleven o'clock and this had to be one of the longest stretches that Greg has been in front of an array of computers and monitors without his green can of pick-me-up but he did find a substitute in Jorja's now dissipating perfume; a whiff was all that was needed but it didn't do a damn thing for his stomach. Greg was not going to cry uncle when it came to his hunger, not in front of Jorja and he didn't have to—Jorja broke the concentration and silence with her stomach growling. Greg looked at her and before he could say anything, she asked, "What do you want on your pizza?"

"Pepperoni is fine, actually anything except black olives or anchovies will do, whatever you like is fine."

She picked up the phone and dialed her favorite thin crust specialist. After she reconfirmed her pepperoni and Italian sausage pie with her phone number, she hung up the phone and stared at the paper with the list of numbers again.

"Greg, ten digits . . . . ten digits, that's a phone number, where is the six oh seven area code?"

"Let's find out . . . oh Google," and within seconds they had their answer.

"Hmmm . . . in southern New York . . . I think we are on to something."

"You might be right, let's do a little investigating shall we . . . a reverse phone search using our computers . . . . and waiting . . . . waiting . . . . bingo . . . . Mr. Royerson, age fifty-eight, here's his address, social, tax bracket, anything else you might want to know? He really doesn't look all that interesting, runs a family bakery, married, two kids, has a nice chunk of money in savings, owns his house, no debt on credit cards, bought groceries last on his debit card . . . again I say not that interesting but . . . but rare."

"Rare?"

"Yes, no debt, tell me what American in this day and age is debt free?"

"Okay, I get your point, rare, try the next number."

"Waiting . . . . waiting . . . . hmmmm phone number not in existence."

"How about the next number?"

"Waiting . . . . waiting . . . . same thing."

"Maybe it's not a phone number."

"I think you are right about that, I think I remember that first set of numbers were shorter on up the list . . . . hey, your bathroom is?"

'There's one down the hall to your left, right before my bedroom."

"Be right back."

"Something to drink?"

"Well I'm sure you don't have my usual, whatever you're having is fine."

Greg took a second or two to stretch his legs and disappeared around the corner. Jorja took the opportunity to make her way into the kitchen and unbeknownst to her, Greg made a little detour. He took a peek in her master bedroom and tried to commit his sights to memory for a later use, that and he just wanted to see where she slept. The light from the hallway was all that he needed for his sights into a wondrous world. He admired the no hanging pictures very stark olive colored walls, though not his first choice of color and he admired the bed itself. It was a very big bed, unmade bed, masculine to a point, dark wood, maybe mahogany, maybe walnut, he wasn't a wood expert. He saw there were none of those frilly throw pillows anywhere—the ones just for decoration that no one uses, just two pillows in their proper places. There was some sort of t-shirt thrown at the foot of the bed and piles of shoes here and there, other than that, the bedroom looked pretty tidy. There was one nightstand with an alarm clock, a small light, and a box of tissues, there were no dressers to speak of, and he correctly assumed all her clothes were stuffed to the gills in the two walk-in closets. He gave the room one more quick once around and proceeded to his original destination. When he came back to Jorja's office he found sitting on the desk his choice of drink and smiled.

"You know me so well."

"Yeah, like no one ever notices the green pyramid of cans you have stacked around your monitors, just think if you applied all that cash into the stock of the company well you'd be . . ."

"Tired . . . and probably fired, but thanks for the drink, had I known, I would have asked earlier . . . I didn't know you drank the stuff."

"I don't," leaving Greg with an even bigger smile, "So going back to what you said before, about being a rare American, let's say that Mr. Royerson and his phone number where not a coincidence, that maybe, maybe this is a database contains more people just like him . . . . debt free . . . wait here me out . . . . I mean a database with that type of data could be worth . . . . well a lot I'm sure . . . and . . ."

"Jorja, let me interrupt by saying first, I estimate there are billions of entries in this database, more entries than people on this planet so your theory is already shot, plus did you forget about the invalid phone numbers?"

"Maybe they are bank accounts? . . . Umm don't answer that . . . same thing . . . billions of entries . . . can you go back to the data again, the one where we got this screen print?"

"Sure thing," and with a few keystrokes the numbers filled the screen again, scrolling and scrolling.

"Look, the second number, the length never changes . . . . it's always nine."

"Yeah, so far so good, always nine . . . . like the nine planets of the solar system."

"Eight."

"You know kids have It so easy today, back when I was a kid we had to learn nine . . . nine . . . . number nine, number nine . . . . number nine . . . . nine minute abs."

"Seven minute abs."

"Are you sure, nine minutes sounds right."

"Seven minute abs, seven eleven, seven doors, you know, seven chipmunks twirlin' on a branch, eatin' lots of sunflowers on my uncle's ranch."

"I know, I know, Something About Mary . . . . I only saw it once."

"Well, one of my favorite comedies, that and Groundhog Day."

"Now that I love, Bill Murray, my favorite part, him sitting around the old folks with a bottle of JD watching Jeopardy for the umpteenth time, saying what is Lake Titicaca, what are the Finger Lakes, and even before they show the answer . . . what is the Rhone," and from there they must have quoted almost the entire movie before the door bell rang with their pizza.

With the empty pizza box aside and a full stomach, things turned back to business. The mind is sharper with nutriments abound and it didn't take long for Jorja and Greg to come up with new ideas.

"Where were we," Jorja asked as she wiped the last bit of pizza grease from her lips?

"Number nine . . . . number nine . . . . number nine . . . ."

"Oh yeah, right . . . nine, nine lives of a cat . . . . it's a perfect square . . . The Ennead . . . . the . . ."

"The what?

"The Ennead . . . Egyptian mythology."

"Sorry, the only things I know are the pyramids, King Tut, the Sphinx, that and they were aliens from a distant galaxy brought here by a stargate."

"Well nine represents The Ennead, the nine deities, you have, Atum the father god or first god, his children Shu and Tefnut, then their children Geb, Nut . . . and I forget the rest but nine in all . . . and there was no stargate or Richard Dean Anderson."

"Obviously you took a few history courses in college and filled your brain with a bunch of useless knowledge . . . . I don't think it's going to help us here my dear."

"Yeah, yeah, yeah, well how about the fact nine is the limit of all numbers meaning all numbers can be comprised of digits zero through nine with nine being the limit."

"How about the fact that a nine digit number has almost a billion possibilities?"

"Can we find a range of those numbers, see if there is a limit?"

"That's going to take a bit of time, not much mind you, but I'll have to write a little program first."

"Wait," Jorja remembered and was a bit hesitant, she went to her desktop, copied a program and gave it to Greg, 'this might help."

"What is it?"

'A little program slash utility that a friend gave me."

"What does it do?"

"It helps to traverse a mumps database a little quicker; he says his company uses it all the time."

"Jorja have you been holding out on me?"

"Just a smidgen, I did some digging this past week, not much, I just poked around and my curiosity got the best of me, I found this database and was unfamiliar with it . . . I did a bit of research to get up to speed."

"Okely-dokely," was his candid reply, Greg didn't say another word on the subject; he knew she was the boss. He just took the program and followed the prompts when he started it and before long he had a range of numbers, a range from one million twenty thousand four hundred fifty-eight to seven hundred seventy-two million three hundred thirty-four thousand eight hundred seventy-seven, or one million to seven hundred seventy-two million, give or take.

"So, that range doesn't start with zero or one?"

"Doesn't appear that way, nothing smaller than a million, I don't know how accurate that little program you gave me is but . . ."

"But can you see how many distinct numbers we have?"

"I'll try, might take awhile, especially if there are about seven hundred and seventy million entries."

While Greg was looking at the screen waiting for an answer, Jorja glanced at her inbox to see if there were any issues she needed to tend to and found none. There were just a few budget reports needing her approval but they could wait until Monday if they had to, there was one from her bank saying her pay has been deposited, two office memos, and a bunch of seemingly unimportant news snipes that the CIA tends to send out to keep everyone informed on the daily events. When she saw the email from the bank she had this nagging twinge in the back of her mind that stemmed from an HR problem she has had since her raise in salary regarding her pension fund deductions. She quickly opened a link to the internal payroll department to view her online pay stub and cursed under her breath. The same deductions were again wrong even after she talked to the head of the department. "How hard could it be?" she thought, then she compared her last pay stub to the present one. She compared every number and amount and sure enough they were the same—it wasn't fixed so she would have to make yet another phone call, maybe even pay a visit this time. Before she closed the window to the payroll site Jorja noticed something on her pay stub and just like the bathing Archimedes proclaiming Eureka and running naked through the streets of Syracuse, she knew she might be on to something but she saved her euphoria and naked romp until she was sure. While Greg was still mesmerized by his blank screen still waiting for an answer, she opened another session into this machine and ran her own test. She ran the nice little utility and entered what appeared to be a random nine digit number. The screen filled with numbers and lo and behold the second number was always the number she had just entered, the nine digit number, the nine digit number that she knew by heart.

"Greg."

"Yes?"

"Take a look at this."

"Oooo . . . more numbers how nice."

"No, take a look at the second number in the list, after the first comma."

"They are all the same."

"Yes, they are, do me a favor will ya, enter your social security into this prompt."

"I don't just give that out to anyone, you know it's illegal for you to ask me," in a sarcastic slur but he did as he was told. As soon as Greg hit return, the screen again came to life with scrolling numbers, his tax id being the second number, "Coincidence?"

"Let me find a few more tax ID's," Jorja went to her employee files and picked another tax number at random, entered it and received more scrolling numbers. She entered another one, same results, thousands of entries, maybe even hundreds of thousands. She tried another employee and realized this was no coincidence. Every number she entered she got a reply—that is until she searched for her father's social security number; she had that one memorized as well due to all the red tape she had to go through since he never had a will when he passed away. It turned up nothing. "Maybe just active numbers," she concluded, so she searched for a few recently deceased individuals using the CIA's computers at her beck and call. Within minutes she had a handful of more social security numbers. Older ones had no records but most of the recently deceased tax id holders, more often than not, were contained in this database.

"One hundred ten million, one seventy eight thousand, four hundred and two"

"What?"

"That's how many distinct tax ID's are in this database at the moment."

"That's about half of the all the numbers."

"How do you know that?"

"More useless facts in that brain of mine, there are roughly two hundred eleven million active numbers in the social security database. Looking back that range makes sense now. Seven seventy two was the last area, the first three positions, that the social security admin issued. Nothing beyond that."

"Makes sense, no zero zero zero area either, so this is a demographics file of some sort."

"Looks that way, I don't recognize any of the other numbers in my portfolio, they are not bank account numbers, or credit card numbers and looking at this, the first numbers are all different and sequential to a point, my tax id second, the third and fourth numbers seem to change but there are a lot of duplicates."

"That first number, you're right, sequential, let's start at the beginning"

6070685194, 462752203, -77.05853462219238, 38.909001254076514
6070685495, 462752203, -77.05853462219238, 38.909001254076514
6070685799, 462752203, -77.05853462219238, 38.909001254076514
6070686098, 462752203, -77.05853462219238, 38.909001254076514
6070686399, 462752203, -77.05853462219238, 38.909001254076514
6070700089, 462752203, -77.05853462219238, 38.909001254076514

"So this first number, it's always ten digits right?"

"Right."

"Is that some sort of a timestamp or something?"

"Sure, it could be, wait . . . wait . . . look . . . . the last five digits get close to eighty seven thousand but not quite . . . in fact it never exceeds eighty six thousand four hundred, they get close, but none over that mark . . . . Fuck me!"

"What?"

"Eighty-six thousand four hundred."

"Yeah?"

"The amount of seconds in a day."

"Talk about your useless knowledge . . . so what does that mean?"

"You were right, it is a timestamp, the last five digits are the time . . . one being one second after midnight, thirty-six hundred is one a m, and eighty-six thousand four hundred is midnight . . . . the first five numbers are the date."

"Date?"

"Yeah, date, in mumps, it's a Julian date, days since a specific date."

"If these are Julian dates, shouldn't those numbers be bigger if using the unix epoch . . . are they truncated?"

"Yeah Unix stores its dates as seconds elapsed since January first nineteen seventy, but no, mumps has some weird date as its starting point, something around the mid eighteen hundreds . . . let me check on Wikipedia for an exact date." Meanwhile Jorja just looked at the numbers on the screen, "O.K. here it is, January first eighteen forty-one."

"Strange starting date."

"Yeah, told you, it has something to do with a hospital and the age of a patient, the originator of the language just picked an arbitrary date that he deemed safe as to the oldest person alive at the time and their birth date."

"I get it, so everyone's birth date would be valid in a database, do me a favor, what is the last entry associated with my social?"

"Just a sec . . . . here it is . . . . six one five seven zero eight six four one nine two"

"Can you do a date conversion for me?"

"I think there is an algorithm that can help us in this program . . . by the way, who did you say you got this from?"

"I didn't, just a friend."

"Uhuh, well looks like there is a function in here, I hope it calculates leap year correctly . . . . O.K. here it is . . . . hmmm . . . today's date."

"Technically it's yesterday's date, it's after twelve . . . but, but what the hell is this other information and why is there an entry in this thing using my social for just before midnight?"

"Good question but look at this, not only is there an entry in this thing for your social security just before midnight but it looks as though there is an entry in here on your social security every five minutes . . . . hold on . . . wait . . . . yeah look at this . . . six one five seven one one two three three . . . . that's about three minutes ago."

"What the hell? Why place an entry every five minutes, that's . . . hold on . . . . that's two hundred and eighty-entries per day . . . wouldn't one suffice?"

"It could be some simulation thing."

"Like what?"

"I don't know, like a game or something."

"Not sitting in the hills of Virginia under the protection of the CIA it ain't."

"True, it could have something to do with actuary tables or . . ."

"Or what?"

"Hmmm I don't know yet . . . I'm trying to comprehend why anyone would need this much power and storage . . . I mean weather simulators don't amass this much data . . . this thing is churning out . . . . let's see . . . a few quick calculations . . . six point six gigs every five minutes times twelve times twenty-four . . . that's just shy of two terabytes of data a day . . . holy shit!"

"Storage is cheap these days so relax . . . . besides I'm sure it gets compressed and stored somewhere down the line."

"Looking at this data, it would help if we knew what those last two numbers are for."

"Data pointers?"

"Could be, good guess, there are a bunch of duplicate numbers, yeah maybe data points into another database . . . for more information . . . yeah those two digits could be x and y coordinates on a hard drive or database somewhere."

"So we have a date and time, and we have a social security number, and maybe data pointers . . . now what?"

"I'm thinking . . . . if we stick to your assumption, this isn't one of those holographic storage systems . . . that would require a z or third coordinate . . . so now I have to find a system that uses this range for storage . . . . maybe that will get us somewhere . . . we have time right?"

"All night."

Again they went their separate ways but stayed in the same room, Greg on one computer, Jorja on another. This was not like hacking in the movies where some whiz kid took a few minutes and presto they have the world's defense systems by the balls or drained bank accounts within seconds using some hidden back door only known by the software's creator. No, this was actually the mundane world of hacking, the most boring aspect of hacking—research, and it took time . . . way too much time, even with the help of some of the world's fastest computers. They were both methodical in their approach, reading and cross checking their facts with one another. Greg dove into the CIA's archives on computer and software companies in search of specifications that would match the range of numbers. Jorja took a more practical approach and used the web as her tool. Jorja googled the word "coordinates" and found a bunch of hits, the first was a link to geographical coordinates and based on this she redefined her search parameters to list hard drives, then she tried databases and from there it was into the world of technologies' inner workings.

● ● ●

Chapter 23

His first order of business was to empty the trash cans in the two hundred and twenty eight cubes. Each cube had two cans, one for just paper that was to be recycled, the other for trash. He knew the cubes by heart. He knew if Eric Campbell was working today there would be two cans of diet Pepsi and a Subway sandwich wrapper—it was that way every day of the week. He particularly liked Chris Peterbergs' cube for each night he would take a cinnamon jawbreaker out of his candy jar which lasted until he was finished with the cans. He noticed all the cube decorations and especially liked the primitive artwork given to the mothers and fathers by their sons and daughters. He liked the hairy fire engine in Bob's cube and the green cotton ball clouds in Kevin's cube, and the big wide grin of a sister's mouth with braces in Shaun's cube, and the sun's rays shining over a lopsided house in Lisa's cube but most of all he liked the photographs in Dane's cube. Dane had several pictures of his daughter in various activities. In one the little blonde was in a blue soccer outfit, number 18, with her foot propped up on a soccer ball. She was with her mother in another shot, and with her older brother in another in what appeared to be a water balloon fight. Since he was the only one working this floor he would spend a few extra minutes just mulling over the pictures, sometimes even sitting down in the chair and taking a break. The little blonde girl in the pictures was what he looked most forward to each and every night . . . . except this night. Tonight he did his regular routine, emptied the trash cans, got his jawbreaker but when he came upon Dane's cube his nightly ritual changed. He took down each picture and simply threw them away, he didn't need his fantasies anymore; he already had his little girl—safe at home. He finished with the cans and grabbed the vacuum. He was done in record time. He clocked out and headed back home.

He made one stop and that was to one of those twenty-four hour mini-marts. He needed some more bananas, although a mini-mart was not the ideal place to buy a bunch, his little girl liked bananas so his little girl was going to get bananas. He also purchased an eight pound bag of ice. The kid behind the counter was bored and tried to make some idle chit-chat but he ignored his every word. He paid in cash and limped to his car. The kid behind the counter watched his every move. When he entered the car he saw the kid was watching. Before he turned the key he thought to himself, then smiled at his ingenuity. He got back out of the car and limped back into the mini-mart. He went to the wall of refrigerated drinks and perused his choices. He picked up another bottle of juice, this time it was apple and made his way to the counter again.

"Forgot my thirst, this is what I came in here for."

"It happens all the time, 99 cents."

"Here you go, thanks."

"You're welcome, have a good night."

"Will do," and he limped back to the car, smiling. He was thinking if someone was trying to hide why would they go back into the store . . . very clever he thought and started the car and headed back to his little girl. By the time he made it home it was a little after three in the morning and the first thing he did was to go down into the basement and enter his watching room. The light was still on but Ripley was sound asleep with the panda bear tucked tightly under her arm. She was precious. He decided to go in . . . . it was time. Just before he unlocked the door he remembered something and stopped. He went back upstairs and went to the second floor. He approached with much forethought, what appeared to be a bedroom door. He opened it and entered, he didn't turn on any lights, hoping the light from the hallway would be enough. It was, there in the corner was what he was looking for . . . a white wicker waste basket and back downstairs he went. He walked into the room ever so quietly. He placed the wicker basket just besides the dresser and placed the bunch of bananas next to the other food. He then brought in a small blue Coleman cooler filled with ice and bottle juice, including the apple juice. He looked around the room like he was checking if anyone was watching. He walked over to the bed and leaned over Ripley. She was beautiful. She moved and it startled him and quickly fled through the steel door. Click. Click. Click. He realized she wasn't ready. He realized he wasn't ready.

●　　●　　●

Chapter 24

It was growing very late but neither of them wanted to quit. They took a quick break and Greg found his way to the fridge for his own personal stash of thirst quenching goodness supplied by his friend. Jorja took the time to pop a few aspirin, hoping to cure her mild headache and knowing full well aspirin's primary ingredient was caffeine, giving her a hopefully added boost . . . . she took three and back to work it was. Closing in on four in the morning neither made too much headway. Jorja wanted to retrace her steps just in case she missed anything. She again googled the word "coordinates". Again she saw the primary links on the page were geographical in nature. She spent some time going through the links, then see tried another search and some of the same geographical links were displayed, even one for Google Maps and out of boredom she clicked on it. She entered the last two numbers into google maps on a whim and waited.

-77.05853462219238, 38.909001254076514

Nothing happened. She was focusing on a blank map. She tried to zoom in and nothing happened, she zoomed out nothing happened, then she zoomed all the way out and she was looking at Antarctica. Greg happened to look over seeing Jorja starring at a green marker on the screen.

"Looking for penguins?"

"No, just bored. I kept getting links to geographic coordinates, latitude and longitudes . . . I still get them confused, well the numbers don't look like the standard geographical coordinates with minutes and seconds . . . anyways I tired plugging in the numbers into google maps and that's what it returned."

"So you end up in good old Terra Australis. Tell me you never heard of latitude are like rungs of a ladder? Lat . . . Lad."

"No but that's a good one, I'll try remember that."

"What happens if you reverse those numbers? Those could be the decimal representation of the coordinates," and he waited for the answer, "Zoom in . . . . again . . . . one more time."

They both sat there in silence but mostly in horror.

Greg broke the silence first, "That can't be, tell me that can't be . . . . Fuck! Please tell me Jorja, please."

Jorja didn't say a word; she was too busy thinking about all the ramifications, thinking how this was possible.

"Jorja . . . . Jorja, please tell me this is some kind of sick twisted joke, you're fucking with me right? This can't be fucking possible, right? You were in the database earlier this week, you set this up right?"

Jorja was still silent. Greg went to the computer and punched up his social security number and looked at the last entry in the database. The last two numbers were almost identical to Jorja's.

-77.058534622345, 38.90900125406733

"Jorja, why the fuck didn't we notice this before? Those two numbers are almost identical to yours. This can't be. Fuck it can't be."

"Let's not jump to conclusions," she said in a soothingly calm voice, "let's run another test before we . . ."

"Before what? Before we fucking panic . . . . it's too late for that," as Greg looked again at the Google map pinpointing the exact location of Jorja's town home.

• • •

Chapter 25

Greg was still freaked out and to be honest so was Jorja but they ran their tests. They picked a few entries from earlier on Saturday and mapped out a route that was taken every five minutes. The maps were dead on. It showed Jorja out and about running errands and even in the grocery store where she picked up some Mountain Dew. Greg's map was dead on too for his daily roundabout through town and to work. Jorja found one of her colleague's tax id that she knew was on vacation. Sure enough she was located in Virginia Beach just where she said she was going.

"How is this happening?"

"Fuck if I know . . . . maybe through cell phone triangulation."

"That's got to be it, probably would only take a few super computers, hack into the phone systems, and . . ."

"That's still a lot of processing power and manpower to set something like this up, not to mention . . . ."

"Mention what?"

"I just realized something."

"What?"

"Well, my battery died about one this morning, I have a charger in the car but didn't bother to get it . . . and there are entries in the files for every five minutes since then."

"Maybe it just keeps defaulting the same location until it comes back on line."

"Yeah probably, so it's cell phone triangulation . . . on everybody . . . . pretty fucking scary . . . think about it, anybody with a cell phone, and that's just about everybody, can be tracked to a location at almost any point in time . . . it's no wonder this thing is locked away in the hills . . . . I wonder how many people know about this?"

"Well the President and Scott cannot be the only ones, they would need a few more key players that's for sure."

"Something like this has to go pretty deep. Fuck! I still can't believe it. I can't believe this fucking thing exists. The sheer big brother aspect is just so goddamn overwhelming"

"Being able to search for anyone anytime . . ."

"There goes the anonymity of the fourth amendment, this goes beyond any reasonable search . . . because of this they have seized our right to declare our innocence, because of this we are now proven guilty through association of location and time, someone somewhere can pinpoint your exact location anytime, anyplace be it probable cause or on a whim all without a warrant."

"But this sort of happens all the time though does it not? I mean we search for people using some sort of data mining techniques and we search people's records without a warrant in order to eliminate them from the original search parameters. It's the people or data fitting those search parameters that need to worry."

"But Jorja, that's my point . . . every time you search for someone now they are in the Venn diagram, they are in that circle enclosed by facts, the facts being the exact place and time . . . I search for you, I found you, you're guilty as charged."

"What did I do?"

"Rob a bank, there you are, murder someone there you are, speeding there you are, sleeping around, there you are, you can't hide, you can't lie, you can't get away."

"See I don't think this would hold up in court."

'Court? Court? Are you kidding me . . . if this system was put in place on a nationwide scale, there would be no court, no freedom."

"Greg if this gets out in the public . . . ."

"Public? No way, no fucking way, the government would implode, crumble, people would just go ballistic . . . . that would be the end of America as we know it."

"I know, I know . . . but . . . but what are we going to do . . . this information is definitely worth more than our lives . . . it makes hacking the President's password seem like just getting a demerit in school for not doing your homework."

"Fuck, I don't know, only God should have this much knowledge."

"Think about it, this is God or God's brain."

"Pretty fucking close I'll give you that."

"No think about it, it is God, g . . . o . . . d . . . government overseeing device."

"God, yeah well fuck this government . . . ummm."

"Overseeing device."

"No, no, oracle, oracle device."

"You mean oracle like in Oracle databases?"

"No, like fucking Oracle of Delphi, the government's Oracle of Delphi, fucking . . . g . . . o . . . d. Fuck we're dead! Jorja, we're in deep fucking shit if they find out we know about their fucking god, if they don't know already."

"This makes the Real ID Act look like it was put together by a bunch of pre-schoolers."

'Huh?"

'The Real ID Act."

"Yeah I know, the national identification number the government wants everybody to have, yet another false sense of security in the name of fucking terrorism."

"Yeah people were up in arms about this one saying the government could track your movements about the country since you need it for a driver's license, plane, bus, and train travel . . . this system trumps that."

"Trumps? More like annihilates it using every goddamn nuclear bomb this world has to offer . . . this is some scary fucking shit Jorja . . . scary fucking shit," shaking his head.

"Just settle down, we need to think things through, we need to, we need to . . . . just think"

"You're right, you're fucking right . . . . but . . . . okay . . . I need to clear my head, I can't think straight at the moment, I need to get out of here, I need, I need . . . . I'm going to walk down to M Street,. I need some air, I need some goddamn fucking air."

"Just be careful Greg," and with that he headed to the door but first checked through the window before he exited the town home.

●　　●　　●

Chapter 26

It was a rather crisp morning for June but the sun creeping over the horizon would soon change that. Greg knew exactly where he was going and walked with a quick step, checking over his shoulder almost every minute knowing full well his precautionary measure was futile. If the CIA wanted to watch someone—they would never know. They could watch from above via some hunk of space junk, they could tell what size a shirt was if the tag was showing, and there was not a damn thing anyone could do about it, except stay indoors and thus becoming an easier piece of prey. They could also extinguish the life without so much of an effort, just like the movies, yes exactly just like the movies, and sometimes they were dead on but he knew how his company worked; he didn't need the silver screen for that. He knew because he saw the internal communications between people in the field, he knew the dangers, he knew the risk, he knew he was in a world of shit for penetrating a system almost as all-knowing as god. The more he pandered about it, the more pebbles of sweat clung to his brows. He was becoming increasingly nervous and paranoid mainly from his body's continued state of caffeine intoxication. He made his way to his destination, grabbed a few twenty ounce plastic bottles, and started to return back. He stopped and remembered. He then walked across the street to a local coffee shop and not the one from Seattle and bought a twenty ounce cup of straight black Joe for Jorja. He remembered Jorja, he remembered they were both involved in this and he needed to return to her, to protect her anyway he could.

Meanwhile Jorja continued to punch in social security numbers and using the web she continued to do more searching. She was very much in denial; she didn't want to believe but the more she entered the more real it became and the more addicting it became. She was able to locate individuals in her department on a moment's notice. She even inputted two individuals who she had suspected were seeing each other and sure enough, over the weekend they were in the same location for most of the time. The power Jorja started to feel was enough to dissipate the sense of anxiousness of waiting for Greg to return. This was taking spying to a whole new level and she was starting to enjoy it. She wanted to know more about her colleague so she brought Greg's file back up on the screen. She looked at the last entry and was a little perplexed. It now had a different set of numbers from hers and she distinctly remembered his cell phone battery had died. She pinpointed the exact location and it was within a few blocks of the Seven Eleven, an earlier entry had him within inside another store across the street—a coffee shop. Her trepidation started to return. She didn't touch the keyboard again and waited for Greg. When he did arrive she noticed the paper bag in his hand, in his other a bottle that was three-quarters empty, and he appeared much calmer.

"You got me coffee didn't you?"

"Yes and . . ."

"And you went down to Thomas Jefferson Street."

"How . . ."

"Do you have your cell phone with you?"

"No, it's on the desk right . . . . right . . . . here it is," then Greg looked at the monitor and it showed his previous location on the screen. "How the fuck?"

"It must be some kind of bug elsewhere."

"Where the fuck could that be, I have nothing else, no watch, just the clothes on my back and shoes on my feet . . . that can't be . . . no fucking way."

"Embedded?"

"Where?"

"Money?"

"Impossible . . . even though people do believe that little plastic strip woven between the linen has something to do with just this . . . no way, too hard to tie a social to all that cash."

"Clothes?"

"No, same reason as money."

"They could be radio frequency ID's."

"In the clothes? Highly doubtful, we could easily find them, and then if you washed them, they'd be history."

"The only other choice really is within the body."

"No way . . . no how . . . . how would they do that . . . . how would you embed something in over a hundred and ten million people?"

"Think!"

Greg pulled up a chair and a keyboard and went straight back into the system. He pulled up the very first records in his file and did the same to Jorja's file. The starting dates were the same.

"Here is your first entry and here is mine . . . they are the same date but different times, mine is like three hours later in the day."

"So what is that date?"

"Over two years ago, back in October, October fifteenth to be exact, ring any bells?"

"Not one, maybe that's when they archived records."

"Maybe, but looking across the board at other records, there are dates in the system of over five years old, the oldest appears close to seven, it wouldn't make sense if they archived records on different dates, then again nothing makes any fucking sense now."

"Agreed. Let me take a look at my calendar and email box and see if anything jumps out . . . . let's see, it was a Wednesday, I had two morning meetings and my afternoon was in the clear. I must have deleted most of the unimportant emails, nothing of consequent that I see."

"Nothing is ever deleted in this place Jorja, you know that, just in case I'll bring up our deleted folders from that date . . . here we go."

"Is all that just from one date, geez there's a bunch of emails in here."

"I'd say about seventy. Did you know the average person spends about four minutes per email, looking at your folder that's a lot of time?"

"Four minutes, I could see that, most of my day is spent on emails.," she briefly read through most of them skipping certain ones in the process and Greg did the same, "nope, nothing here . . . hey, what's that reminder? We both have one," Greg then clicked it open, read it, and the beads of sweat started their return.

This is a reminder for those of you who have signed up for your annual flu shots to report to the meeting hall "A" at the proposed times:

Last names A—L 9:00 to 12:00
M—Z 1:00 to 4:00

This season's flu is expected to be problematic for the healthcare system; any precautions taken will be of benefit.

Sincerely, the Human Resource Department

Without a doubt in each of their minds, they knew the horror was real. The horror was worse than any leather-faced chainsaw wielding demonic could conjure up. It was worse than all the world wars together, worse than any plague, disease, or sickness known to man, and worse than any catastrophes unleashed by the throws of heavens upon this earth. The horror was real, the total loss of freedom was real. The Orwellian society coming of age has happened and it was real; the truth written in data before their very eyes. Big brother was actually inside their bodies knowing every move, the exact location and time of almost every step and just about every breath, maybe listening, maybe even watching. Deep inside the body somewhere, somehow, something was communicating with the outside world plotting the locations of over one hundred and ten million people, every five minutes and Greg and Jorja were two of those people . . . almost one half of America was as well. No where to run, nowhere to hide. The horror was real, the fear was real. With this information and the information already stored on the vast systems of the CIA, the knowledge on any one of these given individuals was almost unfathomable. The person or persons obtaining this knowledge, this power, would be deemed gods to any mere morsel of a man and bestowing true fear into the soul itself. All knowing, all powerful, god-esque, supreme supremacy, yes, these were now all adjectives of the president and the people around him, for god is knowledge and today the hands of god lay in the power of a computer and the hands of Satan lay in those who use it. Greg and Jorja saw the writing on the wall. The president was in his first term of office and already held a firm hand on the American people and their plights. The American people loved him; he did his job and did it well. Another term was predicted and with this type of power behind him, who knows what lies ahead, maybe a possible third term with the help of congress and a new amendment, then a fourth, then dictatorship, then the end of America. With this much power it wasn't inconceivable, nothing seemed too farfetched anymore. What a change of views since the evening of yesterday. Greg and Jorja started out on an adventure and ended up in the pits of hell within a few hours. The only way to—climb out of the depths of Dante's Inferno was to play the same game, to obtain knowledge, as much as possible, before the clock ran out via some accidental death, before their last bated breath at the hands of the devil himself, and hopefully before the end of a nation.

• • •

Chapter 27

Vaccines have eradicated smallpox, placed polio on the endangered list, and have measles on the run. In due time maybe HIV and even certain types of cancer will be on the ropes. Yes, vaccines are an important part in the fight against diseases. They are simple in design. They are nothing more than a delivery method for weakened and even dead microbes to the immune system in order to build immunity against the known destructor. They are also complex to build, to test, and to prove to the public they are safe. Vaccines have been around for quite some time, as far as two hundred years ago when Edward Jenner first inoculated a small boy with cowpox. From there Louis Pasteur continued the work and eventually coined the word vaccine derived from the Latin word vacca, meaning cow, in order to honor Jenner in his work with the cowpox disease. Without vaccines the world population might have been on the decline, either that or the wheelchair business would have been booming. Yes, vaccines are an important part in the fight against diseases, a very important part and governments know it.

That's why legislation has been in place even since the mid 1800's in order to protect its people. In 1840 the UK passed the first law regarding vaccines and in 1853 made it even more stringent by requiring every child between the ages of three and four months to be vaccinated. Included in this Act was a bylaw requiring proof to the local registrar of births that the inoculations have been completed. The U.S. followed suit by providing law upon law and even upholding its laws as in the Supreme Court ruling of 1905 in the case of *Jacobson v. Commonwealth of Massachusetts*. This case marked that the state could require vaccinations for the greater good of its people. Since then, many states require vaccinations before attending public school and even private schools must require it if they want to receive any type of state or federal funding. The federal government laid down the law again with the National Childhood Vaccine Injury Act of 1986. This act mandated that each health care provider must record the name of the individual receiving the vaccine, the date, the manufacturer, and the vaccine lot number into the immune registries or Immune Information Systems. The IIS are nothing more than computerized databases for maintaining a system of record to ensure timely immunizations and consolidation of information. This information is then to be used by schools, daycare centers, and health professionals but must meet strict privacy measures put in place by the Center for Disease Control and Prevention.

The CDC falls under the Department of Health and Human Services and its mission is "to promote health and quality of life by preventing and controlling disease, injury, and disability." Vaccines fall within the guidelines of operations of the CDC and they develop policies and procedures to control the resources and technologies in administrating them to the greater good of the people. The actual manufacturing of vaccines falls under the guidance of the Food and Drug Administration and strictly monitors each and every step of the vaccine's developmental process. They too, do this for the greater good of the people.

Just like with food, the FDA deems what is safe and what is not in creating a vaccine. It dictates what you can add in the way of additives, preservatives, and stabilizers, although it is highly doubtful that sawdust or cardboard be allowed as fillers in a vaccine against rubella, as opposed to the acceptable levels in the average hotdog. Nonetheless, they try to preserve the integrity of all vaccines. These additional materials are required in building a vaccine for many reasons; certain types of vaccines might require live microbes of the disease and need food to survive, while others might need to maintain their environment without becoming diluted once entering the bloodstream, whatever the reason, these additional materials are also governed by the FDA.

If the FDA states an allowance of sawdust in hotdogs, it doesn't state what kind of trees the sawdust must come from or inspects the plants where the sawdust is made; it just accepts the fact that it is a raw ingredient. Just as long as the hotdog manufacturer stays within the acceptable guidelines drawn by the FDA, no penalties or fines will come against them. Now if the hotdog manufacture produces a faulty lot and causes illness or worse, death, then many asses are going to be probed by the biggest of microscopes, including those supplying the raw ingredients. Same holds true with the building blocks of a vaccine. To create an additive, a preservative, or a stabilizer there is no need to follow the same procedures as a vaccine itself and apply for a Biologics License Application (BLA); verification by the vaccine creator is usually all that is required by a company since the FDA considers many of these as just raw ingredients, in other words, the sawdust of vaccines. As long as a biotech company creating the vaccine stays within the acceptable guidelines drawn by the FDA for any additional materials, no penalties or fines will come against them and more importantly, no microscopes. They are free to use any raw materials as dictated by the rules of the business world: price and quality. Mainly the only difference between hotdogs and a vaccine is the vaccine must track each lot number of its raw ingredients, just to be on the safe side.

One of the most popular raw ingredients, actually a stabilizer for a few big named vaccines, is STB5 (what's in a name?). It is very cost effective and is also used in flu shots worldwide making it much in demand. This stabilizer is produced by Etimiz, a biotech company located in the western suburbs of Philadelphia, Pennsylvania. The STB5 is just one of many little sidebars that keep this relatively small privately held company afloat, that and a few subsidized federal funds in the way of annual research grants. STB5 was first created in the early part of the 80's by Francis Simoski, a brilliant but bordering on unstable PhD. holder out of America's seventh oldest college. Francis himself is the proprietor of over sixty different patents while his company is accountable for almost double that figure. Frank's patents range from his now famous STB5 stabilizer (famous only in the biotech world), to cell division tools, and all kinds of nanotechnologies from bonding agents and catalysts, to micro identification tags. He has been a member of the National Science and Technology Council (NSTC) since its inception in 1993 and one of the key founding fathers of the Interagency Working Group on Nanotechnology, later changing its name officially in 2001 to the National Nanotechnology Initiative (NNI) under the Clinton administration. Yes, Dr. Simoski is considered to be one of the biggest names in the smallest of worlds, in other words, the world that is only one billionth of a meter in length, the world of the nano. His nickname of Dr. Smallski is rightfully fitting.

The almost average looking Francis Simoski is in his late 50's, fifty-seven to be exact, average height, five ten to be exact, and of average weight give or take five pounds, still black hair with wisps of gray in the temples, brown uneventful eyes, and a nose that would help with a down payment on a plastic surgeon's Bimmer. He's unmarried, in fact, his last major girlfriend was in the 11th grade and since then it has been a box of tissues and the first five minutes of any porn movie; his mind has been occupied by many things other than the genitalia draw of a female companion—probably why his nickname (behind his back) of Dr. Smalldick is also rightfully fitting. He doesn't have too many male friends either, only one or two that he has maintained communication with since his college days. To reiterate, Dr. Francis Simoski is not an average man in the grey matter capacity; commonsense seems to dissipate when he's lost in thought and compulsiveness rears its ugly head when he is at a loss for thought but he is never at a loss for words. The man can talk and most of the time it's on a higher plane than his audience but given the opportunity to speak in front of his peers at anyone of the many conferences throughout the year, watch out, he takes no prisoners and speaks his mind . . . right or wrong but the majority of the time Dr. Francis Simoski is never wrong, only because few could ever prove otherwise.

Oftentimes, in college, he was locked in a lab, lost in his theories, but when he did adventure away from the Bunsen burners, test tubes, and beakers he would pontificate about his visions of the world to anyone who would listen—and what a strange world it was, a strange "small" world. His mini lectures (pun intended) were given mostly with a cheap beer in hand talking about miniature robots fixing your heart, creating super glue out of mucus, or spying insects dropped from planes; people just assumed he was intoxicated, while others envisioned his screws were a wee bit loose. Outside of the lab, no one really took Francis Simoski seriously in the days of college . . . except for the one or two people in which he still maintains communication.

May the truth be known, it was these one or two individuals that helped Francis secure his own company. Fresh out of school with sheepskin in hand and no official lab to call home, he thought about staying at his alma mater and teaching but most of all continuing with his passion. He thought about this briefly and quickly vetoed the idea for he wanted no part of prying eyes from deans, other professors, or even students—why be the giant whose shoulders they stand upon when the pay is better in the real world. So it was off to the outside world . . . . the real world. He landed a job at Bell Labs easily; they practically begged him and offered him a handsome salary from the get-go. After seven years he realized this was not the place—here too were prying eyes but most bothersome were the stealing of his credits and his ideas for patents all in the name of the company. He wanted more; he wanted to be on his own, away from the eyes and grabby hands, but was unsure of the first steps. Then out of the blue, a state representative called him, asked how he was, and could they meet for dinner. "Dinner with an old friend . . . . why not?" Since that dinner the world of grants and funding was ripe for the taking. Soon afterwards, Etimiz, contrived from his 11th grade girl friend's name, secured a million dollar grant to study the relationship of microbes and cellular membranes within vaccines, and opened up shop.

Yearning to invoke his own concepts and designs he sought a place very close to his upbringing. With his grant money securely grasped in his fist and a good chunk of his seven year stint with Bell, he leased a fitting environment for his new lab, hired a few people, and got down to business— his business. Although he had other agendas, his first goal at hand was to develop his company into an established identity. Being able to support the company through its own technologies helps to prevent wondering eyes from the takers—mainly the IRS and the grant givers. For the better part of the first five years he teetered on the books that were magenta in color; if it wasn't for the few grants from above, Etimiz simply would have faded away. Then he struck pay dirt. Without getting into the nitty-gritty, Francis was able to increase the effectiveness of a vaccine stabilizer given it an increase of over a three hundred fifty percent in shelf life. This new stabilizer was dubbed STB5 for the five new peptides introduced to its environment and became the corner stone for his company—in more ways than one.

Developing new ideas was now his primary focus. With a decent product to keep the company buoyant, he concentrated more towards his love of all things small—the nano. At his former employer he developed methodologies, tools, and theories, in which he carried forward and used these as a springboard into the pool of nanotechnology. He basically picked up where he left off from Bell Labs and dove, head first, into the shallow end. In actuality nanotechnology was in its infancy stage, still is to much degree, but no one knew more about it than Dr. Smallski. Although he wanted to keep as much as possible under his hat and did, the requirements for federal funding led him to sermonize in front of the masses. With each new grant came more and more responsibility—being placed on the board here, being chair of that committee there, speaking at this conference and that conference, writing white papers and proof of concepts and journal articles, all while treading water in the technology pool—it was more than just an aquatic ballet to entertain the troops. He became a predominate leader in this new world, which meant he alone could almost dictate the direction of a new era, even though most of it was just a façade. With his established leadership and very tight ties with the powers to be, he helped to forge government regulations and mandates from both a government sense and from the populace sense thus creating a moral boundary for this new technology, one that everybody seemed to agree upon, everyone except himself.

Etimiz was his company and to a certain degree it was able to govern itself. Why should anyone question the moral leader of the world of nanotechnology? Most people took him for his word—hook, line, and sinker as they say and his grant givers loved every minute of it. After all, he preyed upon the fears of what this technology could accomplish if left in the hands of just the scientists—the fears of blending the human genome with silicon chips to create a new hybrid humanoid, the fears of releasing a man-made microbe with lethal proportion to that of a plague, the fears of every imaginable mad doctor schema coming to life in an instance. It was these fears he fought long and hard to suppress with the help of his counterparts and their moral ethics. But in reality, their moral lines drawn in the sands were just that, imaginary lines being erased by his left hand. The masses saw his visible right hand, a clear leader in the field but what they never saw was what his left hand was doing. It was more than just sleight of hand, for when being fooled, expect the old "hand is quicker than the eye routine"; no one thought they were being fooled. The tighter the restriction he himself helped place on the companies through mandates and regulations by the government, the more he strayed in the opposite direction. Again, who would ever question his ethics on the subject matter when their fears where his fears as well?

And those fears were all too real in the labs at Etimiz. When Dr. Francis Simoski was not out touring the conference circuit he was busy locked in a lab trying to create his own circuit. That was his main goal in life—to create a circuit . . . a nanocircuit, one fit for the human body. That was the one piece of the puzzle that was his responsibility, the one piece he knew he could deliver given time, the one piece of the puzzle to make the system a reality and not just a pipe dream—his part of the equilateral triangle. Dr. Simoski sleight of hand trick was to step over the boundaries he forewarned his colleagues about and insure the success of his system.

Research and development made strides when no boundaries existed in the labs of Dr. Simoski; he was light-years ahead of anyone else in the field, still to this day his technology is light-years ahead of anyone else. Now it wasn't all him, it wasn't all his ingenuity and time and money and hard work and dedication and because of his obligations it couldn't have been all him; he had help, after all, he owned the company, he told his brain trust, his think tanks, his employees what to do, what to create, what to test, but what he did not tell them was what for or why. Departmentalization was the key to its success. Sure, one or two people very close to the project did ask, and those who did are no longer working for the company, in fact, through some outside intervention, those people are no longer working individuals—in the living and breathing sense. One may have committed suicide based on the pressures of work and marriage and one may have driven off the road coming home from a local bar after spending another Friday night alone. These things happen and one must move along and move along they did—at a rapid pace, at blinding speeds, and mostly under the radar gun of the government and their regulations or basically his regulations.

Advancements were made almost on a daily basis. His lab experimented with quantum dots, hydrogen bonding, ionic bonding, nanowires, nanotextured surfaces (a one dimensional object on the nanoscale), nanotubes (two dimensional), nanoparticles (three dimensional), and a whirlwind of other scientific terms well beyond the comprehension of most individuals. They built nanoswitches able to be turned off and on—a common thread with computers and their binary code of ones and zeros but much smaller in scale. They hammered out theories on conductivity with chemical catalysis and super conductors created from carbon and noble metal particles. They pushed the envelope in regards to passing these substances through the human body and even through the blood-brain barrier in order to power them through the central nervous system. This is where the true fears of the people lie, for once inside a living organism, different reactions can take place and they are almost unpredictable. These nanoparticles can accumulate in areas not destined for treatment or analysis, cause inflammation or infections, stress the immune system, or halt or stimulate the natural production of proteins and enzymes. They can be highly mobile, highly volatile, and highly difficult to trace. They can in fact be highly dangerous within the biological world of the human anatomy but in order to make new strides in the name of science, warnings and cautions are thrown to the wind. Etimiz, the company that made many great strides, never once read the road signs, never once applied the brake pedals, never once looked in the review mirror, they just applied pressure to the accelerator and sped past their competitors.

Somewhere on the open deserted road of where nanotechnology meets biology, speeding along well over the limit, Etimiz made a few discoveries and created an invention the world has yet to know—the patent is pending, not that they would ever apply for one. Again, without getting into the nitty-gritty, they were able to generate a signal through the body from an object smaller than a cell. The object in discussion could in theory be called the world's smallest passive transmitter, passive in the sense that it only transmitted a signal when a signal is received. It contained the most rudimentary components of a transmitter. It contained an oscillator, the circuit that creates a signal, a modulator, the circuit that varies this signal, and a power supply to produce this signal. After the circuitry was mapped for the oscillator, their first major road block was the modulator. In the beginnings, they hard coded the information that was to be transmitted; it was just a single digit number. Over the next few years, the company developed nanoswitches and was able to increase the signal to produce a thirteen digit number, and here's the kicker, they were able to produce specific number sequences, sort of like a serial number. Their next obstacle was the power supply. They didn't need New York City power grid type of energy but what they did need was a constant energy source. They had to look within the body itself for fuel. They played around with oxygen and glucose and even tried to use currents from the central nervous systems and the brain to no avail. Then while in Norway at a conference, Dr. Simoski found the answer. His plane flew over a machine sitting in the North Sea. His curiosity peaked when he found out that it was an oscillating water column. This device created energy from the waves of the ocean, from the constant ebb and flow of the tides. The light bulb almost blew it was so bright. There was a constant ebb and flow within the body as well, the blood stream. If only Etimiz could create a miniature version of the OWC, the power supply dilemma would be solved . . . . it was. On the underbelly of the nano device are fin like nanoparticles that flex to and fro as the blood cycles pass. The flexing creates energy much like one of those handcarts on the railway tracks that are seen in old movies. That energy is able to produce enough power to generate a signal. This signal or wave was infinitesimal and undetectable to any known listening device made by man but in theory it was there. In order to help detect this signal an amplifier was also needed and created, as a result this invention almost doubled in size but still very small even on the scale of the nano. Even with this mini amplification, the signal was still undetectable.

Hearing this signal was indeed the crux of the big picture. The device was useless if it couldn't be heard; if it couldn't transmit its data, its series of unique numerical digits, the whole project would be deemed a failure. They couldn't afford to fail—too much at stake, too many millions would go down the drain, too many man hours would be logged in vain, and too many ideals would go astray. To emphasize, hearing this device was the overall key to the project, to the system. They couldn't afford to fail. They had to solve this problem, no matter what cost.

Like most problems, solutions can be rather difficult to come by at times. Solutions can be found through hard work and dedication, through experimentation and examinations, through simplification and modification, and even by accident or chance in the strangest of places. The amplification was solved through a little bit of all the aforementioned but the big breakthrough came while an Etimiz employee was at home watching the latest blockbuster on Blu-ray. The light bulb was so bright it almost blew. Sitting in the couch and laughing his head off, his wife wondered what was literally so funny. The fact it was so simple was indeed the joke only he understood at that moment.

Everyone, including his boss Francis Simoski also got the joke, for they knew they were one step closer to reality, in fact this was the last major roadblock of the project, nothing but open road lied ahead of them. So instead of having a mini transmitter and an amplifier combined on a single nanochip, they separated them into two components, much the way high-end audio systems separates the tuner, CD player, or turntable, from the amplifier; then if you need more power just add another amplifier or two or three or four. They just had to find the right ratio of transmitters to amplifiers to support their goal and eventually they did.

Yielding enough power to extend the range of a signal beyond the human body, these nanotransmitters and nanoamplifiers are a work of pure genius, not to mention a work of art in their own right to anyone who is privy enough to see them. The sheer beauty of these devices lies not only in their size but to how they interact with one another, how they communicate, thousands of tiny little particles, that cannot be seen by the naked eye or even under a standard microscope, working in conjunction to receive and produce a unique and amplified signal. It is a miracle that they even exist. From his ideals in college, to the papers of theories and proofs in his studies, to their creation within his laboratory, it took little more than twenty years to grasp something tangible, for his/his network's dream to materialize and the real shocker being—it was only a few million dollars over budget. What he received in return from his prolonged dedication was a product that is profound in every aspect of its existence and not one ounce of recognition, no history book footnotes, no television interviews, no magazine articles, nothing. What he received instead was a power unlike anything man has ever held before.

Micro identification tags or nano identification tags or NID's as they are truly known to inside crowd, are ingrained with a unique serial number so to speak and can transmit this unique signal to a specific target or scanner. They are small and almost untraceable and they are not known to exist outside the realm of a few privileged individuals. That secret is well kept unlike its big brother, the radio frequency identification tag. The RFID has been touted as the miracle of all time-saving devices. In this day and age the barcode is slowly beginning to be replaced by the RFID chip that is no bigger than a grain of rice. This small device can track packages, cars, and even lost animals and children. It can make shopping a breeze by bypassing the checkout lines. Just stock the grocery cart to the brim, pass under a scanner and every single product's price is uploaded to the checkout screen almost instantaneously, pay, and then leave—a breeze indeed, except when it comes to bagging, that's another story. The public is just beginning to react to the endless possibilities of the RFID chips and so has the government. In fact, several states have already placed laws on their books to protect its people from the misuse of RFID's. The state of Wisconsin was among the first to protect its citizens with Act 482 which states "no person may require an individual to undergo the implanting of a microchip." It has nothing against the individual who solely permits the implants. A parent may eject a RFID under the skin of their children in order to keep a watchful eye but if the government mandates such a creed then a closer step to an Orwellian society everyone will be. It's obvious through these laws that the government's best interest is protecting its people, keeping the privacy pirates at bay but the truth of the matter—it is a mere façade. Now imagine that RFID, that grain of rice, is replaced by hundreds of thousands of these nanotransmitters and nanoamplifiers aka NID's, being dispersed within the human body without the knowledge of the individual. The possibilities for such devices are endless. Well in actuality, there is only one really good reason for this and the only reason they were devised in the first place. That reason being is for identification purposes—identification without detection. If no one knows of their existence, then no laws can be passed to help protect its people.

Unlike its big brother, NID's are supposed to go unnoticed but just how is this supposed to happen? That's were STB5 comes into play. The inventor used his cost effective stabilizer, STB5, as the delivery system for the NID's. Easy to do, his company owns the stabilizer, his company owns the NID's, his company owns the process of mixing the two and no one is the wiser. Anyone needing a vaccination simply had a small dose of NID's injected into the blood stream along with the needed vaccine. The only side effect from the several hundred thousand NIDs embedded within the human body is feedback, in other words, just a very faint high pitched sound from time to time when a television or another electronic device is turned on in the same room as the NIDs, otherwise the NIDs are totally harmless and can last a lifetime. Each NID transmits a different signal, each individual package of STB5 has a lot number based on a five digit ascii code, and each vaccine's lot number contains the stabilizer's lot number as well and all this information is stored in a database at Etimiz.

Connect this database through an undetectable interface within the IIS database and the power of a system starts to unfold. The IIS database, by law, stores the lot number of the vaccine that was injected into an individual and the best way to identify that individual is through their government identification number aka—social security number. The government has a person's social security number tied to a vaccine lot number, that vaccine is tied to a stabilizer lot number that contains the NID's. The NID's transmit a unique frequency when oscillated by another transmitted wave. Now link this technology with a global positioning system and the worst fears of big brother watching are a reality.

History has never seen the likes of this power. The dominance of the Roman Empire, the horrors of Hitler, the thrusts of the Saturn 5 rockets, the destructiveness of the atomic bomb, the winds of Katrina—all are just flashes in the pan, mere child's play, compare to the power bound by this system. From the moment a person is vaccinated and linked to the IIS database, they can be tracked via the invisible lines of latitude and longitude within this blue marble. Every move calculated and stored. Every move, from their first steps to eventually their final resting place and every step in between is calculated and stored. Every move calculated and stored. There is no hiding. No lying. No secrets. No escaping the eyes of the creators. It's the power of god's all-knowing ability stored as ones and zeros in a database.

Linkages are the keys to this all-knowing power. Linking NID's, satellites, supercomputers and databases creates the true power of the system. The satellites fly over the globe, transmit and receive the signal from the NID's and their exact location calculated, then stored. Each and every signal is processed through the supercomputers. Thousands, even hundreds of thousands signals are turned into raw data in an instant. The data is simplistic in form and contains only four pieces of data, the nano identification number, the latitude, the longitude, and the time. This information is stored in a database only few have access. From this data everything else can be derived through interfaces into other databases throughout the world. Every database that is online can be accessed to provide a wealth of information. They can pinpoint the exact location of any individual that is online and determine who they are with or what they buy or when—almost in real-time and they have access to this information forever. An individual's past becomes stored as ones and zeros. Their entire life is stored as ones and zeros. Their truth is stored as ones and zeros. That truth is knowledge, and that knowledge is the power. NID's, satellites, supercomputers, databases, all tied together create the most powerful system/network in the world—a system that is held within the hands of the government and even the government doesn't know the system exists.

Only a selected few hold the power of God in their hands. It started out as a very small circle of friends, more like a triangle than a circle really, and it hasn't grown much since then. Each primary individual played a significant role, from securing of funds and lobbying for laws, to creating interfaces and databases, to developing stabilizers and nano devices; without each piece of the triangle the system would not exist. The complete system took time to exist, years in fact, years of planning, scheming, and conniving. They had to lay the objectives out in a linear timeline. They had to have laws in place before the public would accept certain things. They had to make friends in very high places. They had to do many things outside the box in order to meet all their objectives. One of their main objectives was for the system to be fully functional with the majority of Americans logged online within twenty years of graduation. They fell a little short of their target date, four years give or take, and mainly because of the delivery method was geared more towards newborns and children.

Vaccination was their primary delivery method, though vaccination is not the only method of delivery. It is the best because of its natural linkage to the IIS database, however other shots help fill in the voids within the complete demographics of a society. Given the fact that within sixty-five years almost ninety-seven percent of all Americans will be injected with NID's through vaccination, this does not help in today's world, in today's tracking ability. Since the system came on line, ninety-two percent of the population under the age of twenty-five has been vaccinated. But what about the adults? Again this is where STB5 comes into play. This stabilizer is also used in flu and tetanus shots and anything else needing a shelf life. Flu shots are meant as a yearly precaution against sickness and are mostly consumed by the elderly via free injections with the help of subsidized funds from the federal government. One of the nice features about the NID's is they will continue to broadcast the older serial number if existing NID's are encountered in the bloodstream; so a patient who receives a yearly flu shot will continue to transmit the embedded serial number on their first injected NID's. The lot number of the flu shot is then connected to the social security number and stored in a database just like the logging of the vaccinations. With only children and the elderly being logged in droves into the system this leaves a huge chunk of citizens still unaccountable but not to worry. The biggest chunks of citizens, known as the baby boomers, are just getting ripe for their annual flu shots and are becoming linked into the system. Still this leaves a large number of unaccountable citizens but again, not to worry. More and more mandates, laws, and government sponsorship are encouraging flu shots in the workplace and in schools. At this point in time roughly half to two-thirds of all legal Americans are online within the system, not too shabby; all thanks to vaccinations and free flu shots but inevitably, people will slip through the cracks and across the borders. The government will play a huge part in this as well. Entering the country will require proof of shots thus linking a passport number to the shot number and again this is stored into a database. But still people will slip through the cracks. A plan was needed to fill in those cracks, to ensure the protection and safety of its people, to promote health and the welfare of its people, to ensure the traceability of its people, to ensure all the people become online.

Early on Francis Simoski considered this problem and early on he had a solution to this problem. Cell phones and OnStar could help fill the voids but they could easily be compromised. His solution was much more simplistic. It was fear, fear for one's life. Simple indeed. He just had to bestow fear into the common man and make them want to be injected. He knew how things worked, how rumors began, how they traveled, so he wrote an article or two under a pseudonym and had them published in a medical journal in Indonesia. Then after a few months he linked the articles to a wide spread story in Asia, again under a pseudonym. Through whisper down the lane the story grew until it was picked up by the mainstream media. Blogs were written on the subject, even a science fiction thriller or two. It appeared in Time and on World News Tonight and in other media outlets even on the internet. It left a lasting impression on the people who read or heard anything about it. Every once in awhile another article or television news report will surface confirming that the fears are true. Funny thing is, no one actually tries to confirm if the fears themselves are based in reality. No one tries to locate the doctors who first made the discovery or wrote any of the other articles. No reporters or medical practitioners are flown to secluded places to examine the bodies of the dead. No one does any true research. They just reference bogus articles after bogus articles, talk to so-called experts, just to generate hype or whip the public into a frenzy, like the bones the media throws in for the eleven o'clock news during primetime shows—"There could be something in your fridge right now that will kill you, more at eleven," and it turns out to be milk older than two years, well duhhh. The scare tactics are easy, make it plausible, make it inevitable, and make it news.

"Yes, I've heard of them, I think the first was the Avian Flu, also known as the bird flu if I'm not mistaken."

"Originally this new strain of the Tanjung Flu was confined to our feathered friends but recent studies from Indonesia have proven that a crossover into different species could exist, same thing happen in Mexico with the Swine Flu, tomorrow it may be goat or cow. This is the worst of the bird flues we have seen in awhile."

"Usually something like this is rare, right?"

"Right, but it has been known to happen, take the Black Plague or Bubonic Plague for instance."

"Black Plague, that's some pretty serious stuff."

"Events like that define history. This flu could very well be another history defining moment for our species."

"So we're saying this flu, this Tanjung Flu from Indonesia has many similarities to the Black Plague?"

"The theory is based on a disease that infected the rat population which also made the crossover to humans, killing almost two-thirds of all of Europe in the fourteenth century.

"From what I gather, the same could happen here."

"Right you are again, it becomes much more advanced than we originally feared, then makes the crossover from species to humans and then begins to move across the globe,"

"Is there any proof to back up such claims?"

"Enough evidence has shown that many deaths throughout Asia and now Eastern Europe are linked to a severe strain known as H5N1, the last reported cases were in Turkey. England had a slight scare about two months ago but it was proven to be false . . . . for now."

"Now is this strain, what was it you said . . . H5N1, something to worry about?"

"Don't really know, this strain may peter out and give way to an even more infectious strain. If that happens then we will really need to worry, it could possibly wipe out up to seventy percent of the entire planet, only three out of every ten will survive and no race, class, or individual will be truly safe. We need to take precautions now."

"Jesus . . . you mean this could be more deadly than the plague, is there a cure?"

"Eventually, well I mean hopefully, it's rather difficult to pinpoint an exact cure for an exact strain but there are governmental agencies and pharmaceutical companies throughout the world working towards that goal as we speak, regular flu shots will help somewhat in the meantime until an actual vaccine is created and to answer your other question, yes, I think seventy percent of the population wiped off the face of the earth is more deadlier than the plague."

"Frankly I'm scared to death now, I had no idea something like this was feasible in our lifetime."

"Fear it because it is possible and probably will happen in our lifetime and if we don't start planning, ramping up on distribution centers, stocking up on medication, and taking the threats seriously, repercussions are going to happen."

"Repercussions meaning seven out of every ten people we know and love could vanish almost overnight in a worldwide epidemic? Sorry we are almost out of time . . . any last thoughts?"

"Epidemic, no. More like pandemic. This is the way the world ends . . . . This is the way the world ends . . . . This is the way the world ends. Not with a bang but a whimper T.S. Eliot, The Hollow Men. Can you envision that world?"

"Yes . . . . yes I can . . . . Thank you Doctor. Simoski, thank you for your time and . . . the truth."

●   ●   ●

Chapter 28

Over the next few hours, the two of them traced their steps and double and even triple-checked their data and always came to the same conclusion—they were being watched, maybe not watched per se but being tracked, their lives being recorded—it was an uneasy feeling. They scoured their backdoor entries into the machine to see if anyone was watching them and as far as they could tell only the president and Scott were ever on this machine . . . . and of course root, aka the administrator, whoever that may be. Greg knew his way around this machine and he made the conclusion that nobody knew they were there, that is after he deleted a few system generated log files that tracked their movement on the box. This was a matter of a few simple keystrokes and their records had vanished and vanished for good, unlike the data deleted on a personal computer, most often than not that data remained stored on the drive and the only thing deleted were the file pointers to that data. This is the reason many would be thieves are caught, just because they can't see the data doesn't mean it's gone. Greg was smarter than that, not only did he delete the pointers but also the data . . . it was gone and so were they when they logged off around 10 am.

"Greg, I'm going to say this again . . . don't go in the system without me."

"I . . . ."

"Just don't, I mean it, just don't okay?"

"Yes, I'm not, I won't . . . . shit I really don't know what to think right now."

"We are both going to have to get some rest, we'll talk more on Monday."

"That's if we're still here by tomorrow."

"Don't go getting all paranoid on me Greg," as she was walking him to the door.

"Jorja, I really think you don't comprehend our situation, there are over half the people of our country in this system being tracked on a daily basis, you and I are just two of those people. Jorja, if they wanted to, they could track us, hell they might even know we were together all night, that will really be suspicious."

"Greg, relax, it's like you said, there are a lot of people in this system, what are the chances that we are the ones being watched?"

"I know, but it's just . . . well we did stumble upon this system, we might have tripped some wires somewhere, they might know we know."

"I thought you covered our tracks?"

"I did but . . ."

"Greg, I trust you, don't go second guessing yourself, we'll talk tomorrow."

"I'm still uncomfortable with the fact that they could find out we were together last night."

"If they ever say anything, we'll just tell them we were sleeping together, now I'll see you tomorrow." That caught Greg by surprised and he took his raised eyebrow expression all the way home with him.

Once Greg was out the door Jorja was left to her own thoughts. The implications to the flu shots were beginning to sink in, really sink in. In what she thought was common sense, protecting her health, that one little pin prick changed her body forever. That one little pin prick changed her perception of her country, of her freedom, of her life . . . forever. Without her knowledge she was a caged animal, an endangered species, able to be tracked anytime, anyplace. Without her knowledge her right granted to her by the Fourth Amendment that guards against unreasonable searches was taken away by tiny little transmitters deep within her body. Without her knowledge, the freedom won through the blood, the sweat, and the tears of the founding forefathers was lost instantaneously. Their declaration that was placed on parchment during that famous date in July is now a mute point deemed a farce of the highest degree and saturated with unequivocal irony upheld by a government spewing righteous democracy and liberties. It goes beyond the United States Constitution. It goes beyond any sanctioned law known to man. It goes beyond reason, beyond fear. It strips the very soul that defines humanity forcing it to comply, to obey, to submit, all without mistake, without assumptions, without faith.

Jorja reached for her left arm, feeling her bicep, feeling for the spot of injections. She felt hot. She felt as though a watching eye was burning a hole right through her. She knew she was alone yet she felt this presence upon her, watching her, watching her every move, and it wasn't her god. Her mind raced with the horrors of her new found prison, her home. She felt the walls closing in on her, a tightness gripping her chest as reality was starting to macerate the boundaries of her sanctuary. Her muscles tensed, she couldn't breathe as she imagined thousands of tiny little robots eating her skin from the inside. Her skin began to crawl as these tiny robots broke the flesh and started screaming as to alarm the hounds of her whereabouts. She heard sirens in her head. She saw visions of the Third Reich marching in unison, police surrounding her house, iron bars on the doors and windows. She started to gasp for air but before she could succumb to any more horrors brought on by her science fiction movie plots, she forced herself to face the fears. She took a deep breath and tried to relax. She took another deep breath and tried to force her mind into an analytical mode. It worked somewhat.

●   ●   ●

Chapter 29

Still a bit startled from what he thought was a close encounter with Ripley, he made his way back to the kitchen and sat at the table for a few minutes to calm himself down. He almost nodded off. He was extremely tired. He had a long day. All the driving, the watching, the working—it was a very long day. He glanced at the clock on the microwave; it read 4:32 a.m. He muscled up the energy to lift his tired body out of the chair and walked to the appliance white refrigerator. He grabbed some orange juice and decided to call it a night. He then climbed the stairs and entered his room. It wasn't the biggest bedroom in the house but this was where he was most comfortable. He flipped on the light, stripped to his boxer shorts and a t-shirt, folded his dirty cloths, and walked across the hall to the bathroom to brush his teeth. He reentered his room, turned off the light and climbed into bed. He turned on his alarm and his head hit the pillow with heavy eyes. He knew that his little girl would be wide awake before him, so he mumbled a little prayer to keep her safe in the meantime, he mumbled a few words of thanks, and blessed himself just before he rolled over and fell asleep.

A few hours had elapsed and he awoke from a dream, the same bad dream he always dreamt. He was crying in his sleep. His eyes were puffy and bloodshot. His hands were sweaty and his body was shaking. Each and every night his ghosts had come back and haunted him but this time they were much worse than he had remembered in a long time. Somehow, someway, they should have subsided; the monsters should have been gone, now that his little girl was in his life but they were still there, plain as the sun shining from behind the dark shades of his room. He couldn't understand it. He was happy; at least he felt happy, like a weight had been lifted, yet his confusion angered him. "Why have this dream again? Why now? Why can't it end? Why did this have to happen? Why?" He glanced at the clock and this angered him even more. It was only ten after eight. He was still tired, very tired and on top of it he was in pain from a headache. He clenched his fist and his teeth. The more he remembered about his dream the more ill-tempered he became. Between his anger, his pain, his tiredness, his confusion, he couldn't hold a clear thought in his head. He was practically seething. He rose out of bed, scuffled across the hall, and entered the bathroom. He turned on the light and winced from the pain the light had caused him. He looked for aspirin, found them, and the bottle slipped out of his still trembling hands and onto the floor—aspirin everywhere. They were scattered across the black, gray, and pink tile floor. The bottle rolled behind the porcelain bowl. He needed the aspirin more than ever now. He fell to his hands and knees and started picking them up one by one. Then he suddenly stopped. He glanced at the dirt and hair on the floor, he glanced at the few pills in his hands, and they too were covered in dirt and hair. He didn't know what to do, where to turn. His anger grew. Then he remembered his little girl. "Maybe she wasn't the one after all. That had to be it, yes it had to be it" and in a flash he flew down the stairs and was in the basement in no time. It was like a light switch—he flipped with rage as he stared at the solid steel door to her room. "How could she?" He let out sounds of his rage and a tapestry of vulgar words through clenched teeth but on the other side of the door they went unnoticed for they were muffled. He became enraged much like a caged animal being provoked with a stick. He sputtered nonsense aloud "How could she not take this away, why did she, that little bitch, why?" He ran towards the door, his forehead scrunched, his fist ready to pound, he seemed ready for battle but turned away as if it were the aggressor wielding a weapon. He backed away. He turned towards the door again. He stood. He stared. He moved a foot closer. A foot more. A foot more. He stared at the beast. He raised his hand. He unlocked one dead bolt. Then another. By the time he turned the third lock, unlike Dr. Bruce Banner, his episode had receded before turning into any kind of monster.

He was totally calm now. He gathered his thoughts and bowed his head seemingly asking for forgiveness. He counted to ten and walked over to his watching room. He entered. He looked through the mirror and saw an empty room. He expected to see Ripley either in bed or playing on the floor. He saw neither. He was perplexed thinking his mind was playing tricks with him for he was still a bit groggy and still in much pain. So he studied the room for he knew she was hiding but where? He noticed two more of the bananas were gone and so were the cookies. There was an apple juice bottle on the nightstand and the small ice chest was open but still no sign of his little girl. He squatted on the floor and peered out the one-way mirror to get a better look under the bed. The duvet cover barely touched the bottom of the bed so he had a clear view. Nothing. He then stood on his chair to get a better peek of the only hiding place he thought she could be and that was lying in the bathtub. Nothing. Now he was getting worried. He exited the room and checked the steel door to see if it was locked. It was. Back to the watching room. Nothing. He pressed his cheek against the mirror to try to see to the far right of the room. Nothing. He did the same with the left. Nothing. He was growing even more worried—almost to the point of panic. He felt his blood pressure start to rise again. He felt the pressure of his headache even more. He felt his tiredness taking control. He was just about to lose it again when he spotted the only place she could be . . . . the closet. "Yes, such a clever girl," he said to himself. He felt so smart for thinking of it, then felt like an idiot. "Why did I put a door on the closet? Why did I even build a closet in the first place?" Quickly he tried to gather his thoughts again, thinking if he should remove the closet door or not, then came to the conclusion, "No, everybody needs a little privacy from time to time; even my little girl needs some privacy." He thought of his next move, "Yes today is the day, today is the day I welcomed her into my life. It is time." He so wanted to walk right in there and open the closet door and and . . . . and he stopped his brain from processing. "She is safe now and I'm still tired," and with that he headed back upstairs for some aspirin and a little more rest. When he reached his bathroom, he saw once again the pills on the floor. He ignored them and opened the medicine cabinet and elected for something a little stronger. He glanced at his watch; he had another four hours before he was supposed to take his prescription but since he completely ignored that rule the day before, he open the childproof bottle with ease and popped two gel tablets down his throat. He never needed any water; to him it was like swallowing a piece of meat. He shut the light off, crossed the hall, and entered his still very dark room, crawled into bed and closed his eyes hoping the headache would soon dissipate.

He was in total blackness and his eyes focused on the back of his eyelids as though he was still able to see clearly. Sparkles, wavy lines, and spots, all green, against a black canvas, his eyes seemed to be still transmitting signals to the brain and he was trying to make sense of it all. After a few minutes his body relaxed and he was back in the realm of his unconscious self. His dreams were muted in colors; boundaries of objects seemed to blend into the background, and his surroundings were not very detailed. Images and visions floated by like clouds of a fast moving storm. They were almost hallucinogenic to a degree, and then a form of reality crept in. There were soda bottles filled with orange syrup on a shelf at a grocery store next to a few boxes of cereal and soap. He reached for a bottle and it slipped from his hands, then he glided his cart around the corner and studied the very goth-like wallpaper that appeared out of nowhere. It was velvet gold and red with bats with red eyes. There were people talking around the corner and he went to investigate. He didn't recognize a single soul yet they all seemed very familiar—like old friends. They appeared to be waiting for an argument to be settled that was taking place in the basement. He chose to walk towards the basement door and open it. There was a child that was holding a toy gun. The child walked into a waiting area and shot a woman. He thought long and hard before deciding it was the parent's fault for allowing the child to find a real gun in the house and went to find the father. He found the father and starting yelling then turned his head and in a calm tone he told a nurse to send an ambulance to Kirbyville. He looked down in his hand expecting to find a bloody gun yet it was a wilted daisy from his back yard. His brain was trying to create some sort of story line from the visions but soon gave up and lapsed into stage four of the sleep cycle, also known as deep sleep.

●   ●   ●

Chapter 30

Their job was no longer the number one priority but they still had to maintain the façade until they could come to grasp with their new found intelligence. Their main concern now was that of survival. They didn't know who to trust so they trusted each other, they had no other choice. They had to find out all the main players and the depth of this, for lack of a better word, conspiracy. Greg and Jorja knew they had a few holes to plug—like the person or persons that had access to create and maintain the machine with all the information—they had to be within the very walls of the Intelligence Community and most probably at the top of the food chain. They already knew President Jonathan Whitaker and Scott Norwood were deep in this shit and through a ton more research they came up with another name that didn't smell like roses, that belonging to Frank Simoski, CEO of Etimiz. He was the other user in the box ending in 12.168 whose username was CEOFS01. Greg was the one who tied him to a college acquaintance of the president. He found the connection between Simoski and Whitaker's with the help of an online yearbook at their alma mater and a causal picture of the two of them talking outside the Sciences Library; there was no caption. He recognized the president since he was structurally the same—his Jay Leno like chin gave him away. Frank's name was found perusing through the rest of the pictures that were online. These two people had no other common connections besides this photograph. It just caught Greg as odd, the way these two seemed lock in deep conversation yet not once did they ever share a class or even the same professor. He found out Frank was big, strike that huge, in the field of nano technology, graduated the very same year as Whitaker, and had a few grants thrown his way by the former representative, former senator and now president. There was a picture clearly forming. Greg surmised that there might be a few more key individuals whose college motto was "In deo speramus" (In God we hope). College is just the kind of place where half-baked ideas derived mainly from a few bong hits becomes an obsession to a brilliant yet borderline psychopath. Then like the Order of the Skulls and Bones, the Freemasons, the Illuminati, or even Microsoft or Google, select individuals are drawn and allied into the inner circle with the illusions of greater power and fortitude . . . in this case they may be right.

Greg ran a quick check of any CIA employees that graduated within four years of the president. He found none. He then did a search through congress and found two other alumni—both senators now, a republican from Illinois, the other a democrat from California; both sides of the fence were covered in the political arena so it seemed. Jorja ran with the names while Greg concentrated his sights based on the source of the incoming data stream. Jorja uncovered some interesting facts. The back then Illinois representative was the one who brought to light the National Childhood Vaccine Injury Act along with support from the California representative. This act brought together the lot numbers of vaccines and social security numbers of the injected, a seemingly harmless trait, in order to provide compensation for individuals injured in an event of a vaccine failure. Jorja quickly recalled the term steganography—the art of hiding or embedding hidden messages in plain view. Here a simple addition to the NCVI Act provided a piece of the hidden agenda. It was in plain sight, yet no one ever questioned the true reason it was there. How convenient it must have been to place something like this in a bill where there was a greater scope involved. She searched for more sponsored bills by this duo and learned quite a lot. She learned they helped passed federal spending on satellites for the NSA, they voted for cell phone regulations in regarding nine one one calls, they provided grants to scientists, they even helped to elect Frank Simoski to the National Nanotechnology Initiative, and not to mention they were strong supporters of inner workings of Homeland Security and the relatively new DNI. Piece by piece they helped assemble the underlying structure for the network. It took years to plan and build but with the help of congress and the tax payers' money it became a reality in about fifteen years.

Over the course of several months the big picture was certainly clear—a network of friends in high places all stemming from college. It was Greg who found the connections again using the online yearbook. A common thread was woven between the pictures of some senators and the would-be-president of the United States—they each wore a ring; it was hard to make out in the pictures but after the pictures were digitally enhanced the insignia became crystal clear. It bore just two simple letters "PS". Through further investigation it was uncovered that in 1821, the university had a secret society that was once called the Franklin Society and was created to pursue the rational investigation of the truths and principles of being, knowledge, and conduct. That struck a chord with Greg as he thought to himself "yeah the pursuit of truths, knowledge, all being taken to the extreme." During its initial gathering it was simply known as the Philosophical Society, hence the "PS". It was disbanded in the early 1900's but looks as though it was resurrected by none other than Whitaker himself with only a few members, maybe six or seven in all. Most of who now work in or with the government in one way shape or form. There was Frank Simoski, biology whiz, two senators, a security expert in the NSA, and the lead chair in Homeland Security. Scott Norwood didn't fit the mold. He was fifteen years younger than the president and went to Georgetown. He seemingly had no other connection to Whitaker before the plan started to formalize. He didn't have special skills in one area or the other but boy was he smart. His analytical skills were top notch. It wasn't until after Jorja pulled his college thesis that the bells of Saint Mary's started ringing. His two hundred page thesis was simply entitled DATA. After reading it Jorja had a better understanding of what the powers to be were capable of doing to this country.

Over that same period of time, both Jorja and Greg had dissipating fears of being caught. They theorized that maybe either A) no one knew that the secret was out or B) that maybe they were watching for reactions and if proven favorable, bring them into the inner sanctum, into god's realm. It didn't matter to either of them for they still could only trust one another and they had to play the waiting game.

And wait they did. In the meantime Jorja's bloodline was starting to show. She was part of the world's biggest spy organization and slowly she was being drawn into the seductive powers that god himself held. Greg was learning about the day to day operations—the how's. He found the data stream supporting the location data. That was a difficult task because it didn't come through the normal channels. It was backdoored by the NSA from Schriever Air Force Base in Colorado and hardwired directly into the database. Schriever AFB is known for its men and women of the 2nd Space Operations Squadron who operate the world's only global utility simply referred to as GPS. Here coordinates obtained from Schiever AFB were downloaded into the database along with a series of digits. Greg's initial conclusion was spot on; that these sets of digits were the serial numbers of whatever was within the body. These serial numbers were crossed referenced with the Immune Information Systems with lot numbers of the vaccines and tax id's, then placed into the file Jorja and Greg first stumbled upon. He also found a replicating database, mirroring any data within seconds of the original entries but one of his more important finds was a GUI—a graphical user interface into the system. It was written so any internet browser could connect to this database in a point and click fashion. It was pretty slick even by Greg's standards. One could prompt for a tax id and a satellite image appeared on the screen or one could click on a location and find all the taxid's within a certain radius and this could be done for both date and time. Clicking on a tax id linked directly to any data known to be stored for that person, almost to the "t" of what Scott Norwood's thesis envisioned. This program was powerful yet simple in form thus leading Greg to wonder who the programmer of this functionality might be; yet another missing piece to the puzzle.

Certain experiments were done by the duo. They wandered in the streets to look for blind spots. They rode subway cars, entered various building including the CIA headquarters, and in all but a very few, they were tracked and recorded, and yes, even underground. The signals were being broadcasted to anything that listened . . . and it seem almost everything listened from cell phones to radios and everything in between, all thanks to a few bills brought to the floor and passed based on the emergency broadcast system and some little known FCC regulations. Looking within the FCC two more PS members were identified—in the yearbook their hands were behind their backs so no rings were spotted—they were both electrical engineers who furthered their careers at MIT and are now big-wigs within this governmental establishment.

It seemed there were many players but only a selected few had keys to the car and was able to take it out for a joy ride. The car itself had low miles on it. It seemed only every now and then was it being used and it was used to further the career of the big man himself, like in the case of the Holiday Mall Massacre, oh, how the president was praised by his swift actions that day. So the big mystery was exactly when was this thing going to become fully operational and to what extent was it going to play in everybody's life?

Jorja and Greg's most difficult task at hand was not putting up the façade of their daily grind, no, actually it was the task of not becoming drawn to the dark side. They had this power at their finger tips, they despised it, hated it, yet were intrigued and fascinated, they could very well see the benefit, the greater good of the people. Criminals squelched almost where they stood, no more lying about your whereabouts on such and such a date; tap in the name, social security, and date and presto, scene of the crime. But all-in-all they promised each other they'd never use it . . . . except in the back of each of their minds they said only if they needed it.

Their next difficult task was to look for the so-called mole within the very walls of their place of business. They tried to find a past connection between Whitaker and the Director of the CIA, nothing was found. The director was a goody-two-shoe who worked his way up the ranks quite honestly. They tried the same thing with the next in line and nothing, yet someone had to prerequisite that machine and it should have been Jorja

"So what are we going to do Jorja?"

"Nothing we can do until we expose the person within the Intelligence Community."

"What if there is no one to expose."

"Impossible, it's not like the president walks into the Virginia site and says, please hook this up."

"True but it could just as well be you."

"Me? I was the one who found it."

"Exactly, you are the one who found it because you knew right where it was, you also have the authority to order the machine and get it connected to our network, plus you had that handy dandy little program, and then there is the fact we are both still alive."

"You have a point but why would I want you to get involved?"

"Trust, face it Jorja you trust me."

"Yes I do but trust is a two way street and right now it seems you don't trust me . . . I too can point the finger at you, you found plenty of hacks to get us into the system, you have the expertise to hide a server on our network, your skills are just as plausible as mine."

"Damn it Jorja, I trust you . . . in fact I . . . . I . . ."

"I what?"

"Well . . . . I care about you," he very much wanted to say that he loved her, "and I have to trust you. I know you are not involved . . . really I do . . . I'm just fucking paranoid anymore . . . these past few months have been driving me insane, they have me second guessing everything I do, where I go, who I see . . . every part of my life has changed . . . and not for the better I can assure you that."

"Whether you trust me or not we are in this together."

"I know, I know . . . but . . . . but . . . . let me ask you this . . . . then how the hell do you act so calmly knowing these people whoever the fuck they are, know your every move?"

"Because I know their every move as well . . . . and so do you . . . . so far all the players we have uncovered are in this system, probably because of their first experiments, anyway . . . . for the most part I tend to believe at this stage of the game we know more about them than they do with us . . . assuming you played your cards right and covered our tracks . . . we have the upper hand and I intend to keep it that way."

"Okay my dear . . . I will never second guess you again . . . so we go back to the cat and mouse game . . . we need some cheese."

"A big piece."

● ● ●

Chapter 31

The day of the shootings at the mall proved to be a quintessential turning point in the fight against terrorism. It took only a mere half of day to pinpoint all of the assailants, much to the chagrin of evil doers worldwide. Yes, that day placed second thoughts in the mind on many would be terrorists. It was that day that every arm of American law enforcement seemed to be under one umbrella. It was the FBI, the CIA, Homeland Security, the NSA, local and state police, and a few black ops that no one knows about, that on that day, the day of carnage, worked as if they were all tentacles of the same octopus. They communicated effortlessly, efficiently—teamwork at its finest. They worked together, they exchanged data together, they analyzed together, they solved together and together they didn't do a damn thing to abolish this perception. Smoke and mirrors, duct tape, chewing gum, lies upon lies, who knows what else was holding this mirage together; in reality the togetherness was just a veneer, a pipe dream, brought on by Homeland Security. Homeland Security was supposed to be the glue, the middle man, the collaborating partner in the fight against terrorism—holding a warehouse of information and communication protocols for everybody's use but behind the scenes there was discombobulation. Agencies were still very protective with the data they gathered and the data they shared but somehow, somewhere, and at some point in time, the pivotal data in this case was placed on the databases of Homeland Security and acted upon, thus providing a perception of alertness and justification—remember perception is ninety percent of the battle.

It was a phone call that started the chain of events that day, a phone call placed by Scott Norwood.

"Listen, obviously you've heard the news about the mall and that two assailants were taken out, I've just talked with the President, he gave the nod, I need as much information within the hour so it can be fed to the proper channels," a click was the next thing heard."

With that, an IP address was dial up on his monitor, a login and password entered, and just like that he had access to a database the world would never see; the very notion of its existence would shatter the world and consume the government's infrastructure, never to be trusted again. He had very few facts to go on: he knew the location, the approximate time, and that two assailants were killed, everything else was sketchy at best. The first order of business would be to gather the complete lists—the before list and the after list. The before list was a list of tax identification numbers a.k.a. social security numbers (everybody in the U.S. had one—it was the law) that were within a five hundred meter perimeter of the mall just before the shootings occurred. The time of the shootings were approximately 2:15 p.m., so the reference time would be 2:10 p.m. since each pass of a satellite receptor was a five minute interval. Oh how times have changed thanks to technology. In the old days the intervals first started out as every twenty-four hours, then twelve, eight, and so on and so forth, to the present day of just every five minutes. Tomorrow it will be every minute and the next it will be instantaneous but until then five minutes will have to do. He then needed a reference ending time and chose 2:20 p.m. The next key information is the approximate latitude and longitude of the shootings easily obtained from any satellite photo or even Google Maps for that matter. Time and place are entered into the prompts of the custom program and in a flash there is a list of 34,302 people who have been identified within the proximity of the shootings that were alive at 2:10 p.m.—the before list. Next he entered the same criteria except changing the time to his ending reference and the information is much different. This is the after list—27,443 social security numbers within the original radius; a difference of almost seven thousand people. A quick analysis yields a mass exodus just after the shootings and rightfully so. Since the

NID's need pumping blood to maintain communication, cross referencing the seven thousand people difference with those still transmitting at 2:20 p.m. yields sixty-two individuals who are no longer transmitting. At 2:25 the number jumps to sixty-four, then to sixty-five five minutes later but when all is said and done—hours later, the number is seventy-eight—the exact confirmed death toll of the Holiday Mall Massacre. Now out of the sixty-two, two of them are the assailants and a further breakdown of the data confirms there are two different shooting locations: location A—the one with twenty-six people no longer transmitting and location B—the one where thirty-six people are no longer transmitting. Now this is where multi-tasking takes place, while at his computer he overhears the television and two different reports confirm that two gunman were brought down outside of Macy's. Checking the exact location of Macy's, he also confirms that group "A" now contains the two dead gunmen—his reference set just got smaller, only twenty-six people. Again listening to news reports, the two gunmen appeared to be in their late teens to early twenties and Caucasian, the reference set grows smaller yet again. Crosschecking yields only six victims in that range, two of which are the gunmen. With six social security numbers at hand and on the computer screen in front of him, further investigating is mere child's play. Of the six people, two are from Wayne, Pennsylvania, one from Philadelphia, one is from a little town in New Jersey, and the other two are from Ohio, he now fully concentrates on the pairs of men. The Ohio men yield some fascinating results in the database. As of five o'clock this morning they were staying in the Holiday Inn right across the mall. Further data mining tells us they were staying there for the past month and appeared to be working at the mall for the past month as well. Just like Interpol in Europe, the United States requires each hotel's database to be online with the Federal Bureau of Investigation and Homeland Security, which can also be accessed by the CIA or DNI. Crosschecking the hotel's database proves they were using aliases for there were no matches based on their social security numbers, however the hotel's database provided the credit card numbers for all persons whose stay was greater than twenty-one days. There were four rooms booked and three of them were to the same credit card number. Using a credit card for three rooms, using aliases with fake id's upon checking, working at the mall, one plus one plus one certainly adds up to a fishy three. Without a doubt in his mind the names of the gunman were found; two of them at least, from Ohio. On a hunch he inputs more search parameters into the program—out of the filtered list of seven thousand who were now missing from the scene within a ten minute window of the crimes, just how many were from Ohio and in the age range of sixteen to twenty-five? Again in a flash, the programs spits out only five social security numbers up on his screen. So where were these five as of five o'clock this morning? One was in Valley Forge staying at a residential address, the other was in Atlantic City at the Trump Plaza, one was staying at the exact Holiday Inn as the others—bingo again, and the last two staying at a Comfort Inn just up the street from the mall. Checking the Comfort Inn's database, and guess what—aliases again. Three more gunmen have been found. A wee bit more checking finds that the five cold blooded killers lived within a twenty-five mile radius of one another just outside of Cincinnati, Ohio. They were Michael Romberger age 18, Matthew Gieger age 21, Steven Tyler (no relation to Aerosmith's lead singer) age 18, Gene Lynner age 18, and Brian O'Neil age 19.

The search took fourteen minutes. The time was now 2:46 p.m. Three of the gunmen are MIA but not for long. Inputting the three remaining social security numbers into the computer and the results are the coordinates and a big "Gotcha!!!" The three social security numbers are just outside Downingtown, on the Pennsylvania Turnpike, at a service station. The three numbers will now have a marker placed on them and the program will begin updating their coordinates every five minutes—they will be tracked and with nowhere to run.

"Just how much more information should be obtained," he asked himself? "Another forty-five minutes worth," was the answer. So let's build a timeline. 2:45 p.m. three gunmen at a service station on the PA turnpike. 2:15 three gunmen are in a parking lot outside the mall, two are dead. 1:30 p.m.

From 1:30 p.m. back to at least 10:45 p.m. the following day, the five gunmen were in their various hotel rooms. Going back a month, they can be seen going to and from the mall and the hotel; all of them working different stores but all in close proximity to the shooting sites. The timeline doesn't vary much but there are the occasional trips outside their realm. For instance, on December 15th all five ventured to a movie theater, based on the time and the theater's database, they watched the latest slasher flick by Wes Craven. Rifling through all sales receipts for the show time proved they paid cash unless they used another alias and credit card. On December 8th all five again went out, this time to Chi Chi's, a local Mexican eatery.

Linking the database from the theater on the 15th and Chi Chi's on the 8th, there is a credit card match—a one Mr. William Parker. Upon closer examination of the restaurant's bill and matching it with the credit card receipt, one can see five entrees were ordered, three appetizers, two sodas, and six beers (looks like there might be some pretty good fake ID's in the mix as well, for only one was of legal age in the state of Pennsylvania and Chi Chi's always, always cards being on probation and one more violation from closing). Coincidence is plausible until the card also has one transaction for five tickets to a Wes Craven film on December 15th. This credit card is flagged for all expenses in the past year along with the cards used at the hotels. Back to the timeline. Right before Thanksgiving, actually the Monday before and before the busy holiday season when stores need the most help, they are located on the Pennsylvania Turnpike heading east but the five are not together—separate cars. At noon the cars are two hours apart but at nine o'clock, three hours earlier, the cars were within one hundred feet of one another. Strange, why the lag time all of a sudden? Car problems maybe? More digging is required. A little before 7 a.m. Monday morning they entered the PA Turnpike—somewhere between 6:45 a.m. and 6:50 a.m. At that point in time the turnpike's computer has roughly six hundred cars entering the exchange so cross check with the credit cards that were already flagged and lo and behold there are two rental cars; one for a grey Chrysler Neon, the other for a red Dodge Daytona. Now it is a matter of querying the Avis data banks and the license plates are obtained. The license-plates are matched to the picture database the turnpike stores and within thirty seconds the software spits out sixteen images, eight of each car. Smile, you're on candid camera. Clear as a bell too. There are great pictures of the Neon, the driver, and two passengers. Same holds true for the Daytona—again the driver and two passengers are clear as the day the planes hit the towers on 9/11.

Wait! Two passengers? Two passengers in each car? A total of six gunmen, not five. What happened to the other gunman . . . the lone gunman? Checking the clock he has fifteen minutes before his report is due to Scott. Still time. Now he must isolate the Daytona, preferable away from traffic as to not to interfere with other social security numbers in the same coordinates. Remembering the coordinates are accurate to within six feet, he also needs to take into account any passing automobiles. At 7:00 a.m. the first search based on a coordinate pairing produces twelve social security numbers—two of the numbers are already identified, so the lone gunmen resides in the other ten. At 7:05 and 7:10 respectively, there is only an elimination of one other number, it looks as though traffic was at a crawl. Spacing out the search by another half hour and the magic number is shown on the screen, belonging to a Simon Trudell, age 18. So where is Simon now . . . . and "Access Denied." Strange he thought and tried it again—"Access Denied." He tried another search, this time for his wife and the same reply was shown on the screen "Access Denied." He didn't get a "Server Unavailable" or a hundred other messages implying database backup or system maintenance. It was he himself that was being denied access which was strange in and of itself for there were only three other people who had access to the machine and knew its purpose and two were at the White House and one of them had asked for his help in the research.

When his phone chirped he simply forwarded the information onto Scott and at the same time placed it anonymously on the databases at Homeland Security. He uploaded all the security photos from the turnpike with some extraneous references and bogus percentages belonging to nonexistent data files. He thought about digitally enhancing the mall pictures but he wasn't a whiz with Photoshop so he decided that it be best left alone, besides he knew how the system worked and it didn't work all that well. He knew it was a rare chance, especially with the President screaming down their necks, that any significant data simply wouldn't be checked for authenticity once it appeared in these databases. He was correct. But give credit where credit is due, within minutes of this newly found information, the people at HS started the ball rolling towards an early Christmas present for the nation.

His session was restored a few minutes later when Scott intervened, he then picked up where he left off, digging for more clues. He wanted to do two things, build a better timeline for past events and find the assailant with cold feet. First things first, Simon Trudell was now in Indiana, living with an aunt, he had been there since the Tuesday before Thanksgiving, he rarely left the house. He's not going anywhere and even if he did he couldn't hide. As it turns out he simply hitched a ride at a rest area and went back home, from there it was to his aunt's. Cold feet indeed and lucky for him or they would have been forever cold while rotting in a pine box.

Next up on the radar scope was pinpointing the exact time when each member of the group was contacted. This was no simple task but within minutes he found them all together at one of the houses prior to their road-trip on a Tuesday evening, in fact they met almost every Tuesday evening for three months prior to their departure. He learned two of the boys went to the same high school and hung out quite a bit. He uncovered an essay on a college application in which, the writer Steven Tyler, was disenchanted with the American way of life. He found many similarities between the other boys when he poked around in their electronic lives and files. He found subscriptions to several white supremacist websites and magazines; he found links to questionable chat rooms, and uncovered a plethora of racist emails that would make the skin crawl even on a seasoned member of the KKK. The words of hatred reached far into the depths of the America ideals associated with its melting pot culture. Hate was the one string that was intertwined through the six boys but something or someone had to be the accelerant, the igniter in order to go from simple words on paper and screen to actions of horror in a mall. It just didn't make any sense. The more digging he did, the more straight laced the boys seemed. Most did pretty well in school; one was even a member of the National Honor Society. None of them had any prior convictions or even a minor altercation with the law; they didn't shave their heads or have any tattoos, yet something or someone made them explode into cold blooded killers.

He spent the better part of the night piecing things together. He found almost the exact times each new member came into the inner circle. It seemed to start with Matthew Gieger and Gene Lynner about twenty-six months before the shootings—over two years in the making. Gradually a new member was introduced roughly every three months and not once did all the members gather until their weekly Tuesday meetings had started. He then put the power of the computer to a laborious data mining task. He created a radius of ten feet around each individual's location and searched for any and all social security numbers found within that circle for each member for the past twenty-six months, then crossed referenced those numbers. Using the super computer's ability, in a few minutes a list of all matching numbers was on the screen. He crossed checked these numbers with his and the DNI's database. One number in particular stuck out in the crowd as if it was in yellow highlighter but it was not a social security number. It was a passport number. It was a number off a Turkish passport belonging to one Ehsan Nejem who entered this country over three years ago and was injected with the recommend dosage of a certain flu vaccine which in turn carried the now famous STBL5 stabilizer and logged into the

Etimiz's database. He was flagged as a supporter in connection to several suicide bombers and shooting instances but has never been charged, just watched from afar. His current location was in northern India and has been there since the beginning of November, however prior to his new surroundings he was in a Tuesday night meeting outside of Cincinnati, Ohio, just two months ago. The plot thickens.

He was too enthralled to notice it was closing in on four in the morning and he hadn't left the office yet. He was starting to unravel a theory in which terrorist cells were using home grown Americans, the young manipulative minds, to inflict its own doings on the general populace. This wasn't a new theory. Back in the nineties Arlen Specter, the famous long-time Pennsylvania Senator, had the same theory during the Oklahoma bombing of the Alfred P. Murrah Federal Building in April of 95. Timothy McVeigh and Terry Nichols took the fall for supposedly two middle-eastern descent looking men fleeing the scene in an old pickup truck just prior to the explosion. After McVeigh refused to give up any names and was put to death, the American public moved on with their lives never wanting to reopen old wounds. He confessed. He did it. Case closed. Next news story please, all while ignoring the Senator's plea for a further investigation. Now several years later, all members of the Holiday Mall Massacre brigade had laid in their own pools of blood and there is not one mention of middle-eastern men at the scene or talk of people plotting revenge on some unknown foreign country. Smart dressed, young Americans gone amuck, just like school shootings—it just happens, and most Americans tend to rely on the sole rationalization that these boys must have been wired differently from the rest or just plain old bad up-bringing. Never would the American people even try to theorize or blame members of Al Qaeda or some other Islamic extremist group. They know all too well they need not look elsewhere for accountability—these boys were sown from the very fiber of the American Heartland. In this case the Americans assumed the parents were at fault, the teachers were at fault, the police, the mall security guards, the government, they were all at fault and to a degree they all were, yet staring him in the face was a number to a passport that told him otherwise, the passport belonging to Ehsan Nejem.

Before he brought up any more files his body cried out for some adjustment and nourishment. He needed to stretch his legs and get a jolt of caffeine and maybe something to eat. He had been sitting in his office; sitting in the same chair, since Scott's call and that was almost twelve hours ago. He flexed his fingers and lifted himself up from the chair which was a chore. His back was stiff with pain. He lifted his hands above his head, rolled his neck once or twice, leaned back, and heard a few cracks. He yawned. He looked around thinking he should have been the only one in the office but on this day it was not the case—answers were still needed so people still worked all through the night, just like him. He exited his office and adventured to the caff. Here all the TV's were tuned to various CNN stations across the globe, with only the American version out of Atlanta still showing scenes of the trauma—that drum will not be fully beaten for weeks to come. He went straight to the soda machine; he thought about his usual selection but pulled out an additional dollar and opted for a can of Red Bull to perk his brain. His change clanged in the coin return but he went straight for the gusto. He popped the top and took a huge swig; almost half the can was gone. He grabbed his change and perused his selections of snacks in the next machine. Something salty, something chocolaty, something crunchy, he couldn't decide. He glanced at a bag of chocolate covered pretzels, all his urges in one convenient little plastic container. He was about to put his change into the bank of unfulfilling calories but a memory quickly flashed in his mind. He turned towards the fridge instead. "Holiday luncheon leftovers," was his light bulb moment. Grant it, nothing much was left since every office has its vultures and here inside the DNI it was no different, but there were a few pickled eggs, various holiday cookies, some cheese, a few slices of meat and a few discarded gherkins. He grabbed a paper plate from the cabinet over the sink and now there were officially no holiday luncheon leftovers left. He made his way back to his office with a plate of goodies in one hand and half a can of Red bull in the other.

He wanted so much just to let his mind rest and take a break. He went straight to his favorite internet site, digg.com. Here was a bunch of techies, nerds, and news hounds posting various articles from throughout the web. They posted just a link and a brief description and if the eyes liked what they saw, one just clicked on the link to read the rest of the article or see the full picture, or watch the video. Again he so wanted his mind to rest but when he went to digg, eighty percent of the articles pertained to yesterday's events. He couldn't escape the facts, the theories, the bloodshed, the sobs, the rage. He couldn't escape a nation in mourning. He couldn't escape it no matter where he went on the web . . . even espn.com had articles on the carnage since most sporting events were cancelled in lieu of the situation. He didn't fight his mind's tension any longer. He ate his last cookie, the one with the Hershey's Kiss, he swallowed his last bit of carbonated sucrose, glucose, vitamin B12 beverage, then forgetting a napkin, he wiped his hands on his jeans, and logged into his computer once again. He realized he had great power. It was he himself that gave the mourning nation the gift of the killers. Yes, tomorrow was Christmas but there was work to be done and more presents to be given but first he had to wrap the one named Eshan.

When he dialed into HS's database he was a bit surprised, Ehsan Nejem had already been tagged and tracked as he exited the country a few weeks ago. He was half expecting he'd be the only one with that information but soon remembered he had pulled this very same data from the terrorist watch list. Ehsan boarded a flight out of JFK and hit a few connecting hubs to arrive at his destination. His last known whereabouts were correct—India, now where exactly in India, only he had that answer, down to a few meters. He really wasn't concerned with that now, when it came time to pay the piper, that information will be highly beneficial to some of our boys in black. He was more interested in the past and thanks to Frank Simoski and his little inventions—that too could easily be done. Eshan's NID's were referenced several times within the cross reference set of the Holiday Mall Massacre members. The first occurrence intersected with Matthew Geiger just over thirty-two months ago Then Gene came on board and it was proven the three of them had a few meetings together. The reference points plotted a story of camaraderie between the boys and their new found friend. He had found the accelerant.

●   ●   ●

Chapter 32

The countdown of twenty-four hours had elapsed and the cops and feds were restless as could be.

"Goddamnit," Lynch said aloud as he looked at the clock, "just who came up with the twenty-four hour bullshit rule anyhow? I mean . . . . shit. Goddamnit!"

"We're not giving up," Josh snipped, "Com'on Lynch, I know you have been working through the night but we are all working on this."

"I know, I know, it's just there's this lead balloon hanging over us and it's about to pop. We are no closer to the truth then we were yesterday."

"True, but these things take time and manpower and yes it's a bullshit rule but you and I both know there has been exceptions to that rule and that's what we cling to, remember not long ago, there was the girl, Russian maybe, or from one of those other eastern bloc countries, I can't remember. She was taken at age ten and escaped at age eighteen, and there was Elizabeth Smart, remember her, they found her after a few months . . . . besides all that, the phones have starting ringing from the news clips . . . where there are facts there are clues."

Lynch's frustration showed on his face along with baggy eyes, uncombed hair, and winkled clothes, his sleeplessness also showed. The twenty-four hour mark had come and gone and it felt like a deadline, literally and on top of that he felt like shit and depressed. In the back of his mind hope was fleeting fast but he knew he had to make a phone call and try to hide his true feelings before he headed home for some needed sleep. He walked into his office, sat down in his chair, picked up the phone and dialed the number to Ripley's parents. It was a brief conversation, very cordial, and to the point. "We are not giving up hope. We have the best people working to find your daughter. We have some leads, We.have. We are. We. We We." He felt sick to his stomach after he replaced the receiver back onto its cradle, sick because of the lies he just told, sick because of the lack of sleep, sick because he has been doing nothing but pouring jet black acid into the pit of his stomach in order to find the cute little blonde who went missing over twenty-four hours ago. Lynch then powered down his computer, glanced at the clock that read five after twelve and stood. He picked up the last photograph the Newenbergs had of their daughter, one where her daddy had her on his shoulders. She was wearing a small Braves hat and was all smiles. Then he placed it into his shirt pocket and walked out the station towards his car. He forewent his daily ritual of the last smoke before calling it a day; the nicotine would have made him even sicker. Within fifteen minutes he was passed out on his unmade bed, shoes and all.

Garfield was back fielding the phones with several of the FBI guys. Ever since the morning news broke, the phones starting ringing off the hook at the suburban Atlanta police station with descriptions of limping men and blonde children. It was a tedious job to say the least. Garfield didn't have direct access to a workstation at the moment so he took notes the old fashion way—longhand making it even more tedious for him. Each phone called was logged; time and facts jotted down, and names and numbers were taken down for follow-ups. Very few people called in anonymously. Those types of calls usually are taken with skepticism but on occasion when the facts are just too detailed the red flags are waved. Once in a blue moon, the perpetrators themselves call in to brag, they slip, and they are captured and convicted due to their stupidity. Sometimes it was easy to catch people in their weaves of lies but most of the time the officers have to be attentive with their ears to the ground. Garfield was anything but attentive. He was feeling the effects of the all-nighter as well; cops are just mere men, not superheroes. His body beckoned for a little shuteye but instead of making the commute back home he hunkered down in a very seldom used waiting room that had a small uncomfortable couch but it wasn't the stiffness in the cushions that kept him deprived of his much needed rest. His mind raced with the many so-called facts from the morning's phone conversations. So much so, he couldn't keep anything straight in the whirlwind of his thoughts. "Red hat. Red car. Walks with a limp. Old man buying children's toys. In Tyler County, near Hapeville, outside of Woosley, in downtown Americus. Young man limps on his right leg. Sports a cane. Green Camaro. Ripley. Blonde hair. Medium build limping in Wal-Mart. Drunken man with red hat at the bar. Limping man getting gas, buying toilet paper, buying coffee, buying paint, buying a child's toothbrush, buying fruit, seen at the donut shop, the bank, the post office, the hardware store, never mows his lawn, never outside, always a strange man, a loner, a pedophile lives next to me, was arrested for child molestation once I think, always watches the kids getting haircuts, very creepy, still lives with mother, house looks dilapidated, never parks in his garage, never a light on, never gives out candy for Halloween, works at night, doesn't work, disability compensation, never talks, in his own world, heard he was in therapy most of his life, since the accident, since his mother died, since his father died, it was his fault, he killed his sister, he left home at a young age, rarely drives, is a thin man, big around the middle, black, white, sort of tall . . . ." Somewhere in there, there just might be a clue, a lead, a case breaker. His mind reeled for another twenty minutes until it just shut down under its own accord.

Josh was a different story altogether. He was still in the sprinting stages and working closely with the FBI and GBI, pouring over phone notes, dissecting maps, and making assumptions. Even though he had lost hope for his own case a few months ago, this was a case that could make amends, maybe fix the wrongs and help his partner, and capture, taking a line from Lynch and Garfield, that sick twisted bastard. Yes, that was his ultimate goal, capture him and put him away for good, although he wouldn't mind spending the taxpayers' hard earned money for the cost of a single bullet—just look at the long run, no high price lawyers, no drawn-out trials, no putting him up for life in a six by six cell, no book signings, no fan mail. For a cost of a single bullet it could save millions, hell, he'd even cough up the cash as to not burden the people for the eighty-five cents. Whatever the means of capture, Josh was back in the game of hunting for a sicko and this time with the help of the government. These FBI guys knew a thing or two and they had a wealth of data in the palms of their hands not to mention a wealth of experts at their disposal. They also had wealth in other areas as confirmed by their dining tabs, also confirmed was the fact man thinks better with a full stomach. Next thing Josh knew, lunch was sprawled out on the table in the conference room—a nice lunch to boot. It was a small catered affair spurred by a quick call to an assistant. The lunch consisted of three types of meat filled sandwiches, pasta salad, chips, sweet tea, soda, water, and a few cookies all with disposable wares. It was brought in and set up by two people who were out the door and onto their next office venue in less than two minutes. With lunch in hand plus his typical sugared filled swill, Josh started to organize the phone notes by geographical location. There was a lull in the ringing of the phones but he knew that would eventually end as the evening news runs the story again and he wanted to get as much done as possible before the next eruption. Organizing the data was pretty much a breeze with the software provided by the feds. It was just a glorified spreadsheet which was later channeled into a database for cross referencing. The only real challenge was reading Garfield's handwriting which he assumed correctly, that he was not raised in a Catholic school. It was atrocious—dots for i's, a's and e's almost indistinguishable, and ones and sevens and fours and nines caused his eyes to squint and blur as well. Heaven forbid that he needed to call any of these helpful individuals for conformation or more details; he'd probably end up dialing a strip club or an adult bookshop.

The men in suits were on the phones most of the day, busy with colleagues back at the home office. They initially had communication problems bouncing through the police's LAN lines, firewalls, and routers, but with the help of some of the best IT people in the world it was a fully workable offsite location with all the comforts of home and all the security of home too. This security was extended to a few of the computers in the station and all three officers working the case were granted a security clearance, login id, and a password to the powerful database located within the J. Edgar Hoover Building back in D.C. They also had access to the FBI's Criminal Justice Information Services Division which holds all sorts of biometric data from finger prints and palm prints to iris scans and face plots used for facial recognition. At the moment Josh was the only officer logged in since the all-nighters were busy catching some z's. He had finished his uploading of Garfield's notes and was given access to a report generator. The software had all the basic prompts he was accustomed to with fields for case number, name, tax id, address, date, time, and practically anything else one can think of, but the real beauty was the graphical interface with point and click capabilities. It was far more advanced and he needed a small amount of tutoring to grasp the full layout of the system. Within fifteen minutes he was well on his way of mining for data. This interface was able to show locations of schools, homes, and businesses, bring up credit history at a click of a button, even filter on last known credit card usages, phone calls both cell and landlines, or anything that was a public record—public meaning a business owned database that was granted access by the government under the Patriot Act (America never really knew how much freedom they lost through that Act in order to keep the façade of liberty in check). The guys from the bureau basically said you're on your own, come up with a plan of attack, get comfortable with the system, and go to town, knowing full well that some of his data/reports will overlap theirs but there is a good chance that he'll come up with something new, something completely different, something that comes from thinking outside the box—this is how a case could break, how this case could be solved.

● ● ●

Chapter 33

"Hey Wide Right, you busy?"

"God I hate that name, I'm in a meeting with the president," as Scott bit his lip in front of Jonathan.

"Just you?"

"Yes, why?"

"Good. I found some more information you are both going to want to hear."

"I'll place you on speaker . . . . go ahead."

"Well I've been doing some more digging on the shootings, turns out there is an interesting plot twist."

"Interesting how," Jonathan questioned?

"Turns out it might have been spurred on by Islamic extremists, there is a one Ehsan Nejem, that has had several meetings with the boys dating to almost three years before the event up to a few weeks ago. He's been on the terrorist watch list since its inception and has been linked to several bombings but never brought in for questioning. He left the country two weeks ago, right now he's in Northern India probably on his way into Pakistan."

"So this Ehsan comes to our country to brainwash our people against us then leaves?"

"It has been done before."

The president looked at Scott and asked, "How should we spin this?"

"I don't think we should, hold on, here's why, ever since nine eleven we as a country know we are not safe, yet there are people out there that are not willing to sacrifice their civil liberties in order to maintain the plight against these extremists and that number is growing by leaps and bounds thus tying our hands. Trying to blame the terrorists again just after we lynched the mob who was responsible will only harden these individuals while they pontificate their conspiracies that the government wants to control its citizens through legislation with the likes of the Patriot Act. We all know that this voice is starting to carry a lot of weight. There is only so much Americans will bend when it comes to protection from outside forces. Yet here is an opportunity to expand their fear and control. Americans against Americans. If we cannot protect ourselves from ourselves what little recourse do they have then to trust their government in order to maintain their freedom? Besides it's not like we can bring this to light, what proof would we show them? It's not like we are going to give a demo of the system, show them their markers, and a map. It really plays to our hand does it not?"

"Scott if I didn't know any better, that sounded a bit rehearsed."

"What are you implying Mr. DNI guy? Are you saying I had a hand in this, killing innocent people prior to Christmas? What kind of fucking monster do you make me out to be?"

"I'm not saying . . ."

Cutting him off in mid sentence, "Good, and to tell you the truth it was a bit rehearsed, I was just waiting for the right moment and I knew eventually another school shooting or some crack in the ice would help solidify our ideals and without trying to sound callous here, this act of violence was really good timing with our proposed bill in its final draft. If the violence within our very walls is going to continue and it will, we can't stop that, the public will be forced to compromise their liberties on their own and hence our bill will be ripe for the passing."

"Good point," the president added.

"So are we just going to keep this under wraps," the voice on the speaker phone question?

Jonathan spoke, "No, of course not. I'll place it in front of the cabinet and maybe run it by the committee of HL and assure them that justice will be served and it will be swift but it's not like we are going to broadcast this on the evening news . . . we have to apply our old rule of thumb, what the American public doesn't know won't hurt them."

"Perfect,' Scott added, "Just like Oklahoma."

"Yes to a degree, besides we don't need to call any more attention to our hidden agenda."

He sat at his monitors and watched with much anticipation. He had the vision of some Tom Clancy novel where the black ops took out an entire insurgence camp and left without a sound. It wasn't the case. After being provided with the exact coordinates of one Ehsan Nejem to within the last five minutes, they were keyed into the firing sequence of a long range cruise missile that was parked in the Arabian Sea. Within four minutes the camp was eradicated and Ehsan's marker no longer transmitted. Cased closed for the mission sanctioned by President's cabinet.

●　　●　　●

Chapter 34

His first order of business with the software was to cross reference the locations of any individuals who called in with tips with the locations of the missing children or the man with the limp. There were one hundred sixty-one people who called in with tips from this morning's news coverage. The result of his first query was a map viewable in either a satellite view or a standard map view, he chose standard, and pinpointed the callers with a blue flag/pin while the victims were in red. There was no seemingly viable connection to the missing at the moment. The callers were scattered across the map and even into other states, even as far a California thanks to the national coverage by CNN. There are always a few nut bags who call in just to tie up phone lines or to chat with someone. Just like the map Lynch and Garfield worked on, he was able to draw radiuses from each of the red flag's point of origin—it was almost instantaneous—"this was too easy," he said to himself. He was able to increase or decrease the radius at a touch of the button and focus on other various statistics such as gender, age, and race. He was able to overlap his results based on different search parameters. He was able to do much more than he could have ever done back at his own station; all thanks to the help of the federal government. He became so engrossed in the new software he never realized the time and was taken by surprise when Garfield walked back into the conference room a little after four in the afternoon looking slightly puckish and wrinkled as hell.

"Did you eat," Garfield quipped?

"Yeah, the guys had lunch brought in, what's left is over there."

Garfield made his way over to the slim pickings, grabbed the only chocolate chip cookie left and a sweet tea. After the boys ate, the word of food spread through the office like, well like leftover food in an office and the vultures left but a few morsels and the sweet tea of course.

"Find anything?" Garfield asked.

"Well first thing, your handwriting sucks."

"Mom says I should have been a doctor but I hate being around the sick. Yeah, ever since my grandfather . . ."

"The second thing.," cutting off Garfield in mid sentence while glancing over his shoulders to see if any feds were in the room, "These guys have way too much data, it's scary. With a touch of a button I can find your credit score, where you bought your last take-out meal, what movie you last rented from your cable company which by the way, I could have told you that Bruce Willis film wasn't any good . . . nowhere near his Die Hard days."

"Yippee-ki-yay motherfucker. Yep, great movie, I'll keep that in mind next time, ... but you know, I just met you this morning, so what have you come up with besides the fact I ate at the Irish restaurant yesterday for lunch?."

"Irish?"

"Yeah, Mickey Dee's but you probably didn't know that since I paid cash."

"One flaw of the system I'm afraid," shaking off the non-funny Mc joke, "but shit they have everything else. I've been using their software since you left, pretty slick I may say, better than anything I've ever worked on."

"That's why they take so much of our hard earn salaries, for toys like this."

"This is no toy, this is some real scary ass shit. Ever since Homeland Security came to be, databases all over the states have been connected to provide a ton of information in the fight against terrorism, this is a piece of software that links them all together."

"Yeah all in the name in terrorism, right, like Al-Qaeda is going to rent True Lies from Blockbuster trying to make a bomb or using the same credit card they used to buy weapons grade uranium, a Timex, and a few rolls of duct tape."

"But I have to tell you, it will sure make our jobs easier. Watch this . . . ," and with that Josh took a bit of his time to bring Garfield up to speed on the program. Then a few of the bureau guys entered back into the room

"How's it going?"

"Yippee-ki-yay . . . I mean . . . fine, nothing major yet but I have to tell you, I'm impressed."

"Most people are when they first log on but it quickly becomes just another tool and there are many . . . . well, many inconsistencies with the data and it's very limited . . . only because not that many business are online yet."

"These databases, who is and who is not connected, and do you hack into outside systems?"

"No we don't hack we leave that to the hacks at the CIA," a slight laugh, "basically anything that is federally regulated must comply with the Patriot Act. Things like phone, electric, cable, banks, health-care all must supply us with a standard way to connect and talk to their database through, now this is geek speak here, an API or, or application programming interface. Things like phone and banking had already created these communication API's so we just created our interfaces based upon their existing protocols but in the case that a standard didn't already exist then our geeky pals back at the ranch created the protocol or basically the standard way to talk to us."

"How about places like Wal-Mart or Target?"

"Anything, a business, with an electronic storage device slash database can be mandated under federal law to supply its information to the government . . . I say can, well because it is not required unless we ask. Now we don't go out knocking on doors and tell everybody to get online, it's like we don't need to know what your average cost in dry cleaning bills are or what Pink Floyd CD you just bought but hey if a business misinterprets the law and wants their database to be connected, we are not going to look a gift-horse in the mouth, we just give them our standard API document and let them do the work, of course we provide all sorts of consultants to help them with the task . . . all free of charge."

"After they are connected how does this program gather all the information?"

"That's one of the true beauties of this software, it has all sorts of filters and enhancements built in plus it's built upon a series of widespread industry standards, those API's I was talking about. Given the fact the data is stored in all types of databases . . . it's hard for a single person to form really good queries. One database may store something in a field called customer address, while another may break it out into billing address and shipping address or even something like A-D-D-R or M-A-D-D-R."

"So how does one compensate for that?" Garfield asked.

"You don't the program does. If you search for address, it will try to find any address fields within all the databases they're connected to. When we query their information, they return the response based on our standard API call that was created by all of our programmers and analysts back at home. So when the address fields reach us we just see it as address one, address two etcetera and it maintains a certain level of, of, ummm, . . . anonymity, meaning it's just a black box to us, you just have to know the keyword or search phrase like address or first name and not what happens or how it happens behind the scene—it's like a miracle to me."

"You asked for a miracle, I give you the F . . . B . . . I," quoted Garfield

"Still can't get Die Hard out of your head huh?"

"Nope."

"They're gonna need some more FBI guys, I guess." said the fed as Josh and Garfield smirked at his Die Hard quote and he continued, without missing a beat, "Now one of the neat things about this program if you right click on a piece of information it will show you the name of the system that particular piece of information came from. You can even limit your queries based on that system. As you can see there is really a ton of information at your fingertips . . . . you just got to dig to find it."

"Man I bet there are some marketing gurus out there that would cream their pants to get a hold of data like this . . . . the demographic files are priceless."

'In today's world, information is wealth, worth its weight in gold."

"Not to mention power," piped Josh and with that the men got back to mining for data . . . mining for gold and feeling the power.

Just a wee bit after five, the first phone rang from the nightly news coverage of Ripley Newenberg's disappearance. Things were a little calm until then. If the guys in the room thought for an instant that they were done talking to a bunch of whackos, they were wrong. The nightly news coverage brought them out of the woodwork, in troves, which made their work even harder and in a way easier. A good cop, a good detective, can discern the truth through voice and story, they pay attention to inflections and facts, they can tell. So this is the easy part. The hard part comes from the sheer volume of calls and the sheer volume of information and this was unlike the mountain of calls from this morning and afternoon sessions combined. But they were ready and no one, Garfield included, needed to take notes longhand this time around. All the information was logged directly into the FBI's database and Josh was rerunning his reports against the new data as it was being uploaded. The team was on . . . except for the original detective for this case, he was still at home.

Lynch woke up groggy as to be expected and a little disoriented and not sure of the time. The sun was just starting to bid its farewell although not quite dusk, it was just enough for Lynch to question if his digital alarm clock was reading a.m. or p.m. His body wasn't used to this, sure when he was a peon in the department he had all sorts of strange bed hours but since he had made detective almost twelve years ago swing shifts were a thing of the past—just one of the perks to his department status. Deciding he better get a move on since it was indeed p.m. he raised himself out of bed and made his way towards the bathroom. He stopped at his chest of drawers and emptied out the contents of his pockets. The last thing was the picture of Ripley from his shirt pocket. He didn't remember placing it there. For a full minute or two he glanced at the picture, she was adorable, and then he remembered she was missing. His hardened heart felt a twinge of pain. He didn't know why but this case was different from the others, he just couldn't place a finger on it but if he looked deep within he would have found his answer. It was the reason he wasn't married. He so wanted to be a father and when he got his college girlfriend pregnant he didn't think it was the end of the world, until she lost the baby and wanted nothing more to do with him—she never loved him but she was the love of his life. Though he never knew the sex of the child he had lost he always assumed it was a girl . . . . daddy's little girl. He placed the picture of Mr. Newenberg's little girl next to his change and keys, walked into the bathroom, and did his business. His shower was hot, maybe too hot for this summer evening. He seemed even more tired upon his exit, dried off, and splashed some cold water on his face, shaved, brushed his teeth, then made his way back into the bedroom. He dressed in the same exact pants he had just slept in but did manage to find a new ironed and starched shirt hanging in the closet. He grabbed his keys and the picture and was going to place her picture in his shirt pocket but this shirt didn't have a pocket, most of his shirts did, not this one. Lynch ventured downstairs thought briefly about a cup of coffee but his stomach was still saying no. He made a quick turkey sandwich with mayo on wheat and walked out the door with sandwich, keys, and picture in hand. Twenty minutes later he was parked in his usual parking spot though he had very little recollection of his drive into work. He just went through the motion, not really thinking of each and every turn or car or sign. He exited his Chevy and made his way to the entrance of the station. His feet felt heavy. His shoulders ached as though he was carrying a dead weight all day. He had too much on his mind, most being the clock. He felt as though the case was lost already and was sinking into that pit of despair he often visited but that all changed when he walked back into the conference room just before eight. There was a buzz in the air and everyone was hard at work. He half expected to see an empty room and then heard Josh say, "We have a few good leads," looking in the direction of Lynch.

"One of those leads was the 74 Camaro again. Some guy called it in. It was spotted right next to his shore home on Tybee Island. Looks like the kid left town but not the state. The local police have been dispatched but there were bigger fish to fry in the pan."

"How so?"

"Well since you were catching up on some z's, and rightfully so, your idea to place the press release out this morning has generated a ton of phone calls. I think we have every man who walks with a limp in Georgia tagged into this system. No names as of yet but again on yours and Garfield's hunch we narrowed down the search diameter to within your original circle which contained all the missing girls."

"I'm sorry, you said no names yet, right?"

"Yes, most people just called in saying there is this man who fits your description that comes in here and buys so and so or was last seen at so and so."

"So now we have to go through all the calls, gather any clues that paint a suspicious portrait of our subject and link them to a specific location and hope we get a break. "That's not going to be easy and it's going to take time, time we don't have."

"It might be easier than you think. Using this software and data the feds have given us access to, we can search medical records for anyone who might have a leg injury, then try to gather buying habits through debit or credit cards on those individuals. In fact we have already started this process. The FBI has gathered a few profiles together to pinpoint certain items such as rope, handcuffs, lubricant, magazines, specific clothes, or anything else a child molester might buy, including toys, candy, or something like bags of lime to help with decomposition."

"So we all think it's a child molester?"

"All signs point to yes."

"I disagree, true we may have a child molester on our hands but the facts remain, we have no idea, the girls could have been taken and sold to some sort of slave trade, smuggled outside the country, killed because this person is a serial killer or something . . . . we just don't know . . . we haven't found any of the bodies as of yet."

"True, so very true but most of this work is about hunches and we again are going with yours and Garfield's hunch because all the girls are almost identical in build. We are going with the bias that most child molesters are creatures of habit. If they like girls they stick with girls, if they like boys then the Catholic priests tend to stick with boys, altar boys I mean."

"Low blow," but said with a smirk.

"In more ways than one . . . . they tend to stay around the same area, and stick to a certain m o . . . . and we see all the signs with these cases but . . . but you already knew that didn't you? We all did."

With that idea lingering in his head, Lynch took a long deep look at the picture he was holding in his hand. The very thought of someone touching this little angel in that way was enough to make him revisit his turkey sandwich. In the back of his mind this theory was always there, that she was taken to be molested and so was the notion she was no longer alive and that made him pissed and at the same time helpless. As all good cops do he simply buried those thoughts and got on with his work.

●　　●　　●

Chapter 35

Scott didn't sleep much after his conversation with the big man during the rivalry match between the Hoyas and Wildcats. His mind was wheeling for weeks on end with many ideas on how to derail a political freight train the size of Anderson and Carson. His mind kept coming back to one word—the one word that has ruined many of men and not just the political type either. This word was a simple word yet was powerful enough to engulf the egos of movie stars, pro athletes, businessmen, family men, and yes, even the fine men who ran the country. The word was sex and given the right opportunity it could take down mere mortals, the presidency, or even a candidate for president. For some reason or another, the American public regarded this natural act as a big taboo when it was aired on the evening news. Don Henley said it best, people love dirty laundry. It was never more proven when an entire population of a country watched in awe as their President tried to convince a nation that a blowjob wasn't sex. Congressed watched. Hillary watched. Hell, everybody watched and really the only people who benefited from the cost of the trial were the teenagers. They were able to vindicate their perpetual lies to their parents based on facts brought on by a congressional hearing, a cigar, and a stained dress.

Whether it was a blowjob or intercourse, it didn't matter to Scott, for Scott, sex was the answer and it was safe—only egos and feelings would be hurt when the dust subsided.

After he had his answer it wasn't long until he had his target. His mind quickly ran through all the logical choices and settled in on Grace Carson. She was the most vulnerable and the easiest one to paint with a bull's eye. Scott could tell that Grace was a lonely soul, couple this with a story of a potential vice president's wife committing adultery and a nation would be salivating, more like foaming at the mouth, for a tabloid scandal of the tenth degree, then the A & C train could start its descent heading downhill without brakes.

Scott had his plan, his target, now all he had to do was set the whole thing in motion which wasn't going to be easy. It wasn't like he could place a call to some gigolo, pay a few thousand dollars, have him seduce the woman that was Mrs. Carson, and ask him to say cheese for the camera. No, this was going to be the mother of all eggshell walks through some undisclosed governmental agency that did the so-called odd jobs of the oval office. Since Scott was the right-hand man he had access to Jonathan's quote unquote advisors. He just needed to use discretion and a wink to imply his actions were authorized by the president himself.

"Hey Reynolds, this is Scott, any plans this evening?"
  Reynolds knew to cancel any plans when the oval office dialed his extension.
  "Nothing that can't be postponed to a later date, what's up?"
  "I got the hankering for some red meat at our favorite steak house."
  "I should be able to pull that off and be on the five thirty-five out of Philly, how's Eight o'clock?"
  "See you then."

Scott had cleared his schedule with the president and was good to go when he hopped into his car at the white house. He arrived at the Prime Rib at ten after eight and went straight to the bar. The Prime Rib was a man's steak house. Dark ebony walls, white linen table cloths, waiters in the traditional tuxes, just picture a 1940's sophisticated supper club . . . . it was elegant and best of all the meat was USDA Prime, the best steak possible without paying the ridiculous prices for Kobe or Wagyu. Even for a Monday the place was pretty busy but Scott found an open seat at the bar right next to Reynolds, who was already done his first Tanqueray on the rocks. Scott wanted to order his favorite but went with a California Cab from Alexander Valley. He couldn't pass up the 2003 Silver Oak by the glass, still a little young for his liking but an excellent full body beginning and finish with minimal earth tones and bold currants. They exchanged idle chit chat while they whetted their appetites with salted snacks. At quarter of nine they were seated in an out-of-the-way very private corner. A single halogen bulb illuminated the single bud flower in the center of the table. As soon as Scott took his seat he simply picked up the vase and handed it to his waiter in exchange for a menu which he really didn't need.

The waiter then started his spiel but was interrupted with a list of orders from Scott—

"If you would please, one sparkling, one still, if you have the Silver Oak, anything older than a 98 please bring it but I want the Napa Valley this time, if not, bring the list, and to start, we each would like an order of your stone crab claws, jumbo, and we are in no rush."

It was rare that Scott got to have a good meal without his boss in tow and he was going to take full advantage of the situation even if it was considered work. A bottle of 95 was brought and decanted at tableside. Scott picked up the cork and felt its moist tip then placed it back on the table. The wine was then poured without a drip on the white linens into some fine Riedel stemware. The first sip was ten times better than his o'three at the bar and he gave the nod to pour away. They each picked up their glasses by the stem and toasted to friendship, then rolled the silky texture of the wine through their gums and over their tongue in order to satisfy their palette. A few minutes later bread was brought to the table. Reynolds went straight for it; he loved bread no matter what kind it was, slab a pat of butter or on rare occasions, some extra virgin olive oil with cracked pepper and he was in heaven, besides he needed the bread to soak up the ten ounces of gin he had at the bar. Scott on the other hand, did not go near it. If there was one thing Scott dislike about this restaurant it was the bread. He was partial to the old country style, very crusty, baked in the same ovens for centuries type of bread, and not some massed produced yeast and water crap that comes frozen and baked on the premise; he simply waited for the first course.

Fresh from Florida, the stone crab claws arrived pre-cracked, accompanied by some lemon, a tiny fork, and the obligatory mustard sauce. These claws were Scott's favorite dish in the world, bar none, and only available from October to May. Although they were already cracked, there was still a good amount of work involved but the meat was definitely worth every ounce of effort. Scott took his time and savored every succulent and sweet bite. He used just a dollop of his sauce on each tasty morsel. Yes it was definitely worth the work. Things were a tad different on the other side of the table; Reynolds needed more sauce and another napkin and couldn't wait for the finger bowl to arrive. He hated to be sticky and wanted the whole ordeal to be over with so he could enjoy his steak. When the waiter came to clear the plates Scott reminded him that they were in no rush and to wait a bit before he brings the salad, then the two men continued their conversation from the bar on Reynolds' life in the suburbs of Philadelphia.

"You're not going to believe me when I tell you this, but the one thing I do miss about D.C . . . . the metro."

"You're right I don't believe you."

"No seriously, yeah it was a pain in the ass to wait for the next train, and many times just way too hot, but I miss the convenience, in the suburbs I have to drive everywhere, even for my morning cup and newspaper, drive, drive, drive, I hate it . . . . oh and then there's the traffic."

"There is traffic here too . . . or did you forget about the belt?"

"Okay, I guess there is traffic everywhere, you think someone would learn to design the infrastructure to support the urban sprawl."

"It's too late, but with the rising fuel cost people will start moving back to the cities just for the convenience as you say, and with that comes new money to help support the railways and other modes of city transportation."

"Maybe we could get some of those maglev trains like they have in Asia. I would love to be at the airport in five minutes whereas it would be an hour by car."

"All in due time."

"Yeah, as soon as you get out of bed with the oil industry . . . ."

And before they could continue on a heated conversation on the injustice and criminal content of the government they were interrupted by hearts of lettuce with Roquefort dressing and vine ripe tomatoes. The discussion thereafter switched to the more subdued topic of sports and continued until the entrees arrived.

This is why they come to this establishment—the steaks. Reynolds ordered the bone-in prime rib steak, medium. The higher fat concentration allowed for a more flavorful mouthful but only when the fat was able to melt at a higher temperature. If this piece would have been ordered like Scott's New York Strip, very rare, it would have been too chewy. In addition to Scott ordering his very rare, he also asked for it to be Pittsburghed or charred on the outside leaving a crunchy crust with a soft interior. They split sides of sautéed button mushrooms, sautéed in butter and cognac and an order of grilled artichokes with stems. Neither one of them had a sauce or a starch to go with the manly helping of heart attack on a plate. With knife in the right and fork in the left, the European way of dining, Scott sliced his steak right down the middle to get a glimpse of its doneness. Perfect. The same went for Reynolds' side of the steer. Neither one of them were in any type of rush to finish their meal. They were both slow eaters when it came to the main course. At a little after eleven their plates were cleared, the table was de-crumbed, and two cups of black coffee were brought to the table. Both men passed on dessert but opted for a V.S.O.P. made by Martel. In glancing around there were only a few tables left in the 2020 K Street facility.

"That was a great dinner."

"Zagat rated and never a disappointment."

"So why do I deserve such a good meal, such a fantastic wine?"

"Well . . . I want our relationship to continue."

"Why wouldn't it, Jonathan and I have been long time friends?"

"That's not what I'm saying . . . I mean with the American people, another term."

"The approval ratings are still way in your favor, I see no need to worry."

"Not good enough, never is, that can turn on a dime as we have seen in the past. We need a sure winner."

"And you think I can help?"

"We need you to go to," then a slight hesitation, "BAT for us," with both men knowing the code for bait and trap.

"BAT, that's an acronym from the past, old school, I didn't know a youngin' such as yourself knew it."

"I didn't, the big man himself told me," a knowing lie.

"What are we talking about for the bait, money, sex, drugs?"

"We need a . . . well a compromising position so to say with a certain female."

"So it's sex."

"Yes."

"Photography?"

"Snap snap, grin grin, wink wink, nudge nudge, say no more."

Reynolds broke into a slight laugh and almost couldn't get a hold of himself with Scott's reference to the Flying Circus skit but then popped the question, "On?"

Scott grabbed a pen from his jacket and wrote two initials on the edge of the cocktail napkin. Reynolds took a few seconds as he scanned his memory banks for a match; it didn't take long, the reply took a bit longer as he once again probed his inner workings to see if this was really feasible or not. He then wrote RA on the napkin and slid it back to Scott. Scott nodded as these were the second letters of both the first and last name.

"Okay, I might be able to find someone within the group but it's going to take some time."

"The sooner the better and we need it before the big day."

"That's a given but we'll need to setup the back storyline, a few months maybe, and there is a chance, strike that, a good chance that the bait remains on the hook."

"Understood, I know it's a tall order and if anyone can pull this off it's you."

"Even though I've been retired for the past five years?"

"You and I both know that's not entirely true, we both believe in the world power that is America, that's why you are not collecting social security."

"That was a world power, that's why I'm doing this, so we are again the dominating character in this play of life, deserving the respect we had lost."

They each picked up their snifters clanked the rims together and finished their remaining sips. With that Scott signaled to the waiter, the international sign for the bill, writing a check mark on his hand, and seconds later it was promptly delivered. He opened his billfold and chose his platinum card. The waiter returned with the receipt and Scott applied twenty percent and attached his signature, and rose from the table. Reynolds followed suit.

The two men walked towards the door, Reynolds stopped by the maitre d's stand to order a cab and picked up his duffel bag. Scott summoned his car via his cell. He would have given Reynolds a ride if he wasn't heading back to the White House. When his car arrived they shook hands and departed.

While in the cab Reynolds punched up his old standby for hotel rooms in the city and booked a standard room with no problem at all, his gold status helped in the sold out hotel. As soon as he entered his room he fired up his laptop and scheduled a meeting with his group nine o'clock sharp and did a bit of research on his assignment. He logged off, shut down, and then the ton of red meat and the alcohol took over, he was asleep in five minutes.

● ● ●

Chapter 36

Reynolds was up at his usual time of 4:30, did a few sit-ups, push-ups, put on his sneaks, and headed out into the drizzle to do his five miles. The hotel had a state of the art fitness center complete with pool but he was never comfortable with machines, nope, he settled for what the marines had taught him—use what god has given you. When he returned he showered and shaved then scanned both the Washington Post and Wall Street Journal from front to back, including the comics and sport pages. At quarter after eight he grabbed a cab from the doorman and headed to his appointment. The drizzle had since turned to a downpour. He arrived at his second home a little wet since he never carried an umbrella and after signing in at the front desk went straight to conference room located on the third floor. Thomas Brickman was already there.

"Good to see you Thomas"

"Likewise."

"A tad wet I see."

"Just a tad, I forgot an umbrella . . . well truth be known, I never carry one. I hate the damn things . . . beside it's only water."

"So what brings you here? It's been a few months since coming to the main."

"I got a call from the double o, they need us to handle a use case for them."

"Requirements."

'I need one BA, someone like Blake."

"Do you want Blake? He just got back from Indonesia and I haven't assigned him to any case just yet?"

"Yes I want Blake, I always want Blake."

Thomas dialed a direct number on the speaker phone, "Blake, Thomas here, can you please come up to the conference room on the third, thanks. He'll be here in a few."

Reynolds took the opportunity to grab some aroma in a cup and when he returned Blake was now sitting with Thomas.

"Hey Blake, how's it going?"

"Fairly well, our Flyboys had a pretty good go this year."

"Just need a defenseman or two, they're still a young team."

"Gotta love'em."

"Thomas, would you please excuse us."

Thomas knew full well he wasn't going to get any more information and just as he was about to head out the door, stopped and asked "How long do you need him, so I can do his timesheets?"

"I would say no later than the end of the first month of hockey season."

The door shut behind Thomas who was already thinking of the first Tuesday in November was a safe bet for Blake's return."

"So Blake let me get to the chase, remember Warsaw a few years back?"

"Yes."

"Well, same thing here, only a bit more delicate . . . . let me rephrase that . . . extremely delicate, wings of a fly delicate," then Reynolds handed him a file, "Here's her dossier."

Blake took a few minutes to read it. Reynolds noticed his eyes widened a bit and assumed he had just read her name. He was speechless as he read every word.

"Delicate is a fucking understatement is it not?'"

"Well . . ."

"I mean, I have just one question . . . . why the fuck?"

"She's Floyd's confidant and we need to find out what he is up to, he appears to be Mr. Clean on the outside, but we know he is into some serious shit, scary ass shit, we just need to find out what exactly."

"And you think she can help?"

"A man of great power usually only trusts one person and that person is usually his wife."

"How close?"

"Warsaw close."

"You're out of your fucking mind, you know that," said with a slight sarcastic grin, "Just how am I going to get that fucking close?"

"Well first of all, maybe clean up that fucking language a bit, after all she is a southern bell, and security is nowhere near what it would be if she was Anderson's wife . . . besides no one, and I mean no one, really knows the name of the candidate for vice president's wife anyway . . . hell they don't even know the first name of our VP's wife."

"Oh and that's going to make it better, she's almost twice my age for Christ's sake."

"Come on Blake, bat those baby blues and turn on that boyish charm of yours, you'll be in like flynn . . . . no grandmother can resist that," he said with a laugh.

"They're hazel and you're serious about this aren't you?"

"I'm afraid so."

After the initial shock of the name, Blake turned to all business and reread her file.

"Alright, I might have an angle here, her charities, she seems to be a good soul, raising money the best she can . . . how bout . . . how bout this . . . . I go to one of her charity events, donate money . . . maybe have someone close to me die of cancer, a wife, a brother, ask to volunteer in order to cope with my feelings."

"Okay, I'll buy that for a dollar."

Blake paused before he spoke, "Hey where's that line from?"

"Nineteen eighty-seven."

"Nineteen eighty-seven?"

"When Robocop was in the theater."

"Hmm, not what I was thinking, never saw it."

"So anyway back to the cancer thing, I like your angle . . . . no wife though, you've never married, you're a lost soul, lonely, never finding the right person, she'll warm to you more that way."

"What about my boyish charm?," and before Reynolds could crack a smile, "And since I've never been married, let's go with the brother dying thing, easier to pull off on my part. I'll have to work up a story with the appropriate players and names."

"I'll take care of the legwork when you're ready."

"And I take it the timeline is critical?"

"We only have a few months to get what we can, in looking at her schedule she has an event this weekend to get you started on, a walk for breast cancer."

"Looks like a sister then . . . and it doesn't give us much time."

"You shouldn't need that much to get the ball rolling, just a meet and greet."

"I would stand out if I made a sizable contribution, easier to get noticed and schmooze with a sizeable check in hand."

"Agreed, I'll find out what the budget is but it shouldn't be a problem."

"Anything else?"

"Just remember to skate lightly . . . . this is going to be the thinnest of ice."

"This isn't going to be easy."

"Never is, but that's why you make the big bucks, you'll be able to buy another Porsche in no time," pronouncing it without the "uh" sound on the end.

"So you'll be in touch?"

"Yes or just call the usual when you need me," and with that Reynolds got up from his chair, grabbed his cup, and headed out the door.

"Oh by the way, she didn't have any children or adopted any, so she can't be a grandmother."

"Just be sure to take your dust buster and a can of WD-40" and walked out with a smile knowing he had the right man for the job.

●　　●　　●

Chapter 37

What nobody realized was during the morning pow-wow with the feds and the various investigating officers, there was someone else working the case. When the story broke on the AP wire little attention was paid by the other parts of the country. It wasn't until CNN broke the story that people paid attention and one person in particular. He was already at work and at his computer and within an ear shot range of the television tuned to CNN. Just because he worked for the DNI it didn't mean he was in tune with everything going on in the world, sometimes, just sometimes, the media plays a key role of up-to date news that mattered. Although the news of the serial kidnapper had nothing to do with the worldly business of his employer—it struck a chord with him—a deep chord. When they flashed a picture of Ripley Newenberg his heart skipped a beat; it was a dead ringer for his godchild, his niece—the same buttery blonde hair, the almost exact same smile; he almost called his sister. After getting up from his chair and moving closer to the TV his heart was still in his throat, even though he learned it was not her, he was still in shock. How could anyone, someone, the answers were beyond him, she was just adorable and his imagination ran wild almost to the point that it made him sick. What if he could . . . . maybe he could . . . . yes he could . . . . he had the power . . . . so he believed . . . . the power to help.

While being a Brunonian, he fell into computer science, not really a science at the time since it was a fairly new field, mostly tedious punch card work and magnetic tape backups (old school stuff by today's standards) which earned him credits but couple this with a second major in political science and a barely dry ink diploma from a top notch Ivy school and he landed a fine government job at the Central Intelligent Agency. If someone would have asked him the typical freshman question, "what do you plan to do after college?" the farthest thing from his mind would have been to work for the government. But that's what college is all about, finding yourself, being exposed to new ideas, new concepts, meeting new people, and making new friends. By the time he turned a junior he was well on his way of becoming a changed man; one with new ideals, new beliefs, so much so he actually believed he could change the world . . . of course with the much needed help of a few new best friends. It was a snap getting accepted into the agency—again the schooling didn't hurt but neither did the recommendations from his friend's parents—some of them being among the most powerful in Washington. After the agency was persuaded by his potential he fit like a well tooled cog within the bowels the CIA's central nervous system; its computer core. Unlike anything he had seen or even heard of before, the room or in this case rooms upon rooms, maybe even warehouses of massive machines filled his comprehension almost to the brink but after six months of working with the beasts they had succumbed to his every command. He was a natural and climbed up the ladder with ease and could have moved well beyond his pay scale but he realized he could make more of a difference if he stayed right where he was. And he did until the president persuaded him to take a new position with the Office of the Director of National Intelligence. His primary job or his official job title quote unquote states database administrator; meaning he was responsible for the entire realm of data within the entire intelligence community, what data was stored, how it is stored, how it got there, who had access to it, and how it was accessed. At this stage in his life he was the head honcho of the department, basically there were no other watchdogs beyond him that knew anything about database architecture, only managers with their budgets and project plans. Being a manager himself meant he wasn't supposed to do any coding, only delegate the work to his peons, his subordinates but he ventured outside the lines on occasions much to the knowledge of no one.

He spent years, literally years, at his computer typing out lines of code that no one would ever see. Code that connected computers that no one would ever see. Code that connected databases that no one would ever see. And that was his part, his part in the overall scheme concocted so many years ago, the part of connection without detection. Of course he was just a side of an equilateral triangle but his part made it come alive just like the three of them planned . . . so many years ago. One interface in particular downloaded data instantaneously from the Immunization Information System (IIS) into a database located in the hills of Virginia. This was the starting point for all. This data contained the lot number of all vaccines and the social security number of those who received the injections. From there it was a matter of downloading the data from Etimiz containing the lot numbers of the stabilizer and the NID's encoding numbers through yet another interface. The last interface and the most important was one that was piggybacked onto a few satellite uplink interfaces and cellular phone services. Since he was responsible for interfaces as well, it went undetected. This interface was responsible for uploading the positions of the NID's every hour into their database. With these three interfaces in place they could track every hour the position of everyone who ever received a rubella vaccination or something containing the STBL5 stabilizer and since it was practically law to be vaccinated, pretty much ninety-nine point ninety-nine of the injected people in America could be tracked from space to within an hour of their last known whereabouts and that time frame would grow smaller as technology progressed. From there it was just a few clicks of the mouse to cross reference databases to get names, ages, addresses, and pretty much any piece of data within an electronic file. With this type of information he could become god-like, he could find people, track people, and help people and no one would ever know.

And that was the key, who would know if he helped little Ripley Newenberg? Who would know if he helped the little girl with blonde hair that looked like his goddaughter? Who would know if he helped a little girl age five taken by a monster? Just who would know? He thought about calling the others to "ask permission" but quickly squelched that idea in fear of their typical response—"You just can't go around helping everybody in this world who needs help, people will start asking questions." And that was indeed the biggest fear of the group.

Her pictured flashed again on the screen and he felt a pit in the bottom of his stomach once again . . . he could help; he knew it, and again who would know? That question weighed heavily on his mind. He learned from the rest of the newscast that twenty-four hours hadn't elapsed . . . that too was key. The weight grew heavier. Time grew shorter so he thought, he also thought it just might be a mute point, it just might be too late anyway but he could try, just this once, who would know? And so the wheels of rationalization were put into motion and once the wheels start spinning, rarely was there any turning back. He headed back to his desk and with a few keystrokes he was in the system, the most powerful system in the world . . . . he felt like god for an instance, then the beads of sweat appeared on his brows and then he prayed he did not get caught.

Within minutes his answer appeared on the screen.

32.728303, -84.012891

She's still alive, still alive as of four minutes ago, and still alive roughly eighty miles outside Georgia's capital, still alive and in the home of one Kyle Kraner, age thirty-seven, and no relation whatsoever to Ripley Newenberg. He contemplated about just picking up the phone and calling the hotline or police or FBI but he would need a cover story and it would have to be convincing enough for them to act upon the information, not to mention, it would have to be done through an untraceable line and that alone would a raise red flag. No, if he were to help, he would need to come up with another way, a better way, a plan, and so he put his morning chores aside and racked his brain.

●　　●　　●

Chapter 38

He kept a watchful eye on the clock and did a refresh of Ripley's biometric readings every hour, twenty-one minutes after the hour. He waited with bated breath each time, and each time let out a sigh of relief. She was still alive, although he didn't want to think dark thoughts; he knew because she was still alive, she would need tons of therapy to enslave the torturous moments this beast had laid upon her. He could only imagine. And speaking of beast, Kyle Kraner, age thirty-seven, lived alone, as do most pedophiles and that was his foregone conclusion, even though there was very little information to go on. There were no major credit cards, only a Home Depot credit card, an 86 Ford Taurus in his name, although no auto insurance, very little phone calls either to or from his home phone, no cell phone, no cable or internet bill, two regular prescriptions from a local pharmacy—one for a pain medication, the other a sleep aid, only one bank account that he used for cashing work checks that contained a whopping total of exactly $47.00, no mortgage payment or rent payment and he found that was quite odd until he did a bit more research finding both parents were deceased and having just enough coverage to pay off the house and live free and clear excluding the taxes. He found Kyle was once a cook, a construction worker, and now part of an office cleaning crew. Kyle's low credit report showed he had been delinquent a few times on both his utility bills and Home Depot credit card but for the most part he tried to pay everything on time. No speeding tickets or other violations were found and has almost a year left on his driver's license before expiration. And that was about it for the offerings from the electronic world. Again, there was not much to go on and nothing in the data screamed "Look! Look! A pedophile! Over here a pedophile!" He didn't work at a Chuck E.Cheese or Toys R' Us, he wasn't a registered sex offender—there was nothing, just a painted picture of an average someone who basically lived day to day given his income. Just how were the feds going to find this sicko if he blended in, if there are no big red arrows pointing in his direction? Sure, he found Kyle Kraner quite easily thanks to his tetanus shot four years ago for stepping on a nail but it was going to be a daunting task to the men in blue without some help.

He accessed the latest police report and studied the notes. Still nothing popped out. He noticed the names of three additional little girls thought to be part of this monster's handy work. He entered their numbers into the system. He entered Tanya Drake and nothing. He entered Becky Timberstone and nothing. He entered Colleen Rhinehardt. Nothing. Not one hit, either they were never injected or his first assumption was spot on. He then searched the database to see if they were ever uploaded to the Virginia site. Colleen Rhinehardt was the only one who had not been injected; actually none of her siblings were as well. His next order of business was to find their last known transmissions. Tanya Drake's last record in the system placed her in Butler, Georgia, just a few blocks from her home and by a small park. Kyle Kraner was also in the same location based on his NID readings. Coincidence at this point was slim at best. Becky's last transmission was a few months ago, the location was very close to Kyle's home address, almost right in his backyard, also not a coincidence by any stretch of the means. When he brought up the exact coordinates of Becky via a satellite uplink, he saw a gut wrenching site. He seethed with anger and rage as he stared at his monitor. Becky's last known coordinates, the last known transmitting coordinates proving she was still alive were pointing smack-dab in the middle of a small water reservoir. She just might have been alive for a brief amount of time after her body hit the water. Being so close to his house he probably did what he needed to do and disposed of her the best he knew how. He let out a sound of frustration that came through clenched teeth. His seething continued. He just wanted to pack up, get in his car, and finish this monster off with his own bare hands. His mind wondered as he envisioned several ways of taking out his anger, most involved some sort of torture to the groin area.

He again wanted to reach for the phone and call, call someone but took a deep breath instead.

He pushed back his feelings and continued onward only to be interrupted by a phone call. It was work, yeah he was already at work but Ripley's case was way out of his jurisdiction and the real work at the DNI was requesting his assistance. The phone call wasn't anything major, only time consuming. One of the databases was throwing integrity errors and since it was a very secure database he had to find someone who had the security clearance to repair it. He knew right away that the only person besides himself that could fix it was out due to illness; therefore he would have to reset permissions and file the necessary paperwork in order expedite a new resource to take care of business. Sure he could have done it himself but he didn't want to spend the better part of his day on mundane work when he had other pursuits. He satisfied his major responsibilities, answered a few emails, and was logged back into the system within an hour. He checked her NID's. She was still alive.

He picked right up where he left off. Although Colleen wasn't in the system, Kyle was. It wasn't entirely clear if Kyle was accountable for Colleen's disappearance since his closest markers were approximately fifteen miles outside of Colleen's last known whereabouts and at this point in time the markers only logged once an hour. Yes, it was hard to say with one hundred percent certainty that Kyle was the predator in this case but sure as shit, he knew without a doubt in his mind what had happened to this little girl. Yes sure as shit he knew and that's why he had to stop this monster. He could have devoted more time searching for even more victims whom he feared there were but he had to take matters into his own hands and help his latest victim now.

He read Ripley's case file again. He read it again and one phase stuck out—"walks with a limp". "Walks with a limp, that's why the pain medication." He found the pharmacy records on his first search and reread those as well. He had been taking the pain meds sporadically over the past two years and always seemed to be on some sort of very mild sleep aid since Dr. Bergerman became his physician five years ago. The latest sleep aid he prescribed was no more effective than Excedrin P.M., although the doctor wouldn't have gotten any free pens, paper, or a nice dinner with drinks included if he had given Kyle an over-the-counter pill. There was no indication why he needed either of these pills on the pharmacy records nor would there be; he would need Kyle's case history. He would need to see Dr. Bergerman's medical records to get a further insight. Again this was possible all thanks to the modern marvels of the computer age. Years ago this would have been a difficult task since most of the medical databases were on closed systems, meaning no connection to the outside world, yet in today's world the medical profession couldn't exist without this interaction. As luck would have it, Bergerman's records were online in order to expedite insurance claims—his filing system left a little to be desired. It was no wonder Kyle's medical records were not found the first go around—it brought to mind the mantra of one George Fuechsel, an IBM techie who coined the phrase "garbage in, garbage out" or simply "GIGO" in nerd speak. This database was atrocious much like his or any doctor's signature for that matter. There were misspellings, lack of data such as no addresses or phone numbers, incomplete histories, pages missing, inconsistent entries for date of birth such as abbreviated month, numerical month, two and four digit years, and the list goes on and on. He scoured the entire database and pulled together what he believed to be a complete profile on Kyle Kranner (with two n's), based on Dr. Bergerman's system of records. There were very few details. There was no mention of accidents. No mention of operations or outpatient procedures, just a few symptoms—"can't sleep," "pain in hip and leg". There was not even an indication if it was the right or left leg. The only other thing within his file was a referral from Dr. Polasky dated almost nine years ago.

He went to the same medical database to dig for Dr. Polasky. Nothing. He searched the white pages. Nothing. No Dr. Polasky within Kyle's vicinity. Odd. He then searched Georgia's database for licensed practitioners and had several hits—none near Kyle though. He then entered Polaski with an "i". Again several hits. Again none near Kyle. On a whim he entered into the search criteria "expired licenses". Again he received several hits. This time one was near Kyle, a one Dr. Henry Polaski, this had to be him but there was one problem—he was a pediatrician, okay two problems, he was also deceased. A dead-end, literally. Again this was odd—why was a pediatrician giving, at the time a twenty-eight year old man, a referral to a new doctor, very odd indeed. He needed more information but none of Dr. Polaski's files were online—it was so long ago and he was probably set in his ways while practicing medicine for over forty years. He found the doctor's old address and phone number. The phone number was still active.

The doctor's wife, Neili Polaski, was still alive. There were other ways of finding information, outdated and old fashion some would say, but they have a lot to learn. He questioned—"should I? What are the chances?" He rationalized—"she was probably his receptionist, his file organizer, there is a good chance." He glanced at the clock and picked up the receiver, his rationalizing was over.

After about four or five rings, "Hello."

"Mrs. Polaski?"

"Yes."

"Hello, I'm an associate with doctor Bergerman."

"Doctor who?"

He so wanted to laugh as he remembered the British television show but didn't, "Doctor Bergerman and this in regards to one of doctor Polaski's patients."

"Dr. Polaski is not here."

Thinking now she has a little bit of dementia, this was going to be difficult.

"I know Mrs. Polaski I . . . ."

"Yes, he passed away a few years ago I'm afraid. I miss him but I always say I'll see him soon. So want can I do for you my dear?"

"We have a former patient of doctor Polaski's and I'm wondering if there are any other files or records that the doctor might have?"

"I'm afraid whatever we had we gave to either doctor Swisher or doctor Bergerman but most of them went to Swisher."

"Why?"

"He's the closest pediatrician in the area."

"I see, who did you send to doctor Bergerman then?"

"Children on the cusps . . . ages fifteen and older I think, I thought you said you were with Bergerman."

Now knowing this gal was pretty with it, "I am . . . well I'm associated . . . . I just started last week and was going through the files, we don't have much information on his patient Kyle Kraner."

There was silence.

"Mrs. Polaski?"

"Yes . . . ."

"Can you shed any light on Kyle Kraner?"

"Is he okay?"

"You remember him?"

"Yes, yes, I'll never forget Kyle, such a nice boy at one time, although I haven't seen him since my Henry retired."

"At one time . . . . what do you mean by that?"

"The last time I saw him, well it was very upsetting, my Henry had told him he was retiring and Kyle went into this rage, we never ever saw anything like it before, after that he never came around again."

"Was Kyle his patient?"

"Sort of . . . . hard to explain really . . . . Kyle just really needed support. My Henry became somewhat like a father figure to him after both his parents died. Kyle was young, very young when he came to us the first time when his sister had become ill. He really didn't have any money or insurance so he did odd jobs around the house and office, you know like mend a fence, mow the lawn, stuff like that. He was seemingly here once a week helping out my Henry anyway he could, more so after the accident."

"The accident?"

"Yes, the one where he lost his sister, such a sad day, very sad day. His sister was a beautiful little angel, the bluest of eyes and almost white blonde hair, just adorable. Her funeral was probably the saddest day of my life . . . . only Henry and myself were there, such a shame. Now when my Henry moved on that was sad too but he lived a long life . . . . a good life, but when a child is taken, very sad."

He could hear she started to sniffle as long lost memories were returning.

"Can you tell me about the accident?"

"Not much to tell, Kyle was driving down to the lake and lost control."

"Is this where he injured his leg?"

"Yes. He was pretty banged up, a crushed femur, a broken hip, a broken arm, he spent several weeks in Peach County Hospital. My Henry checked on him almost every day, he was so young, so alone."

"How old was he when he had his accident?"

"Seventeen or eighteen, he was just devastated when his sister had perished in the accident, he was never quite the same after that. My Henry kept a watchful eye on him, he just needed to."

"Was he unstable?"

"Do you mean physically or mentally because physically, yes, his femur and hip never healed properly causing a slight limp. Mentally, that too was unstable, losing your entire family at such a young age plus blaming yourself each and every day for your sister's life, that would take its toll on anyone but he managed as best he could. Like I said before he started stopping by even more. My Henry convinced Kyle to find a better job and he became a cook somewhere . . . ummm Apple . . . no . . . ummm . . . . I forget where . . . he made a really good ravioli . . . my Henry loved them. Yeah Henry never ate that much pasta but anytime Kyle would bring them over he couldn't wait to sit down and eat. I miss those times with Henry, sitting at the kitchen table and talking over dinner. He was a kind soul my Henry."

He got the feeling Mrs. Polaski was also lonely as she was starting a journey down memory lane.

"Mrs. Polaski . . ."

"Yes?"

"What was his sister's name?"

"Who?"

"Kyle Kraner"

Silence again.

"Mrs. Polaski?"

"Yes, I'm still here . . . . I'm thinking . . . I know it's in here somewhere . . . . right on the tip of my tongue . . . it was a long time ago."

"That's okay, I'll find it."

"Why do you need to know anyway . . . . doctor?"

"Doctor Bergerman."

"Wait, I thought you were an associate of doctor Bergerman?"

Realizing his mistake as he was trying to comprehend all the facts she had given him, he quickly looked for an exit.

"Mrs. Polaski I want to really thank you for your time, is there anything you want me to tell Kyle?"

"There is one thing."

"Sure, what is it?"

"Tell him . . . . no, no, never mind."

"Are you sure?"

"Yes."

"Well okay, thank you again Mrs. Polaski and have a nice day."

"Always do, bye."

"Bye Mrs. Polaski."

Like shaving with a five bladed razor . . . that was close, almost too close, anyway what would she have done had she suspected anything . . . .

"probably nothing," was his conclusion. She did give him a lot to chew on during the brief conversation and though he wasn't a psychiatrist he pretty much gathered the whole trauma thing with his sister sparked some sort of mental imbalance leading him down the road of becoming a pedophiliac. Yeah, he didn't need a PhD to know this guy was pretty fucked up. Somehow, someway Kyle was misplacing the love for his sister within any blonde, blue-eyed little girl that reminded him of his lost and Ripley Newenburg was his current memento. And if he had anything to do with it, she was going to be Kyle Kraner's last keepsake that's for sure.

He went back to his machine and searched for Peach County Hospital only to discover that it had been renamed in 1997 to Peach Regional Medical Hospital. He was hoping that not only did they revamp their name but also their filing system—they did and he dug into the system with the ease of a shovel into dry sand. Doctor/patient privilege was a thing of the past in the digital age all thanks mainly to the insurance companies who rely on facts instead of the actuary tables. If a person is fat, smokes, has cancer, the insurance companies think they have a right to know so they can hedge their bets in the mortality payoff game. Whatever the case may be, it was a blessing disguise as a backdoor to the government agencies prying for the believed to be private information of one's health. Next up for those prying eyes was Kyle Kraner.

The hospital's official online records started in 1997 but its archived records where searchable back to 1976 so it should have been fairly straight forward to find the goods. It wasn't. Finding the buried treasure took some backbone. All of his initial queries returned null. He plugged in all sorts of naming configurations, social security numbers, and zilch was the return each time. He checked his connection to make sure he was hitting their database by running a simple wildcard query. He selected all names and ages and waited for the results. Sure enough he was connected, his answers filled the screen. Names and ages filled his screen. He paged through several thousand names that were in alphabetical order. He just kept hitting the return key like he was on autopilot or stuck in a trance. Return. Return. Bates, Batman, Batts. Return. Return. More names. Return. More names. Return. He didn't know his next move. Return. More names. Return. Cabera, Caden, Cadwell. Return. Return. He paused. Return. He stopped. He stared. A thought Return. He perused the names. He perused the ages. Return. With even more conviction he hit return again. Paused.

Perused. Return. Paused. Perused. He stopped. He didn't hit return; he rewrote his query first and then hit return. He waited for the screen to fill again. He had his answer. He had rewrote the query ordering by age in ascending fashion. There was not one person under the age of eighteen in this database. He then remembered Mrs. Polaski saying Kyle might have been seventeen at the time of the accident. This database did not contain any children. No minors. Interesting. He had a new quest. He needed a new place to dig. Two minutes later he found his new "X". A minute later he found the chest, the buried treasure, the one containing Kyle's medical records.

Here it was, all in black and white, the reason Kyle walks with a limp. Most of his femur is supported by metal rods. His records had very detail entries stating the time of the operation, medications received, the names of the anesthesiologist, the nurses, and even his dietary needs. The only thing that was missing was any mention of his sister or of the depression that surely followed. His mission was clear to him as soon as he read Ripley's case file and "walks with a limp." Now that he followed his map, found the "X," dug deep, and found the treasure, it was like being on a deserted island with no mode of transportation. He had his treasure chest, how exactly was he going to use it was another story . . . . a story that wasn't written yet.

● ● ●

Chapter 39

Greg no longer cruised the internet in his spare time; he had a new hobby now. Even though he promised Jorja he wouldn't play with god, he became obsessed. It became his life, his existence, his daily bread. Plus, he knew damn well Jorja was doing the same, she was good but not that good at removing her footsteps from the sand. Greg on the other hand was an ocean wave, there was no way Jorja was ever going to find out his little secrets and he had plenty. He kept files on various people and their routines and habits. Jorja Carson was top on that list. He knew when she went to the gym, the grocery store, the gynecologist, when she went to bed, showered and logged onto the system; he even knew when she was lying to him. With clues of her whereabouts and his colorful imagination, it was blind voyeurism at its best.

Though tracking Jorja's every move seemed to be his utopia, he loved peeking through the windows of the oval office just as much. Greg's other entries in his files were the president and his staff, after all he needed to keep a close watch on the creators of this machine, and for good reason. He was astonished to even find their identification tags in the system right alongside most of America but he concluded they were probably the first guinea pigs of this absolute power or it was used to enhance their security in some manner. Whatever the reason, their entries into the database made obtaining information on them that much easier. Greg figured that if they ever found out about Jorja and himself he would have enough proof to procure his and hers safe passage from prosecution or stop a bullet to the back of their heads . . . so he thought. He gathered the majority of his information automatically. Being the geek Greg was, he didn't need to sit in front of his array of computers, he just built little snippets or scripts of code that ran on the database machine and stored everything on little files; then each night he would move the files to his machine and analyze them via other snippets or scripts. Again that was for the majority of the information but out of pure addiction he did sit in front of his array of computers and watch the world through god's eyes. The level of detail he could accumulate was simply mind boggling. For instance, last month he knew the president's meal didn't agree with him and he'd be talking with his private physician in the morning because he spent half the night in his bed and the other half in the bathroom. Greg almost called the doctor himself. He knew when the Vice President had meetings with the top brasses of the oil industry way before the press ever got wind or when his chief of staff went off the ranch in search of vaginal juices. He knew lots of things and he kept a record of those lots of things, every last detail.

It was in these details he saw the devil himself. He saw the true evil, the true power this contingency held over the American people. Woven within the fabric of data he saw lies and conspiracies that the American people could not even begin to fathom and this wasn't even including the greatest power of them all, the power of god's watchful eyes. This evening proved to be just the case as Greg stumbled upon vile venom that oozed from the data. He was watching Scott Norwood through the system for he was out of the White House and not in the President's back pocket. The last time Greg followed Scott he ended up getting the name of his piece of ass and adding another memento to his keepsake box. Tonight Greg thought he would be adding yet another name to Scott's snatch collection. He was wrong. Scott went to a steak house for a meal and it took Greg until about 10:30 to find the name of his dinner mate. He was having dinner with Captain Jack Reynolds, ex—U.S. Marine. Was he a buddy or colleague, was it business or pleasure; only time and more digging could tell?

Greg quickly starting doing research and traced Reynolds from Philly to Washington aboard the Acela Express that dropped him off at Union Station just after 7:30. He predicted his hotel since he was a gold card member with Hilton and at about 11:30 proved he was correct, as he was staying in room 242. And so it began, Greg followed the rabbit down the hole, through twist and turns, digging down, way down through layers upon layers of data to the inevitable wonderland stored as bits and bytes. Without working up a sweat, Greg found his military pension records, his tax records, and found he made a pretty decent buck doing his so-called consulting work for the Beta Group of D.C. Now what he did as a consultant was still pretty much up in the air but it did have something to do with software, software for the government. He found phone records of a call from Scott earlier in the day, which he assumed correctly, that's what spurred his travel plans on Amtrak. He found his medical records, his real estate taxes—he found anything and everything pertaining to Captain Jack Reynolds and it was all at Greg's finger tips, awaiting a turn at his analytical skills in order to produce a story, a life. Before Greg turned his attention to the mounds of data that he just unearthed, he decided to take his new toy out for another spin.

His new toy was a piece of software that he wrote using the data stored on god's eyes. It was simple enough to use, just input the tax id and a date into the prompts and hit play. It had controls much like a video player, fast forward, reverse, pause, and controls for speed. It also had a screen of a map. Greg placed in Reynolds' tax id and today's date and hit reverse. He then watched a video of Reynolds movements, starting in room 242 and moving backwards in time across the map and across the globe at five minute intervals. He initially had his speed setting set on two seconds per hour, meaning it took two seconds to watch an hour of Reynolds movement, at that rate it took just under a minute to watch a full day's movement. He increased the speed just a tad and sat back and watched. He watched it like a baseball game with very little thrills. Greg didn't know what he was looking for, if at all anything, so he just watched until it ended and it ended at Reynolds inception date into the system. The location of his inception was the Hospital of the University of Pennsylvania, just over four years ago. He then hit the play button, this time in fast forward motion. He again watched the dot dancing across the screen. He paused the screen when the dot was over the Atlantic. He did a bit of research and found Reynolds was on flight BA 68 heading to Heathrow. Greg continued and watched the dot as it danced across Europe and back. When the dot ended up back in room 242, the reverse button was hit again and the dancing continued. At a random point in time Greg hit the pause button. He then used some of his very cool function keys he built into the software. He hit

F8 and another prompt filled the screen, he entered twenty-five and hit the return key. This opened a new panel in the window and displayed all the names and tax id's within a radius of twenty-five feet from Reynolds at that given time. This was how he found Reynolds to begin with using Scott as the dot. Greg then continued with the backwards video for a second time, then a third, then a fourth. He couldn't recall, maybe it was the fifth or sixth time running through the video that Greg's new found friend scattered his life. For whatever reason Greg saw the dot over a particular place and recognized it instantaneously. Maybe it was imbedded in his brain after all the aerial views on the news or in the numerous power-point presentations Homeland Security had piecemealed together and forced everyone with a level clearance to watch, but there it was, plain as day, the site of the Holiday Massacre and the date was December 23rd—the day of the massacre and Reynolds was smack-dab in the middle of it.

"Son-of-a-fucking-bitch," Greg said aloud, "Jesus, I can't fucking believe this. Fuck, fuck fuck!" shaking his head, "Fucking son-of-a-bitch. This can't be, it just, it just can't . . . goddamnit! Fuck! Another fucking conspiracy, goddamnit. Just what I fucking need."

Thinking to himself as if he weren't in enough trouble already and now this. He reached for his phone and without thinking dialed Jorja's number, then realizing it, he quickly hung up. The last thing he needed was to involve Jorja, actually the last thing he needed was to disobey his boss' direct order.

Then it started, all the data was beginning to process within his cerebral cortex.

So here it was in all its ignominy, Scott and Reynolds in deep shit, up to their fucking eyeballs and then some. Did they really conspire to draw a bloodbath in the middle of an American mall, killing the innocent, killing the young, killing the old, killing over sixty Americans, just before Christmas, just so the President could look good with quick and decisive actions? If what he theorized was true, this was even bigger than the United flight 93 conspiracy. Bigger than the second shooter in the grassy knoll. Bigger, much bigger. This was a plot to kill Americans by Americans, by Scott and Reynolds, by the President of the United States, by Jonathan Whitaker, by Satan. This was pure evil. The venom so vile, so dark, Greg's stomach was beginning to turn in knots and he felt like he was about to vomit. He started to tremble and even though he didn't smoke he wanted a cigarette, he wanted a drink, something to calm his nerves. He made his way to the kitchen and opened the fridge and grabbed a Victory Hop Devil, the only beer he liked. He popped the cap and drank it down it one long gulp, just like his college freshman days. Within seconds his stomach rejected its contents and just like his college freshman days he spewed it back into the kitchen sink. He wiped his mouth and clasped on the floor, leaning against the cabinets, where he remained for the next forty-five minutes in utter shock.

Greg eventually propped himself back up and again opened the fridge, this time removing his old standby, the Dew. He opened it and took a swig, swooshing the neon green liquid between his teeth and gums to remove the nastiness of the stale beer puke from his mouth. He then wisely chose to spit his first sip rather than swallow. The same with his second. The third sip went straight down and to his surprise, didn't return, though his stomach was still in knots. He then made his way back to the computer to face reality, to face the evil.

Again Greg wanted so much to pick up the phone and tell Jorja of his findings but now it was up to him to save his own ass because if they ever found out he knew, his ass would definitely need saving. He turned his attention to the past and tried to scrounge up any data, any other coincidences, anything in order to back his claim. He just couldn't believe that Reynolds just so happened to be in the right place at the right time and take out two of the assailants. He envisioned Reynolds was there as a security blanket making sure the plan went down as it should and maybe it did and maybe it didn't. Maybe nobody was supposed to get hurt or killed and the assailants acted under their own accord. Maybe it went down without a hitch. Maybe just wasn't good enough and whatever the truth Greg wanted answers and maybe with his trusty little tool he could find them.

He spent the next few days deeply entrenched in the system, both at work and at home. It was easy to do while in the office since nobody except Jorja, really knew what he did in the office but supposedly he was one of the best in the business. His firewalls proved just that. If the mainstream hackers knew Greg's mind was preoccupied they would have tried to dance around his security systems to find, if any, their vulnerabilities but as luck would have it his firewalls went unchallenged and his playtime with god's eyes expanded almost exponentially. From the moment he logged in until he called it a day he was pounding away trying desperately to find something, anything but to no avail. Now awhile ago when he first started toying with the system he had found the name Ehsan Nejem and assumed he was the mastermind of the mall massacre since some form of black-ops extinguished his ass in the hills of Pakistan less than a month after the mall shootings. Only a few key individuals, the president's inner circle, and Greg's prying eyes ever saw the red stamped memo and the rest of America was none the wiser. He did find it quite odd that these people who knew of Ehsan didn't expose him to the rest of the world and decided to keep a known terrorist and his deadly deed at bay. It was a conspiracy in the making. Greg's thinking at the time was that maybe this Ehsan Nejem guy used to be on the books of the American spy network and turned out to be a bad apple. That would be a good enough reason to send him to his awaiting vestal virgins without bullhorning the fact that Islam extremists were once again responsible for American bloodshed. Fitting this piece into Greg's new found conspiracy puzzle he now assumed Ehsan was just a scapegoat for the black-ops and the rest of the red stamped memo in-crowd. Greg feared the true conspiracy was to bestow even more disquietude into the hearts of Americans by accusing the very people who live within its borders. America was becoming lackadaisical and numb to the "T" word since it has been used at least once during each and every episode of the evening news since nine eleven. America was also growing sick of the loss of sovereignty the Constitution upheld. A few wackos who took innocent lives for their twisted cause gave the government an excuse to take away the liberties America was built upon. More people die in a year from walking across the street than all the combined terrorist acts on American soil, yet the streets are not made any safer; instead wiretapping is legalized, database records are open to the government, and the private lives of the America's citizens becomes more difficult to protect . . . all in the name of terror. But America is awakening from its deep slumber and removing the wool from their eyes. They have seen their freedom being slowly stripped away but America is starting to learn. America is starting to understand. America is starting to fight back, fighting back for their lost freedoms taken away by the Bush Administration, the senate, the house, their government. Greg's new theory was that this government was trying to disrupt their new found renaissance in freedom by turning

America on itself. Hire some rogue agents to band a group of derelicts and racist pigs together, brainwash them, and let them loose on the *masses* with guns and ammo. Make America cringe in fear again. Make it wilt as it tries to protect its citizens from its very own backyard. If American can't protect itself from its own people . . . enter the Whitaker Administration with swift and decisive action. Pull the wool over their eyes again, protect them from the terror, protect them from themselves, and take away even more civil liberties by hiding behind the legal mumbo jumbo peppered throughout the bills of the senate floor and America would be none the wiser. This was a conspiracy in the making for sure; adding yet another layer of deceit, a conspiracy neatly wrapped in another conspiracy. No one would ever believe it.

●　　●　　●

Chapter 40

Greg thought about his dilemma, he was one hundred percent sure that The holiday massacre was some scheme concocted by the Oval Office but he found nothing pertaining to that fact, even with all the technologies he had at his beck and call. He decided to look in the future for clues of the past. He knew Reynolds had dinner with Scott, he knew Reynolds was at the scene on that bloody day in December, and that's all he knew. So he decided to put some tags or traces on emails to and from Reynolds. Scott's emails went through the servers at the NSA which had protocols he could circumvent given the time and proper credentials but he would need Jorja's assistance. Since Reynolds worked in the private sector his email was more or so public domain now that the Patriot act, the Foreign Intelligence Surveillance Act, and a slew of other acts littered with lawyer speak made it legal

Greg easily rerouted all of Reynolds' email to a government router and he was then able to access each one he sent or received. This was very low tech by Greg's standards and anyone could trace the path of the email but close to one hundred percent of the people had no idea how to view or even read the header information contained in each email. If Reynolds ever bothered to look he could simply open the email, navigate to the tools menu, click options, and then view the header information. He would then see the path that each email traveled. If he looked closely enough, he would spot a router's/IP address that was common to all his emails besides his proper email server's address at The Beta Group. And like almost one hundred percent of the people, he never viewed the header information. As a result, this email popped up on Greg's screen on Thursday evening.

> **From:** *J. Reynolds*
> **Sent:** *Thursday, May 07, 2008 8:58 PM*
> **To:** *Scott Norwood*
> **Subject:** *Rules for software purchasing*
>
> *Proprietary software is expensive. Leasing is usually an inexpensive solution. And tax deductible. Never go with the first solution. In certain circumstances it is cheaper to build your own. Search for the best solution don't take a consultant's word. Avoid unnecessary requirements. Gather only what is needed for the initial phase of the project. Open source should be avoided at all cost within the government—it's free for a reason.*

Reynolds didn't send many emails, if he did it was from another account Greg hadn't found just yet. This one was odd. Why would he be sending Scott what seemed to be spam or very out-dated rules for engaging in a software request from vendors? It's not like Scott was in charge of purchasing software for the oval office. Maybe he was in charge of enhancing the interface to god's eyes, something along the lines of what Greg had already accomplished but why all the talk about cost? Cost would be the last thing this regime would worry about, especially if it pertained to the system. No, there was something very strange about this email and Greg couldn't quite place his finger on it. He reread it again and again. The more he read the stranger it had become. The sentence structure just didn't seem right. He was sure there was something else, he was sure there was more to the message. He tried to read between the lines, was software a metaphor, was cost a metaphor, was the consultant's word actually Reynolds' word, Scott's word, or the President's word, was it a word of warning? Why start a sentence with an "and," why use the word "avoid" twice, why use the words "tax deductible" and "government," why? He wasn't sure why. He regrouped the words of the message, cataloging them as nouns, verbs, and adjectives and played around trying to make new sentences, like an anagram of sorts. Nothing made sense. Greg wasn't a cryptologist by any stretch of the means and his sudoku skills weren't going to help in this situation, nor his computer hacking skills for that matter, but he tried nonetheless. He spent hours on the email, then he took a break when he realized he was getting nowhere and decided to call it a night. Besides a fresh brain is a better brain. The next morning he printed the email out, folded it, stuck in his front pants pocket, and took it to work. When he had some downtime and by downtime it was meant when nobody was looking over his shoulder, he again played with the email and again got nowhere. He stayed well past office hours and continued working the email and again got nowhere. Closing in on ten o'clock and still getting nowhere, Greg decided to do what he did best, he used his math skills. He wrote each sentence on a separate line and placed an equal sign next to it.

Proprietary software is expensive =
Leasing is usually an inexpensive solution =
And tax deductible =
Never go with the first solution =
In certain circumstances it is cheaper to build your own =
Search for the best solution don't take a consultant's word =
Avoid unnecessary requirements =
Gather only what is needed for the initial phase of the project =
Open source should be avoided at all cost within the government—it's free for a reason =

He counted the words in each sentence and wrote the number to the right of the equal sign, 4, 6, 3, 6, 10, 10, 3, 12, 16, then matched those numbers with their respective letters of the alphabet, D, F, C. F, J, J, C, L, P. What he found was no vowels. He then went back and counted the letters in each sentence and wrote that to the right of the equal sign. For the first sentence he counted 32 letters and since he couldn't match that to a respective letter to the alphabet he subtracted 26 from the number and came up with 6 which matched to F. He did this for each sentence again and found the letters F, K P, A, U, V, B, Z, R. This time there were vowels but what word could that possibly be? He was grasping for straws. He felt like Homer Simpson in the episode entitled "My Mother the Carjacker." Homer so badly wanted to win an "Oops Patrol" T-shirt like his wife Marge by finding a blooper in the headlines (Marge's headline was Mayor's Erection instead of Election). He searched and searched, trying desperately to find something funny only to find nothing funny.

Greg felt just like Homer, trying desperately to make some sense out of his mumbo jumbo but finding no sense whatsoever. It hurt his brain. Letters and numbers filled the page, so much so he barely saw the original email through all his gobbly-gook and scribble-scratch. He stopped thinking and just gazed, then Greg starting laughing, uncontrollable laughing, and loud, so loud that his office neighbors, those who worked the late shift, went to investigate. After he calmed down he simply told them it was an inside joke that just caught him off guard; an inside joke indeed. In that same episode, during Homer's search for his funny headline he found an article entitled "World's Biggest Pizza," and since Homer and food go hand-in-hand he starting reading the article, only to find it was talking to him. Each line in the article spelled out "Homer" and continued with "meet me at the 4th street overpass". It was a hidden message within the article. It was the same here, only it was the first letter in each sentence. It was just dumb random luck he found it, that and his bona fide expertise in Simpsons' trivia. If he were to tell the story that the cartoon played a major role in thwarting the logic of cryptography he'd be placed in a nicely padded room with just his maddening thoughts.

His head was now clear of the cryptology cobwebs that filled his brain for almost two days, so was his goal—now the only thing to do was to find out what plan they were talking about and why it was a go but first he needed to make a call.

"Hey Jorja, it's Greg."

"What's up, it's a little late don't cha think?"

Looking at his watch he then realized it was slightly after eleven, "Sorry, but it's only eleven on a Friday evening, I figured . . ."

"Relax Greg, I was only joking, I was just getting ready to go out."

"Really, I'm sorry."

"Again Greg, I was kidding, getting ready to go out, yeah I know those days are behind me, now I'm lucky to make it up to see midnight. So anyway why the call?"

"It's about tomorrow, I know I said I would be in but I can't make it tomorrow, something's come up."

"Anything serious?"

"No, no, nothing really, just some personal business to attend to and I don't want to put it off for another day."

"Oh, okay," with slight hesitation, "I was so looking forward to it, I haven't been in the system for awhile," which they both knew was a lie.

"Listen, go ahead in without me, just be careful."

"I'd rather not, how about Sunday?"

"Possibly, if you don't hear from me tomorrow, I'll see you on Monday morning."

"Greg, are you sure you're okay, nothing serious?"

"Jorja, I'm fine, really, I'll tell you all about it on Monday, I swear."

"Promise?"

"Yes, and really, I'm sorry for calling you so late, and sorry for ditching you last minute."

"That's okay, really, like I said to you before, call me anytime you need me, knowing what we know, well we'll just leave it at that shall we. But you know, you are acting a bit strange and it's got me wondering now."

"Please don't Jorja, listen, it's nothing serious, I'll try to call you tomorrow and hopefully we can do Sunday, okay?'

"Okay, just call if you need anything."

"I will, thank you Jorja, good night."

"Good night."

Now he had two things to do . . . one was a bit more research, the other was to construct a lie. He realized constructing the lie was the easy part. He knew Jorja couldn't keep her hands off the system and she'd be keeping a close eye on his tax id, so he would just play the "I was sick card" and leave it at that. Then it just dawned on him that Jorja was actually worried about him

● ● ●

Chapter 41

Lynch didn't go back to his office; instead he grabbed an empty seat in the now dubbed war room and was commissioned a top of the line laptop by one of the feds. He was now plugged into their secured network. Garfield gave him the same lesson as Josh had given him and Lynch was up in running in no time. After testing the tires for about thirty minutes he realized the potential of this system and just how unnerving this amount of data can be.

"Hey Josh, Garfield can we take a few minutes to revisit and collaborate? I don't want to waste any time stepping on the same toes now that I'm up to snuff on this system."

"Yeah sure," Garfield quipped.

Josh turned around as well as the two feds who were in the room.

"So is it safe to say that the kid and the Camaro are not our priority, that our effort here is trying to find a man in his late thirties to mid forties with a limp, and that's still the only thing we can go on?"

"That and a badly drawn pencil sketch and our assumption he is located within the LGC and a pedophile," added Josh.

"LGC?"

"Yes. It's a TLA."

"TLA?"

"Three letter acronym . . . . The Lynch and Garfield circle that's what our federal friends here are calling it, there's nothing that deviates us from this mind set."

"So we are concentrating our efforts within the diameter of this circle, that's a twenty-five mile radius, that's a lot of ground, a lot of people . . . . let me see . . . . twenty-five squared, that's six hundred twenty-five, times pi . . . . hmmm that's close to two thousand square miles"

"Like you said a lot of people as well, almost three hundred thousand if you take the average population of a hundred and forty-one people per square mile in our state," calculated Garfield.

"I'm not even going to ask how you knew that. So roughly three hundred thousand. How many registered sex offenders in that area?"

"Two hundred fourteen, with a hundred and thirty-seven of them within Macon alone, of those, fifty-one have been against children, we have their names on our hot list right here, but there is also a good possibility this person is not in that system."

"Point taken, o.k. what do you think is the average number of people who walk with a limp is . . . . one in a hundred, a thousand, less, more?"

"Well we all know this guy probably has walked this way for some time now, the two slated witnesses are almost a year apart, so that means it probably wasn't just a broken leg unless it didn't heal right."

"War injury, birth defect, accident of some sort?"

"Have we looked at the service records for discharges due to injury?"

"Yep, we all have those, only two people fit the bill within that circle but we doubt very much one of these guys is our man, it has been our indication that trained military personal, plain and simple, do not become pedophiles, they are trained to serve and protect," supplied by a fed from the back of the room.

"I never heard of that."

"You could probably count the number on one hand where this has happened in the tri-state area."

"But still . . . ."

"Don't worry we've compiled as much info on these two as possible, just to be safe. We have also thought of the birth defect issue, this one is going to be tricky, especially if he hasn't seen a doctor in years. The early medical records of someone in their forties are pretty much non-existent when it comes to the online world."

"So we are pretty much back at square one."

"Yes back to square one . . . . did you ever wonder where that phrase came from?"

"Hopscotch," answered Garfield to Josh's question.

"Hopscotch?"

"The game with chalk and squares."

"Yeah I know it."

"Well, you always go back to square one."

"You're a wealth of knowledge, that sleep did you well my friend."

"It wasn't knowledge, just a guess, but say it convincingly and people don't question the facts."

"Yeah like a hundred and forty one."

"I'm not questioning the facts in this case because there is very little to go on, do we have any medical records with leg injuries for the past few years," Lynch injected as to get back on track?

"Yes, it's quite a list, there are three major hospitals in that area. We didn't get any from the Atlanta or Columbus regions, since they are outside the LGC. We could if we need to expand the circle at some point but that list is going to be huge."

"O.k., so we have a list of medical records, I'm afraid to ask just how many names are on that list, we have the hot list of sex offenders, the two military personal. Have we crossed checked the fifty-one sex offenders with medical records."

"Yes, no matches."

"What else do we have, how about driver's license?"

"Already checked, we looked for both C and J restrictions."

"Mechanical and prosthetic aids, good, any hits?"

"Just one, on the hot list but we're unable to locate him, we have an unmarked at his current address and we pulled all the relevant data, he's actually a transplant."

"So this could be our bastard? Why wasn't I told about this earlier?"

"He is out of the age range, he's fifty-eight plus nothing really jumps out on his spending habits."

"Right, has a prosthetic and is a registered child sex offender, and just so happens to be within the LGC, that's just way too many coincidences. Where is he transplanted from?"

"Arkansas, and we have already checked police records there, no missing children within the same radius."

"I want to take a look at his priors."

"Here, just one, it was a he said she said type of deal."

"Most always the case is it not?" After a moment of reading the file, "Listen, I want to find this, this James Wartner guy and I don't give a shit how it's done, we'll start by knocking on doors, someone has to know where this guy is."

"Day late and a dollar short," snapped one of the G-men, "GBI is doing just that, the neighbors knew nothing, they checked his place of business and he scheduled the day off, they also started combing through his phone records and calling numbers, and nothing yet."

"I have a strong feeling about this guy."

"We all do."

"Alright I need to bring that kid in here again or closer to home, if we catch this guy I want a positive ID asap, and right now he's the only one who can do it. What else is there besides the prosthetic sex offender, anything else on the plate?"

"All the so-called leads spurred on by the press conference, sixteen markers are located within the LGC, they're represented by a blue pin."

The other G-man from the back of the room spoke, "We are doing cross checking on those sixteen markers as I speak, it is already generating a list of hits that will have to be crossed referenced again. It's a daunting task. Basically we are taking the information called in, such as always shops at this store or always seen in this laundry mat, then we run all the credit card information from those locations through our filters or cross reference files so to speak. Then any hits we may have we'll dive deeper into their files, see what they have purchased, where they have been, who they called."

"You know that's not proper search and seizure etiquette."

"Listen we have heard this before and to a certain degree it has been upheld in court under the Patriot Act, besides if we find the little girl who really is going to mind how we found her?"

"The scum sucking lawyers that's who."

"True but we can't worry about that, our number one goal right now is to find a little girl, find the guy who took her using the best tools at our disposal. If we don't then we are not doing our job. I for one am not going to do this job with both my hands tied behind my back while our digital freedom is being squelched in the courts."

"Our digital freedom? What do you mean by our? This data is not ours, it's mine, it's Garfield's, it's Joe Shmoe's, it's private, private information, just because this information is contained in a file somewhere, it's not yours, it doesn't give you or me the right to see it. Remember I've played with that system of yours and the information on me alone is . . . . is overwhelming, we and I mean we, as officers should have no right to pry into anyone's file just because we can without proper jurisdiction."

"I beg to differ, it's just information like this that will help us in these types of cases and in our fight against terrorism."

"Oh fuck that shit, every time you guys are backed into a corner you throw the fucking T word around. Just because some wackos flew a plane into a building does not give the government a right to peak into everybody's file . . . . into everybody's life."

"I understand where you are coming from, I do, but shouldn't we use the gift horse, especially in this case or should we bring the parents back in here and tell them we couldn't find your little girl because the government is unwilling to question the facts and that's just what these are facts, nothing more."

"Very private facts in most cases"

"True, but with those facts we are trying to tell a story, a true story, it's not like we go in with no just cause. We are just looking for suspects, given the potential data fits our story line. If it doesn't we move on."

Lynch looked at the picture of the little Braves fan once again; he put his conjectures aside and agreed with the man, "You're right, I'm just playing devil's advocate, besides I guess there are plenty of ways to skirt the issues when the time comes for justification."

"You betcha, just a well documented phone call by a quote unquote witness, a few facts, a clue, and we have a solid case."

"That and we'll have all of America on our side screaming for justice, so yeah I can live with taking it away also," quipped Josh.

"Exactly what did you mean by taking away?"

"His right to the fourth amendment, pedophiles such as this goddamn sick twisted bastard should have no rights."

"No fucking rights," Garfield quickly added, "and when he's convicted he'll get what he deserves," knowing all too well what usually happens to child molesters in prison.

"In the meantime I guess now we divide and conquer until we find our newest key suspect," continued Lynch.

"With the help of our system. So let's each of us take a few data markers and do some cross checking. If you right click on a blue pin you can see the option to lock that marker. Once it's locked no one else can claim it, so we won't step on each others' toes. From there you can each do your needed data mining and cross checking. Any names you find that stick out, you can drag and drop them into the box on the lower left-hand side of the screen. These will be global names that will automatically be checked against all of the blue pins by the system. Once a name has been selected, again right click on the name and chose filters. Here you can run any numbers of filters already identified by the FBI such as bought items or you can construct your own. In order to do that, just pick custom and follow the prompts. So easy a first grader can do it. If you have any other questions feel free to ask and remember the answers are probably hidden in plain sight."

"If you can hear me whispering you are dying," Josh added.

"Huh?"

"Pink Floyd, you know the album Dark Side of the Moon, well the song Great Gig in the Sky, the one where they use the human voice as an instrument?"

"Yeah I know it, you don't need to explain, I've been to college."

"Well four minutes thirty-three seconds into the song."

"Four Thirty Three, John Cage, I love that song."

"I meant three," not knowing who the hell John Cage was, "so three thirty three give or take you will hear a woman's voice in the right speaker say, if you can hear me whispering you're dying."

"Right?"

"No seriously."

"Listen I've heard the song hundreds of times and never heard that."

"Same with me but way back when I was listening to the album with headphones at like four in the morning, I was dozing off when I heard it for the first time, it freaked me out but now I hear it plain as day each and every time, hidden in plain sight so to say."

"We're all dying, shorter of breath and one day closer to death."

"Touché," realizing this was a reference to another song on one the most quintessential albums of rock of all time.

"So where were we?"

"Hoping Ripley still has breath," Lynch stated in a sort of grumpy manner since he was already tired of the tangents.

●　●　●

Chapter 42

She felt excited and hot and sexy. She hadn't felt this way in a long, long time. There was never any time. She felt naive and dangerous and sporadic and dumb—dumb because she was at home in her own bedroom, her husband's bedroom, their bedroom for the last twenty-seven years. He could come home any minute but no, his campaigning always, always ran late into the evenings, if people were paying twenty-five thousand a plate for dinner to sit with the future president and his vice president then late into the evening it will be. She wasn't worried, only but a little. She felt ready and vindicated and scared and felt her knees buckle and she felt as if she were in college again. She felt like time moved in slow motion. She felt butterflies in the pit of her stomach. She felt her blouse unbutton and her skirt unzip. She felt her clothes slip off her body and onto the floor. She felt excited and hot and sexy. She felt his hands, his lips, his breath. She felt his strong hands gliding over her back, her shoulders, through her hair, she felt his lips on her lips and at the nape of the neck and back to the lips, she wanted to feel them in other places as well but all in due time. She felt her hands moving over his body, unbuttoning his shirt, unzipping his pants. She felt her lips kissing his lips, his neck, his chest. She felt her hands moving, gliding over his body, not exactly in command, just moving and gliding, not knowing what to expect next. She felt his hands again on her back and she felt her bra unfastened. She felt her breasts exposed and his strong hands cupping them, then his lips kissing them. She felt the air entering her lungs at a faster pace, releasing light moans as the air exited past her lips. She felt excited and hot and sexy. She felt her hands slip under his boxers, kneading and probing. She felt he was ready. She waited. She felt his lips again on her breast, again on her neck. She felt a slight nibble on her ear. She moved her fingers through his chest hair and to his back. She again felt his strong hands on her back and shoulders. She felt him motion towards the bed. She arched her back. She was ready. She felt her head hit her pillow, her body hit her bed. She felt comfortable. She felt scared. She felt his weight between her thighs and she wrapped her arms around his muscular frame. For a brief moment she gazed into his eyes and noticed they were brown, she quickly closed hers as he went down to kiss between her breasts. She felt his teeth on her nipple and a slight playful tug and she felt the same sensation to her other nipple. She took another moment and inhaled through the nose. She smelled his cologne, she smelled his sweat, she smelled him, his odor, she smelled passion. She was ready. She was moist. She felt his hands move towards her legs. She felt the remaining bit of lingerie gently glide past her thighs and ankles. She lifted one leg to help and then she was completely naked. He immediately leaned in for another kiss on the lips, then moved to the neck, then moved lower to the breasts, and then even lower, this time she felt them on her stomach and then her thighs. She couldn't remember the last time anyone did this. She knew where he was headed. She felt his lips again on her stomach and to the outer thigh. She let out another slight moan, then the inner thigh was kissed and another moan slightly louder was given as an acceptance. He understood. She felt her thighs spread even wider and his lips against hers. She ran her fingers through his full head of hair and then arched her back and pushed her pelvis forward ever so slightly, forcing her neck to strain against her pillow. She felt his breath, his lips, and then she felt his tongue. A tingle shot up her spine and a whisper of ecstasy protruded her lips as his tongue protruded deeper inside hers. She let go of his hair. She gripped the sheets, tighter and tighter, she arched herself even more. Her moans grew louder and louder. She was becoming tense with pleasure. She felt his fingers enter her, she felt his tongue caressing her, her, her spot, yes . . . . yes . . . yes, her spot, that spot. She gripped the sheets tighter. Her breath was short and fast. She felt the urge to scream. She felt his tongue, his fingers, his breath. Yes. Almost. Yes. She felt the urge to scream. She clenched her eyelids shut as she tried to take in the moment of sexual intoxication. It didn't work. She sucked in her stomach and arched forward even more. Almost. She couldn't catch her breath. Yes. She gulped for air but couldn't breathe. Yes. She felt his tongue, his fingers, his breath. Her body tensed. Anticipation. She gripped the sheets even tighter. Yes. Yes. She felt the urge to scream. She tried to take in even more air. She felt his tongue, his breath, his tongue, his breath. Yes. She was ready to scream. Yes. She felt. Yes. She felt . . . she felt . . . her mind couldn't grasp the strange sensation at first. It didn't seem real. It didn't seem possible. Not at this time. Not in this place. But it was . . . in an instant. She screamed. She screamed because she felt . . . she felt . . . she felt pain . . . . hot seething pain. Nothing like she ever encountered. Pain. Hot seething pain and before she could take another breath she felt the same pain in her chest and then an instant later her face. She tried to reel her mind around the pain but couldn't. It was too much for her to comprehend. Her last thoughts were that she was in her bed, her husband's bed. And then she felt . . . . she felt . . . . she felt nothing.

●　　●　　●

Chapter 43

The chauffeured limo, car really, Lincoln Towncar to be exact, pulled towards the gate where it patiently waited. After the passcode was entered via a terminal inside the car, they parted to allow passage on the cobble stone driveway. A short ride to the turnabout and the car was parked right in front of the entrance way to the house. The right side passenger door was unlocked, then opened. Mr. Carson exited the car.

"Thanks Bobby. What time tomorrow?"

"8:30, you have a nine o'clock meeting at the Westinghouse"

"That's right, budget meeting, then downtown for lunch, thanks again Bobby, see you tomorrow."

"Tomorrow sir, have a pleasant evening."

With that Bobby waited for the front door to close before he got back into car and headed back out the way he came in. Floyd was already making his way upstairs to expel some of the liquids he had consumed earlier. Afterwards he returned to his office to finish the evening's business. He briefly thought about a glass of water but rejected the idea for something a bit stronger. When he entered his finely appointed office, he turned on his computer and decided on that stronger drink. His bar was stocked with some of the finest liquors the world had to offer but that stuff wasn't for him, only for his guests. He was still feeling some of the effects from tonight's event, the champagne, the wine, all of it gave him a sense of being light on his feet but still very much in control. He didn't need any more of the celebratory toasts with drink from the gods. He was a simple man with simple pleasures and his pleasure tonight was for a bit of southern swill. He went straight for the bourbon, Kentucky bourbon, Knob Creek, single barrel and still under forty dollars a bottle, a real bargain, not to mention one of his relatives somewhere owned a piece of the business. He grabbed a snifter, plain, not the crystal ones he served his guests, and barely put two ounces in the glass. He walked over to his computer sat down in his hand crafted chair, yes he did splurge on this piece of furniture, but from the moment he sat in it he felt a sense of accomplishment, he felt something good could be done while sitting here. He logged onto the network and wanted to check the night's take on campaign funds and jot down a few notes. There were a few ideas that were bounced around during the conversations at dinner that were worth saving. This dinner was one of the most expensive of the campaign but it was not for the faint of heart. If someone wanted to bend the ear of a possible future president and vice president, this was the place. The twenty-five grand just got them in the door, the checkbooks really opened once the one-on-one conversations started. There were only about twenty people invited who ranged from CEO's of computer software companies to bankers and brokers, to billionaires with nothing better to do—it was the elite of the elite. Each guest got to spend some quality time with either of the two famous runners in the room. Most had an idea to pitch but a few just wanted to hob knob and be seen as a player to the others in the room. This place was filled with all sorts of agendas but again there were a few ideas worth noting from educating the poor to illegal aliens and maybe, just maybe one or two of these ideas would make their way to the senate floor. After all, to this crowd it was nothing more than money.

Before he entered his password, he picked up his snifter and took a long deep whiff. This always enhanced the first sip; it prepared his mouth for the taste that was to follow. The first sip always stung his taste buds, even with the sense of smell still lingering in the back of his throat. It was like they never had the pleasure of meeting this bourbon before, which was a down and out lie . . . they did many many times but he did enjoy this feeling. Once the first sip was down the memory came back to his taste buds and from there on out it was pure heaven. He took a second sip and let it linger even little bit longer, the swirl, the swish; he could now taste the south, the oak barrels, the grains, the craftsmanship of his favorite drink. It warmed the throat even more. He placed the snifter on his desk, savored the flavor, and logged into his computer. He went straight to the secured file share and opened a spreadsheet dated for this evening. There in alphabetical order was a list of the contributors and more important their pledge amounts were already entered by some of his coordinators during his ride home. The total was at the bottom—a nice take, a nice take indeed. From just these twenty people the total from this night alone was in the neighborhood of thirty-five million dollars, well over a million dollars per, with the most bang for the buck coming from the CEO of the software company with more than 5.5 million in a-hem, donations. Whatever he was pitching, he sat with Mr. Anderson, there would be much more discussions to come. Within this spreadsheet there was room to jot down a few notes so Floyd opened his little black book. Floyd was a well minded individual and was very attentive to the people giving him charitable donations so he took notes on every conversation be it a single word, a sentence or two, and sometimes a paragraph or two along with a name and time. He did have a good memory but the more people he talked to the more the conversations blended together; this was his tool for keeping things straight. Before proceeding on entering his notes, he glanced at the clock, just after twelve and all things considering, it was an early evening, he then glanced at his book to find his first entry for the evening. He had a hard time finding it as his eye sight was beginning to take its toll from the libations he had consume throughout the evening. He took off his glasses and rubbed his eyes, that didn't work, never does, so he got up and decided he'd better have that water now. He made his way over to the mini fridge in the bar of his office and opened a bottled water. He was all of a sudden parched. He unscrewed the cap and gulped the first quarter of the bottle. The cool water was refreshing to say the least. He made his way back to the desk with bottle in hand and sat down in his comfy chair again. He glanced at the screen and this time his eyes seemed worse, another rub, and still no difference. He then closed them for a brief second and that was the finishing touch on his evening.

• • •

Chapter 44

If it wasn't for the amount of blood in the bed the scene looked like a set from a porn movie. Camera flashes going off everywhere, clothes strewn across the floor everywhere, and two bodies laid in the bed but not in your typical missionary position. Hell no, nothing like that, let's just say she was getting the better end of the deal at that moment in time. His bloody head was buried in her thighs. A single gunshot was to the back of his head at seemingly close range—it looked like a professional hit. Her chest had a bullet entry as well as her head but the head shot was not a clean one, not as clean as the guy's, and not nearly as professional. The bullet entered just over the right lip, through the teeth and out the left side just below the ear. It was literally a stomach churning experience even for the not so faint at heart. There was even a gunshot to the left of her face that hit nothing but pillow. They took more pictures before they pulled the bodies off the bed to get them ready to be taken for further investigating at the morgue. they dusted for prints, they measured distances, they looked for anything out of the ordinary, they combed the bed for body fluids, body hairs, as with most crime scene investigators they left no stone unturned, especially one as high as a profile as this one.

"TOD?"

"Between eleven and one from the liver temps."

"Can't do any better?"

"Nope, sorry, air condition seems to be cranked up a bit that could have an effect on the outcome"

"COD?"

"Isn't it obvious?"

"Come on, you know in this line of work, nothing's obvious, any sense of struggle beforehand, strangulations, erotic asphyxiation, anything?"

"From what I could tell the cougar and her prey were having a good time . . . more like great time before this happened."

"Cougar? More like saber."

"Saber?"

"Yeah like saber tooth tiger, you know because she's way older than the typical fortyish cat, fast approaching extinction."

"Call TBS because that's funny . . . . so where was I . . . . yeah . . . there was no semen in the, in the condom yet unless this was his second go around but we haven't found any evidence of the first, usually it's somewhere close, so again my opinion at the present time is they were in throws of passion."

"Well he certainly was in the throes of pussy."

"What a way to go hey?"

"If that was the last thing I saw on the way out . . . put it this way, that's a great memory to take with you to the afterlife."

Yeah, I could see it now, standing at the pearly gates and Saint Peter asking you . . . what's the last thing you remember?"

They both had a slight chuckle on that one even though it was twisted and sick, good thing nobody else heard them.

"Hard to say which shot was first," as they were looking at the crime scene photos on a portable laptop.

"I'd say, pillow, her face, chest, then his head, from top to bottom."

"Okay, but wouldn't you hear the bang and move your head out of that position"

"Silencer?"

"I'd buy that but the pain from her face being hit would send her thrashing and even in rapid session, he'd still have time to move some. No, I think the chest shot was first, then his head shot. If he was shot first she would have felt the bullet enter her and that shot would have not been fatal causing even greater momentum from her."

"Sure, I see that, but what about the face and pillow shots, just to make sure."

"That's what I would think, the pillow shot was a miss, then the second to the head as a precautionary measure"

"Any sign of break in?"

"None"

"Murder weapon?"

"None found yet but the bullet dug out from beneath the bed from the pillow shot looks to be from a 9mm, we'll know more once back at the lab"

Mr. Carson sat motionless and speechless in his office since the police entered the house. The housemaid stumbled upon the two upstairs just around 7 a.m. Usually Mr. and Mrs. Carson were up by now having breakfast in the kitchen but breakfast was already being made and still no sign of either of them. She went upstairs to investigate. She saw no signs of stirring. She knocked, she questioned, she knocked again. She went from room to room and nothing. She remembered no special orders in regarding the morning. She remembers Mrs. Carson dismissing her just before six and she remembers hearing Mr. Carson come home but that was it. So she knocked again, harder this time, and still no answer. The bedroom door was slightly ajar so she entered and again she asked for Mrs. Carson and again no reply. She was in the sitting room just before the bedroom. When she entered the bedroom she found her answer. She didn't scream. She just stood in disbelief. Shock took over instantly. Her eyes couldn't focus on the site before her. She didn't recognize either of the bodies, she didn't want to, she just stood there in silence, her mind wheeling trying to get a grip but just couldn't. After a moment or two she picked up the portable phone and dialed 911 unaware Mr. Carson was still asleep in his downstairs office. The cops found her in the bedroom with her eyes closed gripping the receiver not far away from the two bodies.

Mr. Carson awoke with a splitting headache and to sounds of sirens, very loud sirens right outside his window. He peered out to see a few police cars and an ambulance. Before he could do anything two uniformed officers were in his office. He was unable to focus on the situation at hand.

"Sir are you alright?"

"Ummm, excuse me . . . . what?"

"Are you alright?"

"Yes, I think so, why . . . . why are you here?"

"We got a 911 call from this address."

"No, no, we're okay . . . . what time is it?"

"Seven-fifteen."

"My wife, my wife should be in the kitchen."

Then from somewhere upstairs a voice echoed, "up here," and one officer went in search of the location of the voice.

Mr. Carson jumped from his now uncomfy chair and proceeded to try to make his way upstairs before being succumbed by the remaining officer.

"It's best if you stayed here, sir."

"But . . ."

"Please, sir, we have no idea . . . ."

"But I have to see if Grace is okay."

"Please wait sir."

Waited he did, and then a pit fell in his stomach and he felt nauseous, like something really bad was about to come. He waited for what seemed like forever with no one talking to him, no one saying a word. It was though he was waiting for the head of surgery to come in and give him some really bad news of the terminal kind. Another ten minutes had passed when two other cars entered the driveway. That pit in his stomach was very much real now and he was about to vomit for he noticed from his office window that one of the cars was marked coroner. He prayed in silence it was not his Gracie, he hoped it was Robin his long time housemaid.

A detective was now on the scene and in the office.

"Mr. Carson, Detective Ron Synder, can I ask you a few questions? . . . . Mr. Carson?"

Floyd just sat there wanting to vomit, wanting to scream, wanting to cry, wanting to, to, to do something, but not one of his bottled up feelings could escape. His brain was trying to wrap some sense into this situation, trying to comprehend the unthinkable, trying to imagine his last memory of Grace, her voice, her face . . . . he couldn't. He just sat in silence while his emotions froze.

"Mr. Carson, approximately what time did you arrive home last night?"

"I . . . . I . . . . I don't . . . . can I see her? Is it my Grace? Is it my wife?, Please say no . . . please."

"I'm . . . . I am very . . . . sorry that I have to be the one to tell you this . . . . very sorry sir, Mrs. Carson was found upstairs . . . . shot twice . . . murdered."

Those words echoed in his brain but they didn't make sense, shot? Murdered?

"She was murdered sometime between eleven and one and what time did you say you came home sir?"

No answer. He just sat there with a blank expression as a vivid memory entered his mind as if it were yesterday—a memory of his Gracie walking down the aisle dressed in white, with her hair done up just so, her red lips parted in the biggest of smiles showing her perfectly aligned sparking set of whites . . . she was strikingly beautiful. Then he remembered reading her lips, and hearing her voice utter those immortal words "I do." He started to shake as his emotions were beginning to surface, then the first tear, and that was it, he lost it.

Detective Synder was not one for emotions, yet somehow he felt sympathy when watching this grown man cry. He did not ask any other questions at this time.

Mr. Carson gathered his composure after about fifteen minutes. He grabbed the bottled water that was left out on his desk and drank in the now room temperature water . . . it was vile but did the trick. Still silent Mr. Carson sat and stared at the spectacle gathering in his driveway. There were more policemen, even the news was on scene, and then he noticed Bobby pulled towards the gate right on time. Then he notice a black body bag being placed into the coroner's vehicle . . . he knew it contained his beloved but this time he held back the tears. Then he noticed another black body bag being placed into the same vehicle. Then his mind started spinning.

Blair Anderson watched in horror as the familiar stone facade was shown on the screen of his study's T V. He himself couldn't comprehend the scene. There were a ton of speculations from various reports but no true facts as of yet. His wife was upstairs getting ready for the day and oblivious as to what was happening at the Carson's residence. The phone rang.

"Yes."

"Blair are you watching this?"

"Yes, anybody try calling Floyd?"

"No answer, what do you suppose is happening?"

"I have no fucking clue but we need to get everyone together and fast . . . . did you see that?"

"What?"

"This doesn't look good . . . not at all, I just saw two body bags being placed into the coroner's vehicle . . . . this isn't good."

"Do you think it was Floyd and Grace?"

"Jesus, I don't know what to think . . . . god no . . . not them, not now . . . ."

Although his immediate concern was for the Carsons, He'd be lying if he didn't think about the elections, with his top notch sidekick who was more popular then he was, his bid for the white house would end here. He had to find out what was going on and do it fast.

"Okay, send Eric to the house and the rest of the gang come here, I want everybody here by ten after, you got that?" and hung up the phone, then he went in search of his wife to fill her in.

At the exact time Blair was trying to piece together what he saw, across town in the president's study; news was coming in at a rapid pace. The President already had confirmed two deaths, one to Mrs. Carson and the other at the moment is still a John Doe. He gathered his papers, jotted down a few notes, and went directly to the cabinet room just off the oval office. In Washington things happen fast, the room was full with only one key member missing . . . . Scott but he was in route. The President didn't wait.

"People, Mrs. Carson and an unknown were found murdered in the master bedroom with what appears to be a torrid affair."

The room fell silent; none of them had that much detail, and most assumed it was both Carsons.

"The Press is going to have a field day and all sorts of speculations and rumors are going to surface. We need to cover every detail, no stone unturned."

"Mr. President," William Briddle, press secretary, spoke "This could go either way for the election, sympathetic ears might sway towards Anderson, that is unless Floyd killed them but even if he didn't do it he might be too much of a head case to continue and we all know that Floyd was the main event."

Just then Scott walked in, sat down in his regular seat and without missing a beat, injected "What if they try to pin this on our presidency?"

"Excuse me," the President bellowed.

"Exactly what I said, we have to cover all angles which I assumed you already said, well the one angle that scares the shit out of me, is the angle that we had something to do with it."

"If that rumor somehow escaped this meeting that stone will gather moss quickly, we could forget staffing this office in the next election, and probably any republicans in any following for an awfully long time," voiced the Press Secretary.

"By the way Scott, it was not angles but stones," as the President glared in his direction with somewhat of a hidden meaning, "and yes we need to cover our tracks in that direction as well."

"We need to come up with a statement for you, a sincere condolence, and as soon as possible."

"True but the American public doesn't even know what happened yet."

"Mr. President, that cat just got out of the bag as we speak, CNN."

"Start writing Kathy, okay we have seventy-six days until the election, we have a campaign that is on the ropes, we have a lot to do, we'll meet back in here at eleven, I want a speech, I want as many answers as possible, I want solutions . . . and Scott I want you in my office now . . . and Stacy cancel everything on my plate for the next three days at least."

With that the President lifted from his center chair and made his way to the door with Scott in tow. The oval office was his place of business, he immediately walked in and the door was shut just as Scott entered.

"Please tell me Scott, you, you had nothing to do with this."

"Not one iota."

"Don't fucking lie to me, remember a few months ago when we watched the rest of the Georgetown game?"

"Yes, certain words were spoken."

"Yes, indeed they were, so I ask you one more time."

"Jonathan, I would not jeopardize this or any future presidency."

"Don't fucking call me Jonathan in this office, you got that, in here you address me as President, and I'd be goddamn spitting nails if, if . . .'

"Mr. President, just for the record, if I had done anything, wait, here me out, would you really want the answers? Would you really want to be involved?"

●　　●　　●

Chapter 45

Armed with a bit more knowledge each of the officers locked a few pins and went about their way. Lynch was still dumbfounded with the amount of data one could obtain. His first marker was a well known supermarket chain of the south located just outside of Macon. He hit their database with ease and pulled out over three thousand people who were registered for one of those money savings bar code cards. It's these cards that entice the shopper with extra savings and all one needs to do is supply their name, address, and a phone number in order to reap the rewards of a preferred customer. This of course, tracks each individual's buying power, their complaint ratios, their coupon use, along with the typical what and when they buy. The feds had already pulled the same data and were crossing checking the already fore-mentioned data; Lynch was just playing in his new sandbox. He then pared down the number by gender and age—two hundred twenty-six, the same exact number the feds received. He then did a side-bar query and found seventy-eight percent of the card holders were women. "No surprise there," he thought. He then dragged the men's names into the lower left-hand box and applied the filter for their buying habits with the itemized list of buying goods that some hot-shot PhD holder back in Washington cooked up for child molesters. The list had everything from Cap'n Crunch and Sugar Puffs to Jello, KY Jelly, children's Robitussin, to M & M's and Tootsie Rolls. It wasn't surprising that almost ninety-five percent of the males in this group had purchased at least one of these items at one time or another. Lynch pared down the list of males even more by eliminating fatherhood and still over sixty-five percent of the males were on the list. He then started to check items manually; anything with a high sugar content was his first order of business. He was able to do so in groups like cereal and candy and still his numbers were rather high. Then he sat back and questioned his methodology. He realized he was on a spiral downward picking and choosing the right combination of items that a typical pedophile would buy—the permutations were almost endless. He needed a new plan of attack—just what exactly was he looking for . . . . just a name is all he wanted, a name linked to a limp. Once he had a name he then could drill down to the nitty-gritty and pick apart the life of a soulless sicko.

He started over.

Lynch realized the marker was because a man who fit the description was seen in this location/store, so he just had to find the real name of Mr. Limpy. The name just might be in the list of three thousand or so people who carried those cards, more specifically the two hundred and twenty six males between the ages of thirty-five and fifty who carried the store's savings card. Now he was getting the hang of it. He cross checked these individuals with the medical files, then he did the same against the in-store pharmacy's database. No hits. He did the same against the registered sex offenders even though this had already been done by the feds. Still no hits. He pulled the credit and debit card files. Again he pared down the number by gender and age, the list was a bit larger this time, over five hundred give or take. Within seconds he found three individuals that had medical records for leg injuries. Now he was getting somewhere. He clicked on the names and dragged them to the lower left-hand box as he was told. Now he had three names to work with, "so let the games begin," raced through his mind with the inflection of a sports commentator.

He read their medical records. Two of the men had recent injuries, within the past two months. The other had a hip replacement and at such an early age, thirty-four. The date of his surgery was nineteen months ago placing him well within the range of the abductions which had a witness. For now he put the first two men on the back burner and concentrated his efforts on Mr. Hippy, a.k.a. Brian Sheldon. Almost on command Lynch had a screen full of data at his finger tips, everything from Brian's brokerage accounts to his Food and Wine subscription. It told a story of a one half the member of a DINK household—married, spouse has a great job, no rug rats. It seemed pretty straight laced, with the one exception of a mistress account from a bank in California, probably not for his mistress if he even had one, just a tidy sum tucked away from the old ball and chain for rainy days or after the divorce whichever came first. The more he read on Mr. Sheldon, the more he seemed consumed with money and more importantly not with children being he had a little snip snip just three weeks ago. Like Brian's sperm he was dead in the water on this so called suspect so Lynch moved on. After bringing up information on the other two men with battered legs he needed to look elsewhere. The supermarket pin had nothing more to offer. The next pin was a Home Depot store which he had locked earlier. Before he clicked the pin he got up from the table and walked out the room. He was back with coffee in hand and then picked up his yellow pad. He glanced at it again and reread the notes from yesterday. "Damn it . . . . son of a . . . ," he said under his breath. He never did a follow up on Terry Farnsworth, Lindsay Newenburg's ex. He had a new tool, he had a new suspect, he then entered him into the prompt and was just about to hit return when . . . .

"Hey Lynch, Jim Warner is here to see you."
   "Who the hell is that?"
   "The prosthetic sex offender you just wanted rounded up."
   "Boy, my boys are good," saying like a proud father in the war room.
   "He came under his own accord."
   "Set him up, I'll be right there," saying as if he was a little deflated in front of the guys.

Everyone in the room stopped what they were doing and filed out of the war room, everybody except Josh.

•   •   •

271

Chapter 46

At the same time everyone else was finding out today's events so too was Jorja. She too was already in the office and logged onto the network. She immediately got a high priority popup on her desktop that hid all her open applications. The time was 7:07. It was marked Carson Residence. Each congressman, be it senator, or representative, judge, and political well doers, if they live in Washington or the surrounding area, was logged into a special 911 directory. They didn't have to compete with the daily crime rate of D.C. and be waited on by close to minimum wage, barely trained operators—it was just another added perk to being an elected official.

Jorja's heart skipped a beat when she read "Carson Residence". The message contained the entire 911 transcript from this morning's call that ended only three minutes ago. It also contained a direct link to the actual call. She clicked on the link and turned up her volume.

"911 operator, please state the emergency."
    "Yes . . . . uh, uh . . . this is . . . this is . . . Robin."
    "You are calling from the Carson's residence?"
    "Yes . . . . Mrs . . . Mrs . . . Carson is dead."
    "Dead?"
    "Yes . . . . there's lots of blood . . . . she isn't moving."

"I'm sending officers to the scene now . . . Robin do you understand, do you or anyone else need medical attention?

"Uh . . . . uh."

"Robin . . . . Robin are you still there?"

That was the extent of the call. She replayed it. Again. Again. She heard Robin's all too familiar voice. She heard her say Mrs. Carson is dead. Aunt Gracie is dead. She tried to gather her composure. Her mind was caught between personal and business; caught in a conundrum. She hadn't envisioned this scenario before . . . she was always planning, always preparing for the future but this caught her off guard. For a few minutes she collected herself, then she went to the alert system and punched in the distribution list simply entitled "now". This list contained her goto-guys in the event of a crisis situation. four names total . . . her messages read—'if you're in the office, my office now". Within thirty seconds both Tom and Bill were in Jorja's office.

"I need you two to keep me covered, keep me posted," knowing all too well they each received the 911 transcripts.

"Where are you going?"

"Where do you think . . . . I'm going over there."

"Is that such a good idea?"

"I need to, you know that . . . I have to see my uncle . . . see if he's okay . . . he's all I got left."

With that she was out the door and just about to pass Greg.

"Sorry, I was in the server room."

"I need you to do the digging, find out everything . . . everything you can," and with that she was in the elevator heading down. Her mind was now in full gear. Thinking. Remembering. Thinking. She was thinking on the best route with morning traffic, remembering the last time she truly saw her aunt happy, she was thinking about the 911 call, thinking about her daily agenda, remembering if she had any important meetings scheduled, thinking about the what if's, what if there is another crisis today, what if her uncle was dead too, what if . . . Before she knew it she was already in the car and in route when her phone rang. It was Greg.

"Yes?"

"Listening to the D.C. finest in blue's play by play, crime scene squad, coroner, and detectives are in route. There are two bodies."

"Uncle Floyd," with a shuttle in her voice?

"No, he's alive and okay, found downstairs in his study . . . second victim is a John Doe at the moment. Appears to be in bed with Grace. They were both shot . . . that's all I have but I'm working on a timeline for you."

Click. Thinking. Remembering. Thinking.

On the drive over she started to tear up. She remembered her aunt Grace's face plain as day, she remembered helping to stuff the turkey on her big island in the kitchen, she remembered sleeping over, waking up early and walking in the gardens to pick flowers for the kitchen table. She remembered her aunt's voice as she used to sing Ray Charles' Georgia, to her. She remembered all the good times, mostly because there were rarely any bad times with her aunt. She remembered her aunt as being the only female that was there for her, when she had her first period, had her first kiss, even when she lost her virginity to her long time college boyfriend, Jay Simpson. When she remembered that fact she had to dry her cheeks and laugh a bit, only now did she get the irony of being inundated with Simpsons quotes from Greg.

It took her just over an hour to reach her uncle's house and there was already a circus parked in his driveway. She saw the coroner's car and Bobby's town car. There were no additional phone calls. She was just about to call for a much needed status report when she saw her Uncle from behind the window. She flashed her badge and walked around the uniformed officer and into the much too familiar hallway. Again she flashed her credentials to yet another uniformed officer but this time she was denied. The door to the study was closed and she knew Uncle Floyd was being questioned. She turned back towards the hallway to find someone in charge and she spotted Bobby in the living room sitting patiently as he always does.

"Bobby."

He stood up to meet Jorja. "Jorja, what's going on? They told me to sit tight and don't leave."

"Did they question you yet?"

"About what?'

"Anything."

"No, I have no idea what's happening . . . . I was supposed to take Mr. Carson to the Westinghouse for an eight thirty meeting."

"What time did you bring him back last night?"

"Pretty early . . . I'd say right before twelve, he wanted to get a good night's sleep for this meeting, he didn't want to leave last night's dinner too early but he had to."

"Who was the meeting with today?"

"Don't know but like I said it seemed important . . . can you tell me what happened . . . is he okay?"

"Aunt Gracie . . . my Aunt Gracie," as she took a long pause as to not really believing what she was about to say, "was found dead this morning."

Bobby sat back down and Jorja grasped his shoulder in a very loving way. She left Bobby to his memories for he had known Grace and Floyd for the better part of ten years now and they treated him like family as they did with all their help. With that Jorja went to seek out the person in charge when her phone chirped.

"What have you got?"

"Just speculation at the moment, nothing solid, but police reports and rumors are saying T.O.D. was between eleven and one."

"I just learned that Bobby, the driver, dropped Uncle Floyd off at just before twelve which makes him a prime suspect."

"Jesus . . . you think he did something like this?'

"No, no way in hell but . . . ."

"But what?"

"I'm thinking . . . . do you know if he called anyone yet?"

"Hold on . . . . no outgoing calls, a few incoming . . . . same for his cell."

"Gotta run," and Jorja punched in a new number, as she was listening to the ringing in her blue tooth adapter, she heard a phone ring from her other ear.

"Calling someone?"

As Jorja spun around she saw Eric Riedal, the owner of the last question and Mr. Carson's confidant, one of his best friends, and most important at this time, his lawyer.

Jorja clicked cancel on her cell and Eric's phone stopped ringing.

"No one in particular . . . . . they won't let me in."

"Come with me."

Even though Jorja's credentials are top notch, there are certain situations which they are out of their realm . . . . criminal investigation in the downtown District of Columbia is one of them unless they involved Homeland Security or terrorists in one shape or another. Murder was simply a crime so it was bestowed upon Eric's credentials to get them past the door of the study, where a simple remark was all that was needed. "Yes, I'm Mr. Carson's lawyer."

Upon just glancing at Jorja, Floyd began to tear up once again. No words were spoken and a much needed hug was granted. He hugged her tight and still didn't say a word. Jorja herself was beginning to tear as she glanced at a picture of her aunt on the desk. Then she broke the silence and the hug.

"You okay?"

"Your Aunt Gracie is dead, that's all I know . . . . there was another body bag, another . . . another, someone else with her . . . . I don't know."

"We'll figure it out just for now be calm."

"What have you told them," asked Eric?

"Nothing much, just that I came home around twelve and fell asleep in the study, woke up to cars pulling in my driveway."

"Not to alarm you but they are putting the time of death somewhere between eleven and one which means you might have been home at the time this happened," mentioned Jorja.

"So I'm the prime suspect?"

"Probably so, did they do anything to you while they questioned you?"

"They swabbed me for gunshot residue and took a DNA swab, that was about it. Right now I'm sure the D.A. is fielding the evidence to see if they have enough to hold me."

"Exactly where is your gun?"

"Locked in the gun safe."

"Speaking of which," said a main with papers in his hand standing in the doorway of the study, "we have a warrant to search the premises for that very gun. We understand that it is a nine millimeter."

Eric spoke up, "Papers please," read them and nodded. With that Floyd Carson unlocked his gun safe, and handed the man a box containing his handgun, a nine millimeter.

● ● ●

Chapter 47

"Pictures. Goddamn fucking pictures was what it was supposed to be," was the notion echoing through Scott's mind, "How in the world did Reynolds fuck this up?" He went to his office, slammed the door shut and flipped his cell. He dialed Reynolds' number and waited. It went straight to voicemail.

"Listen, call me asap, not later today, not in a few, call me right fucking now, you got that?," in one of his most demanding tones. He then sat at his desk and logged into the network but was so pissed-off he couldn't concentrate. Within a few minutes his phone rang. It was Reynolds. He saw the last incoming number and dialed it immediately, never listening to the voicemail message.

"Where are you and why didn't you answer?"
    "I'm heading to the rotten apple, I must have been in a bad cell, why, what's up?"
    "You haven't heard? Not listening to the news?'"
    "No, I'm listening to an audio book, it's"
    "I couldn't give a shit, right now you're up to your goddamn eyeballs, Grace Carson was murdered last night."

"What?," as Reynolds tried to comprehend that Grace Carson was dead, he quickly signaled for the shoulder and came to a dead stop along the New Jersey Turnpike somewhere between exits 7 and 7A

"Grace Carson was found dead in her home, found by her housemaid, she was murdered somewhere between eleven and one but I suppose you're going to say you have no fucking idea how this happened."

"I don't, I'm just . . . I just I don't know."

"There was another victim as well."

"Who? Not Floyd?"

"No not Floyd, they are still working on it, right now he's just a John Doe."

"I swear to you, I have no idea how this happened, I knew we were getting close but . . ."

"Hold on a sec," as he was reading a priority one message," they identified the John Doe, does Blake Linge ring any fucking bells?"

"Jesus Christ!"

"This Blake, who is he?"

"He was the bait, Blake Remus actually, good guy, worked with him for a few years now, I just don't understand how this happened."

"Who was your handler?"

"It was going to be Lieutenant Colonel John Smith, retired marine, special ops."

"John Smith?'

"Most common name in the book, never had a problem with him, followed my every command to the letter. He's done just about every type of covert operation there is and then some. Like I said I was going to use him but we never placed him into action."

"And you said you didn't get anything from Blake."

"I didn't say, but right, nothing, if he was over at the Carson's residence then he was pretty damn close to his objective. It's not like either one of these guys would go off the reservation."

"We need to find answers and find them fast, JW is breathing down my neck."

"I'm turning around now, I'll touch base with the office and let them know I'm coming."

"Wait, where exactly are you?"

"Five or sixth miles from seven a."

Scott then pushed a few keys and brought up a map on his monitor, "okay, get to McGuire's, I'll arrange transportation for you from there, we need to save as much time as possible and you need to get me answers asap."

Dial tone was all that Reynolds could hear. As he keyed in the location of McGuire's Air Force Base into his trusty GPS device, Scott was in his office keying in the numbers to the head honcho there in order to arrange Reynolds' transportation back to D.C. When the office of the Commander in Chief calls, people listen. Reynolds would be in the lobby of the Beta Group in under ninety minutes if all goes well.

After arranging transportation, he then went to the military's database and entered the common name John Smith luckily attaching retired Marine Lieutenant Colonel to the name wasn't so common. He received a plethora of information, even the fact that he was deceased as of forty-eight months ago but understood that this was the requisite for a black op of his caliber. He then keyed in John Smith's tax id into the system and came up empty which prompted another phone call.

"Yeah it's me, I have a question for you, I have the name of a deceased marine, John Smith, he was a Lieutenant Colonel. Born in Baton Rouge."

"Yeah I see you queried him, so?"

"Answer me this, is he truly dead or just off the grid?"

"Good question give me a minute," which was a mere forty-five seconds later, "he is or was, special ops, blackest of blacks."

"So shouldn't we have an eye on him if he is still alive, we should know at least where he is, there is no record whatsoever of him in the system."

"You are correct, every dark op can and should be seen by us. I take it this has something to do with this morning's events?"

"I'm just trying to find out as much info for the big guy."

"Well I've been digging as well, that name didn't come up in any of my searches, neither did the name in the last priority one, Blake Linge, it was Blake Remus and it looks like he was undercover as well, well in more ways than one."

"Interesting . . . . but see if you can find this John Smith, whatever it takes."

"How about this Remus guy?"

"Well, I don't think he's going anywhere, I think the priority here is to find this Smith character and why he's not in the system."

"And why should this John Smith mean something?"

"I don't know, it was given to me by JW."

"I'm on it . . . I'll let you know what I find."

Just like with the shootings at the mall Scott didn't have time to dig for answers, he had his inside man do that. He needed the time to piece together a cover story, something to keep the president off his back. The fact that Reynolds' inside man was off the grid made matters worse. Scott's only involvement was he wanted to invoke a scandal with Mrs. Carson and he had asked for Reynolds' help. In turn Reynolds hired Blake Linge aka Blake Remus for the seduction piece of the plan. From there things get a little dicey, the said black ops guru and in this case, the photographer, aka John Smith, is off the grid and both Blake and Grace have been murdered. It wasn't much to go on and Scott knew the man with the plan was either the hero or the goat and in this case the coals in the roasting pit were prime for his soon to be rotating dead carcass.

● ● ●

Chapter 48

Greg did as he promised and piecemealed together as much information as he thought Jorja would require. He found Blake Remus age thirty-eight and with a little digging he uncovered much about this single man. He was an employee of the Beta Group of D.C., which was software consultant company that QA'd major applications for various governments before they were released into official use. Blake graduated from Georgetown with a three point three three in mathematics and never went for his masters. He was recruited for his logical skills by the Beta Group when they were in their infancy stage and never really moved along with his peers into upper management; he stayed the course of a business analyst, probably because he liked to travel. He traveled the world on their dime. Within the past month he was in Indonesia and before that Warsaw and Zurich, in fact over his fifteen year stint with the company there wasn't many places on this blue marble he hadn't visited. His passport was constantly in the shop for adding more pages to it. He drove a nice car and had a nice condo in a pretty wealthy neighborhood. He was a typical white collar middle of the road single kind of guy. What he was doing in the political circle and more importantly in the bed of Grace Carson would take a deeper drill bit.

With Greg's new toy, penetrating the sedimentary rock of the data world was quite simply a piece of three layer chocolate cake, though he still had to take the precautionary measures before dialing into the machine Jorja had nicknamed God's Eyes. A click here, a click there, and even Greg was amazed and that always took a lot to do. So why was Grace Carson shacking up with a BA from the Beta Group? Where did they meet? That was really his top priority. He quickly formed a timeline and tried to find their first meeting. Through cross references he found two weeks prior to their death they were together at the JW Hotel near the white house. Before he jumped to any conclusions he brought up the hotel guest list from that evening along with the hotel's booked functions. There was a political benefit for Mr. Carson and neither Blake nor Grace booked a room. He searched again and found the JW Hotel was not their first encounter but again the question arose as to why Blake was on the political radar, he has yet to vote in any elections, and seems to have no influential ties to a party affiliate. He had the uncanny idea that this was not a chance meeting. He then checked phone records and email services. Nothing on the phone records. Email was a tad more difficult to obtain. The Beta Group wasn't part of the In-Q-Tel links so those systems couldn't be hacked as easily, it wasn't impossible, it would just take some time. Before Greg took that road his search came up with another possibility. They both had a gmail account, which isn't unusual, since gmail had a wealth of users but since this was an internet based email system Greg was able to slide past the security features like a bowling shoe over the maple flooring, quite simply there was a relationship with the people at Google when the government needed help. What he found after his peeking into these accounts were his answers as to why. There were about a hundred seventy or so email exchanges between the two parties, each one becoming more and more intimate. The first several were simple exchanges between two strangers, exchanging conversations based on a breast cancer walk. The move from Blake's non existing sister Melissa to Mrs. Carson was subtle to say the least. This then moved from friendly talk to flirtatious speak, and later towards a more romantic boundary. Pictures were exchanged along with much personal stories of their past. Greg found stories of Jorja interlaced within Grace's emails. He read them with much interest. Blake's emails were well written but didn't seem genuine for one reason or another. The more he read the more he could see Blake was baiting her like a spider spinning a web.

Blake was a good writer, writing mostly of his thoughts on the road and how his heart ached for he has really never loved.

From: Grace [mailto:grace@carsons.com]
To: Blake
Subject: Re:The Walk

Blake—

I found your story very sad and heart touching. I too am lonely at times, well quite frankly most of the time. I have felt true love once and that was in college when I fell in love with my husband. He was a passionate man in both his ideas and goals and need I say, within the sheets.

As his career started to take off I felt left behind. Sure there are still good times to be had but they are few and far between. I feel the daily droll of life is taking a beating on me I wish I could change things. I do not have the power to do so. My urges are strong at this point in my life but I can count on one hand the times we have made love or had sex since my forties had started . . . AND THAT WAS WAY TOO LONG AGO!!! I'm tired of the game that seems never to end, tired of this being the good wife while I wither away into nothingness.

It took several hours for Greg to read each and every email. It was like a good novel that was written over the time span of six months. Greg knew it was a setup and it was interesting how Blake handled himself as he waited for just the right time to spring into action. But then Greg thought, sure this was Blake's plan to seduce Mrs. Carson, the woman of maybe the next vice president, the aunt of his dearest Jorja . . . but why?

He pulled the timeline of Blake right up until his death, and he pulled Grace's as well. He entered the house somewhere between 8:30 and 8:35; though in his last email message to her he was expected around eight. For the next few hours the two dots on the screen were inseparable up until their last transmission. Greg then honed in on the man now in question . . . Senator Carson himself. His suspicion grew when the timeline coincided by place and time of both murders. He was at his dinner but came home just before 11:30. He was home for roughly five to ten minutes before the bed was stained with blood but never did all three dots overlap.

There is that missing window of five minutes which is ample time to do the deadly deed but not enough evidence to say otherwise. At 11:45 Blake and Grace were in the bedroom, the senator was in his office. At 11:50 only one dot was active and it was Senator Carson in his office. Somewhere between those two time stamps the murders occurred and anyone could see why Virginia's elected official was the prime suspect.

●　●　●

Chapter 49

Jorja called Greg into her office. She had just come back from seeing her uncle and she was standing beside her desk looking out the window.

"You okay," he asked

"Sort of . . ."

"Why did you come back? You need to take some time."

"It's just that I need . . . I need . . . . ," and with that her eyes filled with tears and she grabbed a tissue from the box. Greg really didn't know what to do; he felt very uncomfortable but approached her anyway. He put his hand on her back but she quickly turned around and fell into his arms. He hugged her, he had no choice, and he didn't say a word. He just thought.

"I'm sorry Greg, you don't need to be here right now," and she pulled away almost as in disgust.

"Jorja, listen, I'm here for you, we're friends."

"I know, I know . . . I thank you for that but really . . . ," and she dried her eyes and changed gears like a formula one racecar, "Did you find out anything . . . I mean through GE?"

"I found a bunch of information on Blake Linge."

"That was his name?"

"Not exactly, and by that I mean the police report now states Blake Linge, but his social is tied to a Blake Remus in the system, he was thirty-eight, single"

"A lot younger than my Aunt."

"Worked at a company called Beta Group."

"I heard of them."

"Well anyway, he seemed to have had some sort of agenda, I found a bunch of gmails back and forth between your aunt and him . . . pretty personal stuff at times."

"What do you mean hidden agenda?"

"You'll have to read them, it will take a few hours but see if you come to the same conclusion, plus I mean, this Blake character has an alias and a pretty good one at that."

"What else?"

"You're not going to like it . . . but . . ."

"But?"

"But your uncle looks as to be the only one home at the time and Robin of course."

"Greg there could have been someone else . . . you know as well as I do that not everyone is in that system, it could be some punk kid, a jealous girlfriend even a burglar or something."

"Yes Jorja but can you be so sure, remember those finger prints and . . ."

"Don't say another word, just don't, that has been with me all goddamn day, haunting me, don't you think I know that, I'm wondering myself if my uncle was somehow responsible again. This time my aunt Gracie . . . . she was like a mother to me, another mother . . . . it just doesn't make any sense."

"It sort of does, there is a motive of jealously . . . it's a strong motive . . . . if your uncle walked in on the two of them . . . he could have been enthralled with rage . . . seeing the woman he loves in bed with another man . . . his political career going down the tubes."

"Political career yes, seeing the women he loves . . . well that's a different story. I know my uncle really never loved his wife, maybe at certain points in time there were subtle flashes but true love was never the case. He only really loved one woman . . . . and that was my mother?"

"Huh?"

"It's a long story Greg, maybe I'll go into one day but not today, not now, we need to find as much info as possible, maybe he is guilty, maybe not, he's still my uncle who has helped me along the way, he deserves the truth, and justice. Can you get me a copy of the police report?"

"Sure thing, only take a minute, may I," and Jorja stepped aside to let Greg use her computer. "See this never made any sense to me, this is a criminal investigation by the D.C. police. Why they have to load every tidbit of info to homeland is beyond me?"

"In this case I'm glad they did."

"Here's what it says so far, are you sure you want to hear this?"

"Yes, go ahead."

"It says, two victims, Grace Carson and Blake Linge, four gunshots. One to the back of the head of Blake Linge through the pelvis of Grace Carson. One to the face of Grace Carson penetrating the left check, exit right cheek. Third gunshot to the chest of Mrs. Carson. Then it goes into detail about blood splatter, phone was off the hook, lights were out, and other forensic material along with pictures."

"Let me see those pictures," Greg was hesitant, "just bring them up please, I can handle it". There were one hundred four pictures all together. Jorja was alright until she saw a close up of her Aunt Gracie's face. She turned away in horror. That is not how she wanted to remember her aunt but the image was already burned into her brain. She began to cry. "Greg, if you would, please leave." Greg was all too uncomfortable and gladly walked through the office door.

Jorja cried for a solid twenty minutes before she sat back down at her desk. "Memories, too many goddamn memories to contend with," she said aloud. She tried to push them aside but every time she saw her aunt's name on the police report she would tear up as the memories returned. She decide to drop everything and concentrate on those memories, "get it out of my system," she thought, besides there was a full box of tissues and so she relived as many memories as she could.

It was closing in on seven o'clock and not once did she even look at her monitor. She was disturbed only by a knock at the door.

"Yes."

"Jorja, it's Greg, are you . . ."

"You can come in."

"You alright," noticing her bloodshot eyes and a trashcan filled with tissues.

"Yeah . . . . I'm okay."

"You sure . . . it looks as though a bunch of old ladies emptied their pockets in here."

She laughed a bit, "Yeah, I'm sure, tough day but I need to get back to work."

"What you need is to go back home, relax, take a hot shower, take the day off tomorrow."

"I'm not going to do that and you know that, so why don't you take a seat and we can pick up right where we left off. Did you find out anything else?"

"No, but don't turn on any TV's . . . it is all over the airwaves."

"Not to mention it is all over for my uncle's political career."

"That does seem to be the case. Speculation of murder does not sit well with the American public . . . when there is speculation it's guilty until proven innocent when it plays out on the networks."

"And that's not fair but I know that's how it is . . . ."

"So what is your gut telling you Jorja?"

"I really don't know, I saw my uncle this morning and he was a wreck."

"Was he a wreck because of Grace or his career?"

"He looked genuine for his emotions regarding his wife, but he could have been channeling his emotions from a different source in order to portray his innocence. I keep thinking about those fingerprints on my mother's boat."

"It's like the Kennedy's all over again."

"Don't go there Greg, . . . I . . . I know how it looks . . . and it doesn't look good. Right now we are the only ones who know about those fingerprints and we are thinking of maybe two crimes involving my uncle."

"It does look fishy but also very circumstantial . . . but what doesn't look circumstantial is that your uncle was home at the time of the murders . . . that is a fact . . . you know that and I know that . . . . the police report gives an estimated time of the murders between eleven and one . . . our window is within five minutes . . . and that is a fact that only certain individuals know . . . you and me included and that doesn't leave much wiggle room."

"Let's restate motives here . . . why would my uncle kill his wife?"

"Rage?"

"I just don't buy it."

"Jorja, think about it, he comes home from a late dinner, he's been drinking, he has another drink in his study, then hears something . . . he goes to investigate and he see his wife in bed with another man—that's enough to put any man over the edge."

"There is more to it than that . . . I told you before he really didn't love her."

"There is also his political career, he sees her in bed with this man and right away he thinks betrayal being so close to the white house, his career ruined over a romp in the hay . . . again it's enough to drive a man over the top."

"What doesn't make too much sense, if my uncle heard a noise why would he take a gun to investigate, the house has state of the art security, he would have known something was up."

"Maybe he was tipped off beforehand at the dinner somehow, he was home rather early from one of those events. He builds up rage the closer he gets to the house, he enters the study to get another shot of courage, grabs his gun and walks upstairs."

"The police report states the man was in a very compromising position, that was probably the first shot."

"If I were that pissed that's probably where my first shot would have been."

"The second shot was fired directly at my . . ."

"Wait, let me bring up your uncle's cell phone records from last night," a few minutes elapsed, "Jorja, look at this, right about eleven he gets a call . . . . the number is blocked."

"Blocked, come on now, we know that number."

"Hold on, hold on . . . someone tried to block it . . . I have the number . . . . here it is . . . . now that's strange."

"What?"

"When is the last time you saw a public pay phone in this day and age?"

"So someone called my uncle from a pay phone at eleven o'clock on a Thursday evening, minutes later he is in the car headed home, moments after he arrives, my Aunt Gracie is dead, along with Remus . . ."

"Either way, if someone tipped him off it still looks like he pulled the trigger."

"It could be a setup, you said so yourself this Remus was using another name. Maybe he was the bait, kill them, then lure my uncle and it becomes a solid frame-up."

"You're stretching a bit don't cha think?"

"Yes I'm grabbing at straws, but that call tells me someone else is involved, you said so yourself that this Remus seemed to have an ulterior motive in his writings to my aunt."

"Again either way, setup or not, each has your uncle pulling the trigger since no one else is around, except for Robin."

"I know in my heart she would never."

"Okay, so we have this elaborate setup, hire this Remus character to portray a lover, a phone call, your uncle is home at the time of the murders, and a person to be named later . . . I just don't buy it . . . that's a pretty elaborate plan and all for what, who would go to that much trouble."

"The who is the easy part . . . the president."

"Jonathan Whitaker?"

"Yes, he has the most to gain, another term in the white house. Now that's a big motive . . . is it not?"

"One of the biggest I say, if the tandem team of Anderson and Carson goes down, the democrats are pretty late in the game to contend with this election, they're pretty much screwed."

"Not that my uncle and Anderson were going to make it . . . . Whitaker's approval rating is still pretty high."

"But they were closing, besides, they were going after the lower to low middle class, and although approval ratings are supposed to be across the board most of those people could care less when the phone rings for their questionnaire. I think they would have turned out in droves to elect a president and vice president who stood behind them . . . and they are the true majority of this country. Yes I think Whitaker knew he was going to be up against the ropes during this election."

"See he has the motive and most important the potential to pull something like this off."

"But murder, murder of a senator's wife that is certainly extreme and one hell of a frame up job. I'm sorry Jorja but I just keep coming back to those fingerprints on your mother's boat, I have a strange feeling it was not a coincidence considering that you told me earlier that your mother and your uncle where together at one time."

"I have that CIA training too . . . question everything . . . and believe me that is a juggernaut in my thinking, right now I cannot condemn my uncle until all the facts are in."

"Jorja, if the president was behind this . . . just how do you propose to take him down."

"As Indiana Jones once said, I'm making this up as I go along."

"Just remember Jorja, this isn't our case, never was, you have other priorities being the deputy director of DS and T."

"On my own time, on my own time . . . speaking of which it's getting late . . . I need to get home."

"You wanna grab a bite to eat?"

"Tough long day, some other time maybe I just need a long hot shower right now and maybe some Xanax."

Greg was disappointed at how that event went down. He was sure that Jorja would point the fingers at her uncle considering the timeline. Her quizzical nature was enough to drive him mad. "Damn her," he thought, "this could have been the perfect opportunity."

Jorja went straight home, after the news of her aunt, Jorja thought of only one thing . . . god and it had nothing to do with the spiritual salvation of someone moving on from this world to the next. She wanted answers and she wasn't going to pray for them; she quickly logged into the system as the president—risky since she didn't check the president's itinerary first. Although she promised not to enter the site without Greg by her side she deemed this time necessary. She punched in her uncle's social and pinpointed his location. Then she backed up the clock time and plotted out a timeline for his whereabouts. She confirmed for herself that her uncle was home during the murder, not a good sign. She quickly punched in the coordinates and a radius and tracked everyone within that radius. There were only three people, her aunt, her uncle, and her aunt's rendezvous partner . . . . Blake Remus . . . age thirty-eight. Robin, the house maid was not listed; probably never had a shot that contained the tracking devices.

After her conformation she did indeed take that hot long shower but skipped the Xanax and opted for a glass of wine instead. She went to the bookshelf in the family room and pulled the only family photo album she had. With each turning of the page, a new set of tears rolled down her cheeks. She loved her aunt Gracie more than she ever told her. With each turning of the page she vowed to herself that she would find the answers.

•   •   •

Chapter 50

"O.k., James Wartner, so what brings"

"The t is silent"

"What?"

"The t is silent."

"Oh, ok. Mr. War . . . . ner. Did you change that when you moved from Arkansas?'"

"No, it was the pronunciation I was born with."

"I see, so getting back to my initial question, what brings you into my station this evening?"

"You know as well I as do, so let's cut the crap, it's because my name is on that goddamn list, and every time something happens the police come knocking on my door."

"So what did you do to deserve this?"

"Being broke."

"Excuse me?"

"You heard me, being broke, poor, I couldn't afford a better lawyer, if I had you wouldn't be talking to me right now and I'd still be living in my hometown back in Arkansas but that didn't happen so I'm here and I thought I'd save you the trouble."

"Well I'm afraid you didn't save us any trouble, we've been looking for you all afternoon."

"So I've heard."

"Did you now?"

'Yes, on the radio, I figured there are not too many people on that list that walk the way I do."

"And how did that happen?"

"Car accident, over twenty-five years ago, before our fire department got that jaws of life thingy, my foot was mangled up under the dash. They couldn't save it, hence the prosthetic, hence the limp, hence the reason you were looking for me, hence the reason I'm here."

"That's not the only reason."

"Goddamn list," sort of mumbled under his breath.

"So where were you this afternoon?"

"The doctors."

"For?"

"For none of your," and he so wanted to use a choice profanity but thought otherwise, ". . . . business really, but if you must know, a colonoscopy."

"A colonoscopy?"

"What is it with these simple questions, a colonoscopy for Christ sake, you know where they shove a camera up your ass, I thought a man of your age would have had several done by now."

"I haven't"

"Well you should, I was glad I did, turned fifty-one, they found colon cancer, been going back and giving them a shitty grin every year since then."

"So where were you yesterday, around eleven?"

"Same place."

"The doctors?"

Yes . . . the doctors"

"Why?"

"Same reason"

"Same reason?"

"Yes, the same reason . . . . colonoscopy," saying it in disbelief, "I was scheduled for eleven thirty, they ran late, then an emergency, then a reschedule for today, call them it you want, they'll confirm. I spent the better part of two days reading Ladies Home Journal from nineteen seventy–two."

Lynch knew if his alibi held up this was not their man, "Can you stay awhile?"

"Why did you ask? It's not like I have a choice now is it?"

"Well can you?"

"Sure I'll wait until your witness shows, I'll just be sitting here smiling at that damn mirror until you say otherwise."

Chapter 51

Scott knew this ordeal was about to come to a head when once again he was summoned to the oval office. He thought long and hard about his role in the plot to derail the Anderson and Carson ticket. It wasn't just his role it was his plot, his plan, his evil doings that somehow caused the death of Grace Carson.

"Have a seat Scott," no one else was in the room.

"Mr. President, I need to know, do you really want the entire story?"

"I'll find out either way, you know my techniques."

Without taking a seat and drawing a rather deep breath, "then yes, I did have a role in the this morning's deaths, I was the one who put the ball in motion," as he saw the steam about to bellow, "please let me finish sir, I was the one who put the ball in motion and that ball was to have some pictures taken of Mrs. Carson, the so-called loving wife of senator Carson. It was supposed to be just some tabloid scandal. I received and viewed one of Grace's personal emails to her husband discussing her marriage, she wasn't happy, and it got me thinking, besides since she didn't have any seventeen year old daughters to get knocked up, infidelity seemed the next best thing, it never sits well with the American public and an elected official. So with the help of our friends at the Beta Group we had a man get as close to her as humanly possible. Again photographs were all that we wanted. Photographs were all it was supposed to be. I'm, I'm still at a loss for words and as shocked as you are over this whole thing. It seems Mrs. Carson is dead because of what I might have started, at this time I was trying to gather as much information as possible before I filled you in sir. I still have nothing to go on and for that I apologize. The system is telling us nothing."

"Have your letter of resignation on my desk within the hour."

"I want to see this out Mr. President."

"And you goddamn well better, I want to know what the fuck happened, what went wrong, we've been through a lot, and you know way too much, but, but mark my words, you will be the one who takes the fall should this get out, just have your goddamn letter ready and pray I don't have to use it."

Scott went back to his desk and pulled up a letter that he has had on file since the day Whitaker took the oath. He just changed the date, printed the thing out, sealed it in an envelope, and handed it to Stacy. Within ten minutes it was on the President's desk.

His cover story really wasn't much of a cover story, more like the truth taken from the pages of Parson's Weems book *"The Life of George Washington with Curious Anecdotes Equally Honorable to Himself and Exemplary to his Young Countrymen."* Sure the story of little George fessing up to the brutal destruction of one of his father's favorite fruit bearing trees was indeed embellished a bit but the heroic nature of a boy or in this case man telling the truth in front of the utmost power and in the midst of almost utter annihilation speaks volumes for his integrity even when the circumstantial evidence states otherwise. Yes, Scott was a smart cookie, he could bluff with the best of them but it became clear to Scott to fold for he decided the end game was more important than the single hand and he wanted very much to continue playing in the highest stakes of a game.

The president was also a smart cookie, you don't get to be president of the United Sates otherwise, though some would question George W. Bush. In any case, President Jonathan Whitaker had an ace up his sleeve but it just so happened to be the same ace that his chief of staff uses from time to time. He dialed his direct number.

"Scott was just in my office, he confessed to being involved in this morning's breaking news."

"I've already been doing research for him."

"And?"

"And yes he's involved but from my brief conversation with him this morning he's looking for the same answers as everyone else."

"What else?"

"I found that the John Doe from this morning who police are now calling Blake Linge a banking consultant, is actually Blake Remus, and get this, he's a Beta Group employee."

"Scott mentioned that he had the group involved, I guess he was their inside man?"

"Appears that way, pretty good cover, records in all the right places. He did basic work for the group, nothing too outside the lines, mainly drop-offs and pick-ups, with the occasional gray area here and there but right now I'm looking into finding John Smith."

"Who?"

"Lieutenant Colonel John Smith."

"I'm not following you."

"Scott mentioned him to me, actually he said you were the one looking for him."

"And his story?"

"Not much to tell at this point in time, he was a marine, a deeply undercover op, retired, and as of almost four years ago, deceased."

"So I'm betting he's not eighty-sixed, where is he now?"

"That's the million dollar question. He's not in the system, he should be by our standards, but he's not, never did exist in the system as far as I can tell at the moment."

"Has he worked for the group?"

"His past bank records appear that way, looks like a heavy hitter, you don't get this kind of cash without being totally covert."

"Scott said this was just a scandal, just pictures, then why use a man of this stature?"

"Another million dollar question, I'm sure this guy could handle a camera just as easy as a berretta or a glock, but mix in the fact that he's not in the system and I think it's a bit of overkill for just some snap snaps."

"Okay, Scott's hiding something and I need you to find out what it is and when you do"

"You'll be the second to know."

"Second?"

"Yes, I'll be the first."

Jonathan wasn't in the mood for his pissy little semantics and hung up without so much of a closing remark. It now looked liked his morning plate was full. Although Scott called first, just like in the game pinochle, trump wins and in this suit the trump was the president.

He logged back into the system but before he could do anything something happened. He came face to face with one of the most cursed-out-loud screens a computer monitor could display and on cue he uttered, "fuck me." It was the "blue screen of death." A critical system error had occurred. His computer froze and the only thing he could do was power it down and then back on again. Things like this just happen; it could have been overheating, faulty memory, a bad video driver, or a thousand and one other things inside the black box. If it happened again he would have to investigate further but he didn't want to cross that bridge unless he had to, plus there was no way in hell he was going to let the fellas of IT near his computer.

While his computer rebooted he took the opportunity to take a restroom break, clear his head, and make a trip to the cooler for some hot water and a teabag. When he got back to his office he placed his steeping cup of tea on the desk and again uttered, "fuck me." There it was again, the "blue screen of death." This wasn't good, not at all. He powered it down again and realized the amount of time he would need to do a restore if this continued to happen. Before he turned it back on, he got down on his knees and removed the side casing of his computer. This time he uttered, "son-of-a-bitch," in almost disbelief. His cpu fan was choked full of dust and debris. He was almost certain the computer was overheating. Being a computer expert he should have known better then to let his machine go maintenance free for so long, but being the computer expert, he had the remedy on hand. From the bottom drawer of his desk he removed a can of compressed air, placed the little plastic straw in the end and fired away, blowing dust and debris everywhere. Within a minute he had the casing back in its proper place and fired up his machine. When his desktop reappeared he was relieved that he didn't have to do a restore from his backups since that would have taken the better part of the afternoon.

Then like puberty hitting Aquarius, it dawned on him, in order to do a complete restore it would take his latest backup, with backup being the operative word here. Why he didn't remember this before was beyond his grasp at the moment but he took a few of those moments to point his application to the secondary database. Upon a major malfunction of the real-time database the secondary/backup would kick in automatically without so much as a hiccup to the end user. Since the regular database was running smoothly he had to manipulate his settings and change the port number (the computer address to the database) in his property file. Since he rarely did this he had to locate the exact number buried in or on his desk somewhere. It used to be written on a scratch piece of paper but he had no clue where that could have gone—he didn't care either since anyone who would happen to glance at the number would assume it was a five digit zip code if left out in the open. Since his desk was a lost cause the easiest way to find the number was to search his system and he found it in an obscured extraneous file. Now it was a matter of inserting it into his application and rebooting the program. When his application came back online he was connected to the secondary database and started checking for any errors he may have missed the first time around.

●　●　●

Chapter 52

The Chief of Staff wasn't in a good mood but his neck was the one in the noose and he wanted to breathe a little easier and remain in the game. He thought about the current hand that he was dealt. John Smith was the key, yet he wasn't in the system so he wasn't going to use the system, instead he opened the military's database once again. From there he doubled checked that John Smith was injected with Frank Simosiks' bio-nano concoction in October over three years ago. He also found that he was in the IIR's database for immunizations and the lot number was tied to his social security number. He should be in the system, "unless," he thought, "unless, just how feasible could it be a faulty lot," as he reached for the phone. He dialed his buddy's number and waited. Four rings, five, six, seven rings. It never went to voicemail. Eight rings, then nine, and this happened almost all the time. On the other end his buddy would be so engrossed in whatever it was he did, the ringing of a phone became ambient noise; even a fire alarm once went unnoticed by him. Ten rings, eleven, twelve . . . .

"Yes?"

"What, you're not busy today, you answered rather quickly Frank?"

"Well, I was just thinking about perfume, why do they always have to smell flowery, I mean if a woman had perfume that smelled like steak or pepperoni pizza, they'd have men all over them."

"Like that one commercial where a woman has a taco or something in her purse at the bar, next thing you know the men are all over her."

"See that's my point, men are attracted to smells they like, not what women like, I'm telling you, if she smelled like pepperoni pizza, I'd eat that. I was also thinking of developing a line of candles strictly for men, fuck that vanilla and mango shit, how about wet asphalt, fresh cut grass, or even gasoline."

"Frank, what are you lighting with that Bunsen burner that's making you so high?"

"Huh?"

"Nothing, listen I have a question for you, for your bio injections, that stabilizer with the radio nanos, have you ever had a faulty lot."

"Sure."

"So that might explain it then."

"Explains what?"

"Well we had a person get injected and was never put in the system."

"It's not a faulty lot."

"But you just said . . ."

"What I said was an answer to your question, do I ever have a faulty lot, and that answer is yes, but each lot is checked before it leaves and if it leaves then it is not faulty and besides these things have a good five year shelf-life. What was the lot number?"

"BR7"

"One sec . . . . okay, here it is, out of the 300 hundred people injected with that lot number, two hundred and ninety seven people are in the system. The three who have gone to meet the maker and are bereft of life are Kathryn Gilberts, a one John Smith, and Stacy Bel . . . . Bel . . . fuck it, there's no way I'm pronouncing that name."

"What system are you looking at?"

"I'm doing a combination search, my database, the IIR's and the system."

"Okay, but see John Smith, he was injected but his records were never in the system, doing a quick check both Kathryn and Stacey were, not now though, since they are both pushing up the daisies."

"Kicked the bucket, expired and gone to meet the maker, joined the choir invisible."

"Listen John Cleese wannabe, will you please pay attention."

"I got it, I got, he was never in the system, yet this John Smith, real original name there huh? Well, this John Smith was injected with BR77UK which was working as it went out the door of my plant, it was put in my system on October nineteenth and looking at the upload file to the system there were no exceptions reported during or after that upload. He has to be in the system."

"Well he's not."

"Well something's wrong."

"Gee you think? I'm betting that your little nano thingys failed in some way shape or form."

"I beg to differ and I will not accept that until proven otherwise. Who is this John Smith, if that is his real name."

"He's and ex-marine, black ops, now consultant and is off the grid."

"I think you're out of the loop."

"What?"

"Okay, let me get this straight, your guy, ahem, John Smith, was injected with our solution yet was uploaded to the system, yet never appears in that system, so what do you think the chances are that the one faulty lot in BR7 which by the way is not possible but just for your sake I'll roll with it, just happens to go into a person who is black ops . . . come on I'm waiting, . . . I said I'm waiting."

"I know I know I'm just trying to rule out coincidences."

"And?"

"And I hit a fucking wall."

"So do you like the smell of burning wood?"

"Yes, umm."

"How about a locker room?"

"Huh?"

"You know the smell of sweat, dirty cloths, you know for my candle collection."

Click.

After his conversation with the doctor and his smells, he figured Frank's logic was spot on, someone was hiding something and his money was on his partner in crime. There were only four people who had access to the system, the big man himself, Mr. DNI., Frank, and the obvious. Frank and the president dabbled in the system more for their curiosity than for obtaining actual knowledge in crisis situations but his colleague knew the database all too well; he certainly knew all the finer details of data collection and storage so he was the blood-doping favorite to blame in this race.

● ● ●

Chapter 53

It was rare that the president took his toy out for a ride but this time he was curious to find some information on his Chief of Staff from firsthand knowledge. It was an even rarer occurrence that he got an ACCESS DENIED error.

"Son of a . . . . ," and before he could finish, the reply came from the phone.

"I know, I know . . . I'm in the process of bringing it back up, the system was down."

"Why?"

"Doing research."

"Yes, but"

"I was going on," and paused for a rather long time before he continued, "going on a hunch, I was just restoring the application to point to the secondary database . . . . and . . . . whoa . . . whoa . . ."

"Whoa what?"

"I found him."

"Who?"

"That lieutenant colonel Scott wanted me to find."

"John Smith."

"Yes, it looks as though on October nineteenth, about three years ago as per company regulations, a one John Smith was injected with STBL5 from a lot produced by our friend from the Etimiz Corporation and on that very same day was placed into our system."

"And?"

"I'm getting to that." The President could hear his typing on the other end. "For three years his entire travels where tracked by the eye in the sky and his last entry was . . . . less than twenty-four hours ago at twelve thirty-seven a.m. just after the shootings at the Carson Estate."

"What do you mean his last entry," as he could hear the feverish clicking of keyboard strokes, "is he off the grid?"

"Yes but I think it's a bit more permanent than that, I think he's dead, his last marker readings were just before one this morning, probably right after the murders but the interesting thing is someone manually removed him from our system, erased him, then literally erased him."

"Then how did you find him."

"Whoever erased him forgot the backups, like I said we have a few redundant systems in the hills here and there, and he was in the secondary database but not the primary."

"So this who?"

"Only one person it could be, that is unless you or Frank recently graduated from Lincoln Tech."

"Scott?"

"Bet the house but you have to ask yourself why, why give us the name of the marine in the first place."

"To throw us off the track, you know the complicated headgames this dick can play, the master chess player he thinks he is."

"Isn't that why you hired him?"

"Yes, but he's still a dick."

"So do you want me to tell him or what?"

"Can you monitor him?"

"That's not a problem, it will take some time to put listeners on his cell, email is pretty easy as well as his office phone."

"Then, when he calls you, go ahead and tell him John is dead."

"And when he asks how I know?'

'Tell him what you told me and see how he reacts."

He bit his tongue because he was about to say some smart-ass remark regarding the fact he couldn't see Scott, just hear him, besides he needed his ass to sit in the chair, "Do you want me to accuse him of deleting John Smith."

"Let's not go there, if he wants to play chess, let's see his next move before we take his queen off the board."

●　●　●

Chapter 54

"Whatcha got for me?'

"I was just about to call you Scott, that marine you wanted me to find, well I found him, sort of."

"What do you mean sort of?"

"Well I found him in the backup database, only he's no longer transmitting."

"Are you saying he's dead?"

"Well he was in the system, now he's not, like I said he's no longer transmitting which for all intents and purpose means he's dead, he was extinguished just before one this morning."

"By who?"

"I don't have that information but it looks as though whoever did this did not have any marker injections or it could very well have been the senator."

"Was John around the Carson's residence at the time of the murder?"

"Yes and so was his last marker reading."

"Okay, now you said you found this out how, a backup database?"

"Yes, he was erased from the primary."

"Erased . . . who erased him?"

"I'm not saying, not all the facts are in at the moment."

"But you suspect me?"

"I didn't say that Scott."

"Yes but I could tell, there are not that many players in the game and we both know Jonathan nor Frank have that ability, so your only logical choice is me."

"Well deduced Mr. Spock."

"Well just for the record I didn't, besides why would I ask you to find him if I knew he was dead?"

"Good question Mr. Fisher."

"So you are saying I'm doing this as some kind of freakin' chess game, you know what, go fuck yourself, I'm trying to find answers for the president."

"Then why did you tell me the president wanted to find the lieutenant colonel."

"Listen, my ass is in hot water big time, things didn't go as planned and right now I suspect you had something to do with this."

"Me?"

"Yes you, you have access as well my friend, you're smart enough to pull something like this off, you have other connections within the CIA, and I know for a fact that I did not erase him, so that leaves you, only problem I see is why?"

"So that leaves us at a stalemate, because I know I didn't fucking do it."

"Okay, okay, for a moment let's say neither one of us erased him, did the president authorize access to anyone else?'

"No because that request would have to go through me."

"How about, how about a malfunction of some sort?"

"Can't see it happening, the primary gets the record first then it's copied almost real-time to the secondary."

"Then how about this, either the president or Frank gave someone access that we didn't know about, through their own computer?"

"Plausible."

"That's it, plausible? I think that is a likely scenario, first off who does the president trust more than us?"

"Yeah but still, your point is valid but I don't think in a million years he would just open his computer up for a little show and tell, after all the work, the years, the planning it took to get this system up and running. Why take the chance to expose something greater than the moon landing cover-up? I don't think he could trust anyone with that type of information except, except maybe for Tamra."

"The First Lady? Ha. He would never."

"That leaves Frank."

"I just don't see it, he's too busy with scented candles."

"Huh?'"

"You know how he is, that brain of his is always in Einstein mode, once his next train of thought leaves the station, the last one is completely forgotten, besides he has no political agenda whatsoever, I don't even think he knows Whitaker is a republican."

"So it looks like we are right back to square one . . . you think I did it, I think you did it."

"We're missing something?"

"Yeah, checkmate, but I'm going to be planning my next moves."

"You do that, I suggest you keep an eye on all your pieces, and I'll do the same"

After he was done with his phone call with the president's chief of staff, his first move was to lock him out of the system.

● ● ●

Chapter 55

When he woke he felt refreshed even before his bathroom visit. The drugs worked. They always worked. There was no feeling of guilt or pain, no usual remembrance of the demons that haunted him. The usual was that almost every night he would slip out of consciousness and into the frightful worlds of his dreams. Almost every night his demons would return as his mind softened the logical boundaries of the physical world. He hated to sleep for he hated to dream. Most of the time they started innocently enough, with the mind shifting from glimpses of his daily mundane routine to the snapshots of the entertainment world of television. He flipped between the projected cerebral sequences like changing the channels on the TV, stopping only when something caught his attention. He stopped mainly for two things and like most men it was cars and women but in his case it was always one car, a 74 Mustang, and one little six year old girl.

The 74 Mustang was one that his mother left behind. It was bright red or 2B based on Ford's color codes that year, with spots of rust around the wheel wells and fenders, pitted chrome bumpers, a white interior that had seen better days, and a white vinyl top—that too had seen better days. To the eyes of most it was a piece of shit, to the eyes of the beholder it was the shit. When he slipped behind the steering column and turned the key in the ignition he was easily transported into another world, his world, one where his demons simply faded with the static sounds of pop music filling the interior from the center dash speaker. With the music playing it washed away the sounds of a poorly maintained vehicle, he never heard the clunks, the knocks, the rattles. The car always started and got him from point "a" to point "b" in what he believed "in style". He loved that car; he loved it almost as much as he loved his passenger.

His passenger was the little blonde hair blue eyed six year-old doll baby that he truly loved. She was cute as a button and when both his parents vanished from the earth she was all he had left in the world. His father passed from this world with the help of a mid-morning heart attack at the plant. By the time his mother and him made it to the hospital all that was left was a lifeless shell of a fifty-two year old man, which seemed fitting since even alive he was lifeless. He would come home from the factory, have dinner, and plop himself in front of the boob tube. Not once did he remember his father asking him how his day was or playing catch with him in the front yard, nor his mother for that matter. His mother died shortly there afterwards of lung cancer, which was not a stretch by any means. She was a three pack a day non-filter camels. She looked like she was sixty though only forty-eight when the Grim Reaper dialed her number for the slab. He was just sixteen, a junior at the time, when he was left alone to fend for himself. Even though the house was paid for from his father's insurance, which was an unexpected surprise, he had to drop out of school in order to pay the bills. He couldn't deal with the pressures of school and work and home and on top of all that raising a little girl so he did as any good parent would have done, he sacrificed his own life. He loved her so.

When his sleepy mind focused on one of his loves, his incubus would always return, always the same. The morning was hot and cloudy, it looked like rain but for now the clouds were holding back. It was a Saturday, which meant a day off from work, which meant a long ride with his little girl to a destination unknown until they were both in the car and decided. He helped her into the car, closed her door, and entered the driver's seat. The engine choked a bit, he gave it some gas then it settled into a choppy idle. Any good mechanic would have told you it was a lifter hanging but to him it sounded cool along with the hole in the muffler. He asked her where she wanted to go and the same reply was always given—"I don't care" "Fishing," he said and she nodded with the biggest of smiles. He put the car in drive and headed towards the lake; he wanted to go fishing, catch some dinner, and save a bit of money. The memories of the ride were always a blend of past conversations about her dolls or doll house that he had bought her for Christmas or singing the wrong words to tunes on the radio but mostly it's just an image of her sitting in the passenger seat with nothing but smiles and not a care in the world until . . . .

The rain was no longer holding back. On the way down to the lake via a dirt road it started to spit a little. His windshield wipers needed replacing; they smeared the dirt leaving him with an obstructed view. The sky is much darker now, he can't see. He hears a definite popping sound and losses control. In actuality, the tire hits a good size hole, driving the strut lose and blowing the tire. Since the car wasn't properly maintained, he could only afford the gas, it didn't take much for the vehicle to basically self destruct. The car turned sharply to the left and down an embankment. The sounds of trees and branches scrapping against the metal rang in his ear, along with the sound of his screaming little passenger. Then total darkness. He awoke with the sound of very hard rain hitting the roof. His neck was stiff; his leg was unable to move. He looked around, he saw the windshield cracked in front of the passenger seat; he saw blood at the position of impact. He looked around for his little girl but she was nowhere to be found; her door was open. He cried her name and received no response. He screamed her name and got no response. He grasped for breath, in pain, he tried again. The rain was coming down harder and harder, he screamed again, louder and louder, thunder was clapping in the distance, drowning out his voice and then and then he passed out.

It was this point in the dream where he usually wakes up, clutching the bed sheet, cold beads of sweat running down his face, and unable to breathe but today thanks to his pills, there were no dreams this time around, not that he remembered anyhow. It was a little after one in the afternoon, he was so looking forward to this day and quickly cycled through his hygiene routine. Kyle eventually made his way down to the kitchen; he approached the basement door but wanted to try to subdue his hunger pains first. A quick peek in the fridge yielded three eggs, some butter, and some about to be expired milk. Even though it was officially after lunch, Kyle never missed breakfast. He turned on the stove, placed more than a tablespoon of butter in the pan and while he waited for the pad to melt, he quickly placed two slices of white in the toaster. He broke the eggs on the side of the pan, whisked them to form almost a froth, then added a splash of milk, and whisked some more. The toast popped with a golden hue almost the same time as the fluffy eggs slipped from the pan to the plate. A short order cook in a diner couldn't have timed it any better. He searched for some juice but came up empty handed and poured himself some water straight from the tap and sat down to eat. He traded bites between eggs and toast as if it were a ritual of some sort, almost calculating the amount of each as to be finished in perfect unison with one another. While he ate he stared at the basement door as if it were alive and talking to him. He occasionally nodded as if in recognition. When his plate was empty and the last morsel of toast vanished between his lips, he stood up, went to the sink, washed his plate, glass and utensils, and placed them in the cabinet and drawer as he did a thousand times before. When his daily chore was completed he turned to face the door—he nodded again. He approached the door, opened the door, and proceeded down the stairs to his reward. He stared at the steel door that was before him knowing all too well what lied just beyond its portal. He approached the steel door almost in the same fashion as the basement door but he stopped, then elected to proceed to his watching room, and sat down in his chair.

Ripley was on the floor keeping herself occupied with a pink Corvette and an American icon.

The cogs of his mind sputtered as he watched his little girl, he took a deep breath, then said in a low calming voice, "Ripley," annunciating the two syllables.

Like an acrophobic on top of the Space Needle, she froze. Her body tensed. The supple hair on the back of her neck rose. It was the first time she heard a human voice since being in the pink room. She didn't like it.

He knew he had startled her and he waited a few moments, "Ripley," in an overly concerned mother's type of voice.

She didn't even flinch. Her body still tense. Her young mind was still wheeling, trying desperately to grasp a handle on a similar past situation. Her feeble mind came up empty. She didn't recognize the voice. Her brain scanned her callow memories and she still drew a blank She knew it wasn't her daddy's or Uncle Terry's. The voice was male and came from behind the wall—that she did know; she also knew that it had scared her.

"Now now Ripley, it's okay, I didn't mean to scare you, I won't hurt you."

Her body was still tense but she turned her head ever so slightly towards the wall, the one with the mirror.

"Ripley"

And with one quick motion she sprang up from the floor, ran to the bed, and dove under it. She pressed herself against the far wall, cupped her hands around her ears, then curled up into a ball, knees pulled tightly against her chest, almost as tight as her eyes were shut. Her body started to shake uncontrollably from the fear. She didn't say a word.

He got off his chair and onto his knees. He could barely see an outline of Ripley under the bed due to the heavy shadows. "Ripley," in a very quiet voice.

She didn't hear him. She stayed in her safe spot for the better part of an hour.

As did he.

She was now lying on her stomach with her eyes opened and fixated on the toys scattered about the fuzzy carpet. She was slowing drifting back to a child's land of imagination. She eventually forgot the reason she was underneath the bed and crawled to the allure of Barbie's Dream House.

He didn't say a word. He just watched in awe. He too eventually crawled back into his imagination.

"I'm sorry to have scared you Ripley, I really am sorry."
This time the voice didn't scare her, it was familiar in a way. She still didn't say anything.

"Are you hungry Ripley?"

She shook her head no, not even looking in the direction of the mirror.

"Are you sure?"

Again she shook her head no.

"Is there anything you want?"

Without hesitation she said, "I want my mommy."

Although he knew this was coming, the way she responded caught him off guard. "I'm sorry Ripley your mother isn't here?"

"I want my mommy," being a bit more forceful then before.
　　"Again I'm sorry Ripley, she's not here"
　　"Where is she?"
　　"She's, she's gone."
　　"Where?"

He knew he eventually had to break it to her gently but he so wanted his life to start, his life with his little girl. "She's, she's dead. I'm sorry Ripley your mother is dead," in an eerie yet somehow soothing sort of way.

"I want to see her."
　　"I'm afraid you can't Ripley, she's dead."
　　"I want daddy," she demanded.
　　"I'm afraid he's dead too," said as a matter-of-factly.
　　"I want mommy. I want my mommy . . . . mommy," as she began to cry.
　　"Please don't cry Ripley, please don't . . . . I'll take care of you, I will . . . . I will take care of you Ripley, I promise. I promise I will love you. I promise Ripley. I promise," in the same soothing voice
　　"I want my mommy."
　　He waited a bit, then trying desperately to change the subject, "Ripley, are you hungry?"
　　"No," definitively.

"Are you sure Ripley? I can make you a sandwich. Maybe a peanut-butter and jelly?"

"I'm not allowed to eat peanut butter."

"Sure you are, I'll make you one, okay?," and with that he left his watching room and made his way back up the stairs to the kitchen.

● ● ●

Chapter 56

Something happened and Reynolds racked his brain as to what it could have been during both his Bell H-67 helicopter and Lincoln Town car rides to the office. He arrived at the Beta Group just after nine with his fingers already tired from the constant Blackberry use. He didn't want to work in the confines of the D.C. office but he knew Scott wanted him within strangling distance. His first order of business was to talk to Brickman one on one. No one at the Group knew Blake was dead, not that many people knew Blake to begin with, but nonetheless it was going to be kept that way. Although Brickman was in the dark, given the facts Reynolds was in town and requested an immediate meeting, he had an inkling Blake was connected to this morning news events. His suspicions were laid to rest when he was told of Blake's resignation and request for his login information. He complied with the request for his information and told Reynolds he will be missed and should anything change he would welcome Blake back to his present position. Anyhow he played the game, this wasn't Brickman first rodeo and he knew all too well that his former employee was lying on a slab in a morgue somewhere. They both knew, yet the unspoken word would remain so the game could continue.

Brickman exited the same conference room he last saw Blake and left Reynolds alone with the login credentials to his former employee. Reynolds went straight to work but he was far from being a computer genius, if truth be known he was still pretty much a hunt and peck typist and absolutely hated the touchpad on his IBM laptop. He reached into his over-the-shoulder bag for his optical mouse, plugged it into the USB port and waited for the system to boot. He then logged in as if he were Blake. Reynolds was using his own laptop to logon onto the network but was able to access Blake's email account with the company and any of Blake's information saved on the common folders. His folders were empty and his email account was just as bare aside for a few scattered emails from HR and the monthly newsletters put out by the marketing department. Leaving no stone unturned he visited Blake's desk to see if any clues were left behind. His cubical was as clean as his email account with only a blue highlighter, three pencils in a tin mug from Pussers Pub, fifteen cents, and a nameplate littering his workspace. Reynolds turned into his favorite P.I., Jim Rockford, and did a little more investigating as he visited the HR department and walked away with Blake's home address. He knew Blake for a few years and never once asked where he lived; they were colleagues not friends, so his personal life was left personal.

Reynolds didn't make the trip directly to the address given to him by HR, instead he went to the bank in which Blake had a few personal belongings placed in a safe deposit box just in case of his demise. It was a mandate given to him and all of Reynolds' direct reports. Reynolds was the primary holder of the box so getting the key only required his identification and signature. He went straight to the box numbered forty-two and laughed when he remembered Blake had told him it was the answer to everything as deemed by Douglas Adams in "The Hitchhikers Guide to the Galaxy." Hopefully it did contain all the answers, thought Reynolds but when he opened it, all it contained was a set of house keys and the pin number for his alarm system. The answer would have to be in his home in order for the numerology to hold true.

When he arrived at Blake's townhouse he was expecting to see the police or even yellow tape across the door but then again they were still searching for Mr. Linge so there were none. Upon walking up the steps to the front door he glanced into the garage and noticed his Carrera was gone. He inserted the key, turned the lock, and immediately heard the alarm warning. He simply entered in the pin number and silenced it. Never being in the house before Reynolds was impressed of its cleanliness and proper placement of things and one word quickly came to mind—anal. There was no bric-a-brac or clutter, no piles of clothes, no dishes in the sink, no dust even; if he had a mother she would have been proud. He walked around the house as if peering beyond velvet ropes in a museum. This changed when he reached Blake's office where his laptop's screensaver was running in aquarium mode—exotic goldfish swimming to and fro.

Reynolds sat in the chair and wiggled the mouse. The screensaver disappeared and revealed a webpage for Google's Gmail. On the webpage were dozens of conversations to and from Grace Carson. He clicked on one and read every word and deduced Blake could weave a wonderful web. If he hadn't have known his assignment he would have truly believed the boy was head over heels for the senator's wife. He clicked on the very first email to Grace Carson and read it; he did the same with the last. He read a few more and wanted to read them all but he felt as though a timer was ticking down to its last few seconds so he decided to pack up the laptop and take it with him. Reynolds couldn't think of anything else to search for so he left through the same door he entered setting the alarm beforehand. He quickly nixed the notion to go back to the office and elected to head to his normal hotel since it was closing in on the standard check-in time, not that he needed to wait for that given the status of his hotel rewards card.

Once in his upgraded room he moved to the desk and plugged Blake's laptop into the hotel's internet network and waited for it to boot. He then whipped out his cell and dialed the all too familiar number.

"I was just going to call you, what have you found?"

"Well I was at Blake's townhouse just outside the beltway, not much in the way of answers, however I grabbed his laptop."

"And?"

"And there are a ton of emails between the two parties and from what I gathered some are pretty intimate."

"I think that could go without saying given the positions they were found in."

"The thing I don't understand, his last email stated he was coming over to the house, now reading between the lines, it sounds as though it was going to be a rendezvous of a sexual nature but I never received an email pertaining to the fact . . . but maybe . . . ."

"That might be possible."

"What might be possible?"

"You were going to say that maybe Blake did actually fall for the senator's wife and that's why he never called you."

"Well . . . yes . . . but how did you . . ."

"That was my exact thought as well, maybe he got too close to his subject, it has happened before . . . when's the last time you had communications with him?"

"About two or three weeks ago . . . it seemed things were going as planned, I had no reason to believe otherwise."

"Do you still have his last email to you?'

"Yes."

"Send it to me, in fact send all his emails to me, even the ones he sent to Grace."

"Those are in his gmail account."

"So?"

"Well it would be easier if you logged onto the site yourself, there's a ton of them."

"Then give me his login info."

"Sure, let's see . . . . shit."

"What?"

"Hold on . . . . yeah . . . . it seems I don't know his password."

"What do you mean you don't know his password?"

"Well his browser has automatic login, so it takes me straight to his email . . . . all I see for his passwords are eight dots."

"What browser is he using?"

"I'm not sure."

"Look up in the top left-hand corner, what do you see?'

"A little orange globe, then it says Blake's email address, and Mozilla Firefox."

Great, should be pretty easy to get this information. Follow these steps, go to tools, then options."

"The options box appears."

"Good, now click security and you should see a box labeled save passwords."

'Yep, clicked it . . . wait . . . I see it, show passwords."

"Look for something like gmail or google."

"Got it, carrera nine one one, carrera with a capital c. That was easy."

"I'll take a peek, now that you have his other passwords for other sites besides his gmail account, I want you to do some more investigating, see what else you can learn."

"I'll call you if I find out anything else that might be interesting."

Once Reynolds hung up the phone he went back to Blake's laptop and entered a world he never knew existed. He went to sites such as Facebook, Linked in, Match.com, and Myspace using Blake's logon credentials. He spent the better part of the evening and most of the next day following tangents upon tangents and slipping further from his original goal. He was astonished to find how much personal information people just put out in the open. Sure he read stories in the news on how a teacher was fired for pasting on her website, a picture of herself drinking a cosmo or how an employee was canned after his blog made headlines in the Wall Street Journal but to realize just how stupid people could be on the internet widened his eyes like Alex Delarge in Clockwork Orange. He was so enthralled with pointing and clicking to the nether regions of brainlessness and trying to absorb the display of moronic deposition he never heard the sound of the incoming message.

● ● ●

Chapter 57

Back at the White House Scott read the emails from Blake and Reynolds which didn't leave much to the imagination. They were all straight to the point. He read a few of the emails between Blake and Grace and things were a different story there. They were laced with feelings and innuendos and metaphors out the ass, he felt as if he were reading a Hemmingway novel. He quickly got bored with the subtext of horny talk and focused his attention on the email addresses themselves. Reynolds was the only one who used his Beta Group email address. Blake on the other hand used an alias at hotmail to communicate with Reynolds and he used his gmail account with Grace. He had a gut feeling someone else was involved but couldn't place a finger on it; maybe someone did a blind copy on the emails. Armed with this notion Scott opened up one of Reynolds' emails. He then went to view tab, chose options, and saw the entire email header or the itinerary of the email message itself, where it has been and at what date and time. Although most of it appeared as gibberish to Scott, he did get a sense of the basics and didn't see any other names within the header. He then did a few searches on Google regarding email addresses, read an article on Wikipedia, and learned a few things in the process.

Take for example the email address steve.jones@abc.com. There are two parts to an email address the recipient's actual email name—steve.jones and the part following the @ sign, the domain name—abc.com. There are usually three computers or servers involved in the mailing process. The sender's email server, the recipient's email server, and a domain name server or DNS. The DNS is like a library; it contains all the domain names that have been registered on the internet and the location or IP address for those domains. When an email is sent from a mailing application such as Outlook, it contacts the sender's email server. This email server in turns strips off the domain name abc.com and sends it to a DNS. The DNS looks up the domain name and hands back one or more IP address. The sender's email server then uses this IP address like a phone number and dials the recipient's email server located at abc.com. Much like calling an operator at a huge company and asking for Mr. Peters in accounting, the recipient's email server does the same thing. It searches for steve.jones within the domain abc.com. If it is a valid email address the email server at abc.com will then ask for the complete message to be sent. It then places the entire message in Mr. Jones' inbox. If the email address is invalid or a connection cannot be made between servers, the email is placed in a queuing system where it will try to deliver it again and again for a predetermined length of time.

After his internet search he realized he was out of luck trying to find if anyone was blind copied since he was not the administrator of the email server. He would need to place a call to his liaison in the Beta Group. He flipped open his cell and called Brickman.

"Brickman here, what can I do you for?"

'It's Scott Norwood I need to ask . . . . ," and he stopped mid sentence as he was looking at the printout from the complete header record on Reynolds' email. "Hold on a second will ya," as he kept him on the phone without saying a word for almost a full minute. "Can you do me a quick favor?"

"Sure, what?"

"Just send me an email, no subject or body, just an email."

"Is that it?"

"Yes."

"On its way."

'Is there anything else?'

"Not right now but I might call you back in a few minutes if this doesn't pan out.'

"If what doesn't pan out?"

"Umm nothing . . . . hey I just got your email. Thanks."
"Not a problem, wish they were all that easy."

Scott quickly printed out Brickman's email with the complete header information, compared it to a Reynolds' email, and then highlighted each IP address within the headers. The starting IP addresses were the same on both emails and he went to the web to find its domain name. The Beta Group was the owner of the IP address which made sense since that's where both emails originated. The ending addresses were different and reasonably so since they went to different domains. The thing that he found odd was Reynolds had an extra IP address located within the middle of his header information. When he looked up the address it belonged to a server located at the CIA. He scanned another email from Reynolds and found the same thing. "The plot thickens," he said to himself. He wanted to call his computer guru but since his last conversation almost led to a crucifixion he called in yet another favor from a former colleague at DNI.

"Sam, Scott Norwood, listen I'm trying to get information from an email server."
"What sort of information?"
"I don't know really, maybe some sort of log file, I need to follow a trail from a certain IP address."
"That's possible. What's the IP address?"
"One zero eight dot three three dot three three dot one one."
"Did you say three three dot one one?"
"Yes."
"Are you sure?"
"Yes, why?"
"Well that server resides at the CIA."
"Can you be more specific?"
"Directorate of Science and Technology."
"Interesting, very interesting, can you get the logs?"
"We should be able to get them, no problem whatsoever, wait a minute I'll call."
"No, no, don't do that, listen I don't what to alarm anyone, I need more information first, it's a trust issue, can you get them without asking permission?"
"Sure but . . ."
"Not another word, just do it, you have the president's backing."

"It will take a few minutes maybe even longer depending on the jumps I need to make."

"Whatever you get, just send it to me, I want no other eyes on this, you got that?'

"Yes and will do."

●　　●　　●

Chapter 58

Jorja was back in her office at the crack of dawn after making funeral arrangements for her Aunt Gracie the day before. Services were going to be held in three days giving ample time in order for family and friends in distant parts of the country to join in the celebration of her life. Jorja's mind was elsewhere but she needed the succorance of work along with the diversion it provided. Her morning routine didn't change. She was drinking her free cup of caffeine. She was perusing her inbox debating which emails to answer first. She was even running her IP address report and she was always going to run that report because that's how she found god. She was haphazardly scrolling through the list of numbers on the report stopping only when her mind relaxed from the flashing visions of her youth. She didn't notice anything out of the ordinary but she wasn't looking very hard either. Just before she closed the report she doubled checked the priority hit levels. There were no number ones; one being the highest priority. There were a few twos and some threes, the majority of the hits were five or below. She decided to check the twos and threes and when she did an all too familiar IP address stood out in the crowd like a red feathered penguin. It was their email server. It was always getting bombarded with spam and in a chronic hoedown between the spammers and the spam filters. Luckily they had the very best filters installed even though they were in a constant state of flux and updated almost daily.

Amidst the IP addresses that had logged an incident against their email server was another red feathered penguin. This spiked her interest. She recognized the first few numbers of the IP address to that belonging to the federal government, more precisely belonging to the Office of the Director of National Intelligence. Her immediate thought was someone had hijacked the number somehow which was cause for concern, serious cause for concern, especially dealing with the CIA. She had a new rabbit to chase and did some more digging. She found that the IP address belonged to an individual computer located at DNI but that was all she found. A phone call was in order to her counterpart within the DNI office.

"Hi Doug, Jorja from DST"

"Hi Jorja, long time."

"Yes it has been."

"How have you been doing?"

"So so I guess . . . you know, with all that's been happening."

Then Doug noticed the change of inflection in her voice, put two and two together, and tippy-toed around his next question, "Jorja, were you related in anyway . . . to . . . . to Mrs. Carson?"

"She was my aunt . . . well more like my mom after my mom died when I was younger."

"Jesus, I had no idea . . . I'm so sorry Jorja . . . if you need anything, and I mean anything . . . please . . . please let me know okay?"

"Thank you Doug, I certainly appreciate that . . . really I do . . . and one thing you can help me with now is I have a question."

'Shoot.," and as soon as he said it he felt like an ass and hoped to god she really didn't catch it.

"Can you tell me why someone from your office was hitting our email server?"

"What do you mean?"

"This morning's report shows an IP address originating from your walls and was pulling the log files from our machine."

"That seems indivisible by two evenly," trying desperately to elevate some tension in his voice after tasting his socks.

"My thought . . . well not exactly that thought but close. I know there are some spam filters we share but usually there is a mutual sharing of data between us, not a take and ask later sort of deal."

"Agreed. Jorja, do you have the IP address?"

"Yes," and as she gave it to him, she heard him typing away.

"That IP address is an actual desktop computer belonging to Samantha Green. She's pretty good at what she does, her programming skills are on par with some of the best. Do you want to talk to her?'

"Please."

"Can I put her on conference?'

"Yes"

"Hold on, I was never any good at this, if I lose you, just call me back at my number," and he pressed a few buttons.

"Sam, it's Doug, do you have a minute, I have Jorja Carson from DST on the line?'

"Okay."

"Jorja, you still there?'

"You didn't lose me."

"Good, now Sam I'll get to the point, Jorja has a report that has your IP address on it, she says your machine pulled log files from her email server, is that true?"

"Well uhhh," searching for some words, any words, to explain her predicament and realizing Scott never told her what to do if caught, she decided in an instant to come clean. "Yes that is true."

"Can I ask why?"

"I was asked to"

"By who?"

"Scott Norwood."

"The Chief of Staff?"

"Yes."

"Why?"

"He didn't say."

"And the reason you just didn't call for the information?"

"Scott seemed in a hurry, said he didn't want to call attention to it, he also said he had the backing of the president, besides it was just log files, I didn't delete them or manipulate them in any way."

"Sam," stated Jorja, "How well do you know Scott?'

"We went to college together, I really didn't know him that well, lab partners in a few computer classes, that's about it."

"Why did he contact you to pull the files?"

"I've helped him before with finding certain information but that was before he was the chief of staff."

"Alright, I think a phone call is in order, I'm going to call Scott, Sam thanks for your time, and Doug thank you as well."

"Again Jorja, anything you need, just ask."

"Thank you."

●　　●　　●

Chapter 59

Now the gears in Jorja's mind were spinning at an unprecedented rate. She wondered why Scott wanted the logs to her email server and decided to find out before calling him. She logged onto the server, poked around some, and viewed the log files herself. The log files were huge with thousands and thousands of entries for all incoming and outgoing emails. To find anything one would need another application to analyze the data in any way. Luckily she had just the application on her computer. Jorja uploaded the log file to the application and went to town searching in the haystack. Obviously Scott knew what he was searching for hence his specific request to Sam Green. Jorja didn't have the luxury of searching for a particular needle, hell she didn't even know if it was a needle. In her search for something, anything, she did uncover that her spam filters were working as they should, especially when an email had multiple variations of the same name, such as J.Carson, J_Carson, JorjaCarson, and the list goes on. She also noted who in the office had the most emails and who had the fewest. The one who had the fewest emails belonged to a numbered email address which was atypical for their system, actually it was the only numbered email for her system. The address was 111111@dts.gov. She couldn't find who owned this account but spied a message from the sender in the queuing system that kept failing on its outbound connection.

She searched for all emails pertaining to 111111 and there were very few, five in total. All of the outgoing email addresses were similar in that they had the same domain name which was hotmail.com. This domain offered free email services with anonymity, very popular for the porn surfers trying to hide their already unknowingly exposed identity. The email names were very similar as well with seemingly random numbers and always the letters "sc." There was 83683sc@hotmail.com, 123794sc@hotmal.com, 17400 1sc@hotmail.com. 234318sc@hotmail.com, and 304741sc@hotmail.com.

She clicked on the most recent email:

> **From:** reynolds [mailto:jreynolds@thebetagroupdc.com]
> **To:** 304741sc@hotmail.com
> **Subject:** the tree of life

> *For the grace of god you should love thy neighbor no matter how righteous they may be. Travel by car or foot but spread the wealth of his love by speech or written word. Be his son in the shadows and take his hand in both time of need and abundance. The newly dead will rise to see a new glory upon this earth. Go forth; explain in detail the heavenly kingdom above. Commitment, sacrifice, and complete understanding are essential to eternal life. This is where you shall sit and fill your soul with the appetite of peace. His people are the true believers. It is you who will be the same if you heed his word.*

She quickly noticed the from address of jreynolds was the same company Bake Remus had worked. Interesting. Jorja then read the email encompassed in spiritual rhetoric. She was struck by the odd construction of the sentences. She read it again. She thought it might be just a bunch of text or scriptures taken from the Bible and just mashed together to form some sort of epistle She realized once she saw the word "car" that these sentences couldn't possible come from either the Old or New Testament. She noticed god was in lowercase and no mention of Jesus, just him or he. She looked at the subject "the tree of life" and not once was there any use of metaphors pertaining to a tree within its structure. She also noticed the word grace and immediately her mind envisioned a genuine caring smile on her aunt's face. Then her mind started playing tricks on her. She saw the word grace and right under it she saw the word car . . . grace car . . . . then on the next line she saw the word son . . . . it was as though this email was talking to her personally . . . . grace car . . . son . . . grace car . . . son . . . grace carson. She didn't move pass these three lines. She just kept repeating over and over again grace carson, grace carson, grace carson. She reread the email trying to convey its true meaning but she kept coming back to the words grace, car, and son. "What are the odds," she thought. Grace car, and son, grace carson, grace carson . . . then she noticed the word dead in the next line . . . . grace carson dead. The email was speaking to her. She shook her head as to try and clean out any cobwebs or to restart her logical skills. Grace carson dead. That was a fact but why was this email trying to tell her that. She got up from her chair and walked around her office, still shaking her head and still uttering to herself, grace carson dead, grace carson dead. She went to the window to try to refocus her mind. The very first thing she saw was a tree, the tree of life, she couldn't shake it. She went back to her desk. She took a deep breath and sat back down. She took another deep breath and tried to refocus her mind. She reread the email again only this time she didn't read the first four sentences. Nothing stood out. She reread the first four lines and her mind instantly went back to grace carson dead. Then her analytical skills kicked in. She noticed each of these words was the third word in the sentence. "Was this just a coincidence," she thought until she took the third word in each of the remaining sentences. "Holy," and taking a word right out of Greg's vocabulary, "fuck!" she said aloud.

• • •

Chapter 60

"This is no fucking coincidence," she convinced herself. "This has to be what Scott was looking for, this has to be it." Then she stopped and realized that this email was probably meant for the person who murdered her aunt. She quickly opened the previous email looking for more clues. Her phone rang. She looked at the incoming number and didn't answer it. Her inbox was starting to fill but she didn't answer any of them. She was too engrossed to care as she read another spiritually bullshit filled email:

From: reynolds [mailto:jreynolds@thebetagroupdc.com]
To: 234318sc@hotmail.com
Subject: go forth my friend

These are true blessings to hold close to the heart. It is not for the sake of argument but for the prosperity of his will. One must abandon this creed in order to alleviate one's feelings of lust and desires. The shadows of evening are upon us all, we must look towards his son for light and inspiration. The eternal flames at the gates of hell will penetrate the souls of the condemned. Them, him or her cannot pronounce your acts of violence or disgrace, they are your acts, and yours alone. You are welcomed home only when the wanting stops and realizing the existence of him is enough fulfillment. Always in the after, always in the before, and always will it ever be. It is the eleventh hour for which the soul will falter if it is not true. One must genuflect before the hand of the almighty in order to forgive the sins of the past. Knowledge from all twelve apostles shall shed light upon a darkened soul so go onward and spread their words.

She read every third word and it made no sense whatsoever. She looked for the word "grace" and found none. The only thing close was the word "son" and nothing else. This email was a dead end, nothing jumped out at her so she moved onto the next one.

From: reynolds [mailto:jreynolds@thebetagroupdc.com]
To: 174001sc@hotmail.com
Subject: to each their own

The target of acceptance to his kingdom comes from acts of kindness and love without predetermine actions. The grace of thy holy benefits only those who shall follow in his footsteps. The care for all his creations shall nurture the fruits of its tree with deep roots of strength. The sun will always shine upon those who believe and clouds will follow for those who don't. The senator or congressman do not make his law or shall reign in his spirit. Nor wife nor husband shall dictate false meanings of love to their children. The time will come for justification and redemption but for he who loves only thyself will be turned away to follow the dark angles. Go to the pulpit and listen with open heart, speak of open heart, and bask in his glory. For be the one who proclaims his word, his love, and you will be rewarded. You determine the true path by following the true feelings within thyself and repent from all evil. In order to forgive one must learn from past mistakes and understand their meanings within the soul. To shoot an arrow and penetrate thy enemy's heart is very much like speaking with a forked tongue and damning thy neighbor. The quality of life upon the earth is not just cause for the quality of life forever in his kingdom. The pictures within one's mind are enough to deny entry into this everlasting peace so rid the evil through the baptism of forsaken thoughts.

Those of little faith will have a chance at salivation only
if their hearts are pure. His subjects cannot be condemned
without his final word and shall face him on judgment day.

Her mind was still stuck on every third word, until she came to the word grace again. This time it was the second word in the sentence. She quickly picked out each second word and came up with:

Target grace care son senator wife time to be determined order shoot quality pictures of subject.

She went to the first email she had read, this one had every third word, she looked at the subject line . . . . "tree of life," she looked at the subject of this one "to each their own," and just like that she broke the code. She went to the second email entitled "go forth my friend" and read every fourth word.

blessings for this evening at her home after eleventh before twelve.

This was sent on the day of the murders just before 2 pm.

It seemed this jreynolds had someone working for him, call it an agent or spy but someone was on the other end of the strings. She had three emails from the puppeteer, jreynolds, one was the prime directive, one with the actual time, the last one was asking what went wrong and requested the location of the marionette.

Was this what Scott was after? Was he trying to help or cover up his own tracks, his own mistake, was the president really involved," there were a seemingly a million more questions that followed but she had to focus on just one. She chose to focus on the "who were these emails going to."

●　　●　　●

Chapter 61

When Reynolds finally sobered up from his internet intoxication he opened up his email. In there was an email from 304741sc@hotmail. com. He knew right away who it was from—it was from the man with the answers, it was from the lieutenant colonel John Smith. He immediately clicked it open.

> **From:** 234318sc@hotmail.com
> **To:** jreynolds@thebetagroupdc.com
> **Subject:** first down and goal to go
>
> *Now it's late in the game with the skins down by 6. What they cannot do is lose or they'll be out of the playoffs for sure. How many chances do they get this late in the game? Long yardage is never good on first down, especially being so close to the goal and they are now back beyond the red zone due to the holding call. Should they pass or run? I would pass; running for that many yards late in the game is risky at best. Stay in the pocket, relax, look down field for all your receivers, and only pull the trigger when the coast is clear. Here and now baby, here and now.*

He deciphered the email and wrote his response. Reynolds was quick with his bible talk; growing up a strict Baptist did have its advantages although after the sights and sounds of life in the marine core he was now a strict atheist. He hit send and waited patiently for the response which never came. Usually within minutes his emails were answered. John could churn out sports talk like grinding meat into sausage links. It was going on thirty minutes and still no response. He waited another thirty, then called Scott.

"I hope you have answers Reynolds, if not . . ."
  "About an hour ago I received an email from my handler."
  "You mean John Smith."
  "Yes"
  "I thought he was dead?"
  "What? I never said that, I said I never got in touch with him."
  "Sorry, go on."
  "Like I said, I just got an email from him, basically asking what's next, and how long should he stay at the safe house."
  "Where's the safe house?'
  "I don't know, I was never in contact with him, hold on, back up a bit, well I was, I told him the target and the course of action, but I never told him where or when."
  "Maybe he was in surveillance mode and took it upon himself."
  'Never, he's one of the best I have ever worked with, he would never go against a direct order or take it upon himself to act unless permitted to do so."
  "We need to find him and find him fast."
  "I already sent an email, I'm waiting for his response."
  "What did the email say?'
  "I asked him to explain why she was dead, and to find out where he was."
  "Send me the email."
  "It's in code."
  "I don't care about that, I want to view it."
  "Okay on its way."
  "Now the second he gets back to you . . ."
  "I know I'll call."

Reynolds went back to staring at his inbox while Scott dialed back into the system to see if John Smith was back online. When he entered in his password he got a Permission Denied message. "Son-of-a-fucking-bitch, that cocksucker. First he lies to me, now he locks me out of the fucking system." He knew in an instant that his friend and foe had locked him out. He didn't want to get into a pissing contest but he was going to have to contact his boss sooner than later, for now he elected to review the email Reynolds had sent him.

With little surprise he saw the same IP address as earlier. The log files that were sent to him were pretty useless only because he had no idea what he was looking at or for but at least now he had a clue. He wanted to find exactly where Reynolds' email was being sent; maybe that way he could deduce the whereabouts of the lieutenant. He got back on the horn to Samantha Green.

"Hey Sam, I need you to do me the same favor again, but narrow the search to only the last two hours."

"I have to warn you, Jorja Carson from the DST was talking to me about this very same thing, she knows that I pulled the log files for you."

"Jorja Carson?"

"That's right."

"How did she find out?"

"Seems we turned up on some report in their system when I dialed in to retrieve the files."

"That was fast."

"I'd say, do you still want me to get them?"

"No, looks like I'll have to go through the proper channels this time, thanks, and if I need anything else, I'll call."

"Jorja Carson," he said to himself and then it clicked like a bullet entering the chamber. Jorja Carson, niece of one Senator Floyd Carson, niece of the now deceased Grace Carson, Jorja Carson Deputy Director of the DS&T. "Son-of-a-fucking-bitch!" He was going to have to make a call, a call in which he didn't want to make in any way shape or form.

● ● ●

Chapter 62

Jorja toyed with the idea of getting a hold of Reynolds but he didn't know where his rogue agent was hiding based on his last email. Since his email was never forwarded requesting the rogue agent's location because it was still sitting in the inbox of <u>111111@dts.gov</u> Jorja had the upper hand but there was still plenty of risk involved. She was going to try and make contact with the person who possibly murdered her aunt.

Jorja needed to construct an email. She wanted the "from" email to look as though it was from jreynolds@thebetagroupdc.com but she wanted it to appear in her inbox during the reply. A few years ago she confiscated, from an employee, a handy little program that spoofed a sender's email address. This little program is widely used by spammers and jokesters alike. Her employee played little pranks around the office by sending emails to various colleagues from the likes of George W. Bush thanking them personally for a job well done, the human resource department telling them to take a shower because people are starting to complain of the odor, or doctor so and so stating their test came back positive. It was a good laugh but like all good things in the office world, if it made people laugh, it needs to stop, work should be serious at all times. She never once wanted to use this program, until now. It was straight forward and she ran a few tests to make sure it worked as planned. The only problem was if the person receiving the email reviewed the complete header information they could theoretically find the true sender. She took that chance and sent jreynolds original email entitled "tree of life" to 304741sc@hotmail.com, if he replied without noticing a thing it would be forwarded to her gmail account email address plain and simple.

While she waited, more like hoped and prayed for a reply she had work to do. If she could figure out the next sequence of the agent's hotmail account she could literally become Reynolds. She deleted the message from its inbox on her server and forwarded it to herself along with the rest of the previously sent emails. There had to be some sort of connection in the sequence numbers and given time she could probably figure it out but time was of the essence. She called Greg.

"Hello, you have reached the voicemail of Greg, please leave a detailed message and I will return your call as soon as possible, if you need immediate assistance, please contact Jorja Carson at extension 1134."
"Greg, Jorja, give me a buzz as soon as you can."

She dialed his cell and received a similar response. He was not answering. This was a rarity for Greg, even if he was on the john, that boy answered. She decided to take a crack at it herself

83683, 123794, 174001, 234318, 304741

Each number was greater than the last. Each number alternated between odd and even and she was almost sure the next one would be even. She plugged in all the numbers both separately and as a complete string into Google and did a search. She was hoping they were a sequence within pi or the mathematical constant e or something along those lines. No such luck. When she did them separately she found all sorts of hits ranging from gene sequence numbers to Amazon product codes but nothing was consistent across the board. Off the top of her head she did some quick calculations and found the next number increase by a factor of ten thousand each time. The second number was approximately forty thousand more than the first, the third was approximately fifty thousand more than the second, so on and so forth. She did the actual difference between each number and found the exact increase from one number to the next.

40111, 50207, 60317, 70423

Nothing stood out except each one of these numbers was five digits long. "Maybe zip codes," and she went back to the web. 40111, Cloverport, Kentucky, 50207, New Sharon, Indiana, 60317, didn't exist, and neither did 70423. "That wasn't it." She then searched for these numbers within Google and received the same results as before; there was no string tying them together. She looked at the numbers again and noticed each of these numbers was odd and smiled when she remembered Doug's earlier comment. "Odd, number, odd numbers," she kept repeating to herself, "odd but how about prime, prime being a number only divisible by 1 and itself." She remembered one of her college proofs in one of her mathematics class stating 2 can be the only even prime number. She entered 40111 and the word "prime" into her favorite search engine. About the fourth or fifth hit within the page was a reference to 40111 and a list of prime numbers between 2 and 100,000. She opened the list. She searched for 50207. She found it. She searched for 60317. She found it. She searched for 70432. She did not find it. Then she noticed she transposed the numbers and then found 70423 was also on the list and thus a prime number. "Each one of these numbers was prime, coincidence, I think not." She assumed the next number in the sequence was going to be prime as well, "but just what was the next prime number?" She examined them even more. Each of these prime numbers was roughly ten thousand more than the first, well closer to ten thousand one hundred. If she were to add ten thousand one hundred to the next number she needed a prime number close to 80523. She looked at the list—there were two, 80513 and 80527. 80513 wasn't closer but without going over like as in bidders row on The Price is Right she thought. Then in her head she heard, "80513 come on down you are the next contestant on the number is right." She added this number to the last email and came up with the new email address of 385254sc@hotmail.com. "But what if I'm wrong?" Before she did anything with the email address, she deduced that she had a fifty-fifty chance in picking the right prime given the fact adding ten thousand one hundred, give or take, gives the next prime number in the sequence. "Ah, hell, send both, what's it gonna hurt." So Jorja now had two email address the other one being 385268sc@htomail.com.

She came this far, now the only thing left to do was construct the email to the person who murdered her aunt. Her phone rang.

"Hey Greg, never mind."

"What?"

"I had a little problem on my hands but my math skills solved them."

"Do you care to share?"

"Nah, too long to explain, maybe later."

"Alight call me if you need me"

She was going to ask him where he was but left it to her imagination, besides if she really wanted to know she had god's eyes for that. After her brief conversation she notice her gmail account said, '1 new message." Her heart was pounding in her chest as she saw an incoming message from <u>304741sc@hotmail.com</u>.

From: 304741sc@hotmail.com
To: jreynolds@thebetagroupdc.com
Subject: great teams have character

The boys are back at home but still have not scored in front of their fans in their last three outings here. When it comes down to winning, digging in deep along the boards is essential to scoring goals in front of the net. Pucks, sticks, and pads, are all the same it's the players that determine the outcome of each game. So it really does not matter which location these professional players skate, it comes down to heart. Both the captain and the team's coach need to communicate both on the ice and on the bench. Remember each and every team can call time only once per game so it is critical to use it wisely. If this game goes into overtime, they cannot call another timeout if they already used one, thus forcing a penalty and be down a man. We had to ask the coach "Please explain why you called time in the first period," when the game was still tied at one. "Old and young hockey players must play through pain of losing" was his reply, which did not answer the question. There is a specific conduct or strict code to adhere by when you adorn the jersey and following it to the letter will help a team rise to the top a coach must also follow these rules.

She circled every eighth word and came up with

still in same location need time cannot explain through code.

So back to work she went and kept her fingers crossed that her bible talk was on par with jreynolds@thebetagroupdc.com. After an hour or so she came up with her email.

> **From:** reynolds [mailto:jreynolds@thebetagroupdc.com]
> **To:**
> **Subject:** feeling alive is a gift
>
> *It is god's eyes we feel and not inner guilt when wrongful judgments are made. He knows all we need is proper guidance and knowledge in order to appreciate our gift of life. The gift is given to all but his everlasting love will only be embraced by those who follow. Faith is the key, talk to those who love you, talk to those who don't but forgive those who do not listen. Only then can the one who has given everything will soak in the warmth of his love and feel eternal peace. The road to faith on which you stand may fill with treachery and hate but wither not for the final destination is near and just reward given. Only then can the one who has traveled this road help others along their way. Breathe in new life, tell his people to cherish all they have even if they have nothing. He says never fear me, place faith in his divine truth and there will be nothing to fear. The pure heart is where pure love is found, love for all, love for him, love for love. Drink from the chalice to become one with him, eat from plate to be nourished by him. In time you will meet all the loving souls who you yourself loved along the way and it will be a time that lasts forever and ever.*

It took some time, it was more difficult than she had originally planned but all-in-all she was content as it offered a nice segway from Reynolds' previous emails. She entered in her two prime generated sequence emails addresses and fired away. Now she would play the waiting game not knowing if she would ever receive a reply. She was pretty sure she nailed the decoding and encoding of the messages but she couldn't help but think that there might be another hidden message embedded within the emails.

● ● ●

Chapter 63

He went upstairs to his kitchen that hadn't seen a coat of paint since its established date. It was a dull yellow thanks to his chimney of a father. At one time the metal yellow cabinets were state of the art. He opened one of the cabinets and pulled out a plate and opened the drawer and pulled out two butter knives. From the bread box he pulled out a loaf of fresh white and took out two slices. From another cabinet he removed a jar of creamy Jif and the traditional Smuckers grape jelly and proceeded to build the perfect pb and j. He used two knives as to not cross contaminate; the one thing he hated was peanut butter on his toast in the morning. Once even amounts of spreads were in place he placed the two halves together. He then removed a bread knife from the drawer and removed the crust. He remembered from long ago she did not like the hard part of the bread. He wasn't happy with his result. He picked it up and simply discarded into the trash bin and pulled out two more slices of bread It took him a good twenty five minutes, almost all of his jars, and ten slices of bread to construct just the right sandwich, he was out of practice. It had to be perfect for her. Finally, it was perfect. Once the construction was done he licked both butter knives, washed them, and placed them back in their proper place. He returned the bread knife as well. He next grabbed his favorite, a small bag of cheese doodles, opened it and placed a small amount as an accompaniment to the sandwich.

With plate in hand he descended the stairs one step at a time. He placed the plate outside the steel door on a cheap plastic patio table. He then went to his watching room, hoping this was the last time he would need it. She was asleep on the bed, with panda bear tucked under her arm. That brought a smile to his face, she loved that bear, she always did. She had the faintest of smiles on her face, and he watched as her chest rose and collapsed with each breath she took. It was rhythmical in his mind. Unknowingly he matched her breath for breath. They were becoming one again. His mind slowly focused on the feelings, the tingly feelings from deep inside of him. They brought along memories upon memories which flooded his mind. He took the trip they provided. The faintest of smiles appeared as it parted his lips just so.

He had butterflies in his stomach. Once again he approached the steel door with apprehension. He took a deep breath. He finally had her back in his life, it had been so long. Would she even remember him, he wondered.

It was time.

With his free hand he undid each lock as quietly as he could. He took another deep breath when the final lock released itself back into the door. Another deep breath when he turned the handle. He slowly opened the door and took a quick glance before he proceeded any farther. Another deep breath. He walked in and closed the door behind him ever so quietly. She was still asleep. He moved towards the bed ever so slowly. Calculating and planning every step. He had finally made it to his destination. Another deep breath. She was still asleep. She was just as beautiful as he had remembered. He loved her so. He climbed into the bed ever so gently as not to wake her. He didn't. He was now next to the one he loved. So close, just like he remembered. He was full of delight, joy, and glee. He stroked her pretty blonde hair the way he used to. She loved that. So did he. She did not wake. He kissed her forehead. She did not wake. His life had meaning again. He loved her so. Even more memories surfaced and a sense of euphoria took control of his body. His imagination took control of his mind. He was back in a world of love, unconditional love. He was happy again. She was awake now.

● ● ●

Chapter 64

Scott was going to have to circumnavigate a potentially very messy situation with Jorja and at the same time offer an olive branch for support. He assured himself that they both wanted the same thing, and that was to find Grace's killer, he just had to hide the fact he was the one who instantiated the plan that went awry. The sooner he called the sooner he could come clean and look like the good guy.

"Jorja, it's Scott Norwood calling, listen I have to be upfront and apologize immediately for my actions this morning."

"You mean for defiling my email server."

'Pun intended I hope?"

"Not on purpose I assure you."

"Again I'm sorry, sorry for not going through the proper channels, I realize I should have gone to you first, but with all that's been happening I didn't know how you would react. See, I have some leads regarding your aunt's death."

"What are they?"

"Not over the phone, hold on a sec," as she heard him speak to someone who entered the room, "no, that won't do, what time does he go? Okay then 7:30 is the earliest I can do, take about fifteen minutes. Sorry about that Jorja, as I was saying I have leads, I don't think the senator was involved but I have to . . ."

"Send them over to me and I'll take a look."

"I do want us to work together on this but I have to verify the authenticity of my findings first."

"May I ask, just why are you involved in this in the first place?"

"Sure you can ask and I'll tell you, just not over the phone, it will have to be in person."

"When?"

"Today . . . wait, . . . how about tonight . . . I have a jammed packed scheduled until almost eight."

"You can't do it now?'

'No, I'm sure you understand I can't leave my boss high and dry but later I have some rare free time. Does after eight this evening work for you?"

"Now works for me but I understand . . . . where?"

"Good question . . . . how about, how about Tosca's, on F Street?"

"For dinner?"

'We can have dinner if you want, I'll have someone make the res . . ."

"No, no, just . . ."

"Listen it will be late, they have good food, sort of kill two birds with one stone."

Jorja thought there are a bunch of insensitive assholes of late, "Fine," saying in disgust as he didn't even realize his foot was in his mouth.

"I'll have a car pick you up. Do you want it from the office or home?"

"I can drive."

"I don't want you to go to any trouble, I'll take care of it, I've done enough already so let me make it up to you."

"Office then."

"If you need anything in the meantime, text, call, email, I'll see you around eight."

"This should be very interesting," once again saying aloud, "having dinner with one of the elite members of god's inner circle, should be very interesting indeed."

Just as Greg was walking in the door, a preview of an email popped up on her screen informing her that she received a reply from 385254sc@hotmail.

<u>com</u>. It quickly vanished as Greg took a seat in front of her desk. Her mind was now elsewhere and Greg saw she was a little agitated.

From: 385254sc@hotmail.com
To: jreynolds@thebetagroupdc.com
Subject: never too late

Saying nay or no or even can't were terms of failure and winners strive for the complete opposite. The lure of being a dynasty was our ultimate goal not just one or two championships and a nice footnote in the pages of history. The road was long, filled with cracks, bumps, potholes, but the path remained straight and never wavered. Not last, not this time, oh no, it was first, first for a long long time. To shelter the storm of our slow and methodical start we bonded together to repel the negative energy both the press and our fans laid upon us. The next time we truly bonded was our first win in a stretch of what we knew would be many. Next to winning it all, our first win was special to us as a team, it meant we could do anything and everything as a team. The kiss of death many thought was having our leader on every cover of every sports magazine in the country, again we proved them wrong. Second and third, fourth and fifth, we never wanted to be like them, nobody ever remembers those people, those teams, we wanted it all. The ride to the top was more enjoyable to ourselves then partaking in the view from the top, we knew we would be there again and again. All eleven players on the field gave it their all one hundred percent of the time. In tonight's victory the cream will once again rise to the top and we'll be forever known as a dynasty of greatness, a dynasty of remembrance, a dynasty of legends.

Decoding the message was brief.

●　●　●

Chapter 65

His first obvious thought came long after his initial thoughts, long after he first saw Ripley's innocent face on the news, long after calling Mrs. Polaski, but shortly after his discovery of his treasure chest, that being of Kyle Kraner's medical records. His obvious thought was to place Kyle Kraner on the national registry for sex offenders. It was simple to do and he kicked himself for not thinking of it sooner. With that highly visible warning flag in place it was onto the next task at hand. He had to carefully place breadcrumbs for all the Hansels and Gretels working the case yet make it difficult for them to follow. Too many crumbs could lead them onto the wrong path, one where a quizzical mind starts to question not the end point but the starting point of his directions.

Tick . . . tick . . . tick . . . tick . . . he knew time was of the essence, he also knew Ripley was still alive but he also knew Kyle was home. If he would have stopped to think about it he would have driven himself insane. He didn't. He continued. Armed with his recently excavated data he proceeded to map out a weave of deception backed by facts, his facts and not necessarily the true facts. He knew what the feds brought to the table; he knew their tools, their methodology, their skill set, he had seen them in action first hand. He saw their queries into their database; he saw them trying to find that impossible needle with improbable cause. He was there to help.

He had piles of data and just needed a place to put it but first he had to organize it. He had to think like a pedophile which wasn't easy for him. He did a bit of online research to help with this mindset.

He knew the feds had a list of supplies that one might need to support this addiction. He circled the ones that were of interest and decided to go shopping on Kyle's behalf. He grouped the supplies into three categories. The first was lure. What exactly was needed to entice his victims? Items such as candy, toys, and even pets fell into this niche. The next was sustain. What exactly was needed to support the victims over time? Items such as food, clothing, and again toys made an appearance on this list. His final category was called closure.

● ● ●

Chapter 66

The car had been waiting for Jorja since 6:30 but she didn't leave her office until almost exactly seven o'clock. She logged out of the network, went to the ladies room to freshen up a bit by spritzing her favorite perfume that she kept in her purse, added a little hairspray, and checked her makeup. She walked out of the door almost unnoticed. Greg knew from the moment he walked into her office earlier that day that something was amiss and his nose confirmed it as she walked by the vicinity of his cube. As soon as she walked out the office the driver of the car popped out from behind the wheel and opened her door like he knew her all his life. When she entered the backseat she suddenly felt butterflies in the pit of her stomach, first date like butterflies. She hadn't felt like this in a long long time. She kept saying to herself, "this is not a date, this is not a date." Sure Scott Norwood was a good looking guy, slightly older, unmarried, super smart and the right hand man to the most powerful man in the world but she was meeting him to discuss her aunt's death and nothing more. It was about an hour ride to F Street passing the White House in route.

When she entered the restaurant the maitre d'escorted her to a very private table where Scott was already seated with a bottle of uncorked wine. He promptly stood like all proper gentlemen do and pushed in her chair as she sat. He was struck by her grace but more so by her natural beauty, thinking to himself, "pictures don't do her justice." After the maitre d'vanished from sight only then did Scott utter a word.

"Jorja, I just want thank you for meeting me here and once again I would like to apologize for not contacting you first."

"Water under the bridge as far as I'm concerned, so what's this information regarding my aunt?'

"We'll get to that, I promise, can we at least ease into it, are you hungry?"

"Starved."

He laughed a bit, "That's funny, most women I know don't even admit they eat."

"I'm not like most women, I enjoy a good steak over some dainty greenery any day of the week, but don't look in my fridge at home, it says just the opposite."

"Filled with yogurt and bottled water?"

"Not too far off I'm afraid"

"So let's get back to your, I'm not like most women thing, I've done a bit of research on you, and if I may assume, you are indeed correct in that statement."

She was thinking on just how much research did he do, did he use the system, does he know she knows, but she kept those thoughts away from her lips and simply said, "Research? Well I've done some preliminary work on you as well and you are not like most of the men I know."

"Most men aren't the chief of staff."

She laughed, "true, and so is your arrogance I'm afraid."

He laughed, "I can admit to that, it's gotten me this far," and he picked up the bottle of wine and poured some into each glass, dripping a bit on the linen table cloth.

"Amarone, just how much research did you do?"

"Pardon?"

"How did you know Amarone was my favorite wine in the world?"

"I didn't, I was going to go with the 99 Banfi Brunello but I thought I'd give the tax payers a break."

"Good choice nonetheless," and she swirled the glass by its stem, smelled the bouquet, and took a sip.

As she was savoring the quality of the grape juice, Scott summoned the waiter over and after he went over the specials, "do you like veal?"

"Yes."

"Really?'"

"Yes, I'm not one of those members of PETA, more like a person eating the animals."

"You are certainly not like other women," as he smiled yet again this evening, "try the rack of veal then, simply sumptuous."

And she did.

After some small talk about colleges

"Can I ask, when is your aunt's funeral?"

"Monday, we are waiting for family to arrive."

"I'm so sorry and I'm still in a quasi state of shock, we are doing everything we can but if you need . . ."

"What is that exactly and why?"

"To be quite honest, it was my idea, a pretty selfish act on my part, I thought it would be nice publicity if we were to show support to the other party in time of need, instead of all the mudslinging that we are so accustom to this late in the race, so I sort of jumpstarted the investigations through our federal channels, you know pull a few strings outside the jurisdiction of Washington's men in blue."

"I don't buy it for a second. You bring me here, we have a nice dinner, nice wine, even nice conversation, but then you lie to me. I know damn well the president was behind this in some way, I know it has to do with being reelected, my uncle and Anderson were too much of a threat for his second term."

"Okay, Jorja, you are right, I'll come clean . . . just give me a second," he paused as he was searching for the right words and then said in a somber voice, "It was my fault and not the president's."

It took a moment for the words to register, "Your fault . . . what are you saying? Are you the reason for my aunt's murder, am I sitting in front of a murderer?"

He didn't answer right away.

"Well are you?"

"I may have inadvertently put the ball in motion," then he noticed she was visibly upset and angry, "Listen hear me out, please hear me out Jorja, I'll explain, I don't know what went wrong or how it went wrong but I . . . it wasn't supposed to end like this . . ."

"How was it supposed to end . . . huh . . . how was it?" as her voice grew louder.

'With us winning the election and no one getting hurt . . . but . . .'

"But what," as her voice raised an octave higher?

Looking around the room seeing if anyone was listening within the sparse dining room, "Yes it was my plan, so it's my fault . . . it was supposed to be just a tabloid scandal nothing more."

"Explain."

Taking a deep pause and saying lower than his normal tone, "Did you know your aunt was lonely, I mean lonely when it came to companionship?"

"We talked, but she loved her husband deeply but how did you know?" Baiting him.

"The Oval Office has big ears I'm afraid, I don't remember exactly where we heard it but we found out your aunt was having an affair."

"With Blake?"

"This time with Blake, yes."

"Are you saying . . ."

"No I'm not, they might have just been rumors before but with Blake it was different, different because I truly believe your aunt was in love with him. Now put yourself in my place for a second, I found out that our adversaries, namely Mr. Goody-Two-Shoes' wife is having an affair right in the middle of the big campaign, right in the middle, how could I not exploit that?"

"You don't, I know damn well that . . . ," and she wanted to call him out on the carpet about Blake but she wanted more facts first.

"That what?"

"Nothing."

"Listen, I have to exploit what I found, it's part of my job, whether you like it or not, I have to find the dirt, expand the truth into statistical lies, and throw mud around, that's what we do in a race, your uncle and Anderson would have done the very same if they had caught the president with his pants down."

"Not my uncle."

"Don't be so sure of yourself, yes your uncle was, is, a good man, but he has skeletons in his closet, he has deep dark dirty secrets as well, we all do to some degree."

Jorja stopped in her tracks as her brain flashed to her mother's boat, then to the scan of her uncle's fingerprints; she didn't say a word as Scott rambled on. "So when I was presented with this information, the only thing I wanted to do was to exploit it, I wanted pictures, solid evidence of her torrid affair with a younger man, I wanted to win this race, I wanted another term with my boss, so yes, I took it upon myself to try and win this election. An affair of this nature wouldn't have been swept under the rug, it would have run like a bull in the streets of Pamplona. It would have stopped your uncle's train right in its tracks, maybe even derailed his political career but that's how the game is played in today's world. No one gives a shit about anything other than winning."

As his words went in through her brain without so much of a speed bump, she refocused and said, "Why was my aunt murdered if this was just going to be some pictures? Answer me that Mr. Chief of Staff."

"I don't have an answer for you."

"Then start by telling me everything, and I mean everything."

"Not much to tell, we, I acquired an agent we use from time to time to research a few things for us, I told him we wanted pictures of your aunt and Blake."

"Who was this person, what's his name?"

"Captain Jack Reynolds, he is a retired marine, works for The Beta Group of D.C. now doing something with software, he was a great field op in his prime."

She seemed convinced he was starting to tell the truth since she recognized that name from those emails, "So he was your purposive photographer, where is he now?"

"He was not the photographer, see Reynolds knows a lot of people, I basically told him what I wanted and he was the means to the end, the kindling so to speak."

"Then who was his contact."

"That I do not know for certain, only by what Reynolds has given me, and that name was John Smith, a lieutenant colonel, Reynolds cannot get in contact with him, actual no one can and we have tried every means possible."

"Which are," baiting him even more for the question she already knew the answer to?

"I'm not a liberty to say, but let's just say we turned over every rock and still no sign of him, he may have been extinguished as well."

"So those emails on my machine, these were going to and from Reynolds and Smith?"

"That is correct."

"Then why were they on my machine?"

"We don't know the answer to that either, that's where we could use your help."

"My help, you have some fucking nerve, you know that, I could just bring this whole thing to the public."

Scott was taken aback by her sudden change of wording, "Yes, yes you could, you could try to misdirect the media away from your uncle, after all he is the prime suspect, and you just never know if the smoking gun would surface or not, so I'm giving you the opportunity to work with us, to find the killer, he's still out there, and we both believe it is not your uncle."

•   •   •

Chapter 67

Jorja elected not to take the car back to the office; she had another destination in mind. She looked at her watch and figured she had plenty of time to catch the Metro. It was a short walk to the Metro Center Station at G and 12th and at 10:19 her metro whisked her away to Gallery Place Chinatown. She made her way through the turnstiles and tunnels to the Green Line. She had about a ten minute wait for an eastbound train. It arrived precisely at 10:36. She boarded the car, sat in the closest seat available to the door, immediately glanced at the metro map, and counted in her mind eight stops until Naylor Road. Each time the train stopped she counted down in her mind the number of stops left and glanced at the map to double check her math. During her seventeen minute jaunt she played the "I wasn't looking at you," eye dancing game with the few passengers on the fairly empty car. It was the game where the eyes fixated on a point of interest, usually another person, until that person catches the stare, causing the eyes to dart in a different direction. She played that game until the eighth stop had arrived, she doubled checked the station sign just to make sure and left the car. Her mind was preoccupied with the passengers and the map and it wasn't until she placed her feet on the platform and felt the slight rush of wind from the departing train did she realize why she was here. Her nerves got the better of her as she watched the only other passenger to exit vanish down the stairs and out of sight. The well lit parking lot looked rather sparse from her point of view and looked even more barren as she walked down the steps and made her way towards the last bus shelter. During her walk she kept her eyes and head in constant motion looking for the slightest of movements in the dark shadows beyond the boundaries of the metro station. She saw none. She heard a car start and saw the headlights turn on, then she saw the taillights and figured it was the only other passenger that had exited with her. She checked her watch and it was two minutes to eleven, although perfect timing she was beginning to second guess herself, second guessing her stupidity for coming in the first place, for coming alone, for coming unprotected, for not telling anyone where she was going. She was rattled but tried not to show it. When she reached the last shelter, she tensed; she was very vulnerable and could be seen in every direction—the glass shelter provided no protection whatsoever. It was a chilly evening for the beginning of October, even with all the global warming; she could almost see her breath. She looked at her watch. It was now exactly eleven. She looked again. She peered into the abyss that surrounded her and saw nothing and heard nothing. She waited as her muscles tensed even more. Then she heard a sound. It startled her. It was a vehicle approaching, more so, it was a bus. She watched as it entered the parking lot, she watched as it came closer. All the interior lights were off. She looked around again, then back at the bus. It grew closer, it grew louder. It turned the bend, passed all the other shelters, and promptly stopped in front of Jorja. With the hissing of the air brakes, the lights came on, and the door opened. She looked at her watch again. It was 11:05. She looked at the driver as expecting him to instruct her on what to do next. He didn't say a word. She looked at the bus and saw it was completely empty except for the driver. She had no idea where this bus was headed. She nervously looked at her watch again and looked at the driver and said to herself, "was the driver the sender of the message, he never instructed me to take the bus." Her mind feverishly tried to comprehend the situation. She waved the driver off. He closed the door and she watched it as it exited the lot. She looked at her watch again, 11:06. She had memorized the departure times for this metro stop; the next train back was due in four minutes or she could wait a bit more and take the 11:29. She opted to get the hell out of Dodge. She glanced around one more time and hightailed it back to the platform. She felt slightly winded as she reached the top of the stairs and felt her heart pounding against her chest as though she just raced a marathon. Jorja didn't feel any safer in the confines of the open air station, even when she saw the lights of the train that was right on time, nor did she calm down when she finally entered the metro car. She cursed herself practically the entire ride back to Gallery Place where she hopped a cab back home since she didn't want to make the trek back to Langley.

Her sense of vulnerability while waiting at the glass shelter was warranted as it was a perfect spot for the lieutenant colonel John Smith to view his prey from the second floor of the Econo Lodge. He had an inkling that the last email wasn't from Reynolds, he couldn't pinpoint it exactly, it was just a gut feeling, a hunch, a hunch that panned out. With his trusty Nikon D90 and a telephoto lens he snapped a few quality shots of Jorja Carson without her knowledge and within minutes uploaded the pictures to his laptop. He had no idea who this woman was but his inquiring mind wanted to know. He took twenty photos in all, picked out the two best shots, zipped them, and thought about sending them to Reynolds via email but since his email address seemed to be hijacked by this very same woman in his photos that would be a futile attempt. Instead he sent them to another colleague of his who had some pretty nifty facial recognition software and access to a slew of databases stocked full of photographs from such places as DMV's, FBI's most wanted, the United States Department of State, and the list goes on. He sent the zip files and assumed he should have some sort of answer by tomorrow afternoon at the latest. He glanced at his watch, turned off his laptop, turned on the TV, and watched the rest of David Letterman in his makeshift prison.

At the other end of town Jorja was still uneasy and still cursing herself out for such a stupid move on her part. Only once she was in the confines of her home did her fears dissipate somewhat. With the door locked behind her she went straight to her office, more directly, she went straight to the system. She brought up the location of the metro stop and wanted to see if anyone was watching her, mainly the rogue agent named John Smith. She entered 11:00 pm and a radius of two hundred yards. The screen filled with emptiness. She entered another time, 11:05. Again the screen filled with emptiness. No data whatsoever. She entered 10:55pm. Still nothing. No one. Not even herself. Strange she thought. She expanded the radius to three hundred, then four hundred, then five hundred and still nothing. Only when the radius was over a thousand did she start to see some social security numbers. She was, for all intents and purpose, looking at a dead zone in the eyes of god. She also thought that there was no way in hell this was some sort of coincidence. She didn't sleep much that night with all the extra processing her brain was doing.

By the next morning Jorja's tired cortex was brimming with so many unfocused thoughts that even the mundane tasks of her normal wakeup routine took a bit of time to accomplish. This forced her into a running late mode which she was clearly unaccustomed to and as a result she searched a full ten minutes for her keys before realizing her car was still at the garage. While she waited for the cab, she grabbed a much needed eye-opener in her backup to-go cup. Once inside the cab she felt relieved that she didn't have to concentrate on the morning commute, then she tried once again to wrap her arms around yesterday's events to produce a big picture. She couldn't. She would need help. She could turn to only one person—the person she trusted most, her colleague, Greg. Maybe together they could fine tune the dial and get a picture that was digital in quality. She felt a slight sense of comfort knowing her colleague was there to help.

Once through the doors of DS & T she went straight to Greg only to find he too was running late as there were no signs of disturbance at his desk. As she started to turn towards her office her Blackberry buzzed. It was a message from Greg.

"Running late, have few personal items 2 attend 2, will be in by 12."

Out of all the days to choose his rare non-appearance this had to be the worst. She took a deep breath and just hoped he would be here before her big meeting with Scott and Reynolds so she could bounce a couple of things off of him.

Throughout the morning she was constantly checking her watch, checking her emails, and even checking her text messages for some sort of communication from Greg. She finally got a glimpse of him as he walked by her office just prior to lunch. She immediately rose from her desk and started out the door after him. She saw he was carrying some sort of white bag with him as she followed him to his desk.

When she finally caught up with him, "Hey Greg, I need . . ."

"Sorry I'm late, did you get my text."

"Yes and I need to talk to . . ."

"Like I said I had a few personal things to do this morning," cutting her off on purpose. "So did you do anything exciting last night?"

"No, not really but . . ."

"You left rather late, how come you didn't drive home, if your car was on the fritz you could have asked me for a ride I would have been glad to . . ."

"I . . . how did you know?"

"Jorja, I park on the same level, remember? And I stayed here rather late myself, you had already left but your car was still here. It struck me as odd."

"Well, actually I," and then she noticed the bag Greg was holding in his hand and was sort of lost for words, "I, I, was meeting a friend from, from high school that I hadn't spoken to in years, met of all places on Facebook."

'I never would have figured you to be a Facebook type of person."

"I wasn't, I'm not, I was just curious was all,' and for the first time in her life she was becoming uncomfortable in talking with Greg.

"So did you two get reconnected, is he married, divorced, gay?"

"Well I don't . . . hey I never said it was a man."

"You didn't have too, first time on Facebook, I just knew you were looking up old boyfriends, it's only natural to see what first loves are up to these days."

"We had a nice time, yes, but he was just in town for the evening and happily married I might add, I'm not looking for anything, just catching up," lying through her teeth.

'I'm not judging you, you have your own life I can respect that. So what did you want?'

"Oh, um nothing it can wait, but later on, I need to go over a few things with you, it's about covering for me while I'm at my aunt's funeral."

"Jorja, I was going to go."

"No, no, you don't have too."

"Jorja, I'm a friend, I'll be there for support, you don't have to go through it alone."

"I know but . . . but I don't know . . . I gotta go, we'll talk later."

She spun around and headed back to her office. She replayed the conversation she just had with Greg over in her head. Something was amiss. She knew it as soon as she spotted that white bag he was holding. She tried not to let her eyes glance upon it too long but sure enough the bag had Tosca's name and logo on it; it was the very same restaurant she ate at last night. Something definitely was amiss. He probably already knew who she had dinner with as well. She suspected he was using the system without her knowledge. She started to almost shake as her mind slowly came to the realization that Greg might be watching her, even stalking her. "Was this really happening? Maybe it was just a bizarre twist of fate or something," she said to herself. Before she could question anymore she felt the vibration of her phone and read the text message. Her car to the West Wing was here. She headed to her office grabbed her coat and purse and without double-checking herself in front of a mirror was out the door in under two minutes. It was a short ride by Washington's standards to 1600 Pennsylvania Avenue and she went through the normal security procedures and was seated in Scott's office to await his arrival. Within five minutes Scott entered with who she could surmise was Captain Reynolds.

"Jorja Carson, Captain Jack Reynolds."

"Please just call me Reynolds, "as he took the chair next to her.

"So this is the Reynolds who killed my aunt."

"Jorja . . . . Jorja . . . we have no idea what happened remember . . . . we are on the same side here."

"No we're not, you are just trying to save your asses, it's the fact that my aunt is dead because of some concoction you two dreamed up . . . . remember that. I'm here to find the truth, I'm here to find out who murdered my aunt."

"Well, let's start by trying to find that truth, I have a meeting in an hour with the president to discuss my findings. I'd like to start with a timeline of past events and Reynolds correct me when I'm wrong. It was the second week of February, not sure of the exact date but Villanova and Georgetown were playing. The president was concerned with his numbers and even more concerned with his next term. He wanted to win at any cost. Shortly afterwards I found out that Grace Carson, the wife of a possible running mate was having an affair, I think it was in March or April. Now with the president needing a win and with what just fell in our laps I decided to hold it in my back pocket until the primaries were solidified, a precautionary measure. Only once we had the official November ballot, did I call Reynolds for help with my dirt, that was late September and lucky for us she was still involved with this Blake fellow. I just wanted proof, I wanted photographs and it's not like I could go snooping around in someone's backyard with a camera around my neck."

"That's where I came in, I had a photographer on call."

"You mean your b o, John Smith."

"That's correct Jorja, he's one of the best I ever worked with, he could get up close and personal, probably fuck you in your sleep without you even knowing it. He was the invisible fly on the wall so to speak and he never lost that touch. I wanted him to keep his distance and I was going to inform him when to make his move, only I never told him to move."

"Yet someone did."

"That's where you come in, see I collected all of Reynolds' emails and I noticed all of them went through your email server which struck me as odd, so I called up Sam who always did fine work for me when I was director. She pulled the logs but before I could make any sense of them you called."

"So Reynolds, you are saying you never sent the email to John Smith three nights ago."

"The email," using his fingers as quotation marks, "I suppose you have an email in mind."

Jorja, pulled a piece of paper from her folder and handed it to Reynolds, "So you are saying you never sent this message?"

Reynolds read it, and reread it, then handed it to Scott, "Yes that is my original message."

Scott read the email, "That's some shitty ass writing Reynolds, your coding technique needs a bit of work as well but this is the proof that we just wanted pictures."

Jorja was wondering if Scott had broken the code that fast or knew it already, then said, "How about this one," as she handed Reynolds another piece of paper.

He took a moment, "That is not my writing . . . my code but not my writing . . . . where did you get this?"

"You didn't send this?"

"No"

"How about this one?"

Reynolds read that one as well and promptly said, "No, not that one either, I told you I did not communicate the time or place to Smith, again where did you get these?"

"From my machine, my server, if you didn't send them, then who did?"

'Can I ask you, why are they on your server?"

"I don't know."

"So you are saying that Reynolds' emails are being routed to your server, at the CIA, yet someone is also sending emails from that very same server to John Smith."

"It looks that way, yes."

'So it could be someone from the outside?"

"Possibly."

"I thought DST had state of the art protection against this sort of thing, I mean you certainly knew when I, Sam, tripped your sensors, yet you didn't know someone was taking control of your email server, I don't buy it. What I think is that someone within DST was sending those emails."

Jorja started doing the simple math and she didn't like the summation, "not necessarily."

"It makes perfect sense, that's why your alarms didn't go off, hell it might even be you."

"Me?"

"Yes, you, you have access"

"But why me?"

"Good question, maybe you got wind of what we were up to, you wanted to play your own game, you know, make sure your uncle wins."

"Wins, wins how, by killing my aunt Gracie? You got some," she paused, then through clenched teeth, "some," and wanted to place an expletive in the mix but elected not to, "nerve . . . beside that makes no sense whatsoever."

"I'm playing devil's advocate, we came up with the plan, yet the emails are on your server, the string that ties it all together here is your last name and the evidence is in plain sight. Maybe you wanted to catch us in the act of catching your aunt in the act, so you sent your own agent out to intercept ours but something happened along the way and now your aunt is dead with possibly our lieutenant colonel and that's why we can't find him."

"You still have no straws in your hand with that screen door theory of yours."

"There may be a lot of holes to fill but it is a plausible explanation and you can't deny it's a considerable coincidence that these emails pertaining to your aunt would wind up on the very same email server that her niece is the guardian."

"So why do I come here looking for answers if I already knew the answers?"

"Anticipatory deniability, to throw us off your scent."

Jorja hung on that word, not anticipatory, not deniability, but rather the word scent. She then began searching for words, "Um . . . what if . . ."

"So Jorja you can see our predicament. Your server, your emails."

"No no . . . wait a minute . . . ," she was now back on the same train of thought before she left for the White House. She didn't like it. She felt a pit in the bottom of her stomach. She felt unsure. She felt vulnerable. She felt a pinball of emotions and all of them led to unsettling feelings. "What if . . . ." She felt betrayed. "What if, like you said before someone else placed those emails on my server, someone besides me, someone besides you?"

"Someone from within your office. Who?"

"Listen I got to go," as she stood and gathered her belongings.

"Jorja, who?'

"I want to confirm my suspicions before you call out the firing squad."

"Jorja, I want a name, I need a name now, I'm seeing the President in a few, he's going to want a name goddamnit!"

"I can't give you that now, if I do, your men will get to . . . get to this person first," as she was careful not to give them any hints in using a pronoun.

"Goddamnit Jorja . . ."

"Listen if you are so concerned, give him your name, give him Reynolds, you are the two bastards with the plan, remember that, just give me a few hours, I might, I might have some answers," and she headed back in the direction she came, checked out through security, and was back in the car on route to her office.

● ● ●

Chapter 68

Josh was a pro at the system by now, just as good as any of the feds in the room. When James Wartner's arrival was announced he elected to stay put in the war room for he found something quite interesting in the files. If this information was true he knew the man who walked into the station was Christopher Emmanuel 'Manny' Balestrero, a.k.a. Henry Fonda, a.k.a. The Wrong Man from the 1956 Hitchcock classic and it wasn't a hunch.

Josh was a hard facts type of guy. For the past six or so hours he and everyone in the room had been working on a bunch of lists generated from the computer system. Those lists had been data-sifted again and again both by hand and by machine. To Josh they didn't seem real, just ever changing names on a screen in Times New Roman font. He wanted to use his hands to examine the evidence, just something about hard copies made the facts seem more tangible. It wasn't until he printed them out that they seemed real. It wasn't until he printed them out that he saw the discrepancy. As soon as the paper slid out between the rollers of the laser printer, he knew something was amiss but couldn't place a finger on it until he compared it to the list on the screen. Halfway down the paper a name and age appeared seemingly from nowhere. The name was Kyle Kraner, age 38. The name was on the paper yet not on the screen. He decided to refresh the screen. Kyle Kraner, age 38 was now on the screen as well. He then counted the names by hand. Fifty-two was his answer. Thinking he was pretty close to

Florida, he counted again. Same answer, fifty-two. That is one more name on the national registered sex offender list for child molestation than they had been previously working from. "Odd", he thought.

He opened up the national registration's database like a twist cap from a domestic beer. He went straight to Kyle Kraner's file. It was uploaded in May of 2002. He went to open it and received:

File Not Found.

He tried again, same response. He tried others on the list and was able to bring up their files with ease. "Odd", he thought again. He then entered the name Kyle Kraner into the fed's database and received a plethora of hits, as he should. Their computers did their jobs. At Josh's fingertips were all sorts of links. He went straight for the medical records. Nothing. He went straight for the criminal records. Nothing. He found his tax records and place of work, and insurance information; he even found the pharmacy records and his two prescriptions but like every other lead it turned up empty. He found his license and more importantly his picture on his license. He compared this picture to the pencil drawn sketch. He couldn't tell because that damn pencil sketch could be just about anyone. Then he shuffled through the links and hit his medical records again. This time he could have sworn his mind was playing tricks on him, this time he didn't receive nothing. Maybe he just didn't click the link right, maybe the server hiccupped, maybe there could be a thousand reasons, but one thing was certain, he now had Kyle's medical records. The medical records from Peach Regional Medical Hospital indicated he was in an accident over twenty years ago, injuring his right leg and hip. "This would cause the limp", he said in his mind. He then tried the criminal link again. Nothing again. He was about to dive deeper when the gang walked back in.

"Dead end", Lynch said before Josh had a chance to ask the question.

"Dead end huh, well never mind about that, I think I found another route."

"What do you mean by that?"

"I think I found another name but it's weird."

"What's weird?"

"Let me ask you this, how many names on your sex offenders list?"

"Fifty-one.", piped in one of the feds.

"That's what I thought, yet right before you guys left I reran that exact report and"

"And?"

"I'm getting to that . . . I reran the report and received fifty-two."

"Someone could have just added that."

"That was my thought exactly but the file says it was uploaded in two thousand two but the file is not there, just the name and age, also there are no criminal files to be had anywhere. Oh, and get this, he was in an accident about twenty years ago, he injured his leg and hip and now walks with a limp. His name is Kyle Kraner and just so happens to be in our demographics at age thirty-eight. Here's a picture from his license, looks nothing like our pencil sketch though."

"Why wasn't this name on the list before," questioned Garfield?

"You tell me," looking in the direction of the two feds?

"It should have been, especially if you said it was uploaded in two thousand and two."

"Well it wasn't . . . and it's pretty damn strange if you ask me."

"It happens, I don't know why it happens but it does, we are dealing with machines and stuff like this happens all the time, you reboot and move on."

"But this is a huge coincidence is it not?"

"What? That a sex offender appears to have a limp and was not on the original list? Yeah maybe a coincidence but let's look at the facts . . . what are they?"

"He is Kyle Kraner age thirty-eight, walks with a limp?"

"And?"

"And what? That's all we have to go on at the moment. Like I said before I couldn't open his registration file but I do know his address and was going to do more research until you guys walked in. Again I find it a little strange, that's all."

The other fed in the room spoke, "Alright, I'll see if I can find the missing file, in the meantime I'm still not convinced we need to spend a huge bunch of manpower on this one guy but let's all take a few minutes and dive into our markers to see if anything unusual sticks out."

Lynch sat back down at the table, unlocked the laptop, and eyed the name of Ripley's uncle in his prompt. He would try later to get back to that but now he did a refresh of his screen. Sure enough he now saw Kyle's name on the global list. He quickly checked the name against his original marker.

Roughly ten minutes went by before he decided there was nothing to see so he moved on to his next pin, that of the Home Depot. Not much time elapsed prior to him finding the numbers of Kyle Kraner's Home Depot credit card. It had a balance just over eighteen hundred dollars. The last purchase was well over two years ago. He tried to open the store's database but it wasn't online. He would have to stoop to other means to get his needed information. Lynch looked at his watch and it was almost nine thirty. He was cutting it close, he knew that, but picked up the phone and dialed the number. After a bit of finger dancing and menu surfing it took twelve rings but someone finally picked up.

"Home Depot how may I direct your call?"

"This is Detective Lynch Forest Park Police Department, is there a manager I can speak to, it's sort of urgent?"

"Just one moment."

After about thirty seconds or so, "Hello, this is Rich Arnold, how can I help ya?"

"Detective Lynch here, I need to ask a few questions if you don't mind?"

"Sure, go ahead, glad to help ya."

"Are you able to view old store receipts from your computers?"

"Sure am, do you have the receipt number?"

"No, that's the problem, but I do have a date and credit card number."

"I should be able to locate that one for you, just a sec . . . go ahead." Lynch read the numbers and date and had to reread the numbers for Rich transposed a few the first time around. "Got it, sorry it took a bit, want do you want me to do with it?"

"Well, can you tell me what he bought?"

"Sure will, let's see, some dry wall screws, drywall, a bucket of mud, drywall tape, a few electrical supplies, a few two by fours, total bill came to five hundred and fifty six dollars thirty eight cents, with delivery charges. Do you need specifics like how many?"

"No, so that's everything?"

"Yes sir . . . no wait, there is another receipt for the same date, almost a half hour later, looks like a gallon of Behr paint and a few painting supplies, total of that bill was sixty one twenty seven."

"Nothing else?"

"That's everything, nothing new since that date, he does pay the minimum on time every month . . . . oh wait."

"What?"

"There is another purchase after that date, I didn't see it the first time around . . . . let's see . . . ummm . . . it's only for a shovel, cost nineteen twenty-two . . . and that's it."

"Well thanks for your time Rich."

"Not a problem sir, if there is anything else you need you can call me tomorrow."

He was just about to hang up the phone when a thought pricked his brain, "Hey Rich, one more thing, I'm curious, what color paint did he buy?"

"Color of the paint?"

"Yes."

"Hmmm, hold on will ya", about three minutes later, "you still there?"

"Yes."

"Sorry I took so long, the paint code on the can was an old one."

"Is that color obsolete?"

"No, no, just the code, every so often Behr will change their paints to a new formula, new formulas mean new paint codes, his was an old paint code for the color Pretty Pink."

"That sounds pretty bright."

"It is, probably the brightest pink we have."

"Well thanks again", and promptly hung up much like ending his interviews, before Rich Arnold could reply.

Now Lynch had the same "odd" thought Josh had.

●　　●　　●

Chapter 69

Laying in bed with nothing much to do he was contemplating the differences between Bob Barker and Drew Carey as the host on The Price is Right. Though he grew up with Bob during his sick days from school he actually enjoyed the dry humor from the squinty man behind the glasses though it might have had something to do with both of them being marines. Sure Barker was a military man himself, a navy man but the camaraderie of all things marines placed a big fat plus sign next to Drew. It was during the showcase showdown that Smith's laptop binged announcing an email had arrived in his inbox. It was from his friend that he had sent the pictures to the night before. The email was several megs in size and took a rather long time to download from the server due to its attachment. He read the brief email stating the fact that the four enclosed files were all hits within a ninety-five percent accuracy rate given the distance of the shots.

The first picture was Sarah Conner which looked nothing like the mother from the Terminator series. This photo was from the Pennsylvania Department of Transportation and listed Sarah at 135 pounds with green eyes. He compared them to his photos and besides the hair color it was a pretty good match. The accuracy rate on this photo was in the highest percentile being ninety-eight point seven five. Even though the next photo was in a lower percentile as soon as he saw her name and read the enclosed dossier he knew in a flash Jorja Carson was the person he captured on his smart media card. One didn't have to be a rocket scientist to see otherwise.

Now he had a decision to make. His mind wrestled with the pros and cons and it drew only one conclusion. He had to go see her and explain.

While in route back to the office Jorja came to a conclusion as well. The car dropped her off at the office yet she headed for the garage instead. It was still early in the day and she didn't want any confrontations, mainly with Greg until she was absolutely positive. She wanted to do a bit more research but in the comfort and safety of her home and she was going to have to log into the system to do so.

Jorja's car was still in the garage from the night before and her keys still in her purse so she was good to go, though she was feeling apprehensive for leaving early and unannounced. She tried to formulate an email on her blackberry that would explain her abrupt departure but her mind was elsewhere. She would correct that as soon as she was home. When she finally reached her vehicle on the second level she felt a slight sense of relief like a small personal goal had been reached. That all changed when she heard Greg's voice.

"Jorja"

Ignoring him like she didn't hear him and going for her door.

"Jorja, wait, wait I need to talk to you," from two car lengths away.

"It will have to wait Greg, I'm in a rush," as she unlocked the door and opened it

"You don't understand," now in between the two parked car giving Jorja a sense of being trapped.

"Greg, I can't right now I have to go," with a slight tremble in her voice.

"Where are you going, I can come with you."

"No, it's personal," turning around and looking right at him.

"But," as he came even closer and evading her personal space.

"But what," now becoming defensive, "how did you know I was here?"

Completely taking him by surprise, "I . . ."

"You are following me, spying on me."

"No, I . . ."

"And you are using the system to do it."

"No, no, I . . ."

"Then explain the bag this afternoon."

"Bag?"

"Yes, the bag, the bag from the very same restaurant I had dinner in last night, that is not a coincidence by any stretch of the means."

"I always . . ."

"Don't you lie to me."

"Okay, okay, I wanted to find out who you were with so I went to find some answers."

"You knew who I was with so don't give me that, besides why does it matter who I was with," then it clicked and she waited a bit and said in a sort of demeaning tone, "you are jealous aren't you, yes it all makes sense now."

"No," he said in almost a yell.

"Greg, you are scaring me."

"I just wanted, I just wanted . . . ," she didn't feel safe and she tried to get into her car and he slammed the door shut. "I just wanted to, to protect you is all."

"Protect me? Protect me how? By spying on me?" She reached for the door again.

"No, that's not it, I wanted to protect you from them, they're evil, more evil then you could ever know. I just wanted to protect you."

"Then tell me how my aunt plays into all of this."

"Your aunt?"

"Yes, my aunt, my aunt who was murdered remember, it appears that all these emails were on our servers I'm starting to do the math and in some way it all makes some twisted sense."

"What are you talking about?"

"The emails, you following me, you, you had something to do with my aunt's death didn't you?"

"Jorja, I don't know what you are talking about, what emails?"

"The emails on our servers to and from my aunt's killer. It all points to you."

'Jorja, I would never, never in a million years . . . I swear to you . . . you gotta to believe me."

'No, no I don't, you spied on me, god knows for how long and now you deny your involvement. All this time I trusted you, dammit Greg I trusted you."

"I wanted to protect you, I wanted to protect you from them, from them and your uncle I swear that's all."

"My uncle? So you did have something to do with my aunt's death."

"No!"

"Then why did you just say you wanted to protect me from my uncle?"

"I didn't?"

"You had my aunt killed didn't you, didn't you?"

"No, no, I just made the phone call is all."

"Phone call? What phone call?"

"I just wanted to see what your uncle would do is all."

"What phone call are you talking about?"

'The phone call from the pay phone, I . . . I told your uncle about the affair."

"What?"

"I wanted to see his reaction, see if he could do it again."

"Do what again?"

"He killed your mother Jorja."

"You have no proof of that."

"Those fingerprints on the boat, it puts him there, he did it."

"So you believe my uncle killed my mother and to prove it you placed my aunt's life in danger."

"It wasn't like that I swear."

"Then why all the emails to John Smith."

"I don't know of any emails."

"Liar, you fucking liar!" Again she tried for the door.

He grabbed both her biceps with each hand, she tried to move but he pushed her against the car. "Jorja, it's not like that . . . I . . ."

"Greg you are hurting me."

"I, I just wanted to protect you . . . because . . . because I love you."

"Greg let go of me."

"I said I love you, didn't you hear me, I fucking love you Jorja." as he slammed her harder against the door.

She fought back but was surprised by his strength as he slammed her again against the car

"Greg," she shouted

"I did this all for you, because I love you." His rage was growing and Jorja was about to scream but he spun her around a cupped his hand over her mouth while maintaining complete control over her. She kicked him in the shin with her high heel and he winced in pain. He pushed her body forward; this time her head hit the roof of the car. She was dazed. She felt the pressure of his hands dissipate then she heard some commotion like scuffling feet and then a rather large thud. Her hands immediately went to ease the pain in her forehead as she tried to gather her feet from under her. She felt two strong hands helping her up and a voice say, "Are you alright?"

Still dazed, she glanced down between the cars and saw Greg's lifeless body. "Yes, yes I think, is he, is he . . ."

"No I don't think so," and with that he reached down to check for a pulse, "No just unconscious it seems. I'll call for help."

Jorja was in the midst of gathering her senses as the call to 911 was placed, she looked at the man on the phone trying to place him but couldn't. She waited until he finished the call, "who are you?"

'They'll be here in a few minutes Jorja."

"You know my name?"

"Yes, I'm John Smith, we sort of met last night."

She backed away, "You are the one who murdered my aunt," backing away even farther now.

"Yes Jorja, I was sent to kill your aunt, that is true and I would have completed my mission if it wasn't for the fact they were already dead."

"Already dead?"

"Yes, both of them."

"Are you saying you didn't kill my aunt?"

"Yes that is what I'm saying, I already told you I was sent there to kill her."

"Actually, you were only sent there to take photographs but for some sick and twisted jealousy plot you were set up by that guy over there."

"So either way my mission was a failure, good to know. You didn't answer my earlier question, are you alright?"

"I think so, yes, what are you doing here?"

"I wanted to talk to you, to clear the air, after you tried to contact me last night, I figured you needed to know the truth, the truth that it wasn't me, plus I wanted to meet that woman who had the balls to confront the person who may have killed her aunt."

"How do I know it wasn't you, just because you say it wasn't you?"

"Why would I risk coming out in the open, I could have disappeared never to been seen again."

"Anticipatory deniability."

"What?"

"Nothing, something I picked up from the Chief of Staff, besides they'll find you, no one can truly disappear."

"Maybe that's true with today's technology."

"You know about the system?"

"What are you talking about, what system?"

"Nothing, never mind," as sirens were heard in the distance.

"Jorja, I know it's a tough pill to swallow but I think you have to look in another direction, outside the box in order to find the truth regarding your aunt's death."

"I, I will," still rubbing her head with her hands and apparently becoming more woozy.

The flashing red and white lights were now bouncing off the concrete walls of the parking garage and John went to flag them down and point them in the right direction. The EMT's arrived on the scene and loaded both Jorja and Greg into the ambulance. Jorja awoke on a gurney in the ER with a splitting headache. Greg was still unconscious with IV's dripping into his veins. He already had a CAT scan and some of the best doctors by his side but the prognosis was grim. His brain had hemorrhaged during the ride to the hospital. It was mainly a waiting game now, waiting for family and loved ones to say their goodbyes. Jorja was the first to say her goodbye. She never really knew the strong emotions that played out in her colleague's mind. She never felt that connection but she did feel she had lost a good friend, a friend who had shared one of the biggest secrets held from the populace and now that burden was squarely on her shoulders; in a way he did protect her. She now had some really big decisions to make.

●　　●　　●

Chapter 70

Things started to fall into place like the chips falling into the money slots on the Price is Right's Plinko board. It seemed like everywhere they looked a piece of the puzzle was being revealed like clues on the familiar game show Concentration, though there was not that many pieces and most of it was speculation at the moment.

Josh found the medical records. Garfield pulled up Kyle's home statistics and found no living relatives; he also pinpointed his home address via Google maps. The feds brought up the remaining digital files, such as tax records and phone calls. And Lynch found pink paint and a shovel. Pink was a girl's color, a pretty little girl color. Barbies and easter dresses, and lunchboxes, and braids, and the color of a girls' room were all pink in Lynch's mind. Pink Pink Pink . . . what the hell was Kyle buying pink paint for . . . he knew that answer. The shovel—he knew that answer as well.

Did they have their man, at this point only God knew and in the back of Lynch's mind he knew as well, call it a hunch, a cop's intuition, call it something but he knew, he also knew he needed more facts.

Josh broke the tension, "he doesn't seem to have many neighbors, it would be a good place to take a child."

"That alone doesn't get us a warrant," Lynch ejected.

"Fuck a warrant, I'm tired of playing by the rules," Garfield shouted from behind his laptop."

"We need more than Garfield's Google coordinates and my pink paint, what else do we got?"

"Not much," almost in unison by the two feds, then the dark haired one spoke "pretty sparse, even his phone records look bleak."

"Can you pull them up?"

"Click the phone icon in the upper right hand of the app."

"Okay got it, yeah like you said not much, what maybe two calls a month on average, this guy has no friends or family so it seems."

"Or not many left, pretty lonely if you ask me . . . . hey isn't that one of the signs?"

"Yes."

"Hey can we get a reverse lookup on the calls he made?"

"Sure, see the arrow the points up, click on that."

'Seems like most calls are to the pharmacy."

"Probably for his prescriptions one for pain, the other is a mild sleep aid."

"Here's a strange one, KB toys, what's a man in his thirties with no family or friends doing calling a toy store?"

"Hot Wheels collector or maybe a batman figurine collector, you know like that forty year old virgin guy, a real geek slash hard-up type of guy."

"Okay if that's true, does he belong to any type of club or forum?"

"Not that we could tell."

Josh spoke, "okay this is strange."

"What," the entire room questioned?

"The one phone call he made to KB Toys was two days prior to my little girl's case."

'So?"

"So I'm just saying."

No, no, he's right," Garfield added, "same thing for my case, two day just before she went missing."

"Hellova a coincidence don't you agree?"

"That and seventy-five cents will get you a morning paper and still not enough for a search warrant," the number two FBI guy stated.

"But not the case with Ripley . . . in fact no calls were made this past week, none at all."

"Wait a sec will ya," and Josh pulled up the phone records from KB Toys; he zoomed in on two days before Ripley's disappearance, there were twenty-two calls that day, and a reverse lookup proved insightful. "Who the hell uses a payphone in this day and age?"

"Even money it's Kyle Kraner."

"You think so?'

"Bet your life . . . . same m.o. here, always calls two days before, but as with all criminals they getter smarter, well think they get smarter, the longer they play the game. Somewhere along the line he decided that a payphone is much safer to use then his home phone. Where is that phone located?"

"Just a mile and half from his house."

"That's got to be him."

"So we are saying because this guy is registered as a sex offender, walks with a limp, has no family, bought a can of pink paint and a shovel, and calls a toy store two days prior to his kidnappings that this is our man?"

"Damn straight I can feel it."

"All that is circumstantial evidence and still not enough for a warrant."

"Pull up his driver's license please."

Then Lynch picked up the phone.

"Do you have access to a computer?"

"Yes."

"Right now?"

"Yes, upstairs in my father's room."

"Do you have an email account?'

"Yes."

"Okay give it to me, I'm going to send you a few pictures, okay?"

"Okay," and a few minutes later his email box beeped.

"I got them, hold on, I have to download them onto my desktop, okay, I have them, now what?"

"Open them, do you recognize anyone?'

"Should I?"

"You tell me?"

"Okay number one . . . . no . . . . number two . . . . no . . . . number three . . . . no . . . number four . . . ."

"Did you say number three?"

"I'm on four . . . . wait that was four . . . . number four I mean no . . . . now number three . . . ."

"Did you open it?"

"Yes"

"And?"

"And that looks like the pencil sketch guy . . . . the one who gave me the ten dollars."

"Are you sure?"

"No, he looks different somehow, it could be him."

'But that could be him?'

"Yes."

"Percentage wise how sure are you?"

"Eighty-five maybe ninety."

Dial tone was all he heard.

"Let's roll!"

Since this was now a national case the judge was a little lenient in regarding what constitutes proper evidence for a search warrant plus there was the added fact of the FBI breathing down his neck. It was granted without hesitation and the squad cars and an EMT unit gathered at Kyle's home in Roberta, Georgia. It was a little after eleven pm. Kyle's car was nowhere to be seen, an APB was placed, and even though it was a weekend night, a squad car was sent to his place of work just in case.

The rest of the group assembled and went over entry strategies. Josh, Lynch, and Garfield covered the front while the FBI covered the rear. They knocked and received no reply. They weren't expecting one. They knocked again and still no reply. Garfield checked the door and it was locked but it was forced open with one swift kick. They went in with guns drawn. The only light was coming from the rear of the house in the kitchen, where the FBI had just entered through an unlocked door. They gathered in the kitchen and decided to divide and conquer. Josh and one of the g-men went upstairs, and unlike those CSI TV shows, they actually turned on the lights to see where they were going. Lynch covered the other three very small rooms downstairs. Garfield and the remaining g-man tried the cellar door and proceed down the steps. It wasn't long until the rest of the house heard the commotion.

The steel door was opened and Ripley's body was lying on the floor, her blonde hair covering her face. Garfield checked for a pulse. To his surprise there was one. The EMT unit was quickly summoned, and they quickly surmised annophalitic shock brought on by the peanut butter sandwich that was half eaten and left by the bed. They had seen this many times in their career. Josh, Garfield, and Lynch watched as the two worked their magic. An injection of antihistamine was all that was needed. She was going to be alright. Lynch grabbed his cell phone and punched in the number to the Newenburgs. He was never expecting to make this phone call. He had rehearsed the other alternative over and over in his mind throughout the past couple of days but not this one.

"Hello, Mrs. Newenburgh, this is detective Lynch, we need you . . . ," he was trying to hold back his emotions, they seemingly came all at once, ". . . we need you to come down to the hospital."

"You found . . . you found my Ripley?"

"Yes . . . . yes we did."

Mrs. Newenburg immediately starting crying for she thought the worse.

"She's going to be fine Mrs. Newenburg . . . she's going to be fine . . . I will meet you there . . . don't worry everything is going to be fine."

"Thank you . . . . thank you," in between sobs.

"I will take good care of her until you arrive . . . I promise."

"Thank you."

And before he hung up the phone . . . "You're welcome"

The big man, Lynch, started to cry. The past few days had really taken its toll on him. Garfield was in the same boat. His bottled up emotions that he kept inside for over a year came to the surface as well. They had found Tanya's kidnapper, now it was a matter of finding her body, for he knew all too well she was not alive. Josh was a bit more apprehensive, his case was still hot, and there might be a fleeting chance, all he needed to do was talk to Kyle.

As the EMT prepared Ripley for her ride to the hospital, each man shook each other's hands and exchanged a good bear type of hug; it was an emotional scene. Once outside, Lynch, as promised, took good care of Ripley, he rode in the ambulance with her. Josh and Garfield waited for Kyle's inevitable capture, while the FBI guys called for even more FBI guys.

Josh went back inside. He searched the house again. He found nothing. Before he did anything else he remembered his partner, his partner worked two solid months straight, sixteen and eighteen hour days, his partner needed to be here. It was now after midnight but he made the call anyway.

After the call he learned that he was not going to get the chance to talk to Kyle Kraner, ever.

It was a fitting demise for Kyle Kraner. He saw the flashing lights in his rearview mirror; he hit the gas, and turned the corner. It was the shortest chase in Roberta's history. Kyle turned the corner, hit a pole, and his head impacted with the windshield giving yet another mortality statistic in the case for the slogan 'seatbelts save lives.'

In the hour that followed, the house was a full blown crime scene, with lights, even more FBI and GBI guys, trucks, cameras, and all sort of investigating equipment. It wasn't long before they unearthed Tanya's body from beneath a bed of daisies in the backyard. She was wrapped lovingly in a pink blanket in a little white dress. It wasn't until late afternoon that Josh and his partner could close their case as well. Becky's body was found just a short distance from Kyle's house, in a nearby water reservoir, just off of Kirby Avenue. They found burlap, rope, and a cement block in a small boat by the shed in the backyard. It wasn't hard to solve the equation by putting two and two together. Within a half an hour of dredging they found Becky. Kyle Kraner was responsible for at least three abductions, possibly more, possibly even Colleen Reinhardt, though her body was never found. Their cases could now be closed after a few final entries. Some questions where still left unanswered, like why? Why did he do it? Why did he kill the other girls but not Ripley? Both Tanya and Becky's body were unable to answer the question of any child abuse but Ripley's did. She was unmarred in that nature. As far as she was concerned she lived in a pink room for a few days of her life where she played with a bunch of toys. She'll soon forget the face of her captor, only to be buried in the deep recesses of the mind.

Charles Lynch was bedside by a sleeping Ripley, when her parents rushed in. They couldn't help but wake her; they loved and missed her so. Her smile alone was worth every bit of thankless tasks he had performed through his lifetime of being a cop. It was moments like this that made him proud to have taken the oath to serve the public even though he feared the worst for this little girl. He made up his mind right there and then that he wouldn't be accepting his gold watch this year, in fact, they would have to drag him out the door for he had a new lease on life.

He kept Ripley's picture on his desk from then on.

Josh Cerrito wanted so badly to question Kyle. He couldn't leave well enough alone and wanted to find out all he could. He went to the County seat in order to find something, anything, the only thing we found, Kyle Kraner was an only child with no living relatives. He searched old school records and found he had dropped out during his junior year for reasons unknown. Josh just couldn't put his mind around why this would happen, what would drive a person to do such a thing. To Josh this case would never be closed.

●　　●　　●

Chapter 71

J orja had one question on her mind, actually several that she needed answers and only one person could give her those answers . . . . her uncle.

When she arrived at the gates she entered her pass code but the iron bars refused to budge. Thinking she missed keyed, she entered them again and they still did not move. She buzzed the house only to receive no reply. She buzzed again and waited while she reached for her cell. Then a soft voice came over the small tinny speaker.

"Carson residence, how may I help you?"

"Robin, it's Jorja, is my uncle home?"

"Yes, but . . ."

"Can you just let me in please? My code doesn't work, I need to talk to him."

The gates parted and she pulled up to the front door where Robin was already waiting.

"Your uncle is in his study, but he hasn't moved or said a word since . . ."

"Robin, how are you doing?" in a sincere tone.

"Not good, I really don't want to stay but your uncle needs someone to watch over him."

"Robin . . . . I . . . ," and she turned towards her and gave her a hug, "thank you for being here, it means a lot to us . . . to me."

Robin broke from the hug with tears in her eyes and didn't say another word as she made her way to her private quarters. Jorja went to seek out her uncle and when she arrived at the entrance to his study he was sitting in his favorite chair holding a picture frame that contained his now departed wife. Jorja rapped ever so lightly on the outside wall and without lifting his head he said, "Please come in my dear," in such a somber tone Jorja's heart sank even deeper into her chest. She wanted to just go over and hug him but her brain filled with confusion, torn between distrust and love. She walked in quiet like a church mouse and sat in the hard leather chair trying not to make it squeak as the leather relaxed from her frame. She didn't say a word, mainly because she didn't know what to say.

"I did love her . . . even though I rarely said it, I did love her . . . and yes I admit, with deep regret . . . . that . . . that I took her for granted. Grace was always there for me, she was always there for me and I was never there for her . . . . and now . . . now I have nothing, except for some fading memories and these images printed on paper . . . and I can't touch either of them. I can't tell them how sorry I am or how much I love them. They are worthless. I am worthless. I was too concerned with my career. I always have been. And I don't blame her for what she did. I know I am to blame. I'm to blame for what happened and I'm sorry." He took a deep breath and Jorja just watched as he tried to gather himself, still not uttering a sound. He lifted his head and looked at Jorja for the first time. "I remember the first time I saw her," and she so wanted to interrupt him and ask if he meant her aunt or her mother. "I was a freshman in college and I was going to the movies with a bunch of friends. We were in line and I noticed her behind us, only she didn't appear to have a date. She just had this southern charm that sparkled without saying a word. As the line grew shorter I guess my courage grew stronger. When I approached the ticket counter I bought an extra ticket and without saying a word I turned around and handed it to her. She thanked me and went on her merrier way. The next time I saw her on campus I asked if I could accompany her to the next movie and the rest as they say, is history. She was perfect in every way a man could want or need. I loved her from the moment I laid eyes on her. I just knew we would spend the rest of our lives together."

Before he could continue, the sob story got the best of her, she bit her lip before she spoke, then eased out the question, "What about my mother?"

He was not expecting that and it took him awhile to formulate a reply, searching for words but also trying to ascertain the extent of her knowledge. "Your mother was a different soul and I was very young . . . . very stupid . . . . very naïve and without trying to make an excuse . . . it was college. Your mother caught me by surprise, her beauty her free will, her confidence. She danced to her own tune. Looking back now I guess it was more lust than love and you cannot build a strong foundation on that. I am a lucky man for when I finally learned that life lesson, Grace was there to forgive me and take me back."

"So my mother was not your soul mate?"

'No."

"That's not the way Aunt Gracie remembers it. She says the two of you were inseparable from the moment you saw each other."

"Like I said, it was lust, I've learned from my mistakes."

"So you are saying my mother was a mistake."

"No, no, nothing like that, we were young that's all, too young to control feelings that strong."

"Okay I'm a little confused, first you said it was just lust then you say you had these strong feelings . . . which was it?"

Taking a moment, "If you must know, the truth is, I loved Caroline, I loved your mother, I have never loved anyone else as deeply as her and at the same time no one has ever caused me so much pain. Like I said we were young, far too young and I let my dreams get in the way. If I could, I would reverse time and do things differently, I would gladly give up what I thought were my dreams in return for a life with the woman I loved . . . but I can't. Now I have lost the two women I have loved the most in my life and I have regrets, serious regrets that I must take with me to my grave."

"Aunt Gracie knew that you loved her but she also knew your heart was not entirely hers. She was okay with that. May I ask, what really happened between you and my mother?"

"There were always conflicts mostly in the political realm. She knew I wanted to plant both feet firmly within the government and I believed I could really make a difference. She feared I would succumb to the evils, the corruption, the mainstream agendas. We fought all the time over our ideals. Then one day she grew tired and left. I loved her even more for not giving in. I tried to win her back, I tried several times but I made a huge mistake in the process and I will never forgive myself for it."

"What was it?"

"I don't . . . . ," trailing off as if almost losing his thought, "I don't want to talk it about."

"Are you sure? You shouldn't burden your soul with anymore regrets, no matter how painful it may be."

Taking another deep breath, "You are right my dear . . . it's just that . . . I have lived with this feeling, this image every day of my life and I have never told anyone about it, not even your aunt. It was the moment I lost all hope in a life with Caroline. It was the stupidest thing," as he paused, "utterly stupid," he paused again.

"Go on."

"Well . . . . I could never win a debate with your mother. Never. And I was captain of the debate team. She was full of piss and vinegar that one. She just had a spin on life that I couldn't fathom. She got the better of me and after all my failed attempts I just reacted maybe it was out of some hidden pent up aggression that emanated from the fact that I never ever won an argument. It just happened and to this day I regret it ever since. From that day on things were different between us. Sure we still loved each other but there was always this underlying hint of distrust and rightfully so on her part."

"You still didn't tell me what happened."

"I never ever did this before, and never did it again, but out of shear anger, I raised my hand and slapped her across the cheek. When she turned and walked away without saying a word I just knew I had made the biggest mistake of my life. I tried every way possible to say that I was sorry but to no avail."

"So how many times did you see her during her marriage to my father?"

"Hard to say, not much outside family functions and they were rare, mostly for your birthdays and one or two Christmases. It was very hard on my part. There was always this physical attraction between us, this connection that's hard to explain but like I said before you can't build a foundation on that and on top of that she was married to my brother. And yes, before you say it, I was jealous plain and simple. So I tried not to be around much. I thought of her every single day. So much so I was neglecting my wife. It was sort of this one sided affair in my head."

"I'm going to be blunt. Did you ever sleep with her during her marriage?"

"No, I am not your father, which I knew you must be thinking and no I never slept with her during her marriage. Now before she said her vows it came pretty close but wiser heads did prevail. No you are definitely my brother's daughter but I look at you as the daughter I never had. I never told my brother but I was proud of him raising you like he did." as he shed the slightest of tears, "and I'm not going to lie I wanted to, wanted to tell your mother that I loved her in the worst way every time I saw her. And to tell you the truth she felt the same way."

"You know this for a fact?"

"Yes it was two or three years into my marriage with Grace. I started second guessing my relationship. Getting that grass is always greener sensation. Here was this object of my love within reach and relatively close, a sister-in-law for Christ sake. Like I said we fought a lot but it sparked emotions deep within us and I just knew we could have lived with the lively debates and with each other for we would eventually matured. I needed to know if there was still a chance so I asked her to meet me."

"Where?"

"The place she loved the most. On her boat. She picked me up on the docks. I brought champagne and some glasses. We talked over one of the most beautiful sunsets and as the sun went down the water became as green as her eyes. I learned that evening she had regrets as well. So here are two people who both made choices in their life yet found each other at this crossroad. Honestly I told her I would divorce Grace if she would do the same. She couldn't because of you but said she would sleep on it. And I respected that. She dropped me back off the docks and that was the last time I saw her, never to return to either of us. You can see why I never told your aunt."

Jorja gave her assurances that everything was going to be alright and shortly thereafter she parted ways. Once back in her car she was relieved, relieved because she didn't have to be in the presence of a killer anymore. She knew he was lying the moment he started down the waters of the Chesapeake. He was covering his wake so to speak. Had Jorja not sent him the true AFIS file using Greg's email address he would have never brought up the fact he was even on a boat or had champagne with her mother; that she was sure of without a shadow of a doubt. The senator knew his fingerprints might come back to haunt him. How convenient was his story that she dropped him off the docks and he went his merry way. She didn't buy it for a second. Jorja was a clever girl and she studied her uncle's face as he told the story. It was as if it were rehearsed rather than from memory. He was careful to insert words to proclaim his innocence trying to mold her thoughts as if the events were real to him but real for Jorja was the finality of truth.

• • •

Chapter 72

The database administrator of the Director of National Intelligence was already on the line when Scott walked into the Oval Office.

The President was in the midst of speaking. "So are we saying that this Greg guy over at the CIA was the pivotal point in our situation?"

"It looks that way," Scott interjected, "he reported to the deputy director, Jorja Carson, who you now know is the niece of the senator, seems he knew about the affair as well and wanted to expose it based on some underlying obsession with Jorja, we really don't understand the psychology behind all of it."

"How did he find out about the affair and more importantly how did he find out about your plan?"

From the voice on the phone, "the CIA has a set of big ears, and Greg was a master with email systems and file uploads throughout the intelligence community, he probably saw one of Scott's original emails and just followed the trail because it pertained to his boss in some manner."

"What does Jorja think?"

Scott fielded this question. "She's between a rock and a hard place, on one hand she wants to expose us for our," and he corrected himself, "my plan, for the tabloid photo shoot, on the other, it was her subordinate that initiated the plan to actually have her aunt killed by our rogue agent, not to mention he may have sparked the senator's rampage by his phone call. Truth be told I think she's still on the fence about her uncle's involvement."

"So we still don't know who killed Grace, do we?"

"All signs still point to Senator Carson, he received the phone call from Greg right around eleven which he then manipulated to look like it came from a payphone, probably a tip off, then we have all the circumstantial evidence such as the senator was home at the time of the murders or within our window scope, the bullets were the same caliber as his handgun, and coupled with the fact his gun was freshly cleaned, it all does draw suspicion. Again it's all circumstantial and for all intents and purpose he should be acquitted. If O.J. can get off . . ."

"How about this lieutenant colonel everyone keeps mentioning?"

The voice on the phone again, "We just don't know, we assume he's dead since his transmissions have ended."

"Who erased him in the first place?"

"Scott you wanna take that one?"

"No I don't."

"Just admit it Scott, you erased him to cover your own ass but you forgot the backups."

"But he's still not transmitting is he? You're the database guru, I'm the Chief of Staff, I don't going playing in your sandbox, so unless you have unequivocal proof, go . . ."

"Enough," the stern voice of Jonathan rumbled, "so if John Smith is dead, who killed him, the senator?"

"Very possible, since they both were in and around the vicinity of the Carson's residence, but if he didn't that leaves a huge gaping hole. There are a few scenarios, the first being the senator murdered all three people, Grace, Blake, and our lieutenant colonel but if Smith followed out his change of plans provided by Greg, then the senator could have just killed him, or that gaping hole comes into play, the senator had nothing to do with it, and either Smith or a person to be named later does the deadly deed."

"Okay if Smith is dead, where is the body, the evidence?"

"There is none."

"None? That's totally unacceptable, with all this fucking technology that our system provides, we still can't prove a goddamn thing. We can't even solve a simple murder case."

There was silence, then, "there're still gaps yes, like, not everyone is in the system yet, and the elapse tracking time is every five minutes, which pretty soon, we should have to under a minute, and we haven't blanketed the entire country, there are still blind spots," echoed from the conference phone.

"Still, the wasted manpower, the years of planning that went into this, I expect more, no, I demand more, we have this system to protect the American people from harm, so they can live in a world free from crime, so the American people can be free. We didn't come all this way to fail, yet what I'm seeing here is complete failure, failure through incompetence, and we are very much running out of time."

"Well with Carson out of the race, it does look like another term, and when the senate passes our new bill, then we are one step closer to providing coverage to the entire country, plus if the scare of pandemics continue and they will since we now have officials on the board of WHO, the demand for vaccines will rise. We always knew this system wouldn't be one hundred percent flawless, but with each passing day we get closer to our end goal. Remember in just a few short years we have a little more than half the population being tracked every five minutes, that is one hell of an accomplishment. We are still ahead of our projected timeline."

"I want these timelines moved up, Scott, you take the lead in that and here," as the president handed Scott back his letter, "That better be the last time it's on my desk, now let's get back to business."

"Hold on before you hang up, so are you going to unlock me now," quipped Scott?

"On one condition."

"I know, I know, I should have never doubted you."

"Listen we of all people have to stick together, we alone know the true power of this system."

"So again I never should have doubted you . . . or pissed you off."

As he clicked a few keys there was a slight laugh, "okay, you're good to go."

"Thanks," and Scott punched off on the phone never knowing the true meaning behind his laugh.

That laugh was indeed for Scott because he was dead on to doubt him. He knew the day, the hour, even the second, when Greg and Jorja first entered the system. He knew the very first time they saw through god's eyes. He built the system, he knew the system, he knew all the traps, all the firewalls, all the safety features. When the sensor tripped he kept his watchful eye on them and liked the fact that they had no qualms in disregarding the amendments of the United States. He watched their every move. He knew the length of the leash that he wanted to keep them on. They could be future allies and he knew he needed allies when the system becomes fully operational. He wanted to trust them but that all changed because of Greg, more so with Greg's obsession with Jorja and the system. He spent every waking hour pouring over data, tracking everyone she ever encountered. He was becoming unstable. He was becoming a shaken champagne bottle with its gate released. He alone had to take care of Greg and what better way to do it then frame Greg for the murder of the senator's wife and an easy plan it was. Greg had laid all the ground work with the emails to and from Reynolds, so he merely made it look as though Greg had changed Reynolds' original email from pictures to kills and hid Lieutenant Colonel John Smith's NID's. The rest was a dash of denial, a pinch of paranoia, and a splash of good old fashion jealously. He was just hoping that Greg would be fired and take his rank among the 9/11, grassy knoll and UFO's conspiracy theorists until his encounter with a car fender. Yes, the database administrator for the Office of Director of National Intelligence was the true card player in this game. He knew the real power of the system, the system of justice. He knew that the truth lies in the data and there is no hiding that fact.

● ● ●

Chapter 73

The trial lasted three weeks and was just as gripping as a daytime soap opera yet the general public just didn't seem to care. They already had tough political skin as they've been inundated by everything from coked-up mayors and gay turning governors, to seat selling senators and lying-through-their-teeth presidents. They only cared about the outcome and nothing more—"We the jury find the defendant Floyd Benjamin Carson not guilty." The only so-called evidence was the fact he was possibly home during the time of the murders. There was no GSR on him, no blood, and the bullets' striations never matched his gun. The jury never knew the true meaning behind the phone call he received just prior to the murders since they never knew who was on the other line. It was disregarded simply as a wrong number. The jury never knew that as soon as the senator walked into his study he had grabbed his 9mm caliber Bereta 92 from his gun safe, loaded it, and calmly walked upstairs and shot his wife and her lover. The jury never knew he had cleaned himself, changed his clothes, and more importantly changed the barrel on his gun. They never knew he came back to his study, oiled his gun, placed it back into the box, took a sedative and a sip of bourbon and passed out. The jury never knew that he later disposed the well-hidden extra barrel in trashcan inside the Georgetown Mall. They never knew the power of his rage regarding infidelity. They never knew the weight of his burden, his reoccurring nightmare that took its toll on his everyday life. They never knew it was a constant battle to keep his emotions in check. The jury never knew that he would wake in the middle of most nights with his hands grasping an imaginary champagne bottle and bringing it down on the back of Caroline's neck. They never knew he dropped her overboard in the middle of the Chesapeake. They never knew he ran the boat aground and simply walked off to become a well-respected senator and almost a president. The jury never knew he had a true love before, murdered before, and got away with it before. They never knew but Jorja knew. Jorja knew he was responsible for her empty heart. Jorja knew this man had taken away the two most important people in her life. She knew he had killed her mother. She knew he had killed her Aunt Gracie. After all the redirections, false implications, and conspiracy theories Jorja knew the Lieutenant Colonel John Smith was telling the truth. She also knew that Greg was right not to trust the senator. She also knew now that Greg was gone she had an even bigger burden to carry alone, a bigger burden than knowing your uncle was a murderer gone free. It was the burden of the system, of god's eyes.

As Jorja sat at her desk, the desk of the Deputy Director of Directorate of Science and Technology and gazed at her "Eye" poster, she tried to deny the existence of the system. She tried to deny the allurement of the system, its seductive powers of knowledge and truth. She couldn't. She turned towards her monitor and was about to log in when she heard a rap on her doorframe.

As she looked up from behind her wire frames, "Jorja, do you have a moment, Will Clark from DNI?"

She didn't recognize the face, immediately thought of only one thing, and said, "ah, the famous pioneer, I have some time, come on in."

He shut the door behind him, "so you already know about me?"

"Well without you the world would seem smaller I suppose."

"I suppose and that's what I want to talk to you about."

'What, your great expedition?"

"Well, yes, you can call it that I guess," and from her smile he sensed they were not on the same page, "wait a sec, exactly what are you talking about here?"

"It's William right?"

"Yes."

"Well I was referring to your buddy, Lewis," noticing the sort of puzzled look she added, "Meriwether Lewis and William Clark, Lewis and Clark, the Great Expedition?"

"Yes, okay, I'm with you now, as a matter of fact I do want to talk to you about the great expedition."

Now it was Jorja's turn to have the puzzled look on her face, "you do?"

"The one you and Greg took April of last year."

Jorja looked at her monitor, then looked at the man before her, she noticed his insignia ring, she noticed the "PS" and then tried to formulate a question "Are you talking about the . . . the . . ."

"Yes, I am talking about the system, I've known all along Jorja, I'm its creator, well one of them anyway . . . I'm coming to you because I need someone I can trust."

She felt the weight of her burden lightened.

●　　●　　●

Chapter 74

William Clark was at his desk when a calendar reminder popped up. It stated one word—Ripley. It was exactly one year to the date that Ripley Newenburg was found alive thanks to him and a few good cops. He broke the rules. He skirted the Constitution. And he would do it again and has. It was a feeling that the greater good must always prevail.

He quickly went to the system and dialed up the now six year old's id. It was a Sunday and he found her at home, in the backyard. Little did he know the parents were keeping an even closer watch over her from the kitchen window. This particular sun filled summer afternoon, she was playing with her brother Sam and his favorite new found game, hide-n-go-seek . . . . and she could be heard from the window . . . "I found you, tag your it."

●　　●　　●

Epilogue

The director of the FBI was at home sorting his mail and came across a certified letter obviously signed for by his wife since she was home during the delivery. It was an ordinary plain white envelope and he assumed it had something to do with taxes. When opened, the envelope contained a single sheet of paper. He unfolded the paper and was a bit perplexed. He didn't know what to make of it. It was a list of the FBI's 10 most wanted ranging from murders to terrorist and bank robbers to sexual deviants and next to each picture was either an address or the word "unknown" cut out of newspaper/magazine print. There were five addresses and five unknowns. "Some kind of joke," he thought and simply tossed it with the outgoing flyers he would soon dispose. When he was finished with the rest of the mail he gathered the flyers, the opened envelopes, and any other disregarded piece and tossed them into the trashcan. He noticed the registered letter was on top. He reached for it and once again read it. He dialed the Philadelphia office.

"Hey Dale, I need you to send a few agents over to 718 West 57th, apartment 2C"

"For?"

"Just following up on a hunch."

"You a hunch, since when are you back in the field, it's been quite awhile hasn't it?"

"Yes, it was just something I got in the mail, make sure your agents are familiar with the Jason Brown case."

"Jason Brown? Something in the mail? Are you kidding me, he's been on the list for a few years with no such luck."

"Just tell me what you find out will ya?"

"Sure thing boss."

Within two hours the FBI's ten most wanted list was whittled down to nine. Within two hours after that there were stakeouts at the four remaining addresses. Three more criminals were apprehended during the next two days and just like that the list was cut to almost in half only to soon be replaced by the next in line. The envelope was sent to the lab for further analysis. The paper and envelope were generic in nature bought at any office supply store. Both the stamp and envelope contained no DNA from saliva since they were the self-adhesive kind. No fingerprints were found except for the director's. Not a single clue as to where this letter originated. Not one. Yet thanks to this letter somehow in some way shape or form, four of the most dangerous criminals that ever walked this earth were behind bars, just like that.

On the other side of the continent a similar envelope arrived at the doorstep of one Mrs. Ling. It simply had a picture of her missing daughter and an address in East L.A. Turns out the runaway was seduced into a life of tricks for the trade and stoked out on heroin. The two were reunited and although a long way from returning to a normal life, they're on the right path.

In the state of Arizona in a town just off the beaten path a recently self-made millionaire receives a second letter with the same information as his first. It's a copy of some accounting records showing the embezzled funds from a well known charity and the simple words—"So you think you can hide."

Corporal Thomas Leavitt received the Bronze Star with a deeply weighted heart. Two of his men were taken captive during his last mission in Iraq never to been seen from again. His letter contained the dog tag numbers along with final mass grave burial site of both men.

Every so often, about once a month, a letter or two finds its way into the mail transforming a life of wonderment into life of enlightenment, the deceased into the living, the thought of the living into the deceased, hope into certainty, hope into finality, and giving assurances to those who need it most.

●　　●　　●

CPSIA information can be obtained at www.ICGtesting.com
260254BV00003B/2/P